## Advance Praise for *Death of the Great Man*

"Peter Kramer has created an arch political satire that also offers a deep consideration of the modes and meaning of psychoanalysis. A sly novel of many pleasures, it is at once entertaining and enlightening."

—Geraldine Brooks, author of *Horse*

"*Death of the Great Man* is a diabolically clever and truly original novel about power, paranoia, and the uses (and abuses) of psychoanalysis. Filled with insight and witty asides, Peter Kramer's dystopian not-quite-fable has caught the deflated but ever-hopeful spirit of this cultural moment with unerring skill and unfailing intelligence."

—Daphne Merkin, author of *This Close to Happy*

"*Death of the Great Man* is like nothing else written from our political era—in a good way. Peter Kramer's lifetime experience as a psychiatrist and his lifelong skill as a writer and storyteller combine in a riveting and thought-provoking book. It is fantasy, it is reality, and it is very much worth reading."

—James Fallows, NPR commentator and former chief White House speechwriter

"I've been a Peter Kramer fan for years. His professional training, coupled with his innate curiosity

and compassion, results in a voice uniquely his. Add to that the creativity of a novelist and you have in *Death of the Great Man*, a mesmerizing story and a moving account of a psychotherapist in crisis."

—Abraham Verghese, author of *Cutting for Stone*

"Peter Kramer, whether in his nonfiction guise or in his fiction writing, is a thinker I return to with reverence and esteem often. He has an intuitive and poignant and funny take on the deeper questions that nag struggling humans, one that he comes to with such wisdom."

—Rick Moody, author of *The Ice Storm* and *The Long Accomplishment*

"So many delightful surprises in here! For starters, I didn't really know that Peter Kramer, one of America's most celebrated Serious Thinkers, is also an absolutely crackerjack comic novelist. Nor did I expect this entertaining and timely story to take the thoughtful and thought-provoking twists and turns it does. *Death of the Great Man* is serious fun."

—Kurt Andersen, author of *Evil Geniuses: The Unmaking of America*

"An unusually astute psychiatrist gets ensnared into treating an unusually narcissistic US president who has brought the country to its dystopian knees. What could go wrong? Plenty does, all of it threaded with insights we've come to expect from

Peter Kramer's fiction and landmark nonfiction, and injustices and outrages we've come to expect from such a president—the 'Great Man' of the title. Dr. Kramer's satiric tale is bold, sly, and frighteningly in tune with the moment—and the moments to come."

—Elizabeth Benedict, author of *Almost*, *Slow Dancing*, and *Rewriting Illness*

"Reaching with his storyteller's wand into the swirl of the Now, Peter Kramer has created a fanciful, but in other ways deadly, political and psychological mystery. Deploying the tropes and truisms of psychotherapy, feasting on our collective fears and fantasies, *Death of the Great Man* is a narrative full of crackle and surprise. A mind-worm for our moment and beyond—its atmospheres will be hard to shake."

—Sven Birkerts, author of *The Art of Time in Memoir*

"Political satire with remarkable depictions of the workings of a psychiatrist's mind, meditation on the proper aims, of psychotherapy, and speculation about the dystopian contour of our future should a 'great man' return to high office."

—Sally Satel, author of *Brainwashed: The Seductive Appeal of Mindless Neuroscience*

# DEATH of the GREAT MAN

a novel

PETER D. KRAMER

A POST HILL PRESS BOOK

ISBN: 978-1-63758-796-6
ISBN (eBook): 978-1-63758-797-3

Death of the Great Man:
A Novel


Cover design by Conroy Accord
Cover illustration by Matthew Kramer

Post Hill Press, LLC
New York • Nashville
posthillpress.com

Published in the United States of America

**Also by Peter D. Kramer**

*Ordinarily Well*
*Freud*
*Against Depression*
*Spectacular Happiness*
*Should You Leave?*
*Listening to Prozac*
*Moments of Engagement*

As always, for Rachel

# DEATH OF THE GREAT MAN

I am Henry Farber, the psychiatrist. You will have heard my name, if only lately. The Great Man was found dead in my office in Providence, Rhode Island. That's my couch he's draped across in the photo, the one that ricocheted from device to device, delivering the news. In case you have not seen the image, I will describe it. My lawyer has advised me to begin with the photo.

I took it three days ago under the direction of a security guard who goes by the nickname Muscle. Don't be misled. Muscle is thoughtful and perceptive. Facing a predicament, he turns all its facets to the light.

That morning, Muscle rescued me. Standing before the corpse, I had been overwhelmed.

But why? There was little to miss in the Great Man. He had destroyed our democracy. He was responsible for deaths beyond counting. On a minor note: he had threatened my family. He was unpleasant to be with. In his presence, I had tried to maintain a psychotherapeutic posture—withholding judgment, remaining curious and open, looking out on the world as he did. The effort had pushed me to my limits.

Still, I had tended to him. The death of someone we have cared for is wrenching.

The words *tended* and *cared for* reflect my experience. The Great Man rejected the label *patient*. He warned me never to claim or imagine that I was his doctor. He said, You will serve me as a consultant.

He abused those who served him. He ignored consultants.

All the same, I had sat with him and acted as I do with patients, trying to construct a space in which new accounts of the self might emerge. Seeing him sprawled before me, it was hard not to conclude that I had failed. Worse, I feared that I had sent him to his death.

The Great Man had been a villain, but a lively one. The contrast between the Great Man in motion and the Great Man struck down was stark.

I found myself unsteady on my feet. Before my knees could buckle, I lowered myself into my chair, the one I used when I saw patients. Immediately, it was as if I were in session—as if I were required to make sense of the response that the figure on the couch evoked in me. I found that I resented him for an idiosyncratic reason.

My wife, Miriam, died in the time of the plague. My mourning involves joining her in imagination. The least reminder will throw me into a meditative state. If I am lucky, in that trance I will catch a glimpse of Miriam or recall a gesture or turn of phrase. Sitting across from the Great Man, it confused me that death made no distinction between the kindly and the cruel. My concern was not that the righteous perish but that self-seekers do. I found it wrong that the Great Man should be invited into the space that sheltered Miriam.

We speak of Death's Kingdom. In my dislocation, I realized that I had been envisaging a modest republic, New England in a good year. Walking in Providence in the months after Miriam's death, I would turn a corner and be struck by a vista she had admired, Narragansett Bay in the distance, framed by branches of leafless trees. I would pause to look for patterns in the white chop. I would feel her squeeze my arm to be sure that I shared in her delight. I was angry with the Great Man for intruding on that urban paradise.

It took Muscle to rouse me. He is a former Marine. He believes that crisis tests character.

I never asked Muscle about his nickname, whether it is a reversal or straight up. He's strong and broad-shouldered, but he carries extra weight. He has an Irish lad's roguish face that can make it seem like he's joshing when he's dead serious, which he is, almost always.

Muscle had been circling the room, taking inventory, assessing contingencies, planning a next move.

That day, he had not been tasked with protecting the Great Man. Still, a security guard does not want to stumble over a client's corpse. I wondered whether Muscle would come to blame himself for having been elsewhere when the Great Man was in need.

Muscle said, Our situation requires handling.

He said that no one would wish to be linked to this event. It was momentous, provocative, explosive.

A death along these lines had been desired, intensely, by the public at large.

Wanting to show that I was not out of touch, I said that my patients, some of them, had dreamt of the Great Man's death or disappearance.

There were many variants: illness, murder, a miasma settling on the capital and extinguishing every member of the Regime. One academic had a dream in which aliens from a superior civilization (they looked like his former teachers, a tweedy lot) consulted him. The extraterrestrials had seen our species slip off the rails. Was it okay if they whisked the Great Man away? He would vanish without further injury to the body politic.

Better than any earthling, the advanced social psychologists understood the factors that had brought a shallow egotist to power. They confided in the professor-patient, expert to expert. On waking, he found that he had lost hold of the scientific explanation for our plight. He did recall the story arc. Pushed to make a judgment call, he had said, Thanks, buddies. Beam him up, and enjoy the use of him.

That was the hallmark of the Great Man's rule, Muscle said. No satisfactory solutions short of science fiction.

Everyone has had those dreams, Muscle said.

Everyone, he said, except the Great Man's remaining partisans, the EverGreats. Even they had foreseen his passing. It was a constant in their propaganda that the Regime's opponents would aim for that most illiberal of expedients, assassination, as a way of frustrating the people's will. The Great Man himself had been apprehensive. Straying from the text of a speech, he might begin a sentence with the words *If I go suddenly*—and request mayhem to follow. *If I go suddenly, you must wreak havoc.* He owed his second term to havoc. He had made havoc a staple of governance.

Would the Regime cling to power through more uprisings, more chaos?

Muscle catalogued grim likelihoods.

In the wake of the Great Man's sudden death, there would be talk of foul play. There would be scapegoats.

Muscle pointed to my electronic tablet. I had brought it with me, to take notes as I listened to my quasi-patient.

Is it charged?

In our time together at the Great Man's retreat, I had told Muscle about the device and its capabilities. Patients from my paranoid men's group had configured it for me. It was deeply invisible.

In contrast, Muscle's mobile device was Regime-issued, electronically thumbprinted, attached to him as a user. Muscle preferred to stay under the radar.

See if you can photograph the scene, Muscle said.

No one could say whether we were still in the Great Man era—whether evidence-tampering by the authorities would remain the norm. In case truth mattered, in case truth would help us mount a defense against spurious charges, we would want, so Muscle said, contemporaneous documentation.

I took snapshots from all angles. Muscle reached for the tablet to begin distributing the files, but I pulled it back. None of the images captured what I had seen from the consultant's chair. Sitting there, I had caught a glimpse of the Great Man as I had known him in our time together.

I sat back down. I studied the Great Man as a puzzle in need of solving. I lifted the tablet. After a moment of hesitation, while still in uncertainty, I tapped the button. The effort resembled psychotherapy as I practice it. With patients, I will listen intently and then find myself speaking. Later, thinking back on the session, I will make sense of my words' meaning and function. Action precedes understanding.

Muscle looked over my shoulder. He said, I'll send that shot, all on its own.

He said that the one had more power than the many. The one was message, commentary, and portrait. The one was resistance and requiem.

I tried to see what Muscle saw.

In the photo, the Great Man sprawls belly-down across a couch. He seems outsize. Splayed helter-skelter, the limbs overflow the space. The right knee bends sharply, angling the calf and foot upward. The left leg, extended, points to the bay window through which the scene is lit. The right arm cradles the head. The left hangs limply, the hand touching the floor where the wood is visible beyond the carpet's fringe.

What might be at play, I thought, was a correspondence between how he appeared in death and how he had been in life.

The Great Man cannot be contained. He is every which way. He demands and commands attention.

Looking again, the hair is oddly askew. The neck twists cruelly. The eyes are wild—pleading or threatening. The mouth is agape.

The camera lens has focused on the lower lip, swollen and liverish, and the spot where spittle runs down it to dampen the fabric, a muted herringbone, below. Above the upper lip, the moustache stubble holds a drop of a thick, glossy substance, perhaps from the nose. Around the mouth, the cheeks are slack, pushed into Shar-Pei folds.

The central lesson of my profession is that people's perspectives differ. The corresponding rule is: never assume; always inquire.

I asked Muscle what he saw in the image.

To his eye, the off-putting details evoked the Great Man as he had been in his prime: frightening, pathetic, distasteful, overdramatic, and grotesque.

No, Muscle corrected himself: Not in his prime. Lately, when he was in decline.

Then, too, Muscle continued, for those who encountered it, might not the picture contain a promise of relief? Except for clownish rouge at the cheekbones, the skin is colorless, as if the Great Man were fading, he and his garishness, from our lives.

I have said that, facing the Great Man, I had tried to hold adverse judgments in abeyance. Perhaps as a result, I lacked Muscle's words, *grotesque* and *garish*. My impression of the Great Man had remained inchoate, and purposely so. In therapy, I did not want it to gel prematurely. And yet, I agreed: the photo was the right one. It reflected the Great Man's character, my unformed sense of it, while, at the same time, demonstrating that he was dead, for certain. That was the magic of the image, the tight conjunction of being and non-being, of news past and present.

Muscle sat at my desk with the tablet and prepared to inform the world.

I took my bearings. Three framed prints were missing from the wall behind the couch. They had been removed weeks before, when an emissary of the Great Man coerced me into service. I looked at the naked picture hooks, displayed in dark rectangles where for years the paint had been screened from the sun.

Otherwise, the consulting room was as it had been. It spoke to me of comfort and, now, comfort disturbed, comfort lost. If the Great Man had died in his hideaway, my sympathies might have been more fully with him. In Providence, a sense of place distracted me. The office retained traces of my patients, their burdens, their humor, their insights, subtle reverberations from forty years of speech and silence.

Work is not incidental to my life. I have always loved my work. The room is an instrument constructed for my needs. Miriam designed the seating, specifying the style, fabrics, and upholstering of each piece. Because my therapy is collaborative, she provided identical chairs for my patients and me. The couch, which seats three, has a compatible scale.

These points are trivial, I know, in the face of cataclysm, but it pained me that the prints were missing. It pained me that the couch would be shipped off, as I was guessing, to a forensics laboratory for minute examination. If I am honest—I am trying to be—I must confess that my thoughts strayed from the Great Man, from that loss, and jumped to consequences, personal ones, consequences for me.

I am a homebody. I was close to home. I wanted to go home.

I live in a small, low-ceilinged house, an eighteenth-century colonial on Beneficent Street. Every room bears Miriam's mark.

My wish to be there remained urgent, as did my wish to see my daughter and granddaughter. That had been the plan. First, a sit-down with the Great Man, or the Great Man and his wife, and then family time for me. Nina was at the ready, prepared to leave her office and fetch Tamara from preschool.

The house beckoned. Tammy would rush to pull boxes of blocks from the lowest bookshelves, which are stocked with her toys. She would babble about schoolfriends. My response would reveal that I had confused their names. Nina would worry over my memory loss and my medical conditions. Tammy would become frustrated with a building project and scatter wooden blocks into the hallway.

I missed Tammy's fussing, and Nina's.

My thoughts leapt to the evening and the chance to sleep in my own bed. I have mentioned my means of mourning, conjuring up Miriam. In the Great Man's fortress, she had made appearances. She was lifesaving there. But she is most present in Providence.

Had Muscle caught me daydreaming? He cut in. You do know, he said, that we'll need to leave town?

Not to be brutal, he said, but you are a shrink. You are an easterner.

His list continued. My education. My religion. My late wife's politics. My daughter's circumstances, and my daughter-in-law's. The means by which I had entered the Great Man's life.

And here he was, dead on my couch.

In his followers' eyes, the Great Man was the epitome of health, mental and physical. The EverGreat crowd would not accept that he had died of old age, of stroke or arrythmia—through weakness. The Great Man had taught contempt for vulnerability.

Surely, so the reasoning would go, he had been tricked into coming here. He had been ambushed.

Muscle said, You don't enjoy imprisonment.

If I were not implicated, my patients would be. That was standard procedure, in the Great Man's era—when possible, to pile blame on the mentally ill.

Muscle asked about my patient roster, whether it contained gay men or men of color.

I did not answer, but I understood the question's intent. I would need to be free, free and hidden, if I was to defend my patients.

Was *imprisonment* a euphemism? The Great Man's times were violent. Perhaps Muscle meant that I would not enjoy being hunted down and shot. Perhaps that image, a bullet to the head, was not fearsome enough.

The Great Man, when his anxiety was high, would say, They will turn on me, the mob.

The Great Man toggled between terror and self-congratulation.

I rile them up. I rule by riling.

He was a man who got caught on words, who rolled them in his mouth.

I'm the master riler. No one better at riling.

And then, They will tear me limb from limb.

He held his arms wide. He looked apprehensive, as if he could imagine the torture of dismemberment.

I looked at him now, splayed on the couch. He had been spared the death he feared.

He had a reputation: the harms that he complained of befell others. In the election, he had cried *fraud!*, and his rivals had been defrauded. If the Great Man had not been maimed, who would be? In my mind's eye, I saw my patients, in hiding or being torn—no, too awful to contemplate.

I told Muscle that I would put myself in his hands, rely on his judgment.

He said, Events will move faster than you can imagine.

Muscle sent out the photo, using what he called anonymizing technology, blind remailers and the like, meant to mask the source of the transmission. If, despite his efforts, the location was identified, the discovery would reveal only the obvious. Whoever had taken the photo had been on the scene, in the office.

The file went to prominent social media users with a reputation for trustworthiness—ex-journalists, mostly, who could be relied on to post or forward the photo and who would be believed.

I wondered how much leaking of news Muscle had done in the past. He had addresses lined up. Evidently, he had established his bona fides—that is, the unidentified source's bona fides—with what remained of the independent press, mostly Resistance Underground bloggers skilled at bypassing censors.

Muscle also employed a camouflaging service. It added thousands of recipients with professions and social connections similar to those of the target group. Also included were members of the security community. Muscle was on his own list. Inclusion was camouflage.

Hidden in the welter were Glue and Maury.

Glue, Muscle's counterpart, was guarding the Great Man's wife, whom I call Náomi. I wondered whether Náomi would descend into grief. I wondered whether she would rise up in jubilation.

She would have choices to make. Would she wear widow's weeds and march in the funeral procession?

She had become Marie Antoinette, her name a watchword for heartlessness.

Náomi is complicated, but she is not heartless.

When it was known that the Great Man was dead, Náomi too would be a target of suspicion. Glue would know how to respond.

As would Maury. That's what I had told Muscle. I wanted to rely on Maury—Maurice Keys, my lawyer and lifelong friend. When I say that I am writing at the instigation of my lawyer, I mean Maury.

When Miriam learned that she was dying, she said, For your sake, better me than Maury.

The community, she believed, would find me another wife. There can be no second lifelong friend.

Losing Miriam was not preferable to some other misfortune. But she had meant to remind me of a resource. On occasion, she had teamed up with Maury, to push me toward practicality.

You may have stumbled across Maury's name as well. He has represented prominent reprobates—aging mob bosses and our former mayor. In the standard TV shot, Maury pontificates from a rocking chair on the front porch of his clapboarded house. He's tall and sinewy with the old lefty look: graying ponytail, unruly beard, work shirt, sandals.

If anyone could understand my wish to go home, it would be Maury. When the plans for the Great Man's Rhode Island visit were in place, I had asked Maury to stand on alert in case I had time to meet with him. I had wanted to discuss an exit strategy. When might I sever my ties to the Great Man?

Maury has a house south of the city, in Bristol, Rhode Island, on the old Fourth of July parade route. The view from his kitchen is one Miriam loved—again, with glimpses of the Bay.

I had hoped to meet in that kitchen for an early breakfast on the day after the scheduled office session with the Great Man.

Maury phoned as soon as the photo hit his desktop. The call was brief and cryptic, as if he were concerned that my phone was being tapped. His phone, I knew, would be a burner. As a criminal defense lawyer, he had cause to stockpile burners.

Cooz, Maury said.

He used a joking nickname from our junior high school years. New England had been caught up in the successes of the Boston Celtics. Bob Cousy, the Houdini of the Hardwood, was their ball handler.

On the court, I was Cooz, the point guard, and Maury was Clutch, our power forward. Maury was All-State.

Cooz, yes or no: You remember where we thought we might meet tomorrow morning?

Sure.

Can you get there now and shut yourself indoors? Garage your car if you need to.

He would drop everything and see if he could round up the others I had hoped to visit with.

I would be accompanied, I said, by someone trustworthy.

Maury hung up without having said my name or Nina's or his own. Muscle, too, remained anonymous.

Once I told Muscle that I had a destination, he texted the photo and my office address, 190 Prudence Street, to the Providence Police Department's tip line. There was a chance, he said, that local cops might play the investigation straight, before the Feds intervened.

It used to be the other way, Muscle said.

City police forces had suffered from bias and corruption. The Feds had stood for equal treatment under law.

We've lost bedrock, Muscle said. If the country were to be rebuilt, it would need to be from the ground up—but what was the bedrock?

I think of Muscle as a perceptive young person, someone I would have liked to train in the practice of psychotherapy.

I rose to leave. Rather than say more about the dead man before us, Muscle turned to a different consideration that was salient for me: it's hard to say goodbye to your office.

He was suggesting that my life as it had been, normal life, would not return soon.

◊ ◊ ◊ ◊ ◊

That will-o'-the-wisp, normality! When had we last caught sight of it?

The Great Man's role had been to subvert normality. Before the plague upended our lives, the Great Man did. My Mimi—Miriam—was obsessed with the news. No day without its crisis.

When the plague descended, the Great Man preened and boasted and let it spread. We dealt with illness well or poorly. It laid us low.

What a strange and frightful time.

Mimi was ill, but not of virus. She had cancer, in her glands and then in her blood. The hospital cut her final visit short to free up a bed.

After the return home, a guardian angel, a hospital nurse who had worked with Miriam, left supplies at the back door: medications, syringes, sterile drip bags, surgical tape, IV lines, and liquid food supplements. I had treated the nurse's nephew in my practice. Providence is small in that way.

I administered chemotherapy. Arthritis and cataracts and a slight hand tremor complicated the tasks, but mostly I retained the skills I had practiced in internship. That's one upside to life's brevity. The end of a career is not far from its beginning. I placed butterfly needles and indwelling catheters. I saw to nursing duties, and gratefully.

Before I left the bedroom, I would set the radio to a public news station. Mimi listened. I could not bear to. She told me what I needed to know, which was little.

Of the election, she said, Ignore the polls. He has his ways.

Forget the voting, she said. We will never be rid of him.

She scorned the phrase *second term*.

Why call it a term when it will feel interminable? Why call it a term when it will have no end?

I liked hearing her protest. Outrage boosted her morale.

If Mimi harbored secret hopes, she did not live to see them dashed.

She died as the first plague quarantine was lifting. Funerals had not yet made the all-clear list. Just as well. I don't know how I would have borne up.

Months later, all that Miriam had foreseen came to pass. The Great Man rigged the vote count. He stirred up mobs, coerced legislatures, and leaned on judges. He repeated absurdities until they gained currency. He commandeered the media. He called out armies.

He took the oath of office again in a grand and deadly celebration. He claimed a mandate. The Regime became harsher and more erratic. When the economy collapsed, the Great Man declared a state of emergency. He would govern indefinitely.

Govern over what? A shambles.

When I went on walks, the city spoke for itself. Beloved shops remained shuttered. If I strayed beyond my neighborhood—the East Side, College Hill, Fox Point—kindly strangers approached to offer warnings. The streets were dangerous. I was frail. I had better return home.

The police were understaffed, and not through policy. The defunding movement was cause for nostalgia. Remember when cities had revenue?

I was never mugged. I looked too disturbed, or I was lucky.

As I felt steadier—less self-destructive—I stayed closer to home.

In the face of universal disruption, I looked for ways to re-establish order in my life.

I had worked through the time of the plague, but in desultory fashion. At the start of that crisis, I had tried holding group sessions via the web. My patients had lavished me with technology, to no avail. I was off my game.

Was age to blame? Despite the clever interface, I could not follow the group's moods. I had trouble tracking members who were not speaking. Was one drifting off? Was another annoyed or offended? My patients were less engaged than they had been when we gathered in person.

I said that, if they chose, they could meet virtually. I would absent myself. For a few minutes a week, I spoke with each group member individually, by phone. It was not enough care. It was what I could manage.

I took the plague vaccine. So did my guys, paranoia notwithstanding. When we returned to the office together, we were all so pleased that we wasted precious time beaming at one another.

I decided to buckle down and write. That's how I would cope with loss and absence and my own fragility.

I was and am under contract for a collection of case reports focused on medical errors—my own. I had outlined the proposal after a patient of mine behaved imprudently and died of plague in the early going. You might think that paranoia, with its accompanying suspiciousness and isolation, would have offered protection against the virus. But grandiosity can make you feel invulnerable. That's the damned thing about paranoia. The vigilance deserts you when you need it most.

Now, as I resumed work with patients, I also turned to the book assignment in earnest. I adopted a routine. I would review my notes about a series of therapy sessions and then go for a walk no matter the weather, trying, in imagination, to reconstruct the treatment. When the parts fell into place, I headed home and tapped at the keyboard.

This discipline proved only partly effective.

My psychotherapy mentor, Hans Lutz, had a saying: From the bereaved, we hear only elegy.

Grief colors all it touches. Treating patients who had lost a loved one, I was to understand their complaints and behaviors in the context of the mourning.

Assembling clinical vignettes, I produced elegy. The accounts of therapy were sentimental.

I was out of kilter. In the months of Miriam's illness, I had kept the house clean and organized. I wanted Miriam to have the comforts she had enjoyed in health: a shipshape kitchen, a tidy bedroom, and a trim garden to look out on. After her death, everything slipped. Not drastically. The place was presentable for Tammy's visits. But the sinks didn't gleam.

Like an old New England spiritualist, I longed to conjure the dead. Now and again, it seemed that Miriam was present, and not as a voice from the beyond. She appeared. She grabbed my sleeve. She teased me.

I did not imagine that my wife lived on in another dimension. I knew that the illusion arose from within me. But if I had no belief, I had no doubt either. I accepted the gift of Mimi's company.

I helped out with Tammy. I liked to keep her moving: zoo, woods, beach, playground. Did she remember the quarantine months? Whether she did or not, she loved the outdoors. She was precocious in her athleticism. I taught her to ride a bike, a tiny one with fourteen-inch wheels. I took her to the park at the end of Blackstone Boulevard. Nina had learned there on that same bike. With Tammy, I made up for spills with ice cream. We celebrated progress the same way.

On the drive back to Nina's, Tammy would review her adventures. Or she would turn quiet and hum as she daydreamed. I wondered why Miriam had been denied the pleasure that sound brought.

Patient care was my surest refuge. Was my attention less sharp than it had been? In group, I aimed for unfocused receptiveness. I slipped into a familiar posture, listening to the speaker, hearing music more than words. I monitored responses from other members. I processed a flow of information, recalled past correlates, and crafted responses or let them emerge spontaneously. I monitored my inner state, with reference to my character flaws, blind spots, and prejudices.

Spacing out is part of the process. That's why we can practice into old age.

In the consulting room, more than elsewhere, I was my old self. Perhaps for that reason, I showed up there earlier and stayed later than the caseload demanded. Well, it demanded little. This past year, I was down to a single therapy group that met twice weekly.

◊ ◊ ◊ ◊ ◊

I have never blogged before. I can't say that I know what blogs are—what goes into them. I told Maury as much.

He counseled me to write as I always do. There was no need to seek a new approach or style. Quick and steady production was the goal. *Churn it out.* He would take what I sent him and turn it into blog posts.

I should reference the photo—that's how I was known—and then return to the day that the Regime made contact. I would find my way forward from there.

SITTING AT THE LAPTOP, I find that the two directives conflict. Proceed as usual. Begin at the beginning.

I have always written what comes to mind. That's what has made me productive. Organization comes late on. Here, Maury will need to provide structure on the fly—to delay presenting this section or to omit it, if he thinks chronological order is best. I trust him to decide.

For now, I am recalling a recent session with the Great Man. In a moment of reflection, he spoke of his death and what would follow.

He was having a bad night. He was agitated, he was irrational—not a fair way to introduce him. But we came to a quiet interval between rants.

You will be bereft, he said.

What were you living for, until now?

No greater privilege—serving me.

You call yourself a sleep doctor. You were asleep until I summoned you.

What a dull, tiny, insignificant, weak man you are! Fussy, teary-eyed, pussy-whipped, a peon. Nothing special about you, despite the hype. And yet, here you are, attending on me!

It's not just you who will miss me. How did they pass their time before I came?

I did not ask who *they* were. In the Great Man's monologues, he was always the subject. Others rarely came into focus.

He was not thinking of people's ordinary days, spent working and parenting. He was not thinking of the burdens he had added through misgovernance, of the hours spent tending the ill and standing on food lines. He was referring to excitement. He inspired indignation. He inspired devotion. He kept people on their toes.

He believed that before he assumed power, no one had been fully alert.

I'm like those pills, he said. The tiny ones.

He was a stimulant, if we can imagine an amphetamine that does not focus attention but disrupts it.

When I am gone, he said, they will go into withdrawal.

They will do me in, and then they will pray for my return.

Grim, after me! So grim!

He predicted more despotism, but of a less entertaining sort.

The monologue lost focus. The Great Man returned to warning of dissident militias. He complained about his wife. But there had been that moment of looking forward.

The Great Man was right about his own impending death. Was he right on the other point, that grim tyranny is our fate?

I am writing in isolation, cut off from all news. How are we now?

I AM MEANT TO SAY how I came into the Great Man's employ. It's a story of the sort he bragged about: sudden disruption of a life built on routine.

Mid-October. I walked to my office on a Monday although the calendar was blank. There were professional journals to read, bills to prepare, and letters to answer. My case notes were retrievable through my e-tablet, so I could access them at home, but I told myself that location matters. I find the consulting room evocative. Reviewing a chart while sitting in my customary chair, I may hear a patient's tone of voice or recapture his word choice.

If I were honest, I would admit that I went in because I had an opening in that last remaining group, and therapy groups function poorly when the membership drops. I was hoping to hear the landline ring.

Be careful what you wish for.

When I picked up, the voice was loud, and the tone was irritated, as if I had already caused offense.

You're Henry Farber, the psychiatrist.

From the first words, I knew—thought I knew—what I was facing.

For some years, I had specialized in the treatment of paranoid men. Most doctors shy away from work with paranoia. The patients tend not to get better. The unpleasant ones threaten you. The nice ones are heartbreakers, sweet in their hope that you will share their fantasies, ever more anxious about threats and plots. The risk of violence and suicide is constant. Once word got out that I would take on these cases, colleagues were happy to refer them.

My caller, I imagined, had visited a local physician who, in the evaluation session, had made a subtle error. The doctor had winced, a response that betrayed disbelief in one of the patient's delusions. Offended, the patient had headed for the door. Quickly, the colleague had mentioned me as someone sympathetic to this sort of complaint. Now the man was phoning, but petulantly, primed to explode in response to further insult.

The caller said, I can be in town tomorrow. I want to arrange a morning meeting.

Meeting, not session or appointment. Many contacts began this way, with a conversation stripped of indicators of patient status.

I was sorry to disappoint. My practice was closed, mostly closed. If the caller would let me know what he was looking for, I would try to be of help.

Nina did not accept that a wandering mind is part of the therapeutic process. I must stop taking on new patients. Did she know that I was resistant in this one regard? When I came down to a single group, I reserved the right to keep it afloat.

My apology to the caller—*mostly closed*—sounds obedient to Nina. It was, but in strategic fashion. If the prospective patient turned out not to be paranoid, I could say *no* without having raised expectations. And in the context of paranoia, foot-dragging can constitute acknowledgment. The patient finds the world obdurate and its inhabitants cagy. Early on, the doctor may do well to conform to expectations.

I'm looking for you, the voice said.

But why?

I'm looking to meet.

With each show of stonewalling, my spirits rose.

I want to speak to you on behalf of a third party—highly confidential.

Ah, for a friend. Better and better.

This third party has a problem.

Contempt? Arrogance? Those words appear in my phone notes, followed by question marks. Then I wrote: *familiar voice*?

Have we spoken? You've phoned before?

Let's stop going down this path. I'm calling for a person who has learned of your reputation indirectly.

I strained to recollect phone conversations from recent weeks. Had my caller tried me back when there was no group opening? I would have offered a referral. He would have rung off.

Relieved that I knew why the voice was familiar, I returned to letting the man make his case.

Your acquaintance has been referred?

Someone who knows your work recommends you. My principal has deputized me to interview you and form a judgment.

I'll need the names, I said, yours and your friend's.

Instead, my caller asked, There's garage space below your office?

He was not the first to propose this stratagem, driving in through the alley and then climbing the back stairs to ensure privacy.

The caller upped the demands: Leave your car elsewhere. Have the garage door open.

I wrote *entitled* and underlined the word.

It's after ten-thirty now, my caller said. Am I right in assuming that half past ten is convenient tomorrow as well? I'll be in your parking space.

To be clear, I said, I rarely accept patients.

My caller interrupted, My client will not be a patient. We'll bring you on as an advisor.

You can see why I thought that paranoia was at issue.

I said, Even so.

I use that phrase when I want to stand firm without provoking a fight. Here, it meant, We'll see.

Then, my caller said something strange: *Speak to your daughter*.

Was he a friend of Nina's? Or the father of one of her friends? I wondered whether Nina had made the referral and, if so, whether she would give me permission to take this man on, no matter the suitability for group treatment.

I still need contact information, I said, but the line had gone dead.

◊ ◊ ◊ ◊ ◊

Should I have been more on guard? On that day, the day of the brusque phone call, I failed to make an obvious connection.

Nina had texted early that morning, saying that she wanted to meet. She did not reach out often. But even when the disagreeable caller said *your daughter*, I did not imagine that the two efforts to make contact, his and hers, were related.

On receiving Nina's text, I had speculated about her agenda. Did she need help affording an afternoon activity program for Tamara? I would hear the particulars and volunteer to bear the costs. Nina would have paid me back already by lunching with me and discussing her current concerns, a fair exchange.

When it comes to time with my daughter, I'm a perennial optimist. I imagine meet-ups that flow smoothly and end well.

I had suggested lunch at a restaurant, Zervas Diner—no apostrophe—in walking distance of Nina's office and my own.

Zervas had been a favorite of Miriam's. She was particular about restaurants, in an unusual way. Often, the décor irked her. She found Zervas comfortable: scuffed floor tiles, mustard-yellow banquettes in narrow booths with their own coat hooks. The service consisted of thick-rimmed water glasses scratched with years of use and heavy cream-colored plates with a single burgundy stripe at the edge. Not retro, just unchanged.

The original owner, Phil Zervas, had long since sold the place to a family from the Azores. The short order cook, Ildeberto, who goes by Al, reigned from behind the chrome-and-Formica serving counter. Adelina, the waitress and Al's younger sister, ignored or insulted you.

Addie knew Miriam's breakfast order, white grapefruit juice and one egg poached lightly on dry rye toast. When I tried to order the fruit cup, Addie would turn to Miriam and say, Shall I bring the doctor what he wants? Out would come corned beef hash with a fried egg and a side of home fries, a sprig of parsley the sole concession to norms of healthy eating.

When Miriam was still well, Al had told her that he was heading toward retirement. The diner was on the market.

Recently, I had run into Al at the dry cleaner. Al offered condolences. I asked how he was using his new leisure time.

The deal had fallen through. There was no market. The plague closed restaurants. When he reopened, power grid hacks caused shutdowns. Food sourcing was iffy. Customers were scarce. You would think that affordable restaurants would fare better than high-end ones, but his regulars had no disposable income.

The litany sounded rehearsed. Al had run through it in his mind and with other customers. I had never before heard Al put two sentences together.

But he made concessions, Al said, out of the blue.

I took it that Al was referring to the Great Man. He kowtowed to our enemies abroad. It seemed unfair that they should cripple our electric systems.

If I asked Al to explain, I would risk opening a can of worms. Instead, I apologized for not having stopped into the restaurant. In Providence, there were many places I avoided because the next visit would be the *first one since* and Miriam's absence would be palpable.

Al picked up a stack of clean white uniforms and draped them across his forearms.

I got the door.

Before he turned toward his van, Al whispered, I supported him.

People offer me confessions. Occupational hazard.

I took Al to be saying that through errors in judgment he had contributed to his own misfortune. He had supported the Great Man, perhaps even in the stolen second term. Now, Al would never escape the space between the counter and the grill.

Blurted revelations never tell the whole story. What more burdened Al? Had he marched on the centers of power, weapon in hand? I could see it, just about, a final burst of loyalty before Al allowed himself to understand that he'd been had.

The encounter at the dry cleaner's was news, local news, economic and political news, as useful to me as any broadcast roundup.

THE DAY OF THE MYSTERY phone call, I took care to arrive late for lunch. Perhaps Nina's presence would distract me from the setting. I find it wonderful to happen upon my daughter although I know there's a chance of an onslaught. That combined feeling can't be rare, tenderness in two senses, a melting warmth and an awareness that bruises are in the offing.

Here she was, my Nina, with her tough-gal look—close-cropped hair, sweatshirt with ragged short sleeves, well-toned arms, broad beaten-metal bracelets that would protect a knight in battle. She was scowling, and her scowls are something to behold. Parental love washed over me.

Could you have picked a grimmer place? was Nina's opening. Al was at the griddle. She cocked her head in his direction.

Slumped shoulders, downcast eyes, a slow shuffle between stations. Al was the picture of melancholy when what we expect in a short-order cook is briskness and command.

Dad? Nina said, as if my mind had wandered.

His name's Al, I said to Nina. Al has his reasons.

I saw the plates and glasses as Nina did. What had been *period* for Miriam was simply shabby.

I said, Mom liked the ambience. She liked Al.

Nina looked at him as I spoke. Al was giving Nina the once-over.

I had a dark thought. I imagined that Al saw Nina's get-up and blamed her for his predicament, she and her kind, whatever kind he imagined hers to be. She had pushed the culture along too insistently, and he had been moved to support the Great Man, and where were we now?

I worried that Nina would see the once-over as unpleasant in a different way and offer a further rebuke for my choice of lunch spot. *He's leering at me, your Al-who-has-his-reasons.*

However loyally I echoed her condemnation, I would be in the wrong. Nina does not consider me competent to discuss the male gaze or any topic involving gender. She dislikes how I arrived at my views, through work with patients, abused and abusers, through trying to share their terror or despair or sadistic impulses. Nina values sisterhood, solidarity, and firsthand experience. She's had it with men. Men mistreat women. Men mistreated the country, putting it in the hands of a tin-hat despot.

News or no news, there he was—the Great Man—in my consciousness, because I imagined that he was in Al's and Nina's.

Nina said, However do you treat patients if you take five minutes to respond to a simple question and then don't answer it?

Aging is strange. I'd experienced my conversation as on-beat.

Nina said, I asked what you eat here.

On cue, Addie was at our side, order pad at the ready.

Dr. F—the usual? Same for your girlfriend? Man doesn't waste time.

I was relieved that Addie did not chide me for my long absence.

Our daughter, I said.

I shouldn't joke. We miss your Mimi. You know we do, dear. We missed you, too, and I'm glad to see you looking well. Isn't he, hon, looking well?

You, too, Addie said, meaning Nina. You know, when you walked in, I told my brother, Look at that gal, how perfectly that get-up suits her. No, I did. Take a gander, I said. If I could pull it off, I'd come to work in that outfit tomorrow.

Zervas was as I had known it to be, cozy and welcoming. What I had taken as an intrusive appraisal had been an attempt on Al's part to see Nina as his sister did, admiringly. It is good for a doctor who treats paranoia to be reminded of his own. Now, I felt unease on another grounds. Why hadn't Nina snapped at someone—me or Al or Addie? Nina was showing forbearance. Was something amiss?

The house luncheon salad, I said—my belated answer to the question of what Nina might eat. They use imported olives and sheep feta, always have, since Phil Zervas's time—isn't that right?

No longer, Addie said. The importer went out of business. You know, hon, what with tariffs, what with the dollar as it is, restaurants have to go with domestic.

The Great Man reached that far—down to the food on our plates.

Just as good, very nearly as good, Addie said, to Nina now.

Two salads, I said. No, really, Addie. Salad.

If she brought hash, when she set the dish before me, I would fall apart.

When Addie turned away, I asked Nina, There's no big issue you're avoiding?

She moved the salt and pepper shakers aside as if to clear the space between us.

I braced myself, but not well enough.

It's Kareena, Nina said. She's been asked to report to Deportation.

Kareena is Nina's wife. That status—marriage—ought to have protected Kareena, despite the Great Man's on-and-off diktats on residence and citizenship.

Nina had come to her topic slowly. She was out to handle me.

First, we got a phone call warning us that Kareena had overstayed her visa. I explained to the agent that Kareena is legal, that she's my wife, approved provisionally for a green card. While the application is pending, all deportation proceedings are suspended. Her work status should protect her as well. Her employer has her down as a critical worker.

The voice on the phone insisted. The visa was outdated.

Nina said, Today, a guy with a badge came to the door asking for Kareena. He handed me a summons. She has a week to get her papers in order—actually, a week to pack.

We had been through similar crises before. I was ready to slow the conversation, to suggest where we might turn for help. Nina chose to preempt me.

The immigration lawyer who had worked with Kareena had retooled and switched to maritime law. Immigrants had lost all protections. There was no longer any case to argue.

So terrible, I said. I can't imagine.

How had their lives—our lives—taken this sharp turn?

I said, Walk me through it. Tell me what you've learned.

Addie came with salads, and I thanked her.

Trying to be good, she said.

I thought of Kareena. Outside the workplace, she was at loose ends. Kareena was made for the life she had, an orderly life, managed by a hardheaded and dynamic wife.

Can the gaming people advocate for her? I asked.

Kareena worked at a firm that runs state lotteries, one of those countercyclical businesses that flourish when people grasp at straws. The job, the result of it—the poor risking what little they had—caused Kareena discomfort. Hard times forced us all into complicity.

Dad, Nina said. In her speech, *Dad* is an expletive signifying exasperation.

She reminded me how rarely companies stand up to the Regime.

I began apologizing for my impulse to suggest solutions when Nina would have thought through every alternative. But she was looking past me to the door.

I did not need to turn my head to know who was entering. Nina brightened and then found she needed to daub her eyes.

Kareena touched my shoulder and leaned in to kiss me on the side of the forehead.

You're looking handsome, Poppa. And serious. I love it when you take on a thoughtful look.

Sometimes I think that Kareena's impression of this country came from *Gone with the Wind*, the movie. Her notion of appropriate behavior is a breezy sociability in the face of stress. Sadly, she's a poor actress. She grasped the back of my chair for support.

You forgot the backpack, she said to Nina.

It was made of silvery mesh and contained Tammy's pink dance shoes and tutu.

Nina stood to take the ballet gear and give Kareena a distant hug.

Sit down, I said. You need to eat lunch anyway.

But Kareena was rushed, on a quick break from the office. She was racing to get her files organized in case she would need to hand them off.

Please join us, I said. But she was gone.

Kareena is a slender woman, naturally elegant, with an almond-shaped Modigliani face and almond eyes, a wheat-stalk woman who would be bent to the ground in any breeze.

Could I imagine her in rags, subsisting on scraps?

I could, and I could have even without the lightening visit.

Make an appearance, Nina must have begged. Drop in for a minute, to remind Dad what's at stake. You won't have to speak. You won't need to hold yourself together. A quick in-and-out. Here—the backpack—make like I forgot it.

My seeing Kareena was meant to give her plight immediacy, to heighten my commitment to the rescue effort. Should I have been insulted by the thought that drama was needed? I love Kareena. I love her as Tammy's mother and Nina's wife and my second daughter. If she were none of those, I would want to protect her still.

Perhaps Nina was not wrong to manipulate me. She understood that I am driven by the sight of people. When Nina broke the news, I had been desperate on Kareena's behalf. I was more desperate now.

To control my emotions, I returned to sounding practical.

Maury can accompany her to the hearing.

There's no hearing to speak of.

The Deportation Service followed a rapid removal policy. The administrator invalidated you, and you were shipped out.

You go to the hearing with Kareena, I said, you and Maury. I'll watch Tammy.

The tiny ballet togs were hanging from a coat hook at the end of the booth. Vulnerability was on my mind.

Nina took my offer to babysit as further evidence of cluelessness.

I'll drop in on Maury, I said.

Nina turned silent and picked at her salad. After an interval, she raised her face and revealed why she had summoned me.

Last year, when I was at the Immigration Service office downtown—it was still called that, Immigration—one of the administrators asked after you. A bony woman, no flesh on her, anorexic possibly, with an eye twitch? Luiza—Azores-Island Portuguese by origin, I'm thinking. It occurred to me then that this Luiza might have been a patient of yours.

Dad, help me. Am I making this up? A woman in her sixties? A careful dresser, blouse pressed just so. Accent like the waitress's here—local kid, maybe, who came up in federal service? Sound familiar?

Nina knew not to ask that sort of question.

In bad times, every choice involves betrayal. My love of family is absolute, but so is the doctor's oath. *Whatsoever I shall see or hear in the course of my profession I will never divulge, holding such things to be holy secrets.*

You know I can't comment, I said.

The encounter came back to me today when I saw the name on the exit order, Nina said. Maria Luiza de Souza. Kareena agrees—the same woman. She must be a regional director now.

Take a day, Nina said. Sleep on it. Talk to Maury. But no more than a day. We're under the gun.

Knowing that I would hesitate, Nina had prepared this offer. Take a day to forsake your principles.

It was not my wisdom that Nina was seeking, but my influence. Fathering consists of a series of pratfalls. That's one of its virtues. It sets you in your place.

I doubted that I could be of use, doubted that there was a difficulty for which communication with Luiza de Souza was a solution. And yet, it seemed that I would need to approach her.

I know now that Nina and I were both feeling our way in the dark. We assumed that Kareena's banishment was one more instance of the random cruelty that was common under the Great Man. His lackeys would demand action from an agency. Officials would select victims, destroy their lives, and then, following another of the Great Man's whims, change direction.

Arbitrocracy was the name that Nina gave to the form of government, autocracy applied in arbitrary fashion. We were not in a totalitarian regime, she said, if total implies competent, uniform, or consistent. Arbitrocracy might lead to totalitarianism and even persist within it, but so far, we were only en route. The Great Man imposed grave harm capriciously. That was how he wielded power, how he silenced objectors. That was how he shaped our lives—mine, Nina's, Kareena's, and Tamara's.

I see that I am trying to justify my mistaken belief that the threat to Kareena had come out of the blue.

Dad, Nina said, listen. You're a vain man. Your scruples are a form of vanity. Stop being vain.

She gave me a goodbye kiss.

It is a sign of my unawareness that Nina was almost out the door before I thought to ask her about the morning's caller, whether she had referred him.

Nina looked at me as if I were deranged. How could I introduce a new topic? Kareena's plight was all there was. It filled the universe.

◊ ◊ ◊ ◊ ◊

When I phoned Maury's number, I hit voicemail. I texted and set out walking to his office. Grief made me willing to rely on chance, to put myself at its mercy.

Maury works in a substantial row house in a residential neighborhood of College Hill that overlooks the downtown. A century back, an attorney converted the building's first two floors into an office suite for his own use.

There is no pretense to the setting, no hint that Maury wields power.

We had made vows at the height of the plague, hadn't we, that if we ever again got to taste the pleasures we had lost, we would treasure them? I love sitting in Maury's reception area. It is carved out of a hallway, high-ceilinged, dark, and narrow. A couch, upholstered in old, cracked leather affixed with brass studs, sits against a wall. Maury has decorated the space with art nouveau bicycling posters. Riders outrace a tiger. Riders climb mountain peaks at impossible angles. Jaunty riders make toasts with fashionable drinks. When Maury forsook basketball, he took to the roads.

Maury was a cyclist before everyone was a cyclist. He likes to say that he's never braked on a downhill.

Therapists need their therapy. Waiting for Maury was mine. Some of my best writing ideas came to me on that couch.

I felt secure because Maury is unlike me. He gives advice. He solves problems. He leans on contacts for favors. When Maury takes matters in hand, things work out.

My optimism exasperates Nina.

Why is there such distance between fathers and their grown daughters?

Love gets in the way. Nina scowls, and waves of affection sweep over me.

I have said that I studied psychotherapy with Hans Lutz. The name no longer carries weight, but he was admired in his day.

Early in my training, Hans observed me through a one-way mirror while I interviewed a hostile patient. The man spoke of his expertise in martial arts. He could snap me in two. He had that thought.

I thanked him for being frank about his impulses. What had I done to perturb him? What harm did he intend?

Hans encouraged me. If, in the face of threat, we respond with fear or counterthreat, what use are we to our patients? Sometimes it is good to feel what a patient feels, sometimes it is good to feel what a patient aims to provoke, and sometimes it is best to go in another direction. When a patient turns up the intensity, we become curious.

*Inappropriate affect* was Maury's term for the skew response. He considered it a talent, one that I should develop further. That morning, on the phone, as my prospective patient turned ever more disagreeable, I had felt encouraged. *He's one of mine!*

Nina often reminds me that she's not my patient. *Dad, don't try that psychotherapy stuff on me.*

I do not protest, but *that stuff* is how I approach conversation and how I express caring. We choose our careers because of who we are, and then they make us more like ourselves.

Sitting outside Maury's office, I wondered, Does a trial lawyer's daughter forgive his sly questioning, his way of springing surprises and arguing her into a corner?

Sorry to wake you, Maury said. We can't let every bum sleep in our lobby.

Maury waved me into the office.

What can I bring you?

He had whole-leaf black tea from—somewhere—my mind was not on tea.

Clients have no money. Soon, they'll be paying with chickens, Maury said. His father had been a plumber. His father claimed to have been paid with chickens.

I began to lay out Kareena's story, but Maury waved his hand.

We drank tea together out of Jena glass cups.

Maury's fingers were all arthritic nodes, Heberden's and Bouchard's. Was he developing a fine tremor?

Maury was a mirror. In his hands I was seeing my own.

Maury said, Poor girl!

Words you don't want coming from a lawyer's mouth.

Those bastards send immigrants away for any reason and no reason.

Put too little postage on an envelope, and they'll ship you to a war zone.

The Feds may fail at constructive tasks, but they're skilled at banishing innocents.

The law is not your friend here, Maury said. And the courts are worse than the law. They've stacked the courts.

Visas no longer sufficed. Even citizenship offered slim protection if it came through naturalization. Revocations were common.

Maury threw his arms up and sent papers flying, to convey their worthlessness.

Politics, Cooz. When the law won't help, we look to politics.

What had Nina and Kareena done to attract the interest of the authorities?

I had no notion.

Maury said, It's been many months since I've seen this sort of case.

On coming to power, the Great Man had made a show of mercilessness, dispatching women and children to countries where violence awaited them.

Plague surges and mass unemployment had solved the immigration problem. Deportation was no longer a priority, no longer a shtick. With everyone suffering, there was no box office in creating that particular sort of misery.

But then, rotating demagoguery was the Great Man's trademark. He might well return to blaming joblessness on immigrants.

I am always content to hear Maury think aloud.

As if I were a naïf, he reviewed the state of our knowledge.

Do you ever flip on the TV? he asked me.

The Regime controlled communications. Its disinformation services had raided Hollywood CGI departments for talent. They could make the Great Man appear to speak from anywhere. Regularly, Regime News flooded people's screens with assurances that the Great Man governed calmly from the capital.

But the Resistance web had compiled hints that the Great Man was sequestered elsewhere. Foreigners were no longer an issue. He feared his own people—feared uprisings. Live by the mob, die by the mob.

Finally, Maury doubted that there was a new campaign of deportation. Something local was at issue. Had Kareena's corporation interfered with the Great Man's gaming interests? What projects did she manage? Maury would want that information fast.

Where the Regime was out to punish, the courts were useless. No judge would intervene.

Maury promised to call in debts. He would reach out to colleagues north and south of our borders, to see whether Kareena might be offered safe haven. As for interrupting the expulsion: the process turned on pull, not law. Did I have pull?

I said, The nature of my profession....

Ah, yes, Maury teased me. The sacred profession.

As I stood to leave, he put his hand on my shoulder. Touch was welcome.

Discouraging times, Maury said. They go on and on.

He offered me a tin of tea, but I did not want consolation.

◊ ◊ ◊ ◊ ◊

Home alone, I went online, looking for news or propaganda, anything that might offer a hint about *why now*, why Kareena's file had been pulled. Either the Regime had scrubbed the relevant websites, or I lacked the skill to exploit them. I gave up and headed to bed early, intending to settle in with a novel from Miriam's bedside shelf. That was a project of mine, working my way through her books.

I was many pages into a tome by Karl Ove Knausgård, a Norwegian author who had been one of Miriam's favorites. He writes about life in its details, how an unremarkable evening unfolds, how objects look close up, how we feel when shopping for dinner or comforting an unhappy child. Miriam craved the everyday.

At Miriam's bedside, I had found myself jealous. Why spend an hour on Knausgård's reminiscence of adolescence when Miriam could turn to me and share her own memories of the years before our courtship? Was it that reading seemed an achievement? In her sickbed, she had mastered another chunk of literature. She had done something with her time.

In contrast, my time seemed simply to arrive and disappear. I provided companionship. It was good to contribute. But every minute was loss. I was losing Miriam.

To her, Knausgård was a magician. An hour with him offered days of ordinariness. He might take a hundred pages to describe an uneventful evening, but for a reader, even the slow-motion account constituted compression.

In bereavement, I turned to Knausgård as a way to join Miriam.

Reading that night, I was mired in a discussion of epochs. We are constrained to live in our epoch, Knausgård writes, all of us except, perhaps, a few visionaries. A man who is a good husband or father by the lights of a past era may be a bad husband or father today, and not because others say so. He himself will want to be the man that current norms demand.

I thought, The observation has the beauty of a truth that is evident once stated, and still, it calls for a caveat. Around and alongside us are men who want marriage to be what it was in past decades, men for whom that wish is so strong that they will turn to a leader who assures them that old standards apply. We might argue that the nation was ruined by the assumption that we all inhabit the same epoch. The Great Man's genius was in understanding that epochs coexist or lack uniformity.

Perhaps this objection only demonstrates the centrality of Knausgård's point. The epoch and its standards create the context for action, so that resistance to them can define a political movement.

We might also say that the Great Man's ascent signaled the emergence of a new epoch, one whose values we dismiss at our peril. He set the example: grab what you can. Ignore those you injure. I had not entered the epoch.

That was one way to understand Nina's attribution to me, at lunch, of vanity. Who did I think I was, clinging to outmoded ideals?

The book was heavy. I set it down, switched off the light, and lay awake thinking of Kareena and her prospects.

Take me in her place, I said, as one does, to no one in particular.

I wanted life to continue as it had been or, better yet, for time to run backward.

Who did not have that wish, in the era of the Great Man? Repeatedly, we proposed compromises. We could live with conditions as they had been a year before, a month before, a day. To our dismay, we were here now.

Nina had been right to make Kareena drop by, to help me appreciate, intensely, what was at stake. In a refugee camp, Kareena's fate would be what? Hunger? Beatings? Rape? I saw her neglecting self-care, fading into nothingness. Might she have a flinty, rugged aspect, not yet revealed? Even if so, she would suffer.

What, then, of Nina when she recalls that her father did not do his all? From abroad, from the Middle East, Kareena phones, in tears or stone-faced, open or closed off, to discuss the horror or avoid alluding to it.

Nina confronts me: Medical ethics? What ethics are those?

Retiring to bed had brought no relief. I felt stomach acid rising. The sour gut added to my usual nighttime woes, the sore hip and throbbing great toe.

I was distraught with worry over Kareena. I was distraught at the prospect of approaching Luiza and doing harm—to a former patient, to my profession.

How wrong is it to beg a favor of a patient? The act must rank low on the list of compromises in the era of the Great Man. The newly impoverished turned to theft or drug sales. Those who despised the Great Man and his goals signed on nonetheless to serve the Regime, to get square meals. How many veteran bureaucrats had, under pressure, undone all they had worked for—in hopes, vain hopes, of averting worse? What was asked of me must seem trivial.

We have, all of us, less control over our emotional states than we imagine, and not much more over our moral sensibilities. For me, using my powers of persuasion on Luiza would constitute a betrayal of self.

I had been this way forever.

In bed, far from sleep, I thought of Miriam and how she had sized me up in our first hour together. I was in my junior year of college. Maury had dragged me to a Hillel event meant to bring Brown boys and Pembroke girls together. In a sea of tie-dye, Marimekko, Pucci knockoffs, and paisley-patterned paper dresses, there was Miriam in a modest tan corduroy shift. She was lively in herself. She had red hair, wavy, in a bob. She had freckled skin and a mocking laugh.

Maury showed off to her, bragging about how he tapped into phone lines to make long distance calls and how he filched food from the dining service. I had been hanging back. Miriam asked whether I stole food as well.

I didn't—hadn't.

Why ever not, if everyone did?

I reached for an answer. I found not stealing—never stealing—convenient. One less thing to think about. No risk-induced high, no urge to repeat. No getting caught and expelled. No guilt. Why live with guilt? I was doing what was practical for me. I was a pragmatist—a pragmatist with an exigent conscience.

Convenient? Miriam said. A stash of food in your dorm room is convenient.

She held out a paper plate with canapés, to illustrate. We were not yet in the day of hummus or cherry tomatoes. Crustless cucumber sandwiches were still the norm, and similar ones, only on dark bread, stuffed with spreadable pimento cheese.

She said, You're a Kantian.

She had been reading ahead, trying to make sense of an assignment for an introductory humanities course.

She said, For you, stealing is wrong, period.

She guessed that I was embarrassed to say what I thought, afraid of appearing priggish. But I believed that there were things that one should never do—wasn't that so? Putting stealing in that category was Kantian.

She had, as I say, a mocking smile. Her premise was that, on first meeting, she knew me better than I knew myself or knew more than I was willing to reveal.

I said that I would steal to get medicine for a dying person.

I had the example from a psychology course, one that discussed moral development in children.

Miriam said that when it came time to steal the medicine, my friend—Maury—would be better at it, since he was in the habit. He would manage to deliver the life-saving drug. It seemed that I should steal after all, right now, to get practice.

I agreed. Maury was the better man.

To my astonishment, Miriam stayed in touch. Days after the Hillel mixer, she was with me in my dorm room, on the cot beside me, her back propped against the wall, her leg against mine.

She was making margin notes in a Kant essay, the one where he says that truth-telling is a perfect duty, a requirement that we should fulfill at any cost. The best-known example is the inquiring murderer at the door. When he asks whether his intended victim is with us in our home, we are obliged to say what we believe to be the case: Yes, she is.

That's you to a T, Miriam said, picking up where she had left off. You prefer to act on principle, even when principle points in an impractical direction.

Set aside the implications of the analysis, that was I stiff-necked and unworldly. I liked that Miriam had tried to make sense of me.

I protested. If she was the murderer's target, I would lie to protect her, and vigorously. *Miriam in my house? That hussy? I wouldn't let her past the door!*

But you would feel the injury of your needing to lie.

She had me dead to rights.

She had me all wrong.

I would do anything to keep her from harm and feel joy if I succeeded.

Miriam rubbed her leg against mine and rolled toward me.

Afterward, she said that she had found it appealing that I made no claims for myself or my values. Miriam was used to men who had answers to everything. Her father was like that, and her brothers.

The next morning, she told me that her father was a con man, in prison at that very moment. He had been caught repeatedly. Always, the family had paid a price. She was here on scholarship, supplemented by support from an uncle on her mother's side.

Had those early encounters come to mind because of the Knausgård passage? From the start, Miriam had pegged me as not of our time. Her judgment was less absolute than Nina's. Miriam mocked my scruples and was drawn to me because of them.

It helped that I went on to medical school. Miriam loosened me up in civilian life, in the home. I managed to wall off my rigidity by making obedience to doctorly ethics a perfect duty. Professions can absorb a fair amount of attention to right and wrong. Psychotherapists treat people who have been disappointed or betrayed by those they have relied on. Our patients appreciate absolutism if it reads as trustworthiness.

I found crossing certain lines horrific. I would not occur to me to cash in on information acquired incidentally in a treatment session. I asked no favors of patients, did not want even to elicit their gratitude. My impulses were in the opposite direction, to thank them for entrusting me with their care.

That posture is basic for the doctor. When a person turns to me for treatment, I must not try to extract benefit beyond the psychic one that comes, if I earn it, from satisfaction in a job well done.

It was not only my moral fervor that medicine absorbed. I was devoted to the profession. That channeling of feeling—of loyalty and affection—relieved Miriam. She liked when I turned my zeal elsewhere.

Once pledged, allegiances are hard to shift. I badly wanted to put family first, to let my paternal protective instincts guide my actions. But I wondered whether I could, in good conscience, ask Luiza de Souza to intervene for my sake.

In revoking Kareena's visa, Luiza had, I assumed, been responding to a new Regime directive to reclassify certain immigrants. Or else, as Maury had suggested, Luiza had bowed to pressure from superiors who were bending the law for political or financial purposes, say, to advance the Great Man's interests in the gaming industry. If she granted Kareena a reprieve, Luiza might find herself subject to dismissal, pension loss, or worse. Did I imagine that I was free to injure a patient—to ask her to expose herself to reprisals in the workplace?

How did Nina expect me to approach Luiza? I might ask her a favor neutrally, so as not to exert undue pressure. But I was committed to saving Kareena. Surely, I would do my all—act strategically, to maximum effect, tugging on the heartstrings, bringing to bear my skills as a persuader and my intimate knowledge, from the psychotherapy, about Luiza and what might sway her. Failure was unthinkable.

So, in a different way, was success.

Years ago, Maury read me a passage from a book about a bicycle racer. On a mountain climb, as the pitch got steeper, the rider refused to downshift, preferring to bear pain. He reasoned, If I downshift, why am I racing at all?

That's me, Maury said. That's how I am even on a weekend jaunt in Westport.

If I could not keep the relationship between doctor and patient inviolable, why was I practicing? Doctors who cross moral lines do harm to the profession and to our faith in humankind.

◊ ◊ ◊ ◊ ◊

At lunch, I had not tipped my hand, but I remembered Luiza well. I had written about her in *Rest for the Weary*, my first book. It launched me as a writer and let me establish and expand my private practice. Luiza owed me nothing. I owed her.

It's extraordinary how large that book looms—its popularity, its effect on my image. I did not know it yet, but *Rest* was responsible for the bind I was in. In roundabout fashion, the book had brought me to the Great Man's attention and shaped his expectations of me. Without *Rest*, there would have been no threat to Kareena.

I wrote *Rest* by chance.

After medical school at Brown, I had stayed through residency and beyond. Brown's program was young. It had been founded to produce practicing doctors who would remain in Rhode Island. That was the mandate, to improve care locally. For faculty, research requirements were minimal. But soon, a new and ambitious dean arrived. The med school aimed for academic stature. I was expected to produce a steady flow of papers in influential journals.

Luckily, I had a connection to our local sleep researcher, Margaret Muldowney. She was a scientist in a particular mold:

sharp, methodical, uncomfortable with emotion. Conducting an insomnia study, Peggy might mistakenly enroll patients who proved risky and burdensome—depressed and suicidal. I took those cases off her hands.

I doubt that Peggy respected my work. I relied on intuition. She trusted rating scales. What made me useful was that I hated to say no to patients. I took on all comers.

Shortly after I learned that I would need academic credentials, Peggy won funding for a clinical trial that proved unwieldy. She proposed testing two psychotherapies for insomnia. One therapy targeted maladaptive cognitions by training patients to shed fruitless worries about wakefulness. The other targeted maladaptive behaviors by reinforcing good sleep hygiene—no TV when in bed, and so on.

She had intended to contrast the cognitive and behavioral approaches to each other and to a sedative hypnotic drug, but the funding agency required an additional comparison condition, a more eclectic psychotherapy. She thought that my approach might fit the bill. I could let patients speak about whatever came to mind—marital resentments, job troubles, feelings of inferiority. In the write-up phase, I would describe my work, and my name would appear on the resulting monographs—the ticket to continued faculty appointments at Brown.

Peggy's inviting me on board fell just shy of insult. I was to perform a non-specific intervention that was bound to fail. My calling card was ignorance about tailored treatments of sleep disorders. Surely expertise would outperform improvisation.

Randomly, participants (Luiza among them) were assigned me. Besides exhaustion, I asked, was anything troubling them? They would explain what kept them up nights, or they would stay silent, and I would wonder aloud whether something in my approach was inhibiting—until they relaxed and began to confide in me.

When the study data were complied, they showed that my undirected therapy had performed better than the carefully crafted treatments. Better than the sleeping pill too. Ever the honest scientist, Peggy published the results, listing me as a co-author. In her discussion, she speculated that the influence of a single charismatic practitioner had distorted the outcomes and effectively invalidated the trial. She should have spread the control-group work—unstructured therapizing—among a number of clinicians.

*Charismatic* in this usage means calming. As I have suggested, Hans believed that I had that effect on patients.

The day that the sleep study appeared in print, I got a call from a young editor in New York, another Margaret, Meg Galliard. She was tasked with skimming professional journals in search of ideas that might be turned into popular science books. Meg asked whether I was the charismatic healer. She was a fan of free-form therapies, but it was hard to publish books about them because there was no hook, no angle. She liked this idea of outperforming highly designed, technical treatments. Would I gather patient anecdotes?

Fortuitously, I had all the permissions. On entering the study, participants had granted the researchers the right to discuss their cases in print, so long as an effort was made to disguise identities.

I learned a lesson about consent. From the day that I opened my private practice, in every first session or the phone call preceding it, I asked prospective patients for permission to write about them in disguised fashion. I would alter their name and assign them a different job and family size and so on, to conceal their identity—but the disguising might fail. There was always risk of exposure.

Maury had helped me craft a presentation incorporating those warnings. He called it the spiel. I was to say that I was both a doctor and an author. I considered public education to be a critical part of medicine. For those reluctant to be written about, I would arrange a referral to a less demanding colleague.

Was the spiel coercive? If so, I was less of a Kantian than Miriam imagined. But I had trained in the Vietnam War years, when callings needed to be *relevant*—to do public good. Medicine was directed at the populace as well as the individual. And I had no illusions about my special powers as a healer. Patients leery of giving consent would do fine. In practice, few chose to go elsewhere.

The sleep study volunteers were similarly gracious. Not wanting to rely on the research consent form alone, I re-contacted those I hoped to depict in a vignette. All were willing for me to proceed.

But could I? I discovered that I had inhibitions against revealing patients' secrets. Only slowly did I develop a method of translating case histories into narratives that met my standards.

Vignettes were not the only problem. When I handed Meg a first draft, she returned it quickly. There was not enough of me in it.

In session, how did I think? In off hours, might I fret over a patient who had reached an impasse? What is it like to be a doctor?

Because I was uncomfortable appearing in public, I had withheld that material, even though my case notes were filled with it. My ideals demanded equality in all things, including self-exposure. I went back and inserted myself into the vignettes.

The book became a celebration of an old-fashioned way of being with people, an homage to Hans Lutz, whose stance—he called it existential—was passé even when I apprenticed to him. The cognitive or behavioral therapist reads current research monographs and, drawing on them, offers his patients clarity. Hans was a romantic, a reader of Keats. The doctor, Hans taught, tolerates mystery and doubt, without irritable reaching after certainty. Any understanding of the other will be incomplete and transient.

Like Hans, I had no message. I possessed no formula for finding sleep and no understanding of why my methods worked when they did. I was not even doggedly opposed to insomnia. I saw the occasional sleepless night as an opportunity to review what ails us. Meg believed that my open uncertainty helped the book sell.

Luiza appears in a case study. When I asked what troubled her, she had spoken about her career. She had disappointed her late father, with whom she had immigrated from the Azores. He had intellectual ambitions for his daughter, the most scholarly of his children and his darling. But she had not become a professor.

Working her way through college, Luiza had discovered that she was good at managing people. That's what she liked—that, and security and regular hours. She entered government service.

Effectively, Luiza had emulated her mother, who, during Luiza's early childhood in Terceira, before the move to Providence, had been a schoolteacher. Like her mother, Luiza was home on time for her husband and children. Like her mother, she spent her workday helping people.

Now, Luiza worried that she had not invested her talents. She considered herself a failure, a judgment that reflected her father's standards.

There was a Freudian aura to Luiza's narrative. She had displaced her mother in her father's affections and then betrayed him. But were her mother's values dismissible? As Luiza spoke, she came to see that she had been flogging herself over choices that had suited her fine. After early years disrupted by the move to the States, she had needed stability and wanted to provide it for her children.

Perhaps the well-made story was not what let Luiza sleep. The therapy supplied what Luiza's father had not, open attentiveness.

She said, At night, I listen to myself.

Where she had been judgmental, she was inquisitive.

Luiza let me know that she appreciated being written about. At Christmastime, the year my book appeared, she snuck into my waiting room and left a gift of queijadas, homemade custard tarts. The tin was wrapped for the season and tagged *From Annabella*—her pseudonym in *Rest*.

The book entered the market as a quirky contribution by a local doc. Its popularity came late, in paperback. In Hollywood, it seemed, *Rest* had been passed from hand to hand. Actors discussed *Rest* on television. Soon, professional athletes were photographed carrying the book. Talk show hosts gave it a mention.

Film stars flew east to see me, and theater actors came north—by then, I had set up my practice. Maury helped me alter the spiel. The new version included warnings that for people in the public eye, identities might be impossible to conceal. Celebrities seemed unconcerned. They let it be known that they had worked with me, as if *Rest*-style therapy were a luxury good, conferring cachet on the user.

*Rest* was never a breakout bestseller. The paperback sales reached the hundreds of thousands, but over the course of years. The book became what publishers call evergreen, flourishing on the backlist.

When *Rest* was still in unbound galleys, I had sought out Hans Lutz. He had retired to Wisconsin, where his older sister, Gretchen, had taken him in. Hans was in the silent phase of a dementia. I sat with him on a Midwestern side porch. I drank Gretchen's signature iced tea, with fresh-picked lemon verbena leaves. Hans imitated my gestures, sipping when I did.

I told him that the book was a tribute to him.

He listened patiently.

I said that I had followed the path he had pointed me down, sharing my confusion.

He broke into a smile.

In Hans's presence, the sequence of the book's development seemed humorous: my being forced into research, Peggy M's contemptuous use of my talents, the trial's unexpected outcome. Run the same experiment again, and the pill would win out, or the behavioral counseling.

Hans laughed, and tears ran down his cheeks. He was mimicking my hilarity and my sadness.

He said one word: *Lucky!*

I did not imagine that he had understood my narrative. What he had retained, despite the muddling of his mind, was the therapist's ability to discern affect and reflect it back in a word. In his diminished state, this mirroring had become something like a tic. He picked up on feeling and—bam!—out popped the *mot juste*.

Hans had always been an advocate of exclamations, as preferable to interpretations. Short exclamations especially point two ways at once. They validate the patient's feelings, and they invite a look at the other side of the coin.

When Hans said *Lucky!*, I was moved to explain how uncomfortable I had felt doing sleep research. I had appeared to be delivering routine psychotherapy, but in an important way I was not. Patients entered and left the study without my assuming ongoing responsibility for their wellbeing.

Gretchen was gardening beside the porch, deadheading a stand of small-flowered oxeye daisies, which she also used for tea. As Gretchen leaned over her tool basket, she nodded. I thought I was seeing the head tremor, the titubation, of early Parkinson's.

How distant old age seemed to me then, and what a close companion it is now.

To Hans, to Gretchen listening in, I confessed that I had disliked the *as-if* quality of research-based psychotherapy. I had approached patients as if my motivation were healing, when I had signed on in hopes of academic promotion, via publication. As the provider of the *non-specific* treatment, I was not permitted to discuss certain topics—medication, maladaptive cognitions, and sleep hygiene. Likely, it would never have occurred to me to do so. All the same, I had chafed at the constraints. The therapist must be free.

Hans heard me out or appeared to. When I paused, he spoke his first multi-word sentence: *I'm afraid our time is up!* In a mind largely emptied of language, that phrase remained. How deeply encoded the exit line is! I suppose that when I am on my deathbed, I will be able to dredge it up.

And so, the strange day with Hans ended. Should it have led me to doubt the treatment? I had found Hans's silence and random smiles and grunts encouraging. They had led me to dig deep. How important was it to master the nuances of existential psychotherapy if Hans's method could be duplicated by neurological defects?

But then, how easy would it be, in the consulting room, to provide the equivalent of that afternoon's experience: sitting on a shaded porch in early summer, drinking special tea, looking out on beds of wildflowers, and thinking aloud to listeners one loves?

My responses had been shaped by my history with Hans. I had known him when he was an eminence and I, his acolyte. No other old man's grunts would have had the same effect.

This train of thought allowed me to turn a visit that might have destroyed my faith into one that strengthened it. On the flight back to Providence, I leafed through the galley pages, tweaking the wording to emphasize my commitment to existential psychotherapy.

Taking to heart the reservations I had expressed to Hans about my role in clinical research, I quit full-time academics and took a job with the prisons. The funding for mental health care was generous. I saw patients as long and as often as I chose. I formed therapy groups. I learned more about what we are capable of, what drives us to extremes, and what parts of our humanity persist in the face of harsh experience. After three years, state budget cuts forced me out. I ignored offers to rejoin the hospital and instead opened an outpatient practice and taught informally, on the voluntary faculty.

Despite the *as-if* description I had shared with Hans, patients in the sleep study must have experienced me as engaged in their treatment. A number later contacted me for further care.

Luiza was among them. Fifteen years down the road, she phoned. Her husband was leaving. She had decided not to seek reconciliation. Although the immediate course was clear, she wanted to take a life inventory. I met with Luiza for a few months. I sat quietly by as she weighted options and priorities.

Nina's account of Luiza's current appearance worried me. In those refresher sessions, had I missed something? Or was Luiza now facing stress in the workplace, an arena that had brought her fulfillment? During the Great Man's rule, the emphasis would have shifted, from easing the path for immigrants to blocking it. I wondered how Luiza slept.

How much happier I would have been to offer help than to ask for it.

Reviewing my sessions with Luiza, I must have dozed off, because toward dawn I woke possessed by a strange idea. I thought, I can no more shed the doctor's role than I can surf. I don't know why *surf* instead of *fly*, but images of surfers filled my mind.

The onset of arthritis means that getting out of bed is a struggle for me. I thought of the way that surfers lie back-arched and prone and then pop up into an athletic stance with arms and feet aligned. I could as readily make that move as ask Maria Luiza a favor.

No joke. I tried the surfing leap. Easing myself from under the covers, I stretched out on the small antique Bokhara (one of Miriam's finds) that runs along the bedside and tried throwing myself skyward, to what effect you can imagine. Despite my failure at enacting metaphor or miracle, despite my needing to grasp the box spring to pull myself back up, I knew that I would do what Nina asked.

In betraying my standards and the profession's, what result would I achieve? Luiza might be pleased to help, glad to do a good deed in what had lately turned into a deadening job, one from which she ought, in conscience, to have resigned—but for her own family obligations, but for the half-truth we tell ourselves when we collaborate, that in our absence others would do the same work more cruelly.

Or she would be shocked at my asking her to intervene. On what grounds did my daughter-in-law merit special consideration? Treating Luiza, I had done my own job, doctoring—nothing more. I had not earned extra credit.

Part of me hoped that Luiza's response would be outrage, disappointment, and dismissal. I never wanted to live in a culture where pull and connections—*blat*, *protekzia*—mattered in dealings with the government bureaucracy.

I had a horror of the day before me. Ask favors of a patient? I would have robbed for my daughter and felt less compunction.

Before the bathroom mirror, bleary-eyed, fuzzy-headed, bent over as I was, I steeled myself to committing a harm in general and in specific, sullying my profession and weakening Luiza's faith in humankind. I understood that I was fortunate. I had a shot. Kareena's problems might—conceivably—be solved by a misdeed. Many would have envied me that prospect, of committing a transgression that might suffice to get a loved one out from under the thumb of the Regime.

Before I lost resolve, I picked up the phone. I called the local office of the Deportation Service and followed the prompts. They led only to a general mailbox. I left a message. When she arrived, would Ms. de Souza phone Dr. Henry Farber on a matter of some urgency? I did not expect a callback. I would walk downtown and appear in person once my morning work with patients was done. Still, it seemed important to have crossed the line, important to have sinned.

◊ ◊ ◊ ◊ ◊

My paranoid men's group met at eight that morning, as it does every Tuesday and Friday. The attendees use a different name for the session. They call it Executive Networking, and with reason. The members run businesses, mostly self-owned: a regional chain of plumbing-supply stores, a home security firm, a vendor of software for law enforcement agencies, a manufacturer of wall-mounted electric hand dryers for commercial industrial use, and so on. To a man, my guys are self-made. Each was the most successful member of a dysfunctional family. Their parents were alcoholic or depressed, abusive or neglectful. Sisters and brothers fell by the wayside: teen pregnancies, abusive marriages, drugs, jail, suicide, the lot. My guys had found ways out and up—and then a gear had slipped.

That October day, the maples were in their glory. I know, because when I arrived, the group was discussing the foliage. My notes say *autumn leaves—¿avoidance?* which means I wondered what else was on the members' minds.

Was it in hopes of bringing time to a halt that I had lingered over breakfast? Walking in, I had chosen a circuitous route, one that brought me to a gaudy sugar maple that had been a favorite of Miriam's. She was a visual person. For me, the marriage had been an extended course in the art of noticing. I was not an apt pupil. That morning, I searched for details that would have caught Miriam's eye—a spray of leaves foregrounding an ill-tended colonial home, a dappling of light on sidewalk bricks cast up by roots. Without her guidance, I saw nothing special.

The detour and the daydreaming delayed me further. Because I had become prone to tardiness, I had given office keys to the group members. Free access to the consulting room encouraged trust and self-reliance. The discussion could start without me. Often, when I arrived, it proceeded as if I were not there. I had my role, but in groups what matters is the participation of each and the power of the whole.

Duncan is the member of longest standing. I had slipped in, taken my seat, and made note of the foliage talk. Duncan gave me the once-over.

You look haggard, Dr. F.

Duncan is subject to extreme anxiety. Many weeks, he took advantage of the door key. He might roll up a sleeping bag and head to the office in the small hours of a Tuesday to escape the bad vibes in his own house and avoid being spotted en route to a shrink's office. He might go first to the back door of our local bakery. The therapy group would arrive to the smell of Portuguese sweetbread, extra breakfast for all. The session tended to calm Duncan. After the meeting, without undue concern, he had always been able to leave, to step outside in full view of my office neighbors.

Now Duncan was on my case.

The doc's got worries, Duncan said. He's under pressure.

Duncan was a keen observer. He's the home security expert. He had begun in sales, where he discovered that he had a knack for pinpointing the source of a customer's dread and then amplifying the feeling. *You read about that widow over on Lloyd Street? Robbers in her bedroom, drilling into the closet safe, aware she was watching from under the covers?*

Duncan had acted out the deal-closing routine for the group. He's got my build, reasonably trim, but he's round-faced and cherry-cheeked and casual in his dress. It's a comfortable look, free of the lean-and-hungry features we associate with anxiety.

Who's riding you? Duncan asked me.

Yes, I admitted, responding to the prior observation, about worries.

I try not to gaslight my patients. I validate accurate perceptions.

It's your family, Duncan said, reading my face. They're at risk again.

Providence is a village masquerading as a city. One way and another, the guys had learned of Kareena's past difficulties. All the same, Duncan's perceptiveness struck me as eerie.

Another longtime member, Charlie, stepped in to shield me.

Listen to the mother hen! Charlie said. The doc's fine.

Duncan stood his ground.

No—look—not at all fine.

I jotted a note to self. *Duncan: increased agitation? 1/1 §s?*

1/1 means one-on-one. § is my symbol for *session.* I was reminding myself to consider whether Duncan needed a brief course of individual psychotherapy.

Charlie held the floor. He pulled a list from his pocket and waved it.

Charlie is young for the group, late thirties, muscle-bound, squat with an inverted-pyramid build. He knows martial arts. He owns guns. Charlie claims that the City authorities have it in for him, that they harass him, trying to provoke him into doing something that will get him locked up.

It was only with difficulty that I had convinced Charlie to store his firearms in a locker, one controlled by another member of the group. Those sessions had been a learning opportunity for us all, with lessons about rights, trust, and the special needs of the hypervigilant.

Charlie's grievances arose from various beliefs. The police were encouraging dog owners to let their pets foul the patches of grass in front of his house. The building inspector was casting a blind eye on the doings of his next-door neighbor, one Gwendolyn.

In the wake of a recent divorce, accompanied or occasioned by the sort of financial loss that many have suffered, Gwendolyn was using her house as a bed and breakfast. Because the neighborhood was historic, because the old colonial and Federalist homes were firetraps, the rentals were illegal. But (as the group had told Charlie) in the hard financial times, the city had no staff to enforce its laws and no wish to spend resources resolving neighborhood squabbles. Besides, taking boarders allowed residents to pay their taxes.

Meanwhile, B&B guests returned drunk from evenings out and woke Charlie. Gwendolyn's new back-door lighting, designed to accommodate late arrivals, flooded his bedroom, and brightly, at twice the candlepower the building ordinances permit.

The last straw had come in the form of a golden retriever. Gwendolyn had adopted Rexie as a talisman against her ex, who was allergic to dogs. Charlie knew because Gwendolyn had taunted the ex in public, on the sidewalk, at Charlie's front door. Rexie was a prime suspect in the befoulment saga. Charlie spent hours charting Rexie's doings.

It would be hard to overstate the pain my patients feel. The insults that they suffer provoke dismay and resentment. Their behaviors in response cause others to shun them. Nor is it often possible to coax paranoid people out of their convictions.

But with time, with practice, my executive networkers had become skilled at keeping each other's delusions contained. It helped that, for one another, fellow group members were not authority figures. It helped that their efforts often included paranoid elements. My guys spoke a common language.

When Miriam and I turned seventy, she had us give up skiing, but I still think in its terms. Listening to my guys is like heading down the steeps. I try to stay focused, present, relaxed, and alert—enough so that I'm relieved of other concerns. That morning, the group distracted me from my unease over the impending visit to Luiza.

Before Charlie had finished listing the indignities that he was subject to—dog-walkers stopped to chat with him, as if in mockery, or they avoided him, with equal disdain—Arthur claimed the floor.

Arthur had attained special standing. He had made money, or held on to it, in the financial crisis, and group members had invested with him.

Arthur had managed pension assets for a commercial real estate company run by his sister's husband. The pension accounts did well enough that Arthur was able to open an investment management arm, attracting outside funds. In time, the tail wagged the dog. The plague spread. Office buildings sat empty. The Greater Depression rolled in, destroying what little value they had retained.

It was in this crisis that Arthur shined. The great brokerage houses went bankrupt, and their clients were ruined. Arthur's investors—and the real estate firm—stayed solvent. What saved them and him were his apocalyptic views.

When Arthur read of the plague abroad, he bought short-horizon puts on the market—and that was the easy part. The market came roaring back. But around us, in Providence, even during the market recovery, Arthur had seen leading indicators of disaster—declines in public amenities, upticks in petty crime. He translated informal sociology into a guide for action. Load up on inflation-protected bonds. Dump them. Buy gold. Switch to European stocks. Short the market.

Many pundits got parts right, safety plays, investing in what were called chaos hedges: military weaponry and home security. Arthur's coup was in making the final call: *sell everything*. The disaster would be universal. No enterprise would be spared. His timing was imperfect. He sold early. But early was better than late. It was the extremity of Arthur's paranoia that saved his adherents.

Arthur shared his reasoning with the guys. I am reconstructing fragments of the investment moves, from my therapy notes.

Was Arthur visionary? It occurred to me that his investment success may have been like my effectiveness as a sleep therapist—part happenstance. But the Great Man era showed how paranoia can prove adaptive. Arthur had been right on the main point. If you entrust a nation's economy to an impulsive leader with no care for facts, disaster will follow.

As a side note: I have said that I would never try to profit from what I hear in the consulting room, but therapists are not untouched by what they work in. Immersion in paranoia had made me a cautious, not to say fearful, investor. I was not as well protected as Arthur's followers, but thanks to my exposure to my patients, the hits my retirement account took were less catastrophic than they might have been.

Because Arthur's financial moves were grounded in his everyday observations, when he commented on local conditions, the guys took note.

In answer to Charlie's concerns, Arthur offered a dog inventory.

The streets are full of pit bulls, he said. Pit-bull variants, fierce-snouted mutts. Where are the designer mixes? No more schnoodles, no cockapoos.

In the plague, Arthur observed, dogs had been companions. In the Greater Depression, dogs became instrumental. They are shields against violence. Owners don't enjoy dogs; they need them.

The real dog lovers—lonely folks, sentimental folks—work long hours at low-wage jobs. How can they give pets a good life?

That's why there's poop on your grass. The dogs are in the hands of resentful folks, forced into dog ownership. The culture has collapsed. Why should they be civil?

Was life here as bad as Arthur made out? Were frightened residents dining on rice and beans so the guard dog could have kibble? Rice and beans, yes. Produce was less plentiful and more expensive than it had been when the dollar was strong. But Arthur's observations were, in the common-language sense, paranoid. That vision made his comments acceptable to the group.

I imagined that the bleak analysis might mute Charlie's rage, but the dénouement annoyed him. He'd been listening for a stock tip. Instead, he'd gotten a pat on the head. Doggie doo was everywhere. Nothing personal.

Meanwhile, Duncan addressed me directly. It's your daughter—or daughter-in-law—isn't it?

My wife was gone. My daughter and her family were dear to me. Duncan had the advantage of looking at my face while he was guessing. Still, he sounded psychic.

The group, intent on Arthur's takedown of Charlie, disliked the detour. What made Duncan so insistent?

Doc, is he onto something? Jamal asked. Because Miguel is sure that our financial whiz here has your phone tapped.

Miguel is Jamal's husband and an invisible member of the therapy group.

The two met when Jamal was in a bad way. Miguel nursed him back to mental health—relative health. But it had been a case of assortative mating. Miguel, too, proved prone to paranoia and depression. Shortly after the wedding, he turned densely delusional, and he refused to see a doctor.

Regularly, Jamal raised Miguel's concerns for discussion and brought the group's counsel home. Miguel accepted this indirect treatment, via a man he loved and men that man trusted.

I had never met Miguel, but he was important to me. His invisible presence ennobled the group sessions, giving them a charitable dimension. At the same time, the guys were aware that Jamal often hid behind talk of Miguel. Perhaps it was Jamal who suspected that Duncan was tapping my phones.

Today, the guys ignored the phone-tap question. The focus remained on Charlie and his catalogue of gripes.

Ahmed, a specialty food importer, was the only other attendee with a still-functioning marriage, arranged and all but indissoluble. He was quiet and, when he did speak, incisive. Today, he had information to contribute.

He said, As I was parking, I was listening to the local news. I heard something awful. You know the house that burnt down on Freeman Parkway?

A private residence, a modest center-door colonial, had caught fire. What with the closest fire station being shuttered, the hook-and-ladder, diverted from Pawtucket, had arrived late. Too much arson, too few resources. The ambulance took twelve minutes. A mother and infant had died.

Turns out that there was a third body, Ahmed said. The owner had rented out an attic room through an online site. It seems that the new tenant, a working woman who had lost her home, died because there was no way out—no second set of stairs.

The group fell silent. They might be obsessed with fantastic plots, but my guys were not callous. Even when what they foresaw happened, they felt the impact.

You'd be right to drop a dime on your Gwendolyn, Ahmed said. If she doesn't have fire escapes, she shouldn't let out rooms.

Ahmed's update was precise at a level that went beyond anything a therapist could have contrived.

The go-ahead reassured Charlie. All along, the group had been registering his concerns and keeping his interests in mind. The members' counsel had been strategic. As sufferers from paranoia themselves, they knew how acting on your *bêtes noirs* turns out. The cards are stacked against you. Effective action requires perfect timing. The intent had not been to tie Charlie's hands forever. In the face of the Freeman Parkway disaster—three dead—the building inspector might be inclined, briefly, to enforce the housing code.

At the same time, the failed emergency response validated Arthur. The city was on the skids.

No intervention meets all needs. Ahmed's report blocked aspects of the therapy.

No one got to say that part of Charlie's upset came from disappointment over what Gwendolyn possessed but did not offer, warmth. Even with a husband gone, she never thought to cast a friendly eye on her attentive neighbor. Charlie was presentable, productive, insightful, well off, young, and single. But his meaningful glances and dropped hints of conspiracy revealed his disorder.

Nor did the group confront Ahmed. He had lost two brothers to heroin overdoses. How was it for him to learn of another senseless death?

But Ahmed had crafted a masterful intervention, reassuring Charlie and reintegrating him into the group.

Hans Lutz used to say that psychotherapists employ four tools: interpretation, confrontation, manipulation, and safe haven. How comfortable Charlie looked when the group tended to his frustrations! You need supportive sessions in the mix.

I had felt uplift too. The group was functioning well. Perhaps it was strong enough to absorb an arrogant new member.

I HOPE THAT RUN-THROUGH GIVES a clear impression of my guys and the work that they do together. That morning's topics are typical: neighbors, homes, finances, pets, failed city government, communal conflict, life and death.

No one was obsessed with the Great Man. It's not that, while he governed, his name never entered the conversation. He was the deep cause of much that went wrong locally. But the guys' paranoia served to diminish his scale. His rule was one of many sources of oppression.

The press has its stereotypes. The single paranoid male with access to guns appears in the news only as a murderer. My guys check off bad boxes, but they are men of good character. I vouch for them with all the more confidence because they have bonded as comrades. The group moderates and channels its members' impulses.

◊ ◊ ◊ ◊ ◊

As the others straggled out, Duncan turned to me and said, I'm worried about you.

I waited.

He said, I want you to let me have your tablet and cell phone.

Unlock them.

Just for a minute. You need to trust me.

For the guys, *trust* is a sacred word.

Duncan ducked into the entry hall and returned shortly to hand back the devices.

A precaution, he said.

He began extracting objects from his laptop bag: an electric razor case, a credit card, and brown leather belt with a substantial, finely worked buckle.

With a hand motion, Duncan signaled for me to remove the belt I was wearing.

Keep this one on always, he said, of the new belt.

This stays in your wallet—the card.

Put the razor case in your Dopp kit. When you get where you're going, plug the razor into a socket. Whenever you can, store the wallet and belt—the buckle—near the razor. It will keep them charged.

Even if there was reason to keep tabs on me, the number of devices—case, card, belt, and presumably my tablet and smart phone—seemed like overkill.

For no reason that I could understand, Duncan said, It's Beezelbub.

Duncan had reversed the z and l sounds.

Prepare yourself, he said. He's vicious.

Excuse me—Duncan!

I wanted to ask Duncan why he thought I was going anywhere. But he was off to join the guys for the informal after-session they hold in a pocket park two blocks from the office.

I wondered how concerned I should be about Duncan's agitation. On his way downstairs, he had looked back to deliver a final operatic admonition: Beware of Beezelbub!

It is no small matter when a patient suffering from paranoia warns about Satan's minion. During the session, I had written: *D +, awareness of my mental state*. D stood for Duncan, the plus sign for a favorable development. He had recognized that I was anxious and inferred that family matters might be the cause.

Now I worried that I had gotten the trend wrong. Perhaps Duncan was slipping into an interval of heightened sensitivity and delusion that would require a decisive form of rescue.

I wrote myself a reminder. I must check to see whether Duncan had made satanic references in the past and, if so, whether the prior instances had predicted worsening illness. I noted down *LBLD?* and then did a cross-through, ~~*LBLD?,*~~ raising and rejecting the possibility of working Duncan up for a language-based learning difference, because of his having flipped l and z.

I wondered how long Duncan had been ruminating about infernal forces. Had he spent weeks programming the gizmos he'd handed me?

My concerns notwithstanding, I headed to the back room where I keep a gym bag with a change of clothes and a toiletry kit. Finally, I do trust my guys. I stashed the shaver. I rolled up my old belt and slipped it into a drawer.

I returned to my desk and emptied my mind in preparation for a one-on-one encounter with an unpleasant visitor who would arrive by the rear door.

◊ ◊ ◊ ◊ ◊

Those who have read my case vignettes, particularly in the two collections that followed *Rest for the Weary*, may be wondering about my emphasis on paranoia. Early in my career, I loved being a generalist. How many varieties people come in! My patients were neurotic, depressed, obsessive, bulimic, manic, inattentive, you name it. It was eighteen years ago that I began to narrow my focus.

Insurance companies had begun disallowing long-term psychotherapy. I resigned from the preferred-provider rosters, lowered my fees for less well-off patients, and asked everyone to pay out of pocket, but it troubled me to treat people of ample means who had access to every practice in town. I decided to focus on an underserved population.

My patient mix had always included men with paranoia or something like it. When I resigned from the prisons and opened an outpatient office, a trickle of parolees—white-collar criminals, mostly—contacted me to continue therapy. They were plagued by suspicions and, often, certainties about betrayals, conspiracies, cabals, secret messages, sinister trends, and hidden networks exercising malign control.

I'm not speaking of end-stage delusional disorders, where every thought is hostage to the intrusive concern. I treated paranoid patients of a certain sort, those who maintained some capacity for insight. My guys had walled-off apprehensions, isolated areas of mind in disrepair. Often the misdeed they'd been punished for had stemmed from a preoccupation.

There's a resonance between paranoia and the therapist's posture. When a patient tells me what happened and how he felt in response, I accept the account tentatively. I will not be surprised if the story changes. I don't have the fixity of belief that characterizes paranoia, but what I call openness contains an admixture of skepticism. Why shouldn't I tolerate and even appreciate patients' suspiciousness?

I am using the term *paranoia* loosely, but I hope not excessively so. My patients were of a kind.

Because these men knew each other, because group therapy had seemed to help them when they were behind bars, I used the modality in my practice. It may be strange to say, but my teenage experience on the basketball court gave me confidence in group work. A point guard knows where his teammates are, where they're heading, whom they match up against, and what spots they own as shooters. He distributes the ball accordingly, relying on experience and intuition. Complexity did not daunt me, or shifts in momentum. I knew when to switch plays, when to slow the tempo, when to call a time out. I was not afraid to act fast.

The point-guard analogy is inexact. Often, with a group, I monitored the action from the sideline, like a coach with skilled players.

My ex-cons denied their own legal guilt. They saw themselves as attending a prison-survivors' meeting. Otherwise, they could be frank. I was spared the trouble of questioning the plausibility of their delusional beliefs. My guys took that task on for each other.

Later, I opened a second group, for paranoid men who had not served time. My caseload remained wonderfully varied. For many of my patients, the delusion was off to the side, an impediment like floaters in the eye or tinnitus. Other complaints might be primary. I saw paranoia with depression, paranoia with narcissism, social anxiety, marital discord, morbid obesity, and alcohol misuse. The range of diagnoses only hints at the range of people. My guys could be sweet, funny, acerbic, shy, or assertive. I treated men, with an asterisk.

As I neared retirement age, the sticking point was the paranoid patients. Who would tend to them?

Even before she took ill, Miriam had been concerned about my memory.

What if you harm a patient? What if you miss a cue and a patient harms someone else?

I asked Miriam for examples of my forgetfulness. She gave trivial ones: lost names, misplaced keys—accompaniments of normal aging.

With patients, I am—what is the opposite of forgetful?—memorious. I find myself sorting through years' worth of details so that I can offer a targeted response.

There's that problem, too, Miriam said. You're distracted.

Am I? It seemed to me that I was right there with my patients.

Abstracted then—deep in thought, elsewhere—when you should be keeping pace in the conversation.

I had no ready answer for that complaint. By the time I was able to respond, I had illustrated the problem.

Henry? Dear?

In deference to Miriam's judgment, I began limiting my clinical hours. When a patient left, I did not fill the slot. The caseload dwindled slowly. I'd had my shingle out for over thirty years. Sometimes it seemed that half the city's middle class considered me their doctor.

The crunch came when Miriam died and Nina assumed the task of monitoring me.

Shut the thing down, she said. Write full time—it's everyone's dream.

With the double whammy of the financial crisis and the collapse of health insurance, younger colleagues were happy to enroll paying customers without regard to diagnosis. I transferred two or three of my paranoid guys, ones I had not clicked with.

Seeing me drag my feet, Nina called on Stefania Santangeli. Steffi had been a student of mine, the only one, over many years, to develop a serious interest in paranoia. She stayed on at Brown and studied ways to zap the brain with magnetic fields. For years, I had relied on Steffi for patients who became too sick or too dangerous for group work. She filled in for me when I travelled. Now, she took charge of some stray patients and all the group members with criminal records. If I retired fully, she would look after the final group members as well, the businessmen.

As I say, I acquiesced to my daughter's requirement—no new patients—but like a medieval logician, I retained *mentalis restrictio*, crossed fingers in the case of my final group, should it be down a member.

If I had kept those fingers uncrossed, or if I had retired altogether, would I have been spared trouble?

◊ ◊ ◊ ◊ ◊

If you get your news through social media, you will have guessed that Duncan was not delusional. As Miguel had suspected, Duncan had tapped my landline. He understood that my caller, the one who had advised me to speak to my daughter, was the fearsome Beelzebub.

How ill-informed was I? I later asked Muscle, in our time together at the fortress. He told me that, in a notorious moment of indiscretion, the Great Man's wife had been recorded calling his henchman Beelzebub. It became the standard way to refer to him on Twitter, before the crackdown on nonconforming political content. Only a stranger to social media would have failed to catch the reference. I was that stranger, which is why I had needlessly added Duncan to my worry list.

Since I had no notion that it was Beelzebub who was about to arrive, I will call the new patient *B*, to signal my ignorance of his identity. That's who he was to me, B or some other initial, a man who would declare himself in time.

In that session, he did, I think, display his character. I will try to sketch it, in case Beelzebub is in line to become our leader. We wished for that with the Great Man, didn't we, an early sketch by a psychiatrist?

As for the other eventuality, that Beelzebub will become a suspect in the death of the Great Man, should it be judged a murder—perhaps this account will prove useful in that regard as well.

B ARRIVED WHILE I WAS tweaking my notes on the group. He phoned on the landline. He was in my garage. I should head down promptly.

Remember, I thought that I was addressing someone whose care mattered to my daughter or to a colleague who wanted B seen despite the impending shutdown of my practice.

I tried to enter the contemplative mode, avoiding distractions and fully hearing the person addressing me. I was intent on having the engagement phase of treatment succeed.

B had issued a summons: *Join me*. For all that they may balk at constraints, paranoid men appreciate consistent ground rules. My intention early in encounters is to convey reliability without provoking struggles for control.

My apologies. I conduct interviews only in my office.

My caller demurred. He did not require an interview, only a brief conversation.

His voice was steely, impatient, peremptory. My notes begin: *Rx in car? pl.* The crossed-through letters are my private symbol for *unpleasant*.

Affability is a prognostic indicator in the near term. Nasty depressed patients are harder to budge than nice ones, and so on across the diagnostic spectrum. But extra effort can yield rewards. Patients who are vicious on first meeting may in time reveal or develop an especially considerate side. It's like the idea, advanced by dressage riders, that wild horses, after years of training, will show special nobility. I was far from writing off my new prospect, but I warned myself that his progress might be slow.

You've got me on speaker phone? my caller barked.

Anxiety often spurs paranoid people to resolve an impasse—in this case, over the choice of meeting place. B may have concluded that my office window was open and his voice could be heard on the street below. Was the waiting room door ajar? The reverberations that B heard made him think that he might do best to join me and get the lay of the land. He would move to my turf but for his purposes, to satisfy his suspicions.

I need my hands free, I said, for note-taking.

The theme was: doctors need their instruments.

I heard cursing and then something about my goddamn stairs.

I took the outburst as progress. We were each discussing our requirements and expectations. The therapy had been set in motion.

I apologized. I was in solo practice and not set up to offer handicap access. Perhaps the front stairs, although more public, would suit his purpose? They were wide and carpeted, with a sturdy handrail.

Was it that one word, handicap, that brought the negotiation to an end?

I'm aware now of how *handicap* and *disability* stick in Beelzebub's craw, how he hates that there ever were such categories, or that businesses once had to accommodate whiners. He would have found being counted among them intolerable.

Knowing Beelzebub as I do today, I'm guessing that I had misinterpreted the muffled curse. I suspect that he had said, If I climb those goddamn stairs, the next thing I'll do is wring your neck. He studs his conversation with threats of violence.

I opened the rear door to greet a large fellow in safari wear. He stood in the doorway brushing imagined dust off the tunic, as if the back stairs were cobwebbed. Perhaps the point was to make me wait. I had incommoded B and would pay.

Standing before B was unsettling. Across the bland moon face, with its smooth skin and symmetric features, the expressions rotated from contempt to calculation to open pleasure at my discomfort. What harm might he not do? It was a disappointment when his lip curled in horror-movie fashion, stating openly—comically—what had been implicit.

If B's haughtiness reassured me—*one of mine!*—it must have intimidated me as well. In his glare, I recalled an incident from my early childhood. I was three. My parents had gone to a social event and left me in the care of an older cousin, Eugene, a boy who in his adulthood would be jailed for spousal abuse. Waking from having been put to bed early, I toddled out to the living room and came upon Eugene reading a magazine open to an image I did not understand. Innocently, unknowingly, I had caught him in masturbation.

Eugene did not notice the intrusion until he had concluded the act. Then, he roared at me, You spy! He slapped me hard across the face with the offending hand. Because of the moisture in the palm, the blow made a loud snap.

I recalled one of Hans Lutz's precepts: with an unlikeable patient, for the engagement phase of therapy to begin, the therapist must find something to admire. The memory of Eugene had not come to me for years. Its return offered a benchmark or measure of B's hostile presence. Eliciting such acute discomfort in me—that ability might count as excellence of a sort.

Was it possible that B had experienced a childhood full of episodes like my isolated one with Eugene? Finding the e-tablet in hand, I made a note—*[Eugene]*—to remind myself to create opening for B to recount memories, if he had them, of mistreatment, say, by an older sibling.

My effort at admiration hardly gave B a free pass. The level of menace caused me to rethink my willingness to spring him on the group. I don't doubt that my hesitancy was apparent in my manner.

How annoying for B—that is, Beelzebub. He had assumed that when we were face to face, I would recognize him and turn abashed and apologetic. Why ever had I expressed reluctance when I was dealing with a famed actor on the world stage!

Remaining in the dark, I took B's open impatience—the cocked head, narrowed eyes, and tapping foot—as further indication of the disorder. Grandiose patients often imagine that we know more about them than we do.

B called me a stubborn SOB and might have persisted in this vein except—I am guessing—for his uncertainly about the balance of power. He had not managed to shake me from the premise that he was applying as a gravely disturbed patient. What if I phoned the police for protection or to begin commitment proceedings? There would be a paper trail, sightings by neighbors, and phone videos of him being frog-marched from a building that housed a shrink's office.

Seeking surer bearings, B switched to an examination of his surroundings.

The pause gave me an opening to suggest that he might join me in the main part of the office.

I saw what I now know to be the famous swagger.

I'll need this chair, he said.

It was mine—the most used, the most worn.

I sat on the couch, a furnishing associated with the patient role.

You need it? I asked.

The question annoyed him. Perhaps he thought I was asking whether he had a bad back, when he intended to signal his alpha status.

I took the opportunity, while B composed his response, to snap his photo with my e-tablet.

You don't mind? It's for my own use, for the chart. With new patients especially, referencing the image helps me as I review my notes.

B looked yet more irritated. I offered reassurance. The photo, heavily encrypted, had automatically been uploaded to the cloud and erased from the device. If the tablet were stolen, the image would be nowhere on it.

With hindsight, I understand that I had frustrated Beelzebub's bent toward physical violence. When he saw me take his picture, likely he had been inclined to leap from the chair, snatch the e-tablet, and crush it underfoot. My nattering had made him understand that dramatic action would only make him more vulnerable.

If B had voiced a polite objection, if he had said that he preferred not to have his portrait stored anywhere, I would have respected his denial of consent and deep-sixed the image. Instead, his leaning forward and then switching gears gave me the misimpression that my elaboration—uplink and so on—had put his mind at ease about my documenting the session.

On the pad, I wrote: Δ *pov*. With paranoid patients especially, I am on the lookout for flexibility of viewpoint. It was a hopeful sign that B had managed to relent and, in effect, grant permission for me to conduct the interview in my customary fashion.

Intending to build on the breakthrough, I dove into the spiel. If we were to continue, I would expect B to agree to be written about, and so on. As a concession to his delusion of celebrity, I warned that his identity might be hard to conceal.

I wonder why Beelzebub heard me out. Perhaps by then he had decided to sample the wares, to stand in for the Great Man and gauge the effect of my methods.

Still, B did not conceal his exasperation.

You flatter yourself that you're speaking ethics—informed consent, blah, blah—but all that's at issue is control. You're coercing me. No agreement, no consultation. So, you have my permission to write, *but you never will.*

I require a fuller go-ahead before I feel free to write about a patient, which is also to say that I need willing consent before I will admit anyone to a group. I did not get there with Beelzebub, but then, he turned out not to be a prospective patient. He was a political operative who gave consent as a bargain or, better, a gamble whose odds were in his favor. He had power over me, as he hastened to make clear.

Before this conversation ends, my punctilious friend, you will understand that if a hint of a breath of a soupçon of a rumor about my speaking with you gets out, you will be crushed by forces beyond imagining. The media will find you to have molested your patients and your children. Investigators will produce evidence that you have forged and embezzled. I will have your bank account and your balls. You'll be a eunuch, more of a eunuch than you are now. You'll be convicted of rape. You'll be broke and behind bars.

I am softening B's threats, so as to avoid giving voice to his homophobia.

On the plus side: B had indicated that he wished to proceed and had shown himself willing to reveal the depth of his disturbance.

I said, I understand. I am free to proceed at my own risk.

B countered with a sneer, Face enough risk, freedom vanishes. You are free to walk in the path of a steamroller.

Seeing that I was listening attentively, as one would to a patient who denies that he is a patient, he shifted gears again and surveyed his surroundings.

What a strange place, he said. What did you do, reproduce your grandmother's apartment?

His swept his arm wide, to take in the curios on my desk and the prints on the wall.

Learning to ski, I was taught to aim for a quiet upper body and dynamic legs.

Psychiatry, too, requires separation. The face is calm as the mind races to weigh alternatives. How best to respond to B's hostility, with its scattered targets: my profession, my manhood, and my taste? I chose to acknowledge B's verdict.

If you stay in one place long enough, objects accumulate.

Some of this junk you bought recently? Surely not.

When she still had mobility and before the plague shuttered retail shops, Miriam had asked me to take her to the consignment boutiques on Wickenden Street. She was unsettled by what she saw. The shelves and walls were full. To keep current with bills, people were emptying their houses.

Bypassing finer pieces that may have come from our near neighbors, Miriam chose three prints by David Alfaro Siqueiros, from the *Canto General* series. She no longer had the strength to climb the steps to my office, but she told me where to hang the purchases.

The images were not to my liking—black-and-white landscapes formed of harsh pen strokes in which tortured human faces could be discerned. But then, often Miriam's selections made me uncomfortable at first. Always, she succeeded in educating me. Meanwhile I enjoyed my discomfort with the prints—enjoyed remaining in dialogue with Miriam, confident that I would come to appreciate whatever she had chosen.

That quibble aside, B was right. Most of what was on the walls had been in place for decades.

B began naming artists who had made the prints: Diego Rivera, Käthe Kollwitz, José Orozco, George Grosz, Ben Shahn.

Darlings of the international left, circa 1950, he said.

The Kollwitz engraving is not even an original, he said. After she died, some hustler bought the plate and printed hundreds.

It's a sentimental piece, B said. Mother and plump infant instead of gaunt proletarians beaten down by the state.

To view that image properly, you need to put it on a wall with typical Kollwitz images. Starving children with hollow eye sockets. You want to see the grim fate that awaits that precious baby.

Every member of the 92nd Street Y had that saccharine print, B said.

I understood that, while maintaining the air of hostility, he was trying to correct the impression he had created with his boorish threats. He was a man of culture.

The reference to the New York YMHA—did it signal anti-Semitism?

It strikes a false note, I said, meaning that the print did, for B. You are not inclined to trust a therapist who hangs such schlock in his office.

Finding that I would not fight, B lost interest.

What do you think of the Great Man? he asked.

I wondered whether the abrupt change in topic bespoke delusion—and in which direction? B might be imagining that he had a bug in his brain, implanted at the direction of the Great Man. Or B might worship the Great Man as a hero who singlehandedly was preventing the enactment of a grand conspiracy.

We may, I said, talk politics, in time. For now, why don't you tell me about yourself—a story I will never have heard? I know nothing yet about your private life.

I like to make that request to people who have the delusion of being famous. My intention is to avert conflict over the idea that I understand a great deal in advance. Let's see whether, despite the disorder, the patient can perform impromptu acts of self-discovery.

B paused. Tell me first, you're the noted sleep doctor?

Yes and no, I said.

It had been years since I had treated anyone for insomnia.

The couch you're on now is the one where Trude Nilsson nodded off?

Years back, a movie star who had traveled here to headline a play at our local repertory theater was plagued with malignant insomnia—days without sleep. She asked to see me and dozed off on the couch.

On leaving my practice, she asked whether she could photograph the office. She wanted to remember, she said—wanted an image of the couch. She would hang it in her bedroom in Santa Monica.

She wrote an account of the treatment, *Finding Peace in Providence*. Her photo of the couch graced the front cover. Her own image was on the back.

Trude Nilsson, B said.

He was like a lawyer who needed a verbal response for the record.

It's not the sort of rumor doctors verify, even when the alleged patient is the source.

I asked, You're putting stock in a fable—celebrities, dramatic occurrences? No one has magical powers.

B said he'd move to the couch and be obliged if I'd sit where I did customarily. I was slow to stand—arthritis—and B loomed over me.

Take your seat.

I reclaimed my customary chair, but now at his command.

I want to feel what it's like, he said. See how you operate. I will report to my principal, the person who gave me the commission.

I tried to conjure up that boss. The mafia, long suppressed in Providence, are resurgent in the face of widespread poverty. Was B an enforcer for the mob? His malign mojo and the eerie baby face might serve him in that line of work.

More likely, B was about to reveal that he was, after all, the prospective patient.

I said, *Hello*, to indicate a readiness to begin.

B gave a stern look.

For the record, I'm not here for myself. But pretend that I want more sleep. That's the goal.

I said, You want sleep, and I invite you to tell me something informative about yourself.

B said, I can see that you want to hear about abuse, the claim that I abused my ex-wife, my second ex-wife, Sonia.

He seemed to imagine that he was notorious, with a troubled private life that had fallen into the public domain.

Truth is—I lost interest in her. She was a pianist. That enchanted me, the grace. But it turned out she couldn't spend money. My co-workers were all about yachts and private planes. Sonia wanted modest urban prosperity: no ostentation, play-focused school for the kids—her life with her parents. She talked about good values.

I told her, Provide enough money, they won't need values.

Out of the blue, I developed a tin ear. The disability came on me one afternoon. You must experience similar phenomena, Doc? A sudden loss of capacity? The thumb joint worked yesterday, but no longer? I left the office early. I arrived home to find Sonia practicing arpeggios. The music sounded like cats being hit by hammers.

I begged her not to go near the instrument when I was in the apartment.

She took to playing ethereal, impressionistic pieces. I understood the choice as a rebuke. I was coarse and insensitive. She was delicate and aesthetic.

One day, I woke to hear her rehearsing Debussy. I smashed the keyboard cover on her fingers. I sat by while she tried to dial 9-1-1.

Before the ambulance came, I drove her myself in the Porsche. En route, I told her how it would be if she filed criminal charges, what I would allege to get custody of the children, how I would hide funds and impoverish her. If she wanted an equitable divorce, she would need to clam up with the doctors, plead ignorance, fail to validate the obvious.

She was unable to lie or chose not to. Only with effort did I get everything sealed, the medical records, the police inquiry set in motion by the doctor's report.

I regret the end of the marriage, B said. After that correction, Sonia would have been a better wife. Marriage worked for centuries because there was a clear hierarchy.

She went through surgeries. I would have hand-held her—not sure that's the right expression—if she hadn't tried to turn the kids against me. She healed. Still gives concerts, with some pain.

I do worse to people at the office, give them cardiac crises.

The way I see it, I did Sonia a favor. Read the reviews. She has better access to suffering. Early in her career, her music lacked depth. I supplied it. And made her independently wealthy. The insult had to be paid for. And the silence.

Perhaps concerned that I considered him a patsy, B modified his comments.

I paid, up to a point. The divorce settlement was based on funds that could be accounted for.

She complains that her share included overvalued assets.

Who owes whom in a marriage, Doc—am I right? She had mocked me with that gauzy piano playing.

Before the wedding day, she should have inventoried her own capacities. If you like the life of ease but harbor contempt for the man who will provide it, that's entering the contract in bad faith, don't you agree? She injured me.

B was (I thought) subjecting me to a provocative test. Could I accept him as he was, with capacities for physical violence and limitless self-justification?

What B sought was less acknowledgment than submission. He did not imagine that I would embrace his view of fairness: that he had done right to maim his wife and duck paying the price. He wanted to take my commitment to neutral listening and turn it against me. Could I smell his scat and not recoil?

I turned the question to him. You want me to hear you to be that person?

He said, Doctor, you will find me to be that person.

He said, That was relaxing, telling you about my ex. Doctor, I can see how you come by your reputation. I very much feel the effect.

He put his boots up on the arm of the couch—in the photo that Muscle distributed, you can make out a blemish on the roll arm nearest the Great Man's head. Whatever was on the soles of B's boots left a stain.

B lay back and closed his eyes.

I found my mind turning to Kareena's crisis. I had a flicker of insight, an inkling that there might be a connection to the vicious person before me.

When he sat up again, B said, It's no rumor. You have the capacity my client is seeking.

I thank you for having invited me up, B said. Seeing you on your home turf has been an education, although it goes without saying that I have never been here.

I was stuck on the provocative anecdote about the injuries that he had done his wife. The account did not sit right with me.

Enough fun, B said. Shall we speak seriously? I asked what you think of the Great Man.

I'm not one for politics, I said, as I would to any patient in an initial visit.

Would you take him on?

I understood the invocation of the Great Man's name to be metaphorical: as a professional, how would I approach a person who had done wrong on a vast scale? I could handle spousal abuse, but how would I do with massive injury to the vulnerable?

I was still entertaining the notion that B was making inquiries for a mob boss.

I said, If your principal comes and sits where you are sitting, I will assess him as I am assessing you.

Not holding the past against him?

I've treated murderers, I said.

Those murderers, good doctor, they were in a prison? They underwent rehabilitation or were meant to—that was the premise?

With the Great Man, the framework will be different. He does not want to be other than who he is.

B rose from the couch and stood over me.

You are going to assist the Great Man. I am here to take you to him.

I suspect that the public image of paranoia is built around people who think that they're Napoleon, but the choice of icon shows how antiquated that form of the disorder is. Rarely have patients presented me with a delusion like the one I was confronting, an in with a world leader.

I said that I would be more comfortable if he, B, sat back down.

You're clueless, B said.

He opened his wallet to extract an identity card. *Beelzebub*, he said, in case I did not recognize the given name.

I am accustomed to being mistaken. First sessions with paranoid patients will be rife with shifts in perception. Listening to an account of a complex conflict, perhaps a dispute at the workplace, I will take the patient's complaint at face value only to realize, soon after, that much of what I've accepted is frank delusion. Then it's a matter of scrambling to guess at what can be salvaged from the account.

Less often, I will err in the other direction, mistaking an unembellished report for fantasy.

The sequence of misapprehension, correction, and recovery is, I am saying, a given in psychotherapy. Still, it is unusual for me to be wrong at this level. So much to absorb! B was Beelzebub. The Great Man was *the Great Man*. I was being recruited for a peculiar task, to act as his doctor without being his doctor.

Is it strange that I felt relief? For the whole of the meeting, I had been questioning myself. Could my prospective patient be as distasteful as I perceived him to be?

I had not misjudged. I'd been in the presence of a demon.

I would not need to treat him! I would not need to stretch to understand and care about B! Until that moment of uplift, I don't think I had appreciated how draining the effort at empathy had been for me.

Miriam and Nina were right. I had lost a step. I was no longer open to all comers.

Meanwhile, my assessment of Duncan, during the group session, had been on target. He was agitated but not slipping deeper into paranoia. How wonderful, to be able to scratch Duncan's condition off my list of hot concerns.

I understood the specificity of B's threats. Child abuse and embezzlement: Weren't those the false charges that the Great Man's campaign had pinned on his rival?

More crucially, I understood what *speak to your daughter* meant. Beelzebub had been blackmailing me in advance. I could not know whether he would drop the threat to Kareena, but I understood now that it did not originate locally. I would not need to make a further appeal to Luiza. I would not commit further harm in general.

Beelzebub's revelation, I am saying, threw me less than you might imagine. I was focused on the next, the critical question, whether I could work with the Great Man.

Mimi considered him to be heedless and destructive. She complained about the endless degradation of democracy—new impingements daily—but what hurt her most was the mistreatment of migrant children. Mimi was haunted by a newspaper report about a teenaged girl who was sent home, only to be raped and enslaved. Mimi was drawn to read about such horrors.

I would need to open myself to a man who was every bit as distasteful as B and, moreover, one who had pained my wife and, just now, via B, threatened those who were dear to her.

Against this apprehension—*Can I do it?*—there was the sense that the therapy was already in progress. My prospective patient had selected an emissary. I assumed that not everyone in the inner circle was this offensive. Perhaps the Great Man experienced himself as hateful. He wondered who could bear to work with him. Beelzebub was a stand-in. The Great Man and I were in dialogue. The choice of Beelzebub—just maybe—betrayed a hint of self-awareness.

Nina had warned me against vanity. As a young doctor, I had aspired to priestliness. I would welcome sinners. Prison work had been an early test of my capacities. To sit with the Great Man and attend to his wellbeing would be a virtuoso act of caring. I did not want that ambition, or any ambition, to affect my choice. The virtue appropriate to clinical work is humility.

Beelzebub said, The Great Man cannot be seen outside the—location of his choosing. He cannot be known to be in consultation with you.

Beelzebub was careful with word choice again, *consultation*, not *psychotherapy* or *treatment*.

Beelzebub said, You will go to him.

Beelzebub waited for me to insist that I do my work in my office. He continued as if I had, in fact, voiced a tedious objection. In an exaggeratedly effeminate voice, he said, *It's like a surgeon who needs his operating theater*. Sorry. You'll be doing appendectomies on the kitchen table. Our kitchen, our table.

Beelzebub reached into one of the safari jacket's bottomless pockets and pulled out a half-dozen sheets of folded paper. At my desk, he ran the heel of his hand over them, as if to smooth out wrinkles.

He passed me the stack. The first page was an official waiver, signed by the head of the Deportation Service, providing a two-month stay of execution for Kareena.

If you serve the Great Man in good faith, the stay will become permanent.

Beelzebub would not consign Kareena to a war zone—for now. But he had sent thousands.

I looked at his face, to see if it showed.

What are you staring at?

For a moment, my work with murderers, with men who had touched the flesh of their victims, men who used garottes, men who had killed at close range—all that was as nothing. I had never sat close to someone with so much blood on his hands.

Was Beelzebub uneasy? Focusing on him, I picked up hints of anxiety.

The room supported me.

Once I treated a patient who had trouble reading social cues, a guy who was uncomfortable in group settings. He improved his life by moving to Japan. After he had decoded the rules of behavior, they proved reliable. In each setting, he knew what was expected. Like him, the Japanese valued ritual, routine, and attention to detail. What was awkward here was natural there.

The consulting room is my Japan. My reticence serves me, and the trait that Hans Lutz nurtured, the tendency to answer confrontation with curiosity. You may think my calm extreme or unnatural, but because I was in my element, the menace that Beelzebub conveyed was neutralized. It became *material* to be analyzed. So did the offer of reprieve for Kareena. The crumpled pages, the way Beelzebub had shoved them at me, the combination of the breezy informality and peremptoriness—all of it was a bit off.

As there was no need to afford Beelzebub relief, I concentrated on understanding. How was it that he felt shaky?

Here was a man who was fine with mutilating his wife. Triggering deaths of despair was his specialty. A trivial act of coercion, strong-arming me through threats to my family, could hardly cause him discomfort.

I'll need for you to sign, Beelzebub said. Again, exaggeration—this time in the nonchalance.

I studied the consultation agreement. I was being hired to provide services as a private individual, not a doctor. I would be walled off from the world. The fact of my contact with the Great Man was to remain secret, as was every particular in our interactions. For the period of our association, the Great Man was to exercise limitless control over my movement and communication. Breach of contract would result in ruinous financial penalties.

Next, the stay of execution for Kareena. Many of its clauses concerned confidentiality. If word of either document—the work contract or the reprieve from deportation—got out, the grace period would end, and she would be shipped off.

I looked at the man across from me, trying to see as he saw. I picked up disgust. Disgust with me, with the office, with the task. And always an undertone of fear.

Would Beelzebub have approached me had I lacked that Achilles heel, the vulnerable family?

Even now, I might refuse to play ball. What if I broadcast the photo of Beelzebub sitting in my office? Or if I let it be known that the Great Man was seeking psychiatric attention?

It would be bad, for Beelzebub. I was at his mercy and he was, very slightly, at mine.

He had been offered this assignment as a test. *Don't screw up!* Beelzebub was to bring back the brand-name item—without fuss, invisibly.

On that last point, secrecy, I doubted that mental illness—the label—was the issue. What diagnosis had the Great Man not been tagged with? The problem was weakness. The Great Man could not be seen to have needs, only hungers.

Dr. Farber!

Beelzebub wanted my attention.

*Full citizenship*, I said, almost in a whisper. I was not making a demand so much as voicing words already between us, not yet spoken.

The crumpled paper, the one set before me, had the quality of a Freudian parapraxis, a slip of the tongue that revealed a repressed intention. *Citizenship* was the proper end to the conversation that Beelzebub had started when he threatened Kareena.

What did you say?

Beelzebub had heard me. He launched into a lecture. It was easy for him to derail illegals like Kareena, but hard to grant them legitimacy. Naturalization was out of his control.

In therapy, I let my brief interjections remain ambiguous. If they elicit a complex response, if the patient struggles to understand, the intervention is doing its job.

Beelzebub produced a litany of vulgar threats.

I guessed that he was on the outs, trying to work his way back into the Great Man's good graces. Or he was plotting against the Great Man and needed to appear especially loyal and productive.

I thought of my guys, how much faster they would have arrived at those analyses.

There is no other deal, Beelzebub said.

I was thinking about Kant. He argues that we must not lie to the murderer because we may be wrong. Imagine that we tell him that his intended victim is not in the house and it turns out that, indeed, she has slipped away. Imagine further that our testimony—*She is elsewhere*—causes her to be found and killed. We will bear guilt, as people are responsible for the consequences of their lies. Some days, this line of reasoning strikes me as nonsensical. Some days, it contains a deep truth.

Kant says that in breaking general moral rules, we often fail in our purpose and multiply harm. Phoning Luiza, I had betrayed my profession—and with what result? When it came to Kareena's fate, Luiza had been powerless. The most that I could do was to make her feel imposed upon by her doctor. I was responsible for that injury.

What moral red lines would I cross if I performed the task that Beelzebub proposed, bringing comfort to a despotic leader? None, perhaps. Doctors regularly provide care to bad people. I had been taught that in the ER, we sew up stab wounds without asking who started the fight.

Joining forces with the Great Man, I would commit, at worst, a particular harm, if an immense one. If I patched up the Great Man and helped sustain the Regime, I might worsen the lives of millions, but principle would suffer no injury. I would not break my profession's rules.

Disappoint a patient, and the sin is mortal. Provide comfort to a world-destroyer, and the sin is venial.

I saw this assessment as absurd and, at the same time, I embraced it.

You may ask whether I entertained hopes of reforming the Great Man's character. I try to avoid intentions of that sort. My task is to relieve suffering. Sometimes, when a patient feels less fear, he becomes less hateful—kinder to others. That outcome is, and must be, incidental. Willing it to happen impedes the treatment.

Dr. Farber!

From his jacket, Beelzebub had produced another paper.

He had anticipated that I might require citizenship for Kareena.

Fine. Let's get on with it.

He tried to look confident. He was presenting his final offer.

What if I would not serve the Great Man under any circumstance? What if I was an old man who would not leave home?

To my layman's eye, the documents had been assembled scrupulously. They included an authorization for Kareena's attorney, as an officer of the court, to administer the oath of loyalty, and on and on.

My guess was that some element was flawed. An i was missing a dot, almost certainly. On a whim and in an instant, Beelzebub would throw Kareena to the dogs. If I proved disappointing or defiant, her citizenship would be revoked. And yet, the designation mattered. If citizenship and the judiciary were not what they once had been, still, representing a citizen, Maury would get a day in court.

I had not been out to negotiate. Because I had been in the therapeutic mindset, because I was monitoring the tone along with the content of Beelzebub's speech, I had blurted out that quiet exclamation, *Full citizenship*.

How important those two words now seemed. On a par, say, with *I do*, spoken under the chuppah. Two words to save a family and a life.

Nina might complain about my tendency to analyze people who are not patients, but psychotherapy is how I access my understanding.

Hans Lutz said, Your goal is to know how you feel. The rest follows.

We dislike therapy because we associate it with convoluted explanations. When the result is a quick outburst—how useful therapeutic listening can seem.

I'll need to notify my patients, I said. And my daughter. And the doctor who will cover my practice.

Do you want to ask for a retainer as well? Beelzebub asked.

It was a little joke, about the Great Man's reputation for stiffing contractors.

Don't dick with me, Beelzebub said. You get this paper. Think what you'd give for it.

In partial payment, I'll ask you to donate these prints, he said.

Beelzebub lifted a Shahn lithograph off the wall and then two more, all from the Rilke series, men walking, an injured couple, and a solitary figure by the sea. Had those images, too, turned sentimental? In a time of actual deprivation, spiritual alienation can seem an extravagance.

Rilke and Shahn had understood political disaster. One can be hungry and lonely both.

Seeing Beelzebub disturb Miriam's décor, I thought of Karla palming George Smiley's lighter, the one given him by his wife. Beelzebub needed to end with a gesture that demonstrated his dominance.

Time to sign, he said.

I scanned the citizenship papers and faxed them to Maury. He would vet them and get back to me via text to a number supplied by Beelzebub. For verification, I required that the response include Maury's father's name at birth.

I had wanted Maury to examine the employment contract as well, but there, Beelzebub drew the line. Even with identifiers blacked out, the source would be apparent.

As for the rest, Maury would alert Nina and Steffi S to my absence. The cover story, which I worked out with Beelzebub on the spot, was that my editor wanted faster progress on my book and had arranged time for me at a writers' colony where the rule was radio silence. This fiction was not meant to be fully believable, just vaguely plausible. Maury was not to seek me out or to comment publicly on my absence. He was to make Nina aware that the reprieve for Kareena was contingent on complete secrecy.

Under supervision, I sent a terse notice to the patient listserv. I would be unavailable for the foreseeable future, and so on.

Beelzebub handed me a Regime-issued phone for my use. It could receive the okay from Maury. Then Beelzebub took to sending messages, presumably announcements of the success of his mission.

While I waited for Maury's reply, I thought about Beelzebub's vignette—why it seemed a bit off. Across from me, on the couch, he had been stitching tales together—sharing his own memories, but admixing items from the history of the client I would need to serve. Had the Great Man abused an ex-wife? Secreted assets to cheat others of their due? Some such private misdeeds.

I later came to believe that Beelzebub never told the truth straight up. It was as if he were continually guarding against an imagined future court case. If an accuser repeated a story, it would turn out to be false in its particulars.

Time to go, Beelzebub said.

I used the tablet to photograph the business contract and send the images to the ether. I slipped the tablet and the toiletry kit into the gym bag and slung its straps over my shoulder.

You can manage these, Beelzebub said and handed me the lithographs to carry down to his car.

◊ ◊ ◊ ◊ ◊

I wrote that last passage, shut the laptop, went to bed, and woke in a nightmare. Scattered images remain: a grotesque head—a man's—and slobbering mouth. A bruised woman, sobbing.

Since leaving the fortress, I've been subject to these dreams. I'm guessing that mine is only a more intense version of the general affliction, our lingering awareness of the Great Man's overbearing presence. We should be tolerant, I think, of the residue of trauma. We may want to sit with it as, in therapy, we sit with a painful memory before setting it aside.

Disturbed sleep notwithstanding, I'm glad to have made a start on the project I'm meant to be about—recording history, the fragment I was exposed to. All I can offer is the intimate view. Beelzebub was unnerving from the start, before I came to associate him with the harms he caused, unnerving even when I was considering him as a patient and trying to discern his good points. Others will know more than I do about his public persona. In private B was self-satisfied and menacing, and at a disturbing level. Meeting him was, yes, a fit preview to time with his boss.

Oh, the boss. Early this morning, waking from that dream, I thought, *Et in Arcadia ego*. Even in Arcadia, the Great Man's ego haunts me.

My Arcadia is a cozy cabin, four dirt roads in from the nearest blacktop, in the North Maine Woods. A paradoxical weather pattern brought Maine an early winter this year. Mornings, from behind the kitchen table, I see windblown snow rising from mounds that reshape steadily on the frozen surface of a pond. Regularly, I pause the writing and feed the potbelly stove. The task gives me the illusion of self-sufficiency, as if I were providing myself handmade warmth.

In truth, I depend on my hosts, Chet and Ginnie, who are also my neighbors. The cabin is on their land, although their home is not in sight. They have stocked my fridge and larder. Mason jars packed with canned summer fruits and vegetables line the pantry shelves. In the cabinet below, baskets hold potatoes, onions, garlic, and winter squash.

The couple have supplied me with clothing, too, picked up at thrift shops. The purchases have gone unnoticed, or so we hope. Who, in these hard times, does not grab a stray cold-weather jacket when one shows up for cheap, or a flannel shirt?

My underwear, grey Jockey shorts, came in an unopened three-pack that had spent time sitting on a shelf. The light-exposed edges of the undies have faded. Each pair has a pale stripe running down my left thigh. Thick socks, a winter blend, came in a six-pack. I do a daily wash in Woolite and hang the clothes on a drying rack near the wood-burning stove.

From the gardening shed, I have borrowed a pair of cross-country skis, long for me, but with boots that fit my feet. I found a down-stuffed ski coverall in the shed as well. Earlier this morning, in calmer conditions, I made my way along the edge of the pond and onto a trail through the trees. No tracks remain. That's the beauty of the wilderness. It seems to erase us, even if the truth is otherwise, and marks of our intrusion remain everywhere.

I have discovered that I can still split wood, with a light maul. I swing to a trochaic beat: there is magic in the shatter when you hit a sawn end right. Carrying is the hard part. I toss split logs one by one onto the porch without bothering to stack. I use firewood quickly.

I recognize my foolishness, risking orthopedic or cardiac disaster with no help at hand. Splitting logs, I stop at an even dozen. I keep the ski runs short. But I feel good, with the alternation of cold and warm, exposure and enclosure, activity and stillness.

Reading these words, you may think of the plague and the days we spent walled off from social contact. The routine I have described is one that a plague isolate might follow: write, cook, tidy up, exercise, write more, sleep. But the plague demanded vigilance. I worry little. I'm hidden. I'll contribute with this diary, meant to be chopped into blog posts, for a time. I will be caught, or I'll return home and face whatever justice prevails.

Everything here is clean and fresh. I take deep breaths. I touch what I please.

I am off the information grid, without access to Wi-Fi, cellular networks, internet, radio, television, newspapers, or magazines. Chet and Ginnie know not to update me. I receive no mail—or am meant to receive none. Yesterday, a manila envelope got through. That glitch aside, all is silence.

In the fortress, the most by-the-way conversation was tinged with intrigue. The very décor demanded interpretation. In Providence, the shuttered storefronts spoke to me, and the food lines, and the beggars. In contrast, if the woods bear messages, I can make out only the most obvious, that in this vastness, I am insignificant. Otherwise: no chatter. Free of intrusions, the mind finds its balance.

I miss evenings with Tamara and mornings in the clinical office. I miss my old life. But in it, I missed my older, married life. *Missing* comes with age. Missing aside, I feel fine.

I'm guessing that the safe house comes via Glue. She has been in the security game for years. At the fortress, the aides with policing or military experience understood that their association with the Great Man put them at risk, should the second term end. Glue would long since have made contingency plans.

My protector is Glue or another. I am in the Maine woods or elsewhere. It would not do to pinpoint my location. If you envisage a cozy camp or bungalow on a pond in a forest, you have the right impression.

The kitchen has an unusual table made of pale wooden planks with grain in amber waves. Old elm, I have learned, from a stand of trees felled when blight swept through, many decades back.

At that table, I write. My task is to bear witness and to bring myself home safely, to write my way home.

I work on the thick, old laptop that Maury lent me. The keys have a pleasant spring. Before dinner, I copy the day's text file to a thumb drive that I place in an empty milk delivery box beside the front door. In the course of the evening, Ginnie removes the drive and replaces it with a fresh one.

The early stages of transmission vary. Sometimes, Ginnie drives a long distance before beginning an upload. In the electronic phase, the file bounces from blind remailer to blind remailer. After zigs and zags, the updates appear on Maury's computer, and he does with them what he will.

I hope that I will not endanger my hosts or burden them.

CHET WAS DISAPPOINTED WHEN HE first caught sight of me. On the drive here, he made it clear that he had expected a different sort of guest.

Chet is in his middle fifties, with a wiry build. His demeanor conveys a wish for silence and privacy, but in practice, he speaks a good deal.

It was past midnight when I transferred from Maury's Jeep to Chet's light truck. Outside the zone of its headlights, all was black.

Don't expect the Ritz, Chet warned.

You'll have peace and quiet. Do you appreciate those?

I gave no indication to the contrary, but Chet had his doubts. He had me pegged as ill equipped for country living. Sitting beside him, I was aware of being slight and cerebral.

Chet hunts some and farms more. Ginnie is an equal partner. She weeds and harvests. She does the kitchen work, canning, pickling, and freezing. To the extent that they can, Ginnie and Chet live off the land. They grow vegetables organically, mostly organically, if not by the book. They raise chickens. Ginnie barters with the dairyman down the road.

What we don't serve is gossip, Chet said. We don't much like to know what we don't discover ourselves.

Chet has a mobile phone for when he travels in range of cellular service. The truck has a dashboard radio. The farm has a copper-wire landline.

I told Chet that his sounded like a good life, if a hard one.

In my early years of practice, in the 1980s, the back-to-the-land movement hit Rhode Island. I treated subsistence farmers and family members who'd been dragged along.

Farming puts you in touch with your character, is what I had heard. The meet-up was not always reassuring.

I came to associate small-farm life with paranoia of different stripes. Some men—even then, men composed the bulk of my practice—had moved to the country because neighbors made them nervous. Other transplants arrived in fair shape but found farming's uncertainties wearing: crop failures, market fluctuations, time demands, and financial insecurity.

One beleaguered fellow spoke only of pests. He succumbed to despair over a sudden caterpillar infestation. Larvae coated his cabbages. Heads that had been pale green the day before now looked black—and the black was all in motion. He took the outbreak personally. Great forces were conspiring to kill beloved offspring. My patient had nightmares about those caterpillars, and so did I.

That's one of the pleasures of psychotherapy. You learn how it feels to be in different lines of work.

I asked Chet how the growing season had gone.

He said, Not bad.

I said, That good?

He did not mind the joke about his dourness. He aspired to dourness.

The warming trends had been friendly to Maine, Chet admitted. Tomatoes came in early. Melons and peppers thrived. The big summer storms hit further south now.

The heat's downside was pests. He'd lost a planting of summer squash and pumpkins.

Vine borers?

How did you guess?

I did not answer, but as a therapist, I'd heard detailed complaints about squash farming. Borers kill plants with hollow stems. Solid-stemmed vines do better.

*Cucurbita moschata* outperformed *Cucurbita pepo*, Chet said, naming two species of squash. The problem was that the moschatas mostly didn't look or taste like summer squash. He'd given a small plot over to a Korean moschata with fruit that does resemble zucchini. The seeds came from a neighbor. The borer problem was solved, but the blossoms attracted cucumber beetles.

Reconstructing this conversation from just days ago, I see that I was making a clumsy effort at what Hans Lutz called counter-projection. When a patient has me pegged as demanding of intimacy like his emotionally intrusive father, I will turn standoffish, so as to confuse the issue. Perhaps I'm not as predictable as the patient imagined, or as demanding. With Chet, to block the attribution of unworldliness, I introduced practical knowledge I'd gained from patients.

Did I only reinforce my image? I was weak *and* nerdy. Chet may have thought, Because he's heard about borers and beetles, this jerk thinks he knows what it is to be self-reliant.

I was far from imagining that I could endure the hardship that Chet and his wife faced.

If Chet occasionally mistook my intentions, still, I enjoyed the conversation, the way it proceeded in pre-Great fashion. My host spoke about his work. I inquired about its challenges. There was no avoiding reference to politics—freakish weather!—but the themes were mostly on other lines, the bounty and the burdens that nature brings.

It helped that the drive was long, over slow roads. Chet's talk became less pointed. He was passing time, staying awake.

On the farmstead, he had fixed up a falling-down pond-front camp in hopes of renting it out. Then someone—say, an old military buddy—had approached Chet at, say, a platoon reunion. The guy had heard that Chet had gone off the information grid—mostly off. Did the farm have extra lodgings? A group would pay to keep a place stocked and empty, at the ready.

I liked the word *say*, liked that Chet approached confidentiality as a writer of clinical vignettes does, inventing events and altering people's identities.

You're a surprise, Chet said.

He had expected to host a soldier on the run. He didn't take me for a soldier.

How much had Glue explained when she arranged the placement? She must have made me out as important—on a par with the people whom Chet had agreed to hide, fugitives from the Regime. How courageous Chet and Ginnie were!

I didn't believe that Chet had identified me, but he would soon. Even a man who stayed clear of gossip on principle and got his news by car radio would hear talk of the Great Man's shrink and his disappearance.

Chet might find harboring me an unwelcome assignment. I was more high profile than the resisters he had signed on to house.

Surely openness was the ethical position.

What do you want to know about me? I asked.

Nothing. The less Chet knew, the safer he was.

My conscientiousness had caused me to ask a wrong question, undercutting any progress I had made with Chet. He did not want to shelter a blabbermouth.

We may be able to offer only a brief stay, Chet said.

We're in a kind of paradise, he reminded me. Enjoy paradise, until it's time to move on.

SITTING AT THE ELM WOOD desk after a ski run, log-splitting, and a tepid shower, I see Chet's point. We had been set back a century and a half. In the face of urban blight and rural squalor, *Little House in the Big Woods* was once more an ideal.

In my psychiatry residency, my cohort studied the history of melancholy. For centuries, cures were social, and they mirrored concepts of utopia—the place where one escapes mental strain and, so, flourishes. In periods of political chaos, writers imagined utopia as an ordered society ruled by a strong monarch. In times of oppression, writers dreamed of freedom from constraint. In parallel fashion, depression treatment lurched between discipline and stimulation, abstinence and hedonism. But what was the remedy when a regime combined power and pandemonium, despotism and disarray? Then, the wise counsel was retreat. Melancholy, which in other analyses was caused by isolation, now was cured by it.

People believed in these nostrums. Each in turn became common knowledge, the stuff of advice manuals and cliché. In all likelihood, the contradictory prescriptions worked, relieving the mood disorders of the day. If epochs create their own reality, so do regimes. In the wake of Great Man era, solitude heals.

Nina, Kareena, Maury: I feel fine.

The cabin is stocked with books. Someone with Miriam's taste hung out here. I'm thinking it was Ginnie. She must use the cabin when it's unoccupied. There is only one substantial chair, a wingback upholstered in a colonial small-pattern print. When she visits, Ginnie must expect to be alone.

I have said that in her months of illness, Miriam read autofiction. It spoke to her of daily routine and chance encounters and our own fallibility. It memorialized the life and world she was leaving behind. Autofiction—absorption in it—was her preferred form of analgesia. I was her supplier.

I bought endless volumes. The owner of our local bookstore, Books on Brooke, would email when she happened on new work that seemed up Mimi's alley. The shelf here at the cabin displays familiar authors' names: Cusk, Cole, Louis, Lin, Heti, Lerner, Uribe, Modiano, and Marías. Knausgård is unavoidable. I don't recognize every title. The collection consists of scattered volumes, often the second or third in a series. They are hardcovers, lovingly pored over or acquired second-hand, the pages dog-eared and tea-stained.

Sitting in the wingback, I have been riffling through Knausgård volumes, hoping to happen on passages that Miriam pointed out.

In her first hospitalization, a tough one, I asked Miriam whether she wanted me to read along with her.

She said, You get enough in your office.

Enough of what?

Lightly fictionalized memoir.

Miriam believed that I was too inclined to take my patients' tales at face value. That assessment was not entirely fair. My intent is to work with what patients produce until they choose to correct themselves.

On another occasion, I asked her what she understood by autofiction.

Dear, it's what you write.

How's that?

You take creative license, don't you?

She was being wicked. My distortions are in the service of maintaining patient confidentiality. This *taking license* only confirmed my identity as a reliable and unsurprising man. In contrast, writers of autofiction are freewheeling.

When Miriam woke, she clarified or repeated her thoughts about my work: my case vignettes read as fiction. My books read as memoir. I should embrace those identities—be bolder in those ways.

I thought of Meg's edit: *more of yourself.*

Mimi was saying, Yet more.

She directed me to a short passage in Knausgård, a few sentences. In them, he confesses to having invented a dramatic incident. The manufactured scene made it as far as the printed galleys before being excised. Traces of the invention remain in the description of its removal.

The omitted event is set in a fun fair where Knausgård and his then wife, Linda Boström, had taken their young children. Knausgård had depicted Boström whipping a donkey in anger. When Boström read the galleys, she objected. She had never attacked any animal. Knausgård agreed: the episode had not happened. His intent in creating it had been to capture an atmosphere of menace in the marriage. Boström had manic depression and was prone to bursts of rage.

Sitting at Miriam's side while she dozed, I tried to make sense of the rules that govern autofiction. Confabulation is permissible if it conveys emotional truth. Knausgård's wife had been so hostile that a fictive scene in which she beat a dumb beast might best represent her effect on the marriage.

Writing, I turned schoolteachers into librarians, blonds into brunettes. Had Knausgård felt free to simply make up events? Should I take that sort of license?

The account of the excision had an unsettling undertone, as if Knausgård were placating Boström. *Sure, honey. Whatever you say.* I took it as possible that Boström had, after all, whipped the donkey and later threatened to torpedo the writing project if Knausgård didn't cut the section in which she looked worst. He suppressed the incident but brought it in through the back door, by reporting a conversation about the late edit. Boström was now doubly in the wrong, for attacking an innocent animal and for causing her husband to lie about her cruelty.

Or else Boström had never whipped a donkey. For what real-life behavior is that imagined act the fit proxy? Had she hit the children? It seemed possible that while pretending to clarify his approach to writing memoir, Knausgård was sticking it to his wife. But then, he is quick to critique his hostility.

Knausgård tells stories on himself, ones where he pats himself on the back with one hand and, with the other, pulls the rug out from under his feet. In one harrowing example, Knausgård is cleaning the kitchen, thinking himself a fine fellow for doing housework that his wife has neglected—only to discover that the reason she has not come down from the bedroom is that she is in a deep depression. While he was scrubbing counters, she was taking pills in an attempt at suicide.

Repeatedly, Knausgård offers examples of his failure to appreciate the level of Boström's distress. Why introduce donkey-beating? I wondered whether Knausgård, in his role as memoirist, hadn't committed an outrage, bruising a creature, his wife, who lacked the means to defend herself. To the extent that he knew that the passage could be read that way, Knausgård had been offering a confession: as a writer, I am the abuser. I subject others to the lash.

I wanted not to admire Knausgård, but I saw what had moved Miriam. In flat language, he described a mundane event, a conversation about the decision to cut a passage in a book draft. That bare account exposed the ethical ambiguity of memoir.

On a personal level, I was left wondering whether Miriam would have preferred a different husband. If you marry Knausgård, your dirty linen is out in public, but you have had the fun of soiling it together. With me, there was no drama worth hiding.

We want what we don't have, the reverse sort of partner. We also want what we have, what we've chosen for good reason.

Miriam, you urged me to take liberties. I have done that, I hope—and I hope to continue. It's good, late in life, to push old habits to their limits.

◊ ◊ ◊ ◊ ◊

Yesterday afternoon, Ginnie visited. She is gaunt, with deep-set eyes. She wears frayed and faded clothing. If you photographed her in black and white, the image might fit into a collection from the Farm Services Administration, in the Great Depression, the lesser one, ninety years back.

Ginnie arrived carrying a shopping tote and a picnic basket. She set down both. From the basket she produced a Mason jar and a celadon-colored bowl covered with a green gingham dish-towel. The jar contained canned wax beans. The bowl had a portion of venison stew. Ginnie and Chet had been working their way through the meat from a deer that Chet had shot and dressed. They wondered whether I would enjoy some, wondered how much meat I ate.

The act of graciousness cost Ginnie effort. She is reticent by nature. Certain of my colleagues might call her pathologically shy, and then I would need to ask about the burdensome adverb. She appears to lead a fulfilling life.

Did shyness shape her choice in marriage, to a man inclined to settle far from the press of social demands?

After placing the food on the counter, Ginnie stood silent.

I thanked her but thought it best to mute my enthusiasm. I said that seeing the stew was enough to make me hungry. Was it better warmed on the stovetop or in the oven?

It was not only diffidence that Ginnie had to overcome. To enforce the news blackout, Ginnie is meant to keep her interactions with me to a minimum.

Against instruction, she had decided to make a delivery. From the tote, Ginnie produced a manila envelope, the kind with paper buttons on the back and a string running round them in a figure eight. She had come upon the delivery almost by chance, she said. She rarely checks for mail. When she neared the main road, she had noticed that the mailbox door was ajar. She went to shut it, to keep snow from blowing in.

Moisture had spattered the envelope. It carried no stamp and no address except one hand-printed line: *for the Doc*. The delivery must have come via a courier dispatched by someone who knows my whereabouts. Ginnie hoped that I did not object to her having looked inside. She is responsible for my wellbeing. She is on guard for threats.

The envelope contained information she thought I should know, information she had intended to convey to me herself.

She did not mean to disturb me. She might be out of bounds. But to transmit my last posting, she had set off to a distant village. That's how she had happened to pass the postbox, on the way out.

Sweat moistened Ginnie's brow. She put her hand on a chair back, to steady herself. I tried, in my demeanor, to convey patience and encouragement.

On her trip, she had run errands. In the hardware store, she had overheard customers speaking about my blog.

Could I be trusted? they asked. In my posts, nothing added up.

At last, Ginnie hit her stride.

She thought that a writer ought to know when his readers disbelieve him. That's why she was delivering the envelope despite the instruction she'd been given to keep me out of any loop.

She said that I did not look like someone who would set out to deceive.

Expressing support made Ginnie blush. She backed away, head down.

I had not yet copied the day's file onto the hard drive, and I told Ginnie that I might not. If the milk box was empty in the morning, it would mean that I had wanted to reconsider my latest effort in the light of her critique or the one I would find in the envelope.

Ginnie gave a bashful smile, as if she were unused to acknowledgment.

When I was done with the stew, she said, I could leave the bowl on the front porch, but only after scrubbing it well. I did not want to attract vermin or raccoons. Hereabouts, they forage well into winter.

The delivery of those instructions covered the time it took her to make it out the door.

◊ ◊ ◊ ◊ ◊

I set the envelope on the far end of the elm wood table. I wanted to think through the issue that the envelope's contents promised to address, the confusing aspects of my writing.

From the fridge, I retrieved what remained of a puree I'd made the night before from a warty winter squash. I spooned the left-overs into a baking dish, ladled Ginnie's stew on top, and warmed my dinner in the oven.

Ginnie had put thought into the seasoning. Onion, carrot, cel-ery, and garlic. Thyme, for sure. Miriam had been a mirepoix gal. Ginnie's stew made me think of Miriam. Much does.

Pottery canisters near the sink held dried herbs for infusions. The jar marked *Matricaria* had full flower heads for chamo-mile tea, with chopped dried apple mixed in for good measure. I brewed a cup.

From Ginnie's remarks, I understood the manila envelope to contain editorial comments. Receiving them is part of the writer's life. Meg uses the reviewing function in Microsoft Word to append suggestions to my chapter drafts, but in our first collaborations, she used red pencil to mark up my typescripts and returned them by mail.

When a packet arrived, I would set it aside. I wanted to be aware of my own misgivings before I engaged with Meg's. I was never so frank with myself as when a critique was pending.

Eating dinner, storing the remaining stew, scrubbing the bowl, setting it outdoors, I left Ginnie's delivery untouched.

If I came upon my own writing, how would it read to me?

Unpolished, poorly framed.

My routine has been the same with every book I've written. With a theme in mind, I sketch out case vignettes. As the collection takes shape, I write a dummy preface, one that will never appear in print.

I stuff it with preliminaries. How I approach writing. What I intend to cover. Why it matters.

Then I work to erase the preface, to make it superfluous. I reorder chapters. I move explanations into the main conversation with the reader.

With this material meant for blog posts, each evening I send off the day's output. There's no rearranging and no chance to return weeks later and see what needs clarifying. I had hoped that the immediacy—the free flow of thought—would compensate.

It seems that I have sown confusion.

◊ ◊ ◊ ◊ ◊

I will face the envelope in the morning. Better to write.

My trip to the Great Man's lair was uneventful.

It had to be. When Beelzebub motioned me to the back seat of the car—a black Escalade with darkly tinted side windows—he handed me a head-and-face covering, a black balaclava with openings for the mouth and nose but no eyeholes. I was meant not to know our destination.

A clear, thick plastic divider, such as you see in big-city taxicabs, separated the front seats from the rear. Beelzebub would work by phone as he drove. I would ride in silence.

In treating me as untrustworthy, he did me a courtesy. Visually, the balaclava echoed the black hoods used in the torture of terror suspects. I welcomed my assigned status. Better to be a conscript than a collaborator. But mostly, I was glad to have time to prepare.

In my training years, when psychoanalysis was the core psychiatric treatment, therapists tried to enter the consulting room free of advance impressions. The patient lies on the couch and says what comes to mind. The doctor hears the patient through fresh ears.

My practice has never run on those lines. In Providence, on College Hill, everyone is known. Before a prospective patient visits, I will have seen him coach junior soccer teams or heard him speak at PTA meetings. When he mows his lawn or divorces his wife, neighbors will form opinions. Those neighbors will be my patients, too, or my friends. There are few blank slates. Your reputation precedes you.

The same held for celebrities who consulted me. I had seen them on the screen. I had heard of their arrests for drunk driving or sexual solicitation.

Working with prisoners, I reviewed charts before initiating treatment. I learned what crimes my patient had been convicted of and what lines he had crossed during his stay.

I schooled myself in holding advance impressions lightly. Men who had run drug operations carried private burdens. These men had stories to tell.

With the Great Man, did I know too much or too little?

Daily, he had given Miriam cause for bitterness. She had her list of issues: voting rights, minority rights, civil liberties, gun control, climate change, women's health, public health, criminal justice, separation of powers, clean air and water, policing, domestic terrorism, foreign despotism, immigration, self-dealing, and more. On every item, the Great Man took the side of tyranny. He weakened protections, destroyed institutions, undermined trust, favored friends, and took his cut. In conversation, if I looked overwhelmed by Mimi's detailed accounts, she would offer a bleak generality: *He ruined the world.* And that was before the economy tanked.

Prison work had taught me how difficult self-examination can be for men who have caused grievous harm.

I recalled a patient I treated just after residency. Under the influence of a manic state set off by cocaine, Archie had killed his wife and daughter. Months later, he remained psychotic, answering only to a name not his own. Archie was, I thought, where he needed to be, detached from the person who had ended the lives of those who meant most to him.

Archie worked his way toward self-forgiveness based on self-understanding. He accepted his identity and his history. His affect remained flat, as if he could not bear to feel. The prison chaplain was of help. Archie developed a notion of expiation through good works.

There was backsliding toward delusion.

With patients who have done grievous harm, a therapist broaches sensitive topics gingerly. Therapies are easily derailed.

Did Archie's case provide a fit analogy? Even when he could not yet link himself to the murders, Archie understood how fearsome they were. I did not know how close to that sort of insight my new patient would be. What did he believe about the country he led?

But first, I would need to tend to myself. Is *He ruined the world* an advance impression that can be held lightly?

And the Great Man's threat to Kareena, what of that? The best way to avoid betraying hostility is to free yourself of hostility. Again, the problem of priestliness.

I gave no weight to Beelzebub's warning that the Great Man did not want to be other than who he was. Many patients come for symptom relief only to discover that something basic to themselves is at issue.

◊ ◊ ◊ ◊ ◊

I woke famished.

When I inventoried the larder, I should have mentioned fresh eggs. Ginnie brought a basketful when I arrived. The eggshells are bluish brown and heavily speckled. If we get to the point of engaging in small talk, I will ask what breeds of chicken Ginnie keeps.

I got stuck at the basket this morning, inspecting eggs, rolling them in my hands, brushing off dirt, feeling the roughness of the shells, comparing sizes.

I was uneasy. My isolation had been breached by an intruder, the envelope on the tabletop.

At home, when upset overcame me, I would tend to houseplants: deadhead, trim, mist. It's been that way since the ascent of the Great Man. Battered by the commotion, we turn to the natural world for grounding. How good to see that eggs are still eggs.

Or else it's that we have been driven—reduced—to our essential selves. The paranoid are more paranoid, the histrionic more histrionic. I had turned inward and obsessive, stimming with eggs.

Or the reverse: held distant from family and patients, I was awash in empathy, applying it indiscriminately. I viewed the eggs with melancholy. For all their beauty, they would soon be well and truly gone.

Ginnie had provided handling instructions. I was to scrub each egg before using. After cracking one open, I was to crush the shell, drop it in the compost carrier, and wash up well.

We could not afford salmonella poisoning. Ginnie foresaw diarrhea, dehydration, arrhythmias, the need to tend to a sick old man. I did not want to complicate her life. After the stimming, I scrubbed my hands and the counter.

As if making a consequential choice, I selected a matched pair of eggs for shirring in fresh butter, added a third for good measure, and went through a scrub-and-crack routine.

By way of confession: I played with an egg-shaped russet potato, too, before slicing it for home fries. What a privilege, to put this beauty to use.

I ate. I washed and dried the frypan and tableware. I swept the floorboards.

Time to face the music. I unwound the string.

I found what I had expected: a printout of responses to the blog. Whoever compiled them had done a painstaking job. Most trolling had been suppressed. To be sure, a small handful of commenters simply assume or declare that I am an assassin, and a larger handful make me out as a nutcase myself. The latter attribution is par for the course in my profession. The former is expectable under the circumstances. I assume that there are many other, more incisive sideswipes, but I have been spared them.

My anonymous correspondent—the compiler—was out to alert me to one substantive criticism: I am not credible. Note after note says that nothing in the blog posts checks out.

One reader writes that he performed a search of businesses in Rhode Island. There is no software vendor named Jamal. The closest match is a Jamel Jalali, a programmer who died in the plague year. There is no real-estate-company-pension-manager-turned-investment-guru named Arthur. The Deportation Service website shows no Luiza de Souza, or any Souza at the director's level. Nor, for that matter, does my first book contain vignettes about an Annabella.

It was not only patients, current or former, whose identities had been altered. There is no diner in Providence named Zervas Place. No locals recall having been served by a waitress, gay or straight, named Addie. Why muddle fact with invention?

Although the *Providence Journal* is no longer in print, its files remain accessible. They include a list of Rhode Island students named to All-State teams in every sport. A reader complains, Nowhere does an entry for Maurice Keys appear.

Readers who are not outraged express puzzlement or exasperation. What purpose it can it serve to avoid using the Great Man's name, since there is no mistaking him or other public figures, like Náomi and Beelzebub? Assigning our Marie Antoinette a name, why insert the peculiar accent mark? And why refer to Beelzebub's baby face? He is known for his wrinkle-laced, papery skin, aged as if (so one reader writes) hatred caused senescence, in the manner of tobacco use. Beelzebub was never married to a pianist.

Correspondents protest, You claim to be engaged in an act of witness. What can you testify to? If you worked with the Great Man, what was his diagnosis?

From the other direction: Doesn't confidentiality survive death? How can the doctor justify writing about the Great Man if he was a patient?

Why will I not cooperate with the authorities? I should offer what clarity I can about the leadup to my coming upon the Great Man's corpse.

Speaking of clarity, readers complain about Maury's posting only fragments of what I send.

The redactor of the printout left in a few quasi-supportive responses. Readers thought me brave (or suicidal) to write critically of Beelzebub, who might come to power and exact vengeance.

I thank those correspondents. I want to deny any attribution of courage or self-destructive tendencies. I'm following what my lawyer considers a prudent course.

Other readers—thank you all—point out that, when it comes to patients, I have stuck to the practice I employ in my books, where I change identifiers to preserve confidentiality. In these notes, I wrote about the spiel. If Maury has posted that section—and why would he not?—then my methods are clear.

◊ ◊ ◊ ◊ ◊

Although I am not hungry, I have returned to cottage larder and served myself a treat, Ginnie's canned plums. Simple and lovely: purple syrup on a white plate. The plum skins are tart enough to make me shiver.

I can see how my readers might demand honesty, the tang of it.

BEFORE ANSWERING THE QUESTIONS, I asked myself what news they brought.

Here in exile, my first worry is for Maury. If Beelzebub were in power, might he not arrest my lawyer in hopes of bringing me to heel? If Maury has managed to post blog entries, he is at large.

It appears that web users can communicate openly, without being drowned out by noise from the Regime's successor. I see anti-Great and EverGreat comments both. I conclude that our future is up in the air.

None of my guys is named anywhere, which means that none has been arrested. Perhaps none has been located. In that sense, the annoyance over pseudonyms—no Jamal! no Arthur!—is reassuring.

More, I take it that the cause and manner of the Great Man's death have not been determined—else why complain that I'm withholding salient facts?

What I find less encouraging is the anger that the blog has triggered. As a writer, I rarely encounter harsh responses.

I never worry about misinterpretation. Meg warns me not to. It was Meg who suggested the dummy preface technique.

Explain yourself. Erase the explanation.

If I try to convince skeptics, I will lose everyone else. I am to imagine myself writing for receptive readers.

The printout's assembler is sending the contrary message: I am arousing hostility.

How best to respond? By answering a question? Okay.

About Maury: he was All-State, known for his Havlicek-style jump shots, the right hand bent back, arm cocked high above the head. Maury was an all-rounder. He set picks, started the give and go, hustled back on defense, drew fouls.

In the *ProJo* records, he's probably listed as *Moshe (Moe) Schlussel*. In the 1960s, when Ancel Keys, the diet physiologist, was in the news with his cholesterol studies, Maury's father Mordy, the plumber, decided to translate the family name for everyone. In due course, the Schlussels became Keyses. For the teenagers, first names were tweaked as well—Moshe into Maurice, a choice that shows how little Mordy knew about what sounded mainstream.

My buddy, Moshe, did not suggest a different choice. Moe was one of the three stooges. Maurice could become Maury, like Maury Wills, that avatar of grace.

WHEN I WAS YOUNG, I sometimes made that move in therapy. When a patient presented a list of complaints, I addressed one frankly.

My hope was to avoid a stereotyped discussion: *You always answer a question with a question.* With that objection set aside, we might find ourselves exploring a more substantial basis for the patient's upset. Had I made missteps and injured him? Previously, what had his experience been with deception?

The move carried risk. I did not want to be like the husband who, when his wife names grievances, selects the least plausible one and implies that the rest are equally groundless.

Once I specialized in the treatment of paranoia, fact had less weight. How did the patient know that the direct answer was not itself a put-up job?

Am I in that predicament here?

I hope not.

I have reread the files I sent out. I don't see where I come across as someone who would put his credibility at risk by lying about his lawyer's teenage basketball career. Seriously, it's Maury who is selecting fragments of this memoir to distribute. Why would he post false claims about himself?

Rhode Islanders love school athletics. Look for websites where old-timers gather to reminiscence. You'll find aficionados who can reconstruct Moe Schlussel's exploits, game by game.

The challenge is lazy, unless it's meant to obfuscate. That's a worry, that we are stuck in the Great Man era, where his supporters nitpick anyone who speaks in public, to create a false equivalence with the Regime's bold lies. With the Great Man gone, I had hoped that we might start over and give each other the benefit of the doubt.

I AM TEMPTED TO ERASE what I've just written. I dislike relying on fact.

It's only by chance that I can answer that one question decisively.

No sooner do I imagine Maury editing me than I see him in the gym, breaking to the hoop. For me, Maury and roundball are one thing. In our friendship, forever he and I will be those teammates from school days. And of course, there is no way to hide Maury's identity. I assume that he goes on webcasts and speaks for me.

But if Maury had been a minor character, incidental to my story, I might well have switched sports. Say that a teammate was a power forward and I wanted to convey his balance and wiliness and masked aggression. I might (fictively) have made him a fencer. Then, if readers complained, I could not send them back to the *Providence Journal* files.

Would I then have had no way of offering reassurance—of vouching for my own intent to covey basic truths? Because most of what's in this account, the raw material for the blog, has been subject to what I call imaginative translation. That's why it's hard to locate Jamal and Arthur and Luiza.

How should a narrative from a trustworthy psychiatrist read? Professing puzzlement over my having disguised patients strikes me as wrongheaded. We would all want our doctors to extend us that courtesy.

In autofiction, so Mimi taught me, the goal is emotional honesty. Think of Knausgård's defense: I tried to convey the menace that my wife brought to the marriage.

Similarly, in the blog posts, Charlie's facility with judo is meant to suggest qualities that he expresses in quite different fashion. If the clumsy name choices, *Jamal* and *Ahmed*, signal diversity in the patient mix, that's real. The guys have reached across social boundaries and pulled together, mostly reserving their mistrust for those outside the group.

Have I extended confidentiality too far? Acquaintances in my hometown are due privacy. Thinking of Ildeberto, whose business is it that he had trouble selling the restaurant—or (instead, in reality) turned to drug abuse, lost money gambling, or fell victim to fraud? Through one misfortune or another, he suffers despair that has become common in the Great Man's era.

Who cares, finally, where, on a Monday, I met my daughter and learned of her wife's crisis? I have hoped to capture the feel of the city and the encounter.

Writing, I found that I could not bring myself to use my daughter's name or my granddaughter's or to represent precisely my daughter-in-law's line of work or my granddaughter's age. I knew that the invention would not conceal their identities. Nina's wedding notice is accessible online. Miriam and I are identified as her parents. I don't doubt that social media made note of Tamara's birth. But imaginative translation has become a habit with me. For patients, for acquaintances, for family—I offer what protection I can.

AS FOR THE OTHER POINTS of confusion, does the compiler expect me to allay suspicion by addressing every query? When, in the Great Man era, has explanation quieted outrage?

I think of the items that have caused the most insistent cries of annoyance: the Great Man's name and Beelzebub's face. I can't be liable to charges of deception on those counts. We know who died and what his henchman looks like.

With Beelzebub, I tried to capture the experience of sitting in his presence. Future historians won't record that he was smooth-cheeked. There are photos.

As for why I have gone with *Beelzebub*: I could hardly have improved on Náomi's invention. It's apt, and the man is alive to defend himself. I wanted to maintain consistency with the rest of the blog—all nicknames or pseudonyms—and at the same time to call him by his name.

Writing's a strange process, writing and writer's block. Impulses and inhibitions arise for reasons of their own, for psychological reasons.

With Meg, I believe that the text must serve as preface. Clarification will come as the story proceeds.

AFTERTHOUGHT: ONE BRIEF CRITIQUE STICKS with me. *To emerge from the era of the Great Lie, must we not tell the truth?*

Ever since I first composed a case vignette, I have suffered from scruples along these lines. In writing where facts must be altered, what constitutes good faith?

I worry that of late the answer has changed, that the Great Man has given creative license a bad name.

◊ ◊ ◊ ◊ ◊

Two hours into the drive, Beelzebub knocked open the plastic divider.

On purpose, I imagined. He was speaking by phone with an underling. Every third word of Beelzebub's was an expletive, and every third sentence, a threat of mayhem. He would have this or that organ on a platter. He would mutilate sexual parts.

The harangue did double duty, serving as indirect aggression against me. In therapy, a hostile patient will share sadistic fantasies. His intent is less to unburden himself than to expose me to unpleasantness. Duty constrains me to listen.

In session, I can question the mixed intent. In the Escalade, I removed the balaclava. I doubted that Beelzebub would leave me behind.

The road signs told a story. Approaching Stockbridge. Pittsfield. South and east of Saratoga Springs. We were heading toward the Adirondacks.

I knocked on the plastic divider. If there was an easy place to pull over, I would take a pee.

That request was my intervention. I expected ordinary courtesies.

Beelzebub pulled to a stop. I could pee in the woods.

When I returned to the car, he asked, What in life is a sure thing?

He meant death.

He meant that Kareena's citizenship papers counted for little.

The reminder seemed to satisfy his need for dominance.

He said, About your phone. It's registered to Ezra Weitz. You're Weitz. That's how I'll introduce you to the boss. He's not one for names. He'll call you what he pleases. The point is for him not to trip up and disclose your identity.

Beelzebub turned to logistics. The smart phone had limited capabilities. One was refilling prescriptions. Beelzebub named the heart drugs I am on. I could order them with the touch of a virtual button.

For shopping, the phone was loaded with dummy apps that mirrored sites for branded retailers. Inputted requests would pass through a service run by the quartermaster's office. I could choose clothes and toiletries. I might start now, on the road.

We take a cut, Beelzebub said, as if confirming an assumption he expected I'd made already.

When I pulled on socks, when I flossed my teeth, pennies would drop into my host's coffers. I had signed on to serve him. I would find myself serving him constantly.

On the plus side, I saw that Maury's text had arrived. He had administered the citizenship oath to Kareena. He was on his way to the Deportation Service to register papers.

Did I express pleasure aloud?

Beelzebub said, You're like a mentally ill homeless person. You mutter to yourself, and then you take on a satisfied look, as if something had been achieved.

You'll be a fine match for the Great Man.

Now it was Beelzebub's turn to laugh to himself, a sneer given voice. I took it that he considered his assignment absurd. He had fetched one crazy charlatan to treat another.

WHEN WE REACHED THE MOUNTAINS, the sky darkened, and we found ourselves in a downpour. It abated as we arrived at guard towers and the palisade fence. The Great Man was living the life he had pitched for his countrymen, behind a high wall. Through the fog, I could make out, barely, the roof peaks of a substantial building. In outline, it looked like a child's image of a witch's castle. Were there snipers on the rooftops? Too misty, after the rain, for me to be certain.

The guards at the gate wore navy-blue uniforms that featured a shield-shaped arm patch. A private security firm. I guessed that the Great Man mistrusted or feared the Federal service.

Funny. Walking through Providence, when I came upon a house plastered with security firm stickers, I would wonder whether one of mine—a candidate for group work—lived there.

A guard knocked on the car roof.

Good to go, Bub.

Excuse me?

Good to go…Bub.

Bub! Why had it not occurred to me to compact the nickname? With Miriam, I had watched a documentary about fundamentalist evangelical communities that supported the Great Man. The believers were so familiar with devils as tempters that they referred to them in shorthand.

Our Bub paused. Did he consider upbraiding the guard for his cheek? What could Bub say that would not sound oversensitive? *Secretary Beelzebub to you?*

A dog growled, and Bub startled.

I would pay a price, I knew, for having been present when Bub was addressed casually and when he showed fear.

As we approached the compound, security floodlights revealed the main building's outlines. It looked to be a mountain hotel, grand in scale, but divided in sections so as not to overwhelm with its massiveness. In the angled roofs, the structure made reference to alpine chalets. I was guessing that the Great Man had bought a bankrupted resort and repurposed it. The finance mavens in my therapy group had made that complaint. In the name of security, the Great Man multiplied residences by acquiring failed enterprises and having them renovated at public expense.

◊ ◊ ◊ ◊ ◊

We entered through an underground garage and took an elevator to a residential floor. Bub gave me over to the charge of a well-built, long-faced, ruddy fellow and rushed off without a farewell.

Patrick, my new minder said, by way of introduction.

Ezra.

Patrick ignored the false name and said, I read your book, in Afghanistan.

Some of his men had insomnia, which they could ill afford. A tattered copy of *Rest* had made the rounds.

Henry, then.

Everyone calls me Muscle, Patrick said.

He steered me down a corridor lined with closely spaced doors.

It's tiny, but it has its own bathroom.

I had been assigned a room just wide enough to hold a cot and a dresser. Overnight quarters for staff at the old hotel.

The commissary had made note of my big-box order. Muscle would fetch items as they arrived. In the meanwhile, the laundry had sent up military fatigues a size larger than what I had indicated.

Muscle apologized for hustling me along, but he had assignments.

Be ready for a summons.

I washed, changed into camo, and lay down for a nap. When a knock at the door wakened me, my watch read three.

Weitz!

My escort was not Muscle but Bub, whose day must have been as long as mine. I wondered whether he was being subjected to hazing or whether he wanted credit for delivering the goods.

Whatever are you carrying? he wanted to know.

My electronic tablet and stylus, tools of my trade.

I could see Bub calculating. Could he afford the delay that a fight would cause?

We marched along a corridor and up a staircase that led from the staff dormitory to a dimly lit netherworld of kitsch opulence. The décor consisted of large-scale chinoiserie: statues of guardian lions and serene Buddhas, models of tall pagodas and squat temples, paintings of landscapes and of noble couples at rest, and all manner of porcelain. The wallpaper featured cranes on gingko trees and colorful ducks in smooth-surfaced ponds. Perhaps the ensemble signaled a taste that the Great Man favored but was blocked from expressing in public settings, which required patriotic symbols. Perhaps the hotel had come furnished.

From a wide, high-ceilinged hallway, we passed through an anteroom flanked with bronze gongs and, seated beside one of them, in the blue uniform with shield patch, a ripped young woman with a stolid face.

Do you hear that? I asked.

From far off—faintly—a woman crying.

The guard shrugged. Every night, and still I'm not used to it.

She gave a friendly warning, A bit rich in there tonight.

We passed through double doors into what once may have been a waiting area, a place for visitors to adjust their gowns and hair, and then through another set of double doors into the boudoir proper. It was a vast room with little in the way of furnishing beyond curtains, mirrors, and a fussily appointed four-poster bed. From among the piles of pillows, a large head peeked out, strikingly familiar despite the baldness.

The room was filled with a stench that the Great Man seemed not to notice. Bub struggled with it. I was not perfectly comfortable myself, but at least I was not outraged. Bub was subject to a constant double jeopardy, from adversity and the fact that it was happening to him.

Hey, Reaper, the Great Man said, what took you so long? No excuses! You disappoint, except in this sense: I can count on you to disappoint.

What'd you bring me here, a buck private?

I hope you don't expect me to salute. I don't salute buck privates.

Finding the joke fall flat, he changed course.

You're not telling me that this sorry specimen is the wizard?

Bub said that it was.

Then what are you still doing here?

The style was familiar, discourtesy as a mark of dominance. The Great Man had the standing to dismiss the Reaper, as he called Bub, without the least expression of gratitude and to call on me without regard to my age or the hour. I was to learn that behaving just as he chose in all settings was the Great Man's signature.

As Bub made to leave, the Great Man turned to me. How'd you hit it off with our friend?

I said, I can't say that he took a shine to me.

Leaving, Bub was the picture of ressentiment. I imagined him pulling on his forelock in exaggerated submission. I imagined him bowing and backing out on his knees.

The Great Man took no notice.

Do people generally? he asked. Take a shine to you?

When I did not respond, he conceded, You'd be in a select group if he had.

And again, You don't make much of an impression.

More of the same. You're an ugly cuss.

To that point I had barely made note of my patient's appearance.

We aim to view without judging. If a patient is homely and yet has hopes of taking leading man roles on the big screen, the therapist will not react as the world might, with disbelief. But finally, if we are to gauge the patient's grasp of reality, we need to see what others see.

When the Great Man raised the question of looks, that therapeutic discipline kicked in.

He understood that he was hideous. He claimed prerogative to deny the obvious.

Had his fame blinded me? On entering the boudoir, I had simply recognized the Great Man—registered that he was who he was. Celebrity can work on us that way. We note an equivalence: that's him, alright.

The iconic photo may have the same effect. We may not appreciate his obesity. The photo shows the sag of the couch and the breadth of the caboose, but the belly is partly hidden. I don't know a public image that does the gut justice, or the excess flesh on the face.

When the Great Man set his chin on his chest, the mouth addressed me from within a landscape of folds and creases. I thought of Jabba the Hutt, the insatiable appetite. Perhaps the setting elicited the image. The Great Man was eating. A warming cart sat at the bedside. Periodically, he gestured with a chicken taco, splashing me with lettuce shreds and salsa.

I gathered that preemption was the Great Man's method, attributing his own unattractive traits to others. I wondered how far back the tendency went. In the teens, appearance can take unfortunate turns, and adolescents can be cruel.

I had a familiar feeling: therapy in progress.

I'm sure I was beaming. Yes! Continue!

Did my evident pleasure confuse the Great Man? He repeated himself. *Hard to take a shine to an ugly-cuss doctor.*

Was it the stench or the long trip in or the late hour? I was off my game. I responded in cliched fashion. *That's a value for you, likeability?*

He raised an eyebrow.

You dish out that shit at your peril.

He was right. I was ignoring his intent—insult.

I had turned the focus to him, what he cared about. It had been wrong, a technical lapse, to skip past the obvious message, that I am unimpressive. To treat the taunt as routine content was to resist the Great Man's authority. He had wanted me back on my heels.

I considered saying, *You know how to put a person in his place*, or, better, *You have my number*. Even those responses are problematic. They show that the blow has not landed. They ask, *Is that what you intend, self-assertion?*

Jotting down these thoughts took time—another error. I was at work, in role, searching for the intervention that would best suit my patient, when what he wanted was for me to be flustered.

I made note that the problem that I had anticipated while wearing the balaclava had not arisen. The Great Man's misdeeds on a national or global scale, his awareness or denial of them, his aggression toward my family—none of that material had come into play. In the boudoir, the Great Man created an intimate struggle that preempted attention to other matters. As I made small mistakes, he latched on to them. The issue became my competence.

Or was it me that he had latched on to? His method was to clamp his jaw shut and shake his prey.

I felt welcome—newly at home. That is the benefit that inappropriate affect brings and the difficulty that it creates. The Great Man was challenging my right to feel unshaken.

Cohen, he said, you may make that move in—where are you from, Syria? You're not here to examine my values. You do wizardry or go home, to Syria.

Realizing that he had mixed things up, he doubled down.

Izzy, he said, your type doesn't do well in Syria.

In his own, different way, the Great Man was making himself comfortable. Issuing threats and demands set him at ease.

Sleep, he said. Sleep is what I value. You're here to make me sleep.

I had not been invited to sit. Standing, I jotted on my tablet like a waiter taking an order. Appetizer: Syria. Main course: sleep.

You're a lucky man. The luckiest! Lucky, lucky little man. One minute you're a small-town nobody, and the next, you're serving the greatest leader the world has known. Historic accomplishments.

The economy! The Great Man made special mention of the economy, how it was flourishing, how the world gave him credit.

Do you want to take a selfie with me? Very, very valuable. People treasure photographs of the Great Man.

He reached under a pillow, pulled out a wig, slapped it on his head, and made efforts to adjust it.

It occurred to me that the selfie was meant to be payment in full for the consultation. Rather than decline the offer directly, I explained the purpose of the e-tablet. When it made sense in the course of our work together, I might record observations. I might study them between sessions, to serve him better.

In repeating his word, *serve*, I had veered too far in the other direction. One can serve a patient professionally, as his physician, but I had left open the meaning that the Great Man preferred, obeisance.

He listened just enough to gather that the photoshoot was off. The wig went back under the pillow and the monologue continued.

That's okay. Stick to your job. Fantastically important job, consultant to the Great Man. You're a nobody, but for now you're a nobody in grand cause. Work at it. I like to keep little people employed at important work.

I can't say that I enjoyed standing by while the Great Man belched and farted and spewed food. I knew that if I gagged, I would destroy whatever little progress I had made toward forming an alliance.

I breathed slowly and concentrated on the meeting's good points.

Albeit via denial, the Great Man had introduced delicate topics: the economy, the public response, and his place in history.

The Great Man was right. He had granted me a privilege, entrusting me with his wellbeing, letting me practice my profession. Amidst the insults, I discerned hints of acknowledgement. The *consultant* charade notwithstanding, I was his doctor.

So, Lipschitz, you're the wizard. Let's see what you've got.

I stood by, silent.

That's for you, the Great Man said.

I had not seen it, but tight by the pillow, obscured by the food cart and the bedclothes, was a Victorian lady's parlor side chair, small and low to the ground. I moved it to a comfortable distance and sat down.

What is it, half past three? I'm in a terrible state, the Great Man said. Put me to sleep.

With Bub, when he was B, I had denied having magical powers. I did not do the same now. For all that it contained a measure of wishful thinking, *wizard* implied its opposite: I was a fraud. There was no need for correction.

I said, Night after night you lie awake.

The Great Man shook his finger. He saw where I was heading. We would not review his medical history in light of the chief complaint—when he first noticed the problem, and so on.

Look, Pincus—Schwartzkopf—Wizard, you may be a doctor—somewhere else you may be—but you are not the Great Man's doctor.

As is not unusual, my patient had read my mind and was out to correct an impression I had formed. The move confirmed for me all the more that therapy was under way.

The Great Man does not need doctors for the mind. You've heard of my luscious consort, Naomi? She says you're a sleep sorcerer. That's how she sold you.

The fantastic head loomed over me like a Hollywood prop or special effect.

I daunt you, the Great Man said. I have that effect on people, rattling them. At first, I thought it might be my intelligence. Then I realized that it was my charisma. Well, brilliance and charisma. It's the whole package: the wealth, the popularity, the incredible accomplishment.

I'm an intuitive type. I can see that my charisma daunts you—my mojo.

*Daunt*, my note says. The shower of self-praise was the first example I encountered of his tendency to get stuck on a word.

He was changing tacks. Having threatened me—sedate or go home—he turned to encouragement.

Set your admiration aside. Everyone's daunted in my presence. Push past it. Work your wizardry.

As if responding to the Great Man's invitation—not to be daunted—I said, Tell me a story, then. Tell me something about you that I will not have heard already. That's how I approach insomnia. Asking for memories.

The Great Man shook his fat finger. You tell me a story about yourself. Make it a true one.

For new patients who have never been in therapy, I do on occasion model the process.

You're a skier, I believe, I said to the Great Man.

I hoped that the opening would not sound like a put-down. In his first term, when there was still an opposition press, the Great Man had, I knew, been flayed for spending time on the slopes, ignoring governance while the country slid into plague and poverty. Still, he was associated with the sport, proudly, I believed, through his ownership of ski resorts. He had loved being seen on the trails, loved being photographed beside the luscious wife he had just mentioned, her figure set off in sports togs.

I began, My wife introduced me to skiing. She had started young and kept at it. Once we became an item, she insisted that I learn.

I'm not tired, the Great Man said. But I'm tired of hearing about you.

Working with an antsy and resistant patient, I may speak slowly until he leaps into the breach, livening things up with confessions he had considered withholding. I can't claim to have planned the effect here, but I don't know that I was guileless either. It had felt right to begin deliberately.

No one cares about weak skiers, he said.

Or your wife, or your courtship.

Bore me with talk of your wife, and I'll send her to Syria. Syria or Peru.

Goody-goodies with their pathetic marriages! I can see your honey, fetching enough in her twenties, if a little thick-waisted and flat up top, fetching until she packed on the pounds. Did she lord it over you, your wife who hit the slopes in nursery school? I have it: she sent you to a ski class, you twisted your knee, and back in the condo you found her in bed with an instructor, taking her own lessons. You've been forgiving her ever since, you with your pathetic bleeding heart. That's your story, written all over you.

Suddenly, he gave me a hard look, as if the scattered insults had coalesced into a grand insight. She has contempt for you. She's in despair. She's sorry she ever met you.

The Great Man was constructing me, revealing his initial fantasies about the therapist.

They differed from reality—from my sense of it. For example: Miriam had stayed lovely into old age. Thin, too—and, finally, too thin. Nor, to my knowledge, had she ever strayed in the marriage. She made jokes at my expense, but finally, she loved me. I hope so.

The Great Man's fantasies were distinctive. Most patients made me out as fortunate in my domestic life. Some were jealous over my marriage, as they imagined it. That's the advantage of a longevity in the profession. You know how you appear to others—the range of responses. The Great Man fell at one extreme.

He was revealing his character and his concerns. He was unable to listen long to any voice but his own. He cared about his alpha status. As a man, he needed to succeed in every conventional way, excelling at sport, attracting beauties, and humbling his counterpart in any conversation. He would be doing the talking.

Don't tell me about precocious. When my Dad brought me to the slopes, he knew that he was dealing with a natural. He threw skis on my feet and let me figure it out. *Find your way down* is how a man learns.

You can't believe the skier I became. In prep school, we had a sissy in our class, I forget the kid's name, we called him the Widger—piggy-nosed, scrawny little guy, hated skiing, would spend the afternoon in the lodge if he could.

If you ski at all, you'll like this story. The Widger was a—what do you call them today? He should have been born a girl. Liked nothing better than to mother the kindergarteners.

On the mountain, when the teachers pushed the Widger out of doors, the little spaz would find a quiet spot in the woods and curl up with a book. Kid's piss-poor at skiing, slow and deliberate, but he tolerates cold. We were at Glorious, a resort my father owned—owned in part, largely his. That's a great story for another day, how he finagled the land rights. Ruined a couple of old locals, really funny. Anyway, about the Widger: this is before glade skiing was a thing—before trail crews went into the woods to thin out the understory. If you went off-piste, you hit brush and stands of skinny trees, lots of trees. You bushwhacked.

I took the top of Nosebleed—steep drop-off—and as I hit the main slope, I caught a glimpse of something mustard-colored—we had gold blazes on our outfits—mustard, among the trees. I had a notion that it was the Widger, hiding out. The next run down, I head there with my buddies. We swoop in from all sides, whooping and screaming, making turns among the branches, crazy-man skiing.

The Widger startles, and as he stands up, he's back on his heels. His skis slide out from under him. He's headed for a tree, so he bends at the knees—desperately—pulls his feet back, throws his body to the side—fine moves. Moron had never skied so well. It was genius, my terrorizing the Widger—instant instruction, got him to do stuff he would never have attempted, but for the fright.

Throw a kid into the deep end of the pool. Makes a man of him.

Anyway, the Widger squirts out onto the trail and crashes into a five-year-old, one of the very boys the Widger had befriended, another crybaby. Lucky for the Widger, the little guy buffers the end of the Widger's ride. Less lucky for the tyke.

The patrollers throw the Widger off the mountain for skiing out of control. On the bus back, he's a crying mess. Parents of the rug rat threaten to sue the Widger's family for some injury. The Widger's parents pull him from the school.

You're wondering if I faced discipline. My dad never made an investment without holding some edge. It was only after he had enticed the headmaster and the board chair into participation in a deal that, let us say, was best kept private, only after my dad had leverage, that he enrolled me in prep school.

He's like me, Dad told the headmaster.

Don't stifle the boy, was Dad's attitude. He would take it as a personal insult if the school came down on me. He liked hearing that I was a natural leader, insisted on getting that report.

I want you to keep your nose clean, he told me. And if not, I want them to wipe your nose and your arse too.

Widger and the crybaby tyke. In one blow, I'd rid the school of two wimps, but the big get was the Widger. He doesn't say a thing in class for a week, and then he's gone and, for me, with the lads, it's *All Hail the Great Man!* I'm a legend. But forget the acclaim—I'm remembering the day on the slopes. Jeez, we had a time.

Years later, I'm at a fund-raiser for a do-good cause. We're contributing to a charity and then recouping the cash in the form of inflated hotel rental, genius scheme. I sit down at the head table, and there's the Widger, looking mopey as ever. Turns out he'd ended up in a helping profession, like you, Einstein. I pity the guy—no money in those jobs—so I try to chat him up.

I got you skiing! I say. You were a maniac! Good for you, you wild man!

Jerk looks alarmed.

Don't thank me! I say. Whole rest of the school thanked me when we saw the back of you.

It distorts people, the inability to show gratitude. I almost felt bad for the Widger. Born to be a loser, but he seemed to like it, insisted on being a loser.

Forget it. Forget ingratitude. I'm thinking about that day at Glorious, coming down on the Widger like a bitch. Glory is the right word. What glory!

You're okay, Einstein, I'm getting the hang of what you do. Fantastic stuff, reminding me of what I'm made of. From childhood on—a hero.

And like that, the Great Man dropped off to sleep.

◊ ◊ ◊ ◊ ◊

He was crowing one second, snoring the next. The transition was so quick that I considered a diagnosis of narcolepsy.

If the Great Man was not narcoleptic, why did he nod off?

Perhaps the therapy had played a role. Hans Lutz's method is forgiving. I had made technical mistakes, but not so many as to obscure my intent, to know my patient and let him know himself.

I had aimed for moderation, not expressing horror at the Widger story and not roaring with complicit laughter. I had tried to see the bullying as the Great Man did, as a bold child's victory, a successful imitation of his father's style. I had wanted to express openness, a willingness to hear the narrative change with further telling. Had the Great Man, in childhood, been surprised and humiliated on the slopes? Or had he injured a child? Perhaps it was not the Widger but the kindergartener, now grown, who had shown up at the dinner, in a wheelchair.

I guessed that the Great Man did not often find his anecdotes received in this fashion, quietly, with neither enthusiasm nor harsh judgment—unless he believed that he had bullied me into submission, that his tale of bullying was also an instance of bullying. Like the headmaster, I had heard an account of cruelty, bitten my tongue, and become complicit in the Great Man's bad behavior. Patients can read the neutrality—the silence—of the therapist that way.

Maybe the Great Man was exhausted. Even insomniacs can succumb to exhaustion.

On the e-tablet, I recorded a few moments of snoring and one short interval in which the Great Man's breathing seemed to pause. I can't say why I thought to save the files. I doubted that the Great Man would accept treatment for sleep apnea. Likely, at our next meeting, he would call me worthless and deny that he'd slept at all. I would not answer by playing the video. It's not just that I avoid fact-based clarification. Hearing himself snore, the Great Man would find a way to deny the obvious—and he would demand that I ditch the device. I liked taking notes and reviewing them in my off hours.

THE VIDEO IS IN THE cloud. I have no access to it now. What I recall is echoed in the photo of the Great Man in death: the sprawl, the mouth agape, the pathos. Asleep, he looked and sounded as if he might pass away at any moment.

At the bedside, I asked myself whether, if the breathing stopped, I would begin resuscitation.

A problem for the ethicists: Must we rescue a man whose continued existence endangers us all?

I would try. I would give the breath of life. I had no barrier mask. I would I apply my dry, aging lips to the Great Man's greasy, liverish ones and offer air from my lungs. A doctor does not pick and choose. I was trained to rescue strangers. Certainly, I would rescue a patient.

I had these thoughts, and I saw Mimi or remembered her. She was in her fifties, at an age when she found our marriage difficult. She had cropped her hair and forsaken contact lenses for round wire-rimmed glasses, the kind that the British National Health Service once provided. The style said *functional*, as if she were intent on making no concessions to men, including me.

She was scornful. Revive the Great Man in the name of ethics?

Immediately, we were together toward the end of her life. She was failing. We had no certainty that she would live out the month.

Mimi had me reading to her from Knausgård, the last and fattest book in his fictive memoir. We had reached a long passage on Adolf Hitler. In his youth, he was an aspiring artist, shy and ambitious, with sentimental impulses—not unlike Knausgård himself. If only young Adolf had managed to gain admission to the Viennese art academy!

He has an in with an influential faculty member, makes an appointment to meet with him. We see Adolf standing in the entryway, on the threshold, deciding whether to appeal for help. He turns away and carries his resentments into adulthood.

He would have made a *fine* patient, Mimi says. She sounds bitter.

If I had seen the Führer die a sudden death, would I have revived him?

As in the college conversations with Mimi, I deny my idealism. For Hitler, no breath of life. Rules have exceptions.

Mimi asks: Where along the spectrum of monstrosity does Kantian duty end?

Hitler killed many millions. What of a despot whose death toll numbers in the hundreds of thousands?

Miriam recited her litany, the one that linked the Great Man to deaths. Deportation of migrants, caging of children—for her, those outrages were the first among many. The news told of dead journalists, dead churchgoers and concertgoers, dead nurses, dead checkout clerks, deaths in prisons, deaths in classrooms, deaths on city streets, deaths from domestic abuse and botched abortions, deaths from health care denied, deaths from race hatred and homophobia, deaths from floods and fires and poisonings and pollution. The deaths of despair, the suicides and overdoses—how many of those could be laid at the Regime's door?

And that was just at home. The Great Man embraced foreign tyrants, wars erupted, and innocents perished. The Great Man squelched resistance here, and artists and writers died in distant jails. The seas rose and coastal dwellers drowned on distant shores.

For the Regime, death was a matter of policy. Nina's arbitrocracy was, to Mimi, better understood as thanatocracy. The Regime was anti-life. The Regime was pro-death.

Oh, Mimi, I said.

I knew that the thoughts were mine, based on memories of Mimi's recitations. I could hear her, nonetheless. She tapped her foot in exasperation. Walk away, she said.

I was not a heart doctor or a pulmonologist. I had not been assigned to monitor the Great Man's breathing. I doubted that this night differed from dozens that had come before. The question—whether to resuscitate—was theoretical.

Tend to yourself, Mimi said.

If I was to treat my patient conscientiously, I would need rest.

I obeyed my late wife and stood up, intending to head directly to my room.

BEFORE WE LEAVE THE BOUDOIR: the manila-envelope correspondence suggests that I will disappoint if I do not address the question of diagnosis.

I will disappoint in a different way if I do.

For years, observers complained, If only the Great Man would submit to psychiatric examination! People had that wish, for a doctor to interview him and say what was amiss.

The unfulfilled task dominated a sector of the professional literature. Psychiatrists are permitted to diagnose only if they have interviewed the person—and then the person needs to waive privilege. How could those conditions be met?

Folktales tell us that when our wishes are granted, it is rarely in the fashion that we had hoped. I interviewed the Great Man. I had something like a go-ahead to discuss his case—I'll report on that conversation soon. But I am not much of a diagnostician.

I trained in an era when psychiatrists cared most about a patient's ability to tolerate psychotherapy. Does he have a capacity for insight? If the treatment arouses anxiety, will he be able to bear it?

As a result, I'm not dogged in my pursuit of diagnosis. If a patient is reluctant to discuss his past medical history, I back off. The same for symptoms. I'm using that word as doctors do. Symptoms are what patients report. The Great Man admitted only to insomnia. Otherwise, that first night, he cut me off. *None of that!*

I did make note of *signs*—what the doctor observes. The Great Man was obese. Soon, his sleep apnea became evident. If he had narcolepsy, it would declare itself. Any doctor would be on the lookout for those conditions.

But what of his psychological makeup? The sparring, the threats and insults, the grandiosity—they made me guess that the Great Man would turn out to resemble the patients I treat, the men I consider to have paranoia, loosely taken. If I arrived at that verdict, I would know how to proceed—never mind that another doctor would be intent on labels like narcissism, sociopathy, or mild autism. I get a feel for what it's like to sit with a patient. I assess strengths. In which areas is judgment maintained?

To give one example: That first night, I noticed that the Great Man was insightful in the service of mockery. When a jibe missed the mark, he noticed and changed direction. He slung food. He offered me the tiny chair. Then, recognizing that he had not impressed me with contempt or abuse, he switched gears and tried sharing a memory of the sort that a patient might contribute in a psychotherapy session.

There was my diagnosis: *not unworkable*.

Otherwise: yes, in a general sense, I believed that he would turn out to be one of mine.

I was not discouraged when I left the room, but I had not yet felt the full impact of the encounter. The rest of the night would go less well.

◊ ◊ ◊ ◊ ◊

At the door, the bodyguard gave me a wave. All done?

Once again, I heard weeping. Far down the corridor, near what must have been a grand staircase, I made out the figure of a woman. She was loosely clothed, like an actress in an ancient Greek drama. She leaned backward from the waist, arms spread as if to appeal to the heavens. She bent forward and clung to the railing, as if holding on for dear life. She shook, from the sobbing. I was seeing the silhouette of grief.

Is that…?

The guard did not answer except to ask that I wait for an escort.

It was Muscle. He was on night call.

Success? he asked. He could hear snoring from the bedchamber.

I excused myself from answering.

I've always wondered, Muscle said, what a psychiatrist would make of these furnishings, the ersatz Asian artefacts. He pointed to a folding screen, all gilt and lacquer. It stood behind a bow-legged chest on which sat vases with phoenix and chrysanthemum motifs.

Muscle spoke of how the Great Man's bullying had failed. China flourished while we floundered. All the same, the Great Man had ordered that this hallway be appointed in just this fashion. Every day, he walked past objects meant to memorialize a victory that happened only in his mind, if there.

No one else one uses this hallway, Muscle said. The Great Man walks it mornings and evenings, on the way from the bedroom to the elevator that takes him to the office suites.

The hallway was a lie directed only at the self.

Is it strange to say that I took encouragement from Muscle's suggestion that the Great Man embraced his own false claims? Better—simpler—to work with a patient who is delusional than with one who has clung to power through conscious connivance. Even a mixed verdict, delusion amplified by deception, might be welcome.

◊ ◊ ◊ ◊ ◊

Dropping off to sleep, I found myself revisiting the story that I had attempted to share with the Great Man. I was in the Green Mountains in winter with Miriam, a young Miriam introducing me to skiing. We were on a trail named Audacity. It was labeled intermediate, and Miriam must have considered it easy.

I had done well on flatter slopes, but with instruction. I had cross-examined my teacher with the aim of getting every move right before advancing—and then I had not appreciated how hard it can be to hold your form as the pitch steepens. Seemingly, Miriam had overestimated me as well. Midway down the run, she had flown past. She looked up at me from a short plateau.

Trying to match her pace, I flailed, throwing my arms and poles about to correct for my lower body's rookie mistakes. When I reached Miriam, she had an expression that I interpreted as alarm.

I apologized. I'm sorry. I have no balance.

She was laughing but warmly, lovingly.

You could win awards. I've never seen a skier with better balance.

To ski that awkwardly and remain upright was a feat.

I had been ready to share the anecdote with the Great Man. It made me look foolish but not overly so. I had grit. I had a quick and forgiving wife. I did not mind being a figure of fun. The point was to set an example of vulnerability and openness in hopes of coaxing the Great Man to reply with recollections of his own.

That night on the cot, it seemed to me that the vignette, in the version that I had been prepared to discuss, was anodyne, like memories that Freud taught analysts to mistrust—screen memories, toothless substitutes that block access to awareness of a traumatic event.

The Great Man did not waste heat on the servants' quarters. Was it the chilly air that brought me back to the scene on the mountain? I saw Miriam, not, as in an oft-told tale, kindly and understanding, but as she had been, suddenly doubting her choice of partner. Her laugh expressed no tenderness. She passed from surprise to dismay and disbelief.

I had looked composed on the flats, like a natural. As the steepness increased, other elements in my makeup emerged. My strengths might be substantial, but they were idiosyncratic or—doubtless Mimi's thoughts ran in this direction—peculiar.

How trim Mimi was. Compactness and simplicity were her themes. She wore a one-piece ski suit, cinched at the waist with a broad belt. Standing before her, seeing her beauty and her agitation, I thought, *Why should she not reject me?* She was too graceful, too insightful.

*That's you,* she said, but almost as if thinking to herself, *you through and through.*

She'd had an epiphany about her new husband. As I was on the slopes, so I was in life. Although I often arrived at the same point as other people, I got there differently, and the difference was not all in my favor.

She was right. Take basketball. In junior high, I'd pored over college-level coaching manuals and bugged our own coach for pointers. *Eerie* was the word he used when he saw me progress. My passes looked unconscious. He knew otherwise. I was a cerebral player. I talked to myself for the whole of the game. I had *good instincts* which the coach knew not to be instinctive.

Could Miriam see into the future? I would study the body mechanics of skiing. Building on that one innate talent—balance—I would practice perfect turns on gentle slopes and replicate them in progressively tougher terrain. I would achieve separation, the legs shifting angles, the torso providing stillness, no motion wasted. The wild recoveries from bad positions would become a thing of the past. I would be *elegant* on skis as I had been *intuitive* on the hardwood. As for whether the elegance would reassure my Mimi, I did not know.

In daily life, too, I had a strange mix of acquired and innate skills. Long before I met Hans Lutz, I responded to hostility with curiosity. What I learned allowed me to enter other people's viewpoints. With instruction, I enhanced that capacity.

I was not on the autism spectrum—not if we want that term to hold meaning. I loved intensely. I picked up on social cues. But I had an analytic side. Encountering a social predicament, I might solve it as you do a puzzle and reapply the reasoning to similar dilemmas. I had come to some of my naturalness strangely.

Miriam had been drawn to me because I was considerate, well-meaning, and fair-minded. Those traits should signal a certain sort of man, a full human being. Seeing me, ungainly and oddly stable on the slopes, Miriam was overcome with uncertainty. Perhaps she had made a terrible mistake.

Metaphor is powerful. A is like B. My social self was like my athletic self.

Miriam worried that I came to my humanity through distinctive and highly particular traits: an exigent conscience, a tolerance for uncertainty, and a hypertrophied capacity for understanding.

What is it to be married to a man who gives thoughtful presents, supports your career, says the right thing, never threatens infidelity, shows deference in public and private, and pleases you in bed—but all on a basis that seems wrong? As a husband, too, I *had good instincts*, developed instincts.

In my cot in the fortress, as in a repeated film loop, I saw Mimi's face, caught in panic. Why had the image not haunted me? When had the memory changed character?

Years later, when Nina was in ski school, struggling with new ways of relating to snow and gravity and her own body, Miriam would recall how Daddy had looked hurtling down the hill, lurching and waving—silly Daddy! How beautifully he skis now!

She was making up to me, rewriting history. Psychiatrists speak of *sealing over*. In the course of a psychotic break, a patient may express distressing self-realizations. Later, when the patient is thinking clearly, if the therapist ventures to expand upon the insights, the patient will disown them. *I said no such thing!*

Sealing over frustrates psychoanalysts. The insights are still there, so the theory goes, but no longer accessible.

Had Mimi sealed over her doubt and distaste?

But it was my own sealing over that was at issue.

In my months of grieving, I had not remembered the look on Mimi's face when I joined her midway down Audacity. It had taken contact with the Great Man to get me wondering how often I had disappointed my wife.

Mentally, I thanked the Great Man for the therapy he had performed on me. In my grief, my view of my marriage had been sentimental. Better to arrive at a more comprehensive understanding. That's the premise of my work: it's best to know.

How incisive he was! When Beelzebub frightened you, the attack was from without. The Great Man got in your gut and gnawed.

Have other biographers or memoirists made note of that effect, how he eroded your confidence? As diarists, psychotherapists may have an advantage. We are used to sitting with a patient and noting: he's making me doubt myself. We count that capacity—to redirect emotion in others—as an ego strength for the patient, a skill that he can utilize when it serves him.

It gives hope on a second front as well. The Great Man could size people up. He had their number. It followed that he knew what it is to have someone's number—to see accurately. If my patient grasped others' makeup, he might come to understand himself.

Not soon. When we speak of people as defensive, we mean that they have characteristic ways of fending off self-awareness. The Great Man's insight was all in the service of attacking others. Still, the precision gave me hope.

◊ ◊ ◊ ◊ ◊

I'm back at the kitchen table. There's no view this morning, just whiteout. A storm that began as snow has picked up something icy, hail or sleet. The pellets ping against the windows. If you haven't seen a blizzard in the North Maine Woods—it's convincing.

When you're off the grid, weather arrives unannounced.

Don't almanacs have tips for reading clouds? I would like access to that lore—and to one of those charts that helps you judge wind speed, what it means when fir trees creak in protest.

I'm guessing that this storm was not in the forecasts anyway. If it had been, Chet would have warned me.

He visited yesterday.

When I asked what was up, he said that he'd been to a VFW canteen a few towns over. He was unsure what had drawn him. Not the thought of dollar beer.

A couple of guys from his old outfit hang out at the post. One, Angus, is a cop in a town yet farther away.

Angus mentioned that he'd been sent a bulletin asking law enforcement to be on the lookout for an old guy who'd wandered off from assisted living. Not fully demented, but maybe with a screw loose. Stares off into space. In conversation, slow to get to the point. Guy needs to be on medication—should be brought back for his own good. Angus didn't have the printout with him, but he ventured a description. Chet thought that I was in the running.

To Angus, the dispatch didn't read like a conventional APB. More like a Regime product. As the government turned unpopular, it had stopped sending out search notices for political fugitives. Too much risk that locals would think, Let them hide. Instead, it created pretexts to put people of interest on the radar. There was said to be an office that customized inquiries for particular locales.

Chet wondered how tailored that bulletin was—whether the authorities were closing in. I might want to keep my bags packed, live out of the suitcase.

I told Chet that I had no wish to endanger him. I was ready to leave.

He would let me know, he said. It might come to that.

I asked about the skiing, whether it worried him to have me out and about.

Not at all.

The search was for a geezer with shaking hands and a lost look. A tough old bird on skis was unremarkable in these parts.

Here's where the visit turned strange. Chet stood silent, immersed in thought. He stared at Ginnie's wingback chair and then took a step back, as if he had considered taking a seat but thought better of it. I wondered whether Ginnie had sent Chet in hopes that he and I would speak about a psychological problem.

No, he said aloud, as if rejecting a suggestion.

Well, he said, as if we had put a problem to rest.

IN THE STORM, I FIND myself missing Providence.

Late autumn, early winter. The dogwoods flaunt their red berries. Neighbors bustle about, raking leaves, mulching garden beds, rushing to paint fences before the arrival of harsh weather. The students are back. Bicycles are everywhere. Food trucks. Fish restaurants, ethnic restaurants. Used bookstores. Repertory theaters, community theaters.

I am thinking of the bygone Providence where Mimi and I lived.

The polar vortex, if that's what's throwing Maine into winter, will have hit Rhode Island too. It was cold in Bristol, the day of the parade.

Even on mild days, Providence's bookstores and theaters are shuttered. Anthracnose weakens the dogwoods. Noxious vines grow up sagging fences. The homes are bedraggled. That's how it seemed to me when I left the office with Muscle and we began our drive out of town. I saw the streets through his eyes.

I have been meaning to write about our exit. Describing it should answer a question or two. How and why I left. What purpose the blog is meant to serve. We had decisions to make, Muscle and Maury and I.

THE LAST TIME I SAW Providence, it was from the car that the security dispatchers had assigned to Muscle. He had distributed the famous photo. We had said our farewells to the corpse. Muscle asked me to guide him along back roads and over small bridges, avoiding main thoroughfares. He had shut down our phones and the car's GPS. I served as navigation software.

There would be blockades and searches, Muscle said. We should avoid major commercial areas. The local cops would deploy there first, for fear of riots or vandalism. It was not just the EverGreats who would express rage. The unemployed, the disenfranchised, the Resistance Underground—who could say which group was likeliest to rise up? Muscle listed considerations and contingencies.

Is the city always this quiet? he asked. He wondered whether we were seeing the fruits of the Greater Depression, the collapse of commerce. Or had the news gotten out? Perhaps fear was holding people indoors?

I reassured Muscle. Deserted streets were the norm. It had once been customary to say that Providence was a city on the rise. It only ever rose so far. When the economy slipped in Boston or New York, it collapsed in Providence.

But this looks like an upscale quarter, he said.

We passed a Victorian house in bad repair. As the paint chipped and faded, the clever color scheme, flat purples and golden greens, had turned sickly.

A promising location for a horror movie, Muscle said.

How curious it was, he said, for maintenance to go undone when unemployment soars and labor is cheap. In a time of hyperinflation especially, you'd think that homeowners would spend freely. But, no, they are too afraid, too focused on the next meal.

Worse and worse, Muscle said.

Empty houses. Had they passed to mortgage companies in bankruptcy proceedings?

It hurt to hear a stranger give voice to these thoughts even if I had entertained similar ones. When Muscle spoke, the verdict sounded final: Providence has gone to seed.

I had him turn toward the river and into a multi-ethnic neighborhood. The Azores-American Club had become a food pantry. A line stretched down the block. I remembered when the action was at an upscale cupcake shop, a scrum of Gen X-ers and millennials.

So many empty storefronts! Clever signs still offered nondairy ice cream, gluten-free doughnuts, and barbacoa. The businesses were long gone. Loan sharks had moved in, and shops selling burner phones. Drug dealers and their clients clustered on a corner near a building that had once featured pop-up art shows.

The routine activity, however depressing, reassured Muscle. The news had not broken.

He said, Soon the talk will be of nothing else.

I directed him, left and right.

Like a patient processing a new idea, Muscle stared ahead quietly. Then he said, Do you know what passed through my mind while you snapped photos? After they released the bomb on Hiroshima, for almost a minute as it fell—before ignition, before survivors woke to horror, before the pilots sent the alert that went to journalists and generals and politicos—for that brief interval, only a handful of people, the crewmen on three aircraft, knew that the world had entered a new age.

For us, too, in the office, history had swerved. The message had been ours to deliver.

It's a flawed comparison, Muscle said, a perverse comparison.

I mean only that it felt momentous, potentially momentous, to enter the post-Great era.

Speaking with me casually, people often produce loose associations. Therapists serve that function, keeping a door open to free self-expression.

Was it the death of the Great Man or memories of him in action that had brought the mushroom cloud to mind? One link was explosiveness. Others were devastation, pollution, violence, and guilt. And death. Always death.

What were you thinking about? Muscle asked.

I guessed that he meant when I circled the corpse.

His birthday celebration, I said.

Muscle had provided security for more than one. He said, I can see it: burlesque, travesty, menace.

He was referring to qualities shared by the eerie festivities and the corpse in its operatic pose.

I turned back to navigating. Continue straight at the light.

Photographing the body, I had struggled not to think ill of the dead. I scanned mental images in search of any in which the Great Man had appeared vaguely appealing. I remembered a bizarre scene.

Late on the third night of my stay, the Great Man summoned me to his bedchamber. I arrived to find the vast room dark save for lights from bedside lamps. When my eyes adjusted, I saw that the Great Man lay propped up by pillows, his Harpo Marx curly mop topped with a pointed conical paper party hat striped in silver and gold. A thick application of face powder, now marred by tearstains, completed the clown look.

The counterpane was still strewn with confetti. A nearby sideboard held plates bearing pieces of frosted cake, some with blown-out candles. Banners congratulating the Great Man—shiny letters joined at the top by snap-together arms—were draped from the bedposts. I had arrived in the wake of what looked to be an elementary schooler's birthday party.

I found the innocence of the presentation bewildering. Was the Great Man compensating for deprivation in childhood?

My admirers celebrate me, and still I can't sleep, he said.

*Admirers* was what he called his staff and cabinet members.

He gave a rosy account of the evening. His minions had raised glasses in camaraderie and told stories meant to buck him up. Reading between the lines, I gathered that hangers-on had been summoned to a command performance. The Great Man had played at being a favored toddler but failed to convince himself.

They have your interests at heart, I said.

I was inviting the Great Man to affirm or modify the thought.

He snapped at me. What are you implying?

For me as a therapist, his most distinctive quality was this thorough mix of presentations of self. He was at once childish and vicious, absurd and purposive, pleading and threatening.

In the next moment, pathos predominated. He teared up, his cheeks flushing beneath layers of powder, his eyes moistening. He cried out, Why won't she reassure me?

I understood him to mean his wife.

As a therapist, I like non-sequiturs. They signal sincerity. I acknowledge them to elicit more of the same.

I echoed, If only she would!

It was a Hans-Lutz-style exclamation, inviting correction or refinement. In this instance, the Great Man might have said, *I suppose I alienated her*.

Instead, he took a detour.

Of course, the sex is phenomenal. But when it's done, when she's satisfied—she always is, I always satisfy, I drive women wild—once she's had what she wants, she ignores me!

I soon learned that the reference to sex was pro forma. The Great Man never spoke of contact with a woman without making mention of his potency. But the bulk of the session was given over to laments.

She has no heart!

Where will I find comfort?

He meant to appeal to my fatherly feelings or my maternal instincts, if I can be said to have had them.

That clownish face! The farcical appearance made the Great Man's self-pity tolerable. That, and the clumsy, cliched formulation of the appeal.

I inventoried my own parallel sense of deprivation. I, too, was doing without wifely support.

Lonesome! I said.

The Great Man gave a grateful look. Very!

Satisfied that he had been heard, the Great Man fell asleep.

My mind turned to that evening because it contained moments when I entertained hope that coming to like the Great Man might be possible. The memory would have to suffice, as way of respecting the deceased.

Hearing nothing from me, Muscle continued to think aloud, lurching between wonder and apprehension. We had come upon something cataclysmic and sacred. Or we had witnessed a passage of no consequence. A false populist had died. Another would take his place. The kleptocrats would protect their interests. There was no turning point.

Which was why we were on the run. If the country did not recover, if one despot followed another, if truth held no value, then once we were identified, we would be deemed complicit. The Great Man would be judged to have fallen victim to a plot from within, hatched by an evil shrink and traitorous guard.

Muscle turned bitter. The Great Man had no ideology beyond egotism. Democracy and justice were incidental victims. If we were convicted for murder, we would be late collateral damage from a campaign of self-glorification.

I asked, You feel no pity?

You?

I felt emptiness. What was I missing, my patient or the psychotherapy?

I had been intent on correcting my attitude toward the Great Man so that I could conduct the treatment properly. I had a sense of incompleteness, of tasks left undone.

Mimi would shake her head. The nation has a chance to start afresh, and you feel loss.

Seeking common ground with Muscle, I said, I dislike when things go wrong for those I work with.

◊ ◊ ◊ ◊ ◊

Once, in the boudoir antechamber, in the course of a tedious on-call shift, I had asked Muscle how it was that he had come to be where he was, protecting the Great Man.

After Muscle was demobilized, jobs had been hard to come by. Security duty paid the bills.

Psychiatrists are not satisfied with circumstance.

Your father was not easy to live with, I said.

Hans favored a technique that he called putting a mark on the canvas. He would make a statement that was at once declarative and speculative. Daubing on color he invited the patient to paint a picture. I was making that move.

If she had heard my thoughts, Nina would have protested. Dad, you make everyone a patient!

I was curious. Muscle had signed on to sacrifice his life for a leader he despised. I wanted to understand that choice.

Poor Eddie, Muscle said.

Eddie was what he called his stepfather. Eddie was an unhappy man, bitter and resentful, rigid and controlling, with a violent temper.

Eddie died of MDS—do you know what that is?

Like all doctors, I had memorized acronyms. Myelodysplastic syndrome.

Bad bone marrow, I said. Problems making blood cells. Pre-leukemia.

As bad as leukemia, Muscle said. He had a low white blood count. The least infection might do him in.

When I was fifteen, Muscle said, he sent me to summer camp, for boys. It was a basic affair, rustic cabins, outhouses. The idea was to learn construction, a camp where the activity was building the camp, using basic tools. We sawed wood by hand. Knowing that he might die while I was still young, Eddie wanted to make a man of me.

In the last week, I came down with a cold, or something worse—bronchitis. My mom and I decided that under the circumstances, for Eddie's sake, it was best for me not to come straight home. I would stay in the empty in-law suite in a neighbor's house until my illness resolved.

But the family I was with had a daughter my age, and Eddie got it in his head that I was shacking up with her. He phoned in a rage. I'd best get my ass home, pronto. I might have refused, but my mother was pleading in the background. I heard a thud, as if he'd thrown her against the wall.

I was coughing and feverish but well able to get myself home. Eddie greeted me at the door, grabbed me by the collar, and gave me a beating. I got my licks in. I had grown, or I was bigger than he remembered and beefed up by manual labor. But in the end, he laid me out.

That was the last week he showed any strength. He caught whatever I had and died of it, cursing me to the end.

Muscle knew how it sounded. He had killed one angry, irrational father figure and signed on to protect another.

It's a myth that psychiatrists crave the tidy solution, the unmistakable imprint of childhood injury on adult life, but tempting explanations appear on occasion. Letting them emerge can be liberating. We prefer for people to choose a new path instead of being perp-walked down an old one by an exigent superego, that is, by guilt and remorse.

What does it matter? Muscle asked that night, in the antechamber.

Muscle had not wanted this oppressive assignment. In a balmier era, he would have been a political scientist.

I said, It's hard to go through life with a millstone around your neck.

Your being here is a result of coercion—coercion through unemployment and poverty. Both are of the Great Man's making.

A series of oppressive forces had combined to make Muscle a security guard. He could not change that assignment. Times were too hard. But if someone managed to injure the Great Man, I did not want Muscle to experience the second loss as a repetition of the first.

Now, that other shoe had dropped. If there was a parallel, might it not be exculpatory? Muscle was not responsible for either death.

On the drive south, Muscle said, But he was such a son-of-a-bitch.

I said, When a son-of-a-bitch dies, whose fault is it?

Muscle said, I'm fine.

◊ ◊ ◊ ◊ ◊

As we pulled into Bristol, the alarm horn blared from atop the fire station. Muscle turned up the car radio. The news was out.

Everyone will remember what he or she saw and heard and felt in those heady hours, in the way that people recall where they were when war or an armistice is declared.

Activity ceased while people took their own pulse and tried to gauge the pulse of the nation. What did they anticipate? What were they free to say? How was it for them?

Muscle and I had done our self-assessments in the car. Now, in this antique town, this town of flags and clapboards, we had to turn our attention to the future.

Maury lives in a tidy eighteenth-century colonial, expanded twice but mostly original, with low ceilings, shallow fireplaces, narrow mantels, and exposed wooden beams. He collects early American antiques of local manufacture. The pieces are not by Goddard or Townsend, but they are well crafted and well preserved: desks, chests, and highboys. Quilts too. Maury drapes old quilts over everything.

It's like a museum, Muscle said.

Muscle's inclination was to resist the quaintness, to stay in the contemporary world. In the living room, he flung open cabinet doors until he found a television on a pull-out shelf.

We do wish for it, he said. A free press, he added, by way of explanation.

He turned cynical. For networks, what was the prudent position, clinging to the ways of the Regime or pretending always to have been in opposition? In man-in-the-street interviews, which opinions would be featured?

Muscle was ready to read the tea leaves.

What Muscle took as quaint, I found comfy. We live this way, in Rhode Island, those of us who are fortunate. We move into an old house, maintain it, pass it on.

I wanted to use Maury's house familiarly, to do what one does upon homecoming. I excused myself and headed upstairs for a shower.

The guest bedroom has a quirky bathroom, tiny, with a miniature sink and skinny stall. Maury, who learned plumbing from his father, did the design and installation. I was moved by the house's modest scale, the lack of uniformity, the marks of the owner, the series of owners. I longed for civilian life.

The yammer of television news wafted upstairs. Muscle channel surfed.

Assuming that, once in Providence, I would have access to my old wardrobe, on the trip from the secret lair I had brought only one change of clothes, jeans and a t-shirt and cotton sweater. It was good to have those, good to feel clean and freshened, for myself and for Nina and Tammy, if they were on their way.

I looked around in hopes that Maury might have something that would serve to entertain Tamara. What would engage her? In a drawer in a Federalist ladies' desk, I found a set of colored pencils bound by a rubber band. Colored pencils would have to do, and printing paper.

Noise from outdoors drew me to the window. It has small blown-glass panes. I had to squint to peer through. Blurred edges gave the impromptu procession an old-fashioned look. Here we were, July Fourth come months early.

Horns honked as cars inched along the avenue. A convertible, top open despite the chill air, was festooned with paper streamers in red, white, and blue. An Uncle Sam unicyclist passed by, waving small flags and handing them to bystanders. Mothers pushed strollers. Banners were unfurled. Firecrackers popped. A male couple in down coats reenacted the kiss from the V-J Day photo in Times Square. Shivering pre-teens in cheerleader outfits twirled batons and did backflips on browned-off lawns. It was Mardi Gras. The street was blocked to cars. If Maury, Nina, and Tamara were to make it here, it would be on foot.

A high school band appeared, playing New-Ashmolean style, blasting out *The Washington Post March*. When had I last heard duh-doodle-duh-do-duh-do-duh-do? Had the tune been suppressed, along with the journalism it celebrated? A band advisor must have opened the uniform closet and dug out the file-card-sized sheet music. Higher-ups had cast a blind eye. The holiday was all but official.

Muscle rapped on the open study door and entered. He flashed his customary grin, but he was set on business. He'd found a hidey hole for me—believed he had. It was mostly off the grid. Confirming the arrangement would take time.

I was not ready to plan an exit. You were right, I said, about word traveling fast. Is it this way everywhere?

No—yes—mostly.

News had resumed—free speech, or something like it. It's as if the media moguls had made quick calculations and determined that traditional political freedoms might return and that, if so, journalists who held back would be judged collaborators with the corrupt Regime.

We were like Italy after Mussolini, Portugal after Salazar. In our version of history, the Great Man would be deemed an aberration, someone foisted upon us through trickery conceived abroad.

It's strange, Muscle said. How could the press know, instantly, to resume routine reporting?

He did not want to sound paranoid—was it okay if he used that word with me?—but it was as if the moguls who owned the outlets had been forewarned.

Unless it was just real-time assessment of the way that the facts and their implications added up. Or an enactment of a plan held at the ready. We had, many of us, been awaiting the Great Man's disappearance.

Muscle felt impelled to show me the phenomenon he was straining to understand. I should come down and watch television.

Pundits were back on air. Where had they been stashed? News anchors were assembling reports from local outlets.

They showed regional responses, grief in the Great Man's strongholds and relief elsewhere. Between the black crepe and the tricolor spandex, there was too much contrast. Would the republic hold?

It was not yet midday out west. In San Francisco and Seattle, the streets were full—like here. The marchers were unafraid, as if the nightmare were over.

Think of third-world countries, Muscle said. What happens after the death of a dictator? First, bacchanal. Then, violence, fear of anarchy, and a retreat to absolutism. He had put us in this position, the Great Man, by clinging to power.

The openness might not last, but for now—fascinating to hear—on air—something like old-fashioned reporting.

Even on the Regime Network, reporters were doing live interviews, albeit in states where the Great Man still had a following.

A stout woman, salt of the earth, was apoplectic. How can the Yankees celebrate tragedy?

Indignation outweighed anguish.

I remember the catafalque, an older white woman said. She used the word repeatedly: I remember the veiled widow and the catafalque.

Eunice Curry, the interviewee's name was. The camera crew had stopped her in a grocery store parking lot in Dubuque, Iowa. She was stiff-backed and elegant. She dressed to shop.

Eunice had historical memory, she had vocabulary. She set her bags on the hood of an old Range Rover and spoke her piece.

She asked, This time, in the procession, when it's the Great Man in the casket, will they be riding clown cars alongside? Will they be juggling sparkling balls?

I liked the word *juggling*. Children of my generation memorized the Richard Wilbur poem where a juggler takes a table, a chair, and a broom and makes them light. Was that what the Great Man did? Global warming, police brutality, voter suppression, racism. In his hands, weighty considerations escaped the pull of gravity. Damn, what a show! To honor him, to accompany him to his rest, sparkling balls alongside the cortege? Why not?

Suddenly, Eunice dropped her aristocratic bearing and turned red-faced. *Moonbats!* she said. *Globalists! Libtards!*

We had that in common, a penchant for exclamation. Funny how a single word can serve to locate a person. Say *Libtard!*, and you pigeonhole yourself.

As the feed was tossed back to the anchor in the studio, Eunice Curry continued cursing out enemies.

Muscle flipped channels. I saw a building in flames.

Stop there, I said, and Muscle did, but the image had disappeared.

Enough, I said.

You need to hear, Muscle said. The good and the bad, he said.

Were all outlets the same?

On the Regime Network, murder was topic one, murder and its relation to the parades. The news analysts played with the *illiberal* motif that Muscle had mentioned in my office. If the Great Man had been killed for political reasons, then liberals were cheering a rupture in the democratic process. Isn't respect for the people's will a foundational tenet of liberalism?

On other stations, talk of assassination was balanced by talk of death by natural causes. TV doctors made reference to the Great Man's vulnerabilities. He had tree nut allergies. Two years ago, at a rally to celebrate the extension of his authority, he had suffered a fainting spell. Cardiac sudden death was a consideration.

When the Great Man was alive, mention of his weaknesses had been taboo, litigated as slander, used as grounds for firing from media positions.

The structure has collapsed, Muscle said.

He meant censorship and repression.

Think of it, Muscle said. Parades are on the air. The police are not taking names, not openly, visibly, intrusively. The broadcasters are not talking treason—not all of them, anyway.

No militias, Muscle said. The militias that the Great Man had feared, the ones said to be closing in on the fortress or the capital—they were not marching, they were not making a move to secure the seat of government.

How delusional was he? Muscle asked me, not expecting an answer.

A station cut to an older gentleman with a Southern accent and a slow cadence.

He said, In my childhood—now this is a true story—I had one of those nightmares where it's the dark of winter and you're late to the bus stop—I was tardy for school—and I had not done my homework or prepared for the test that day, an important test, and

I was dreading the burden of time in the classroom, the endless duration, for a boy. Suddenly, I was aware of the sun waking me, you know, the warmth and the angle of sun on a summer morning, and I realized that it was vacation, summer break, and, yes, I might have an early chore to do—we kept chickens, and I fed them and gathered eggs—but the rest of the day was mine, that day and a heaven of days after. That's what waking to this news is like. It may be wrong to say it—I know that the man is dead—but honestly, it's been a long time since I felt that it was summer and I was eleven years old, the perfect age for summer, and the world was bright.

The Southern gentleman had a calm smile. No edge to him. I don't guarantee the details of the text, except for *true story* and *honestly*. That was a function of the clip, I thought, beyond the evocation of the moment's sweetness: the suggestion that honesty might be honored again.

Is it an illusion that one side is more gracious than another? It's easy to be genteel when events go your way—although I could not recall the Regime's ever using that advantage. I did like the sound of the Southern gentleman and the fact that the media featured him.

On another feed, a panel discussed the name *Restoration Day*.

You have it backward, a commentator said. Restoration means a return of monarchy.

A historian referenced the Dominican Republic. They have Independence Day and Independence Restoration Day—for the second liberation from Spain.

Muscle muted the sound.

Clearly, the media moguls had reconciled themselves to an interval of freer speech, but of what sort? Speech as it had been during the ascension of the Great Man, free speech overwhelmed by a tide of disinformation, that sort of compromise? Or free speech that would lead to apparent excess, justifying a clampdown supported by a re-energized base, free speech in the service of revitalized autocracy?

Was money the dynamic? Consumers had stopped spending. When business has no profits, tax breaks and state-sanctioned monopolies become worthless. Kleptocrats can no longer justify the bribes that the Regime demands, directly or in the form of political contributions.

The Great Man had outlived his usefulness. He had been disposed of. Now that he was dead, we would have the pretense of democracy, if briefly.

So sad, Muscle said. *Sic semper tyrranis* was one thing—a bad deed in a noble cause, murder to reverse the erosion of civil liberties. But had the Great Man been murdered because he mismanaged the economy?

If Bub had been the assassin.... Muscle could imagine him lining up corporate sponsors.

As if to validate Muscle's speculation, the network turned to a money expert at a virtual whiteboard. She reviewed drags on growth: plague, trade barriers, weather disasters, a sick workforce, erratic monetary policy, hyperinflation, banks bankrupted, no credit, and endless debt.

*Troubled Legacy*, the chyron read.

One station was discussing an issue of immediate interest to Muscle and me. If the coroner ruled death from natural causes, would the finding be believed?

The Great Man's followers were schooled to mistrust civil servants. How will a medical examiner's results be greeted?

Opinion will be fact. Murder will be the opinion. What's assumed will be what's known.

I thanked Muscle and returned upstairs.

I sat at the window to watch the parade through distorting glass. Did I nod off? I had been awake since four AM.

A musical fragment caught my attention, lines from "To the Ladies," sung *a capella* in a familiar clear alto. Written in the lead-up to the Revolutionary War, the lyrics advise against buying British imports: *No more ribbons wear, nor in rich silks appear; Love your country much better than fine things*. Miriam had learned the ballad for a fifth-grade pageant. In the fashion of Jewish children in the post-War years, she was intensely patriotic. She had made her own simple dress for the performance. Each year, she reprised the ballad at the Fourth of July parties that Maury and Lydia, then his wife, held here.

Frantically, I rubbed at the fogged-up window glass. By the time I had cleared it, the singing had stopped. Looking down, I saw a line of women, marching in place with locked arms. Miriam—vigorous, but not young—stood out among them. She had on a deep red wool coat, double-breasted with a flared skirt, that she had bought on impulse and worn rarely. After her death, I'd donated it to a Salvation Army thrift shop.

The marcher on the far end of the chorus line swung a champagne bottle that had made the rounds. The woman closest to me held a placard: *Make Yourself Heard!* The group looked jolly.

Turning to the window, Miriam broke ranks and gave a wave and a thumbs-up, as if I had done well, although perhaps the signal was meant for Maury, a hello to an old friend, should he be home and watching.

How moving it was to see Miriam celebrate the day she had longed for.

As I pushed my eye closer to the glass, the figure became distorted. Placards obscured my view. When marchers reappeared, Miriam was not among them.

If I had been free to appear in public, I would have run downstairs and out the door to look for her. But I was not free and, more, I knew the ways of ghosts, or Miriam's way.

As a therapist hearing a patient give a comparable report, I would oscillate between perspectives, accepting the reality of the revenant and believing instead that my patient was providing himself the encouragement that he would once have received from the missing loved one.

I would understand that the second perspective might take too much distance from the phenomenon.

Later in the day, it occurred to me that Miriam had been offering direction. I should show my love of country. I should make myself heard.

◊ ◊ ◊ ◊ ◊

After an encounter with Miriam, I will feel drained in the way that people do after a migraine or an epileptic seizure. The brain is intensely occupied, and exhaustion follows. I am guessing that I lost a moment or two that afternoon.

When I came to myself, I heard voices from the ground floor.

Nina? I called. Tammy, it's Poppa!

I hustled down to find Maury in conversation with Muscle. They were seated. It appeared that they had been talking for some time.

No Nina, no Tammy.

In retrospect, I could see that my joy in anticipation of greeting them had been accompanied by the understanding that they would not come.

Through the back window, I saw whitecaps on the bay.

You've blown in with the wind, I said. I tried to mask my disappointment.

Maury stood and put a hand on my shoulder, as tall men do. He drew me in for a hug, the one that acknowledges unwelcome news and signals more to come.

Muscle headed for the living room to finalize plans for my time away.

Maury apologized. He had decided not to phone Nina—too much chance of disclosing my location. Instead, he had called Kareena, as if for a routine contact, attorney to client. She was to fetch Nina and Tammy and bring them to my home. She was to check back when they all had arrived safely.

In the course of a second call, from Kareena's mobile, Maury asked her to look out my front window. As he had imagined, a police car was stationed across the street. Nina would be safe—safer, anyway—with eyes on her. But if she headed here, her shadow would follow.

I appreciated Maury's solicitude.

How are they? I asked.

They're well, Maury said. Kareena said that if ever I were to be in touch with you, I should convey her thanks. She wants to tell you not to be a hero.

The implication was that Kareena had put two and two together.

Nina has been on edge since the day you left, Maury said.

She'd never bought the story I'd had Maury tell her. She'd worried that I had undergone a medical procedure and had chosen to recuperate in private. Or that, yes, fine, I was off somewhere writing, but that I'd got caught in a senile loop—that nothing good would come of the adventure. Or that a cult had promised me contact with Miriam via Ouija board, and I'd signed on.

She had pestered Maury, in case he knew more.

Nina thought me an old fool.

I'm joining that cult, I said.

You had been abducted by a cult, Maury said, for real.

I was worried you'd take it worse, he said, Nina's not visiting.

Oddly, it gave me comfort to have come close. Preparing for the reunion with Tammy had been restorative. The glimpse of

Miriam marching helped too. Being in Rhode Island, far from the fortress. Seeing Maury.

He had his hand on my shoulder again. Sit, he said. Let's have tea.

The kitchen looked much as it had twenty years before when Lydia left Maury because he was wedded to the law. Forty years might be the better figure for the age of the décor. When Lydia and Maury bought the house, over his objections she'd insisted on their installing an oven, dishwasher, and fridge in a popular shade called bisque. He'd warned her that off-white comes to look like dirty white. His later resistance to replacing the appliances became an issue in the marriage. Maury sweats solder. He keeps machines in repair.

You want a lawyer who can be stubborn. You want one who likes to fiddle until things work out.

You must have seen a lot these past weeks, Maury said.

No, I said, surprisingly little.

He was bald, I hear, Maury said. Billiard-ball bald. Is that so? In the photo, the hair doesn't make sense unless it's a wig, a millimeter out of place.

Maury was feeling me out, seeing whether I would discuss the Great Man.

People will want to know what you made of him.

I waited to see where Maury was heading.

Let's change the subject, Maury said. Do you know a Dolly Coopersmith?

Was she a state legislator, I asked, when the beer distributor was governor?

Dolly was a career politician, honorable and well intentioned in the days when politicians sometimes were.

Muscle had returned to the kitchen. On television, he said, the Regime's higher ups—Bub and other pretenders to leadership—were strangely absent. They were conferring, Muscle imagined. They wanted a united front, a single message.

Listen, Maury said, setting aside the Dolly story. What you did this morning, what you saw—I don't want to hear about it. Not yet.

I hummed agreement.

Maury asked whether I knew what happened when government officials died unexpectedly.

In recent years, since the plague, we'd seen four cases. In all but one—the exception was the death of a disfavored figure, a foot-dragger—the officials were ruled victims of foul play. Law enforcement found patsies. Judges handed down convictions. The process constituted an insurance policy for the Great Man and his adherents. No death went unpunished.

It was too soon to know whether, with the Great Man gone, government-by-blame would still prevail. But the authorities had become used to fingering fall guys. I was a fair candidate for the role.

Maury sounded much like Muscle.

It will be a conspiracy, and you will be a conspirator.

The last time we saw the death of a national leader still in office, you and I were in high school. After the funeral, a council of elders conducted an inquiry. Half the populace disbelieved its conclusions. That was back when experts were respected.

Today, citizens were at once less trusting and more credulous. Many had swallowed lies of vast proportion.

When the news began with the headline *Great Man Found Dead on Shrink's Couch*, the related story would write itself.

The Great Man had threatened my family. I was a physician. Surely, I knew how to kill.

Maury said, In this simple-minded time, melodrama is our truth.

There was hope. With a change in ruler, the legal system might change too. Much depended on the Great Man's abettors.

What would they demand? Law? Order? Evidence? Some might be nostalgic for them.

Maury wanted to create sentiment for leaving me alone. He wanted my case to exemplify a return to the presumption of innocence.

Were Muscle and Maury tag-teaming me? When your friends agree, it is wise to hear them out.

Maury said that he would work to negotiate what suspects once could assume—impartiality, due process, and attention to standards of proof. The task would take time. He did not want me interviewed prematurely.

Early this morning, the Providence Chief of Police had phoned and asked Maury what he knew about events in my office. Maury said that he had seen the photo and had no information beyond what it showed. The words were true at the time.

The authorities might issue a formal request at any moment. Much depended on what the medical examiner determined, but where a crime is suspected, witnesses can be compelled to testify—if necessary, by subpoena. Witnesses may not absent themselves to avoid being served, with this exception: when they fear for their lives.

Apropos: on the way to Bristol, in the ride share, Maury had been monitoring Twitter for references to me. A diehard group called the Great Posse had posted a mocked-up wanted poster built around my picture. The bounty was a million dollars for me delivered into their custody, dead or alive.

A million was not what it had been, but people were hungry, and the figure still had a solid ring.

Muscle pulled up the page on his phone.

He said, On the plus side, you look deeply understanding.

The loyalists had grabbed an author's headshot from my most recent book.

They asked what the Great Man, the picture of health, mental and physical, was doing on a kike shrink's couch, never mind dying there.

The Great Man had called for havoc and revenge if ever he were found dead. I might well fear for my life.

Maury said that I was getting hit from the other direction as well. The left wondered whether I'd been complicit. In my role as therapist, had I hoped to keep the Great Man afloat, prolonging the nation's suffering?

Dolly Coopersmith, the former state rep, had parked herself on my front lawn. She had been muttering loudly, a long-barreled Ruger in hand. A neighbor had phoned the police.

Normally, they would have done nothing. A handgun was like the flag. Waving one signaled loyalty. But this time, a cop who had the house under observation chose to respond to the complaint and approach Dolly. She had tried to reach into her backpack. It was found to contain a homemade bomb.

Muscle said that images of a young cop cuffing Dolly were running on the local news. He pulled up a clip on my tablet.

The chyron showed the arresting officer's name: Tom Spear.

Didn't you testify for a Theo Spear? Maury asked.

I had, in a child custody case. Theo had been mildly delusional and an attentive father. He'd had a brother named Tom and—this memory was vague—a nephew, Tom Junior. Perhaps Tom Junior had known that he was protecting the family of a man who had stood up for his uncle.

And who is that neighbor of yours? Maury asked.

Letty Sand, I said.

Letty was homebound, with diabetes that had led to leg amputations. Miriam had been good to her. Later, I had filled in for Miriam. Perhaps Nina had too, lately, in my absence. Letty was the block's eyes on the street. Likely it was Letty who had placed the neighborly call.

In the village that is Providence, no one is exempt from scrutiny, but neither is anyone left to fend for himself.

Muscle said, There will not always be a Letty or a Tom.

I asked what had gotten into Dolly Coopersmith.

Maury had googled her. Before the crackdown on political expression, she had chaired a group that advocated for the restoration of accuracy in vote counts.

The poor woman, Muscle said.

There was the answer to the charge against liberals, that through countenancing murder they short-circuited democracy. Change through the ballot box presupposes fair elections. With her loaded backpack, Dolly C. had been critiquing that premise. Every day the Great Man lived was a day when the vote did not count. In her view, I had worked to add to those days.

I saw Dolly as spurred by feeling states that speak to me: suspiciousness, impulsive rage, and a sense of injury.

Maury said, You might well fear for your life. You might reasonably have so much concern that you would isolate yourself—physically, electronically.

He said that he was bound to advise against a total blackout. If I remained off the internet, and if I refused all incoming communication, then if (for instance) a subpoena were issued, I would remain unaware.

For my benefit, Muscle asked Maury to clarify. You're saying that, your good counsel notwithstanding, cutting off contact would be understandable?

A wink's as good as a nod.

◊ ◊ ◊ ◊ ◊

Muscle had located a safe house in Maine, managed by a married couple.

Meanwhile, he was tapping into online back channels to monitor the deployment of security forces. If we had to pass through checkpoints, he would prefer ones manned by local police. In New England, they were likelier than career military to be anti-Great and so, perhaps, less hellbent on identifying suspects.

Maury and I had the kitchen to ourselves.

I said, You're putting yourself at risk.

Maury asked whether I remembered Gil Ganem.

Gil was a client of Maury's who'd gone missing for weeks when Maury needed a trial delay that a judge would not grant. A volatile man, Gil. I had made house calls to treat him—steady him—while he was in hiding.

Maury was reminding me that I had gone out on a limb for him.

It happens, Maury said. Clients vanish. Later, they reappear.

Well, maybe. It's understood that a mafia figure can go on the lam. No one pressures his lawyer, not seriously. My disappearance would be less routine. Stronger forces were at play. And if the authorities threatened Maury—produce Doctor Farber, or else!—he would have no way of reaching me.

Too much to ask, I said.

You know how you care about medicine? Maury asked.

That was how the law mattered to him.

I suspected that Maury had another motive as well, loyalty to Miriam. I don't doubt that he had promised to look after me.

I asked, Once I am incommunicado, how will I know when to return?

I did not want to be like those Japanese soldiers on Pacific Islands after World War II, active in a conflict long since resolved.

Rather than answer my question, Maury asked me to look at something. It was an appeal from the Resistance Underground, an update of one they had first issued in the leadup to the ill-fated election that led to the Great Man's second term. Leaders of the civil-society-in-waiting had appended their names, our Gandhis and Mandelas, our Walesas and Havels, our Vargas Llosas and Nerudas, our Martin Luther Kings. After the Great Man secured his hold on power, some had gone to prison.

The group had promulgated the new version of the document today.

The organizers wanted all who could, the creative vanguard, those who comment or report, who paint or compose, who act on stage or speak on radio or shoot video, anyone with a talent or an outlet, to depict the regime gone by, in the hopes of asserting lost rights, or at least (on the less optimistic view) exercising them in the interregnum, before they disappeared again. The intent was to gather mosaic pieces—*tesserae*—that, assembled, might depict our era. How had it been to live in the time of the Great Man? The goal was to reclaim truth, to shift from truth that serves power to truth that represents events. The goal was the return of reason, mediated and enhanced by the artistic sensibility.

◊ ◊ ◊ ◊ ◊

When the original broadside appeared, Miriam had asked if I was not tempted to contribute a piece of writing to the cause.

She was in the hospital, nauseated from a round of chemotherapy. In hopes of tempting her to eat, I had brought cartons of food from a favorite Chinese restaurant.

He should write, don't you think? Miriam had said to Maury.

The nation was obsessed with the election. What if the Great Man prevailed? He was a dictator in the making. The right of free expression would disappear.

In those days, what was asked for was not witness but creative opposition. Dramatists answered the call, and composers, choreographers, novelists, poets, actors, directors, musicians, producers, comedians, songwriters, and graphic artists.

Later, in the crackdown, many of those outspoken souls were punished. Libel laws were reinterpreted. Treason was redefined. The Regime picked out past critics and made examples of them.

From then on, resistance required courage, and fewer volunteered. Still, there had been that first flowering.

If I stood on the sidelines, it was because I had lacked a relevant craft. As a writer, I focused on my experience as a therapist. In case vignettes, I disguised patients. Bearing witness was a job for an author who told stories straight up.

Making my excuses, I had asked Maury, Do you remember the section about Priscilla, in *Must We Be as We Are?*

That was my second book, written after celebrities had begun to consult me. Maury had insisted on a read-through of a late draft, to see how well disguised the patients were. He didn't want to discover that he could pick out a screen actor right off the bat.

Maury waved chopsticks and shook his head.

Priscilla, I began, was actually Raymond, an attorney in Providence. Raymond was socially isolated, chronically anxious, plateaued in his career—feeling discouraged on every front. In the law, ever lower standards prevailed. The women he tried to date demanded a flashiness he found demeaning. He entered a disabling depression.

By chance, as an elderly uncle failed and cousins gave their excuses, Raymond came to take charge of the uncle's epileptic cat. The cat interrupted Raymond's routine. It disturbed his sleep. Psychotherapy helped him with the transition, tolerating the intrusion—and cat ownership did the rest. The constellation of new experiences—responsibility, caregiving, constant company, the example of playfulness in the face of impairment—proved liberating.

I wanted this sequence, where psychotherapy provides the context in which a cat might serve as an antidepressant, to illustrate points about how people change. I set out to tell the story straight up, intending to alter details later. No luck. I found myself in the grip of writer's block so dense that my fingers could not work the keyboard. Even in drafts for my eyes only, I was unable, simply unable to breach confidentiality.

After that failed effort, I lay awake wondering whether altering particulars would allow me to write. What if Raymond became Francesca, a family practitioner forced to adopt a dog? Those substitutions—woman for man, doctor for lawyer, dog for cat—were easy, but the result felt wrong. That's what prevented sleep: despair over what had been lost in translation. Readers will consider doctors to be kinder than lawyers. Raymond is less exotic than Francesca. Dogs are more demanding than cats. What is absent in Francesca is everything that matters about Raymond, his special combination of sternness and fragility. Meanwhile, the family crisis, with its intriguing particulars, will be familiar to Providence residents and so off limits.

Soon, in imagination, more fitting details emerged. The cat stayed, its epilepsy mildly masked as cerebellar ataxia, and so did Raymond's essence, his timidity and exigency, his fanatical cleanliness, his discomfort with closeness. Priscilla, as the character would now be named, was a minimalist artist, a Buddhist whose studio in its sparseness and functionality resembled a surgical suite. Crucial to the narrative was a time shift, to the early eighties, when minimalism was losing steam and my own career was in its infancy. Only then, when Priscilla was more Raymond than Raymond, did I drift off to sleep.

The next morning, when I sat down at the desk, the task had become trivial. I saw Priscilla. I described what I saw.

When I paused in this recital, Maury objected. I know the lawyers in Providence. There is no Raymond, is there, lonely and cat-loving? You invented him just now. Here in the room, on the spot, eating eggplant with garlic sauce, you reimagined your patient, in the same way that you had turned that patient—someone else, not Raymond—into Priscilla.

I confessed that I had. I'd gotten fluid with disguising, in the name of confidentiality. Besides, the books were never about Raymond or Priscilla. They were about psychotherapy, about what it's like to do that job.

Imaginative translation had become second nature to me. Sitting in the bleachers at Nina's basketball game, I would generate parallel careers, ailments, enthusiasms, and fates for the parents seated beside me. I changed their facial features and their styles of dress. Psychotherapists of my generation looked for ways to access their own unconscious insights. For me, translation was a key. Elaborating fictions made me better able to gauge likely—real-world—outcomes. Try placing a neighbor in an invented setting and telling an in-character story about him. You'll learn what you make of him altogether.

By that point, Miriam had changed her mind about my ability to contribute a tile to the mosaic.

Do you remember that poem about the Breughel painting?

We had all read it in high school.

A boy falls from the sky. He cries out. The plowman goes on plowing.

Henry is the plowman.

Maury signaled agreement. The Great Man makes the sky fall, and Henry walks to his office and sits in his chair.

The push for me to add a tile to the mosaic had turned into something else, a chance for Miriam and Maury to unite in amused recognition of my idiosyncrasies. The two had been having these conversations since the night they met. There would not be many more.

I had no interest in new writing assignments. My mind was on Miriam.

Now, in his bisque-trimmed kitchen, Maury had played his trump card. In the wake of the Great Man's death, there was another call for tiles to compose a mosaic. Disappearing would allow me to do what Miriam had asked.

Never mind your limitations, Maury said. Bear witness.

Before meeting him and after, how had the Great Man touched my life?

Maury wanted fast production. I was to dash something off, giving myself whatever leeway I required.

You will be judged by the standards of melodrama, he said. You will be the villainous shrink—unless you can tell a better tale.

My testimony would counter the competing charges against me—from the right, that I had seduced the Great Man into care and made him vulnerable, and from the left, that I had volunteered to keep him functional.

As my version appeared, I would gain sympathy. A favorable verdict in the court of public opinion was a prerequisite for fair treatment in a court of law.

◊ ◊ ◊ ◊ ◊

Was Maury concerned that I would beg off once again? To convince me that I was free to write, he talked contract law. Nondisclosure clauses…non-disparagement…ignore them.

I drifted during the monologue.

In commerce, Maury said, the consequence for violating promises is financial.… *I will do this, or I must forfeit that*.… Once penalties are paid, the contract is fulfilled.… Obligations are contextual.… If the Great Man had coerced…clause would be voided.… Defending me would be a privilege.… Members of the jury, please, let's do consider the Great Man's reputation.…

I love how Maury marshals evidence. In truth, I had never worried about breaking the contract that Beelzebub had forced on me. It said that I would not act as a doctor. The profession's standing was hardly at risk.

Have you followed so far? Maury asked.

You're saying, Don't worry about the contract.

You bastard! Maury said. You let me go on and on.

Your only concern is your profession, he said. You're hung up on confidentiality, the privilege that survives death.

I was glad that Maury saw the distinction, contract versus sacred oath.

◊ ◊ ◊ ◊ ◊

Early in their training, doctors learn to treat everyone the same. The research findings are uniform: VIP patients suffer poor outcomes. Special care is substandard care.

I had thought of that adage as I made my way to the Great Man's boudoir in the small hours of my second night in the lair.

Einstein! the Great Man shouted, as I came into view. What kind of quack are you? The nation needs me alert and rested.

I dislike hearing bluster—the public self—in a consultation. I stayed silent and was rewarded with a change in tone. The boasts remained, but the voice was more tentative.

If I had failed as a leader, if I were unloved…then I could understand…. Losers and little men lie awake nights. Let them. I, who have brought the country back to itself….

He turned plaintive. The insurrectionists—so disloyal and ungrateful. Why could his troops not provide the security he deserved?

And now this new disappointment, the bumbling sleep doctor.

I detected a sense of injury, a plea for relief that, in paranoid patients, can signal an openness to treatment. -α, my notes read. α is my symbol for affect. -α, for negative affect, signals sadness. In paranoia, -α can be a hopeful sign.

To sketch the scene: the Great Man was in his grand canopy bed, scarfing down a cold-cut submarine sandwich, mustard squirting onto the sheets and comforter. He wore his curly-haired wig only slightly askew and so looked like the icon you see on television, except that he was teary-eyed—teary or bleary. He lacked the sarcastic brightness that he affects in the media.

A man who has saved the world deserves better, he said.

The problem went beyond insomnia as a medical complaint. He had been wronged—as if one could earn sleep through righteousness, as if he had been righteous.

I said, Sleep should come easily.

My intent was to underscore his implicit question. If good works earn sleep, why was he awake?

The Great Man began reeling off achievements.

Guns everywhere!

Full prisons—fantastic law enforcement.

Prosperity! Boundless prosperity! Prosperity for all.

I did not jot down the claims. I was not preparing to write political history.

I see this entry: *demands affirmation*. If I betrayed the least doubt in the Great Man's accomplishments, I would derail the treatment.

I wrote *¿tenacity?* The word relates to delusional thought. Psychiatrists care less about patients' beliefs than how they are held. Unlikely ideas will not alarm us so long as they remain preliminary or conjectural. There are exceptions. Some beliefs are so bizarre that to entertain them at all is worrisome. But flexibility of thought counts for a lot. With that note, *¿tenacity?*, I was reminding myself to observe how the Great Man discussed the public's wellbeing in future conversations.

Stop doodling! he said.

I liked that he was shifting focus from the inflated self to the therapy, even if the theme was the same: he deserved more respect.

I said, Although you summoned me as a doctor, I am also a writer.

I was transitioning to the spiel. It was in the Great Man's interest that I deliver it to him—in his interest that I proceed with him as I do with every patient who is in the public eye.

What's your point, Izzy?

My patients, some of them, appear in my books.

Game theorists advise: *play the card your opponent knows you have*. Through Bub, I was guessing, the Great Man had heard about my books. That was why he had called for me, because I was the name brand.

Consultant, the Great Man corrected me. Summoned you as a consultant.

He bit down hard on the side of the sub, scattering salami and shreds of pickled onion. He hummed as he chewed.

*We're done talking* was the message. I did not heed it.

I'm one thing, a doctor-writer. We don't know about my work separate from my method: taking notes, thinking about patients between sessions, imagining how I might depict their progress.

I said, With public figures, I don't vary what I require.

I realized that my explanation was unempathetic. What did the Great Man care how other public figures are treated? He was beyond category. The saving grace was that the Great Man would hardly want less than what others received. Did he not outshine any movie star?

I ran through the spiel. I would suppress the Great Man's name and change salient details, but it would be impossible to conceal his identity.

He gave a fierce look. He'd have me horse whipped.

I said, Also, I will want to speak to your wife.

I'm used to practicing in a small city, I said, where everyone knows one another. When I treat strangers, I like to interview family members for context.

I was acting as I did with other celebrities. As they were about to object to one condition, I added another.

I did not love the set-up that the Great Man had offered—the stifling room, the flying food, the mid-night summonses. I did not like being limited to one patient. I disliked the threat of violence. I missed my daily routine. But I had my method.

The Great Man gave his theatrical Jackie Gleason look, the one that says he has reached his limit with a fool.

Requests like that are why I am here and you are there.

I was perched uncomfortably on the edge of the low chair.

Still holding the sub remnant, the Great Man raised his index finger and moved it toward my face. Oil dripped on my pants.

You have no idea how negotiations work. You are asking for something worthless. The less something is worth, the more I demand for it.

I love people with obsessions. They're chumps, pigeons, pushovers.

When he paused to lick his fingertips, I signaled agreement. As a writer, my subject was psychotherapy. Who knew whether our work together would prove of interest? The permission I required might be worth nothing.

The Great Man switched perspective.

If you write about me, you'll sell a hundred million copies. If I don't squelch the publication.

Might be good publicity, he said. Fresh audience, all the injured bleeding hearts, the boo-hooers, show my sensitive side.

My insights are superb. No one knows himself like I do.

You're not escaping the contract, he said.

He meant that if word got out about my presence in the fortress, I would forfeit my freedom and all I owned.

He said, I can waive confidentiality, but if you publish, you're in jail, and I own your home and your great-grandchildren.

He had only a vague sense of who I was and how my family was constituted.

He took a dramatic pause, as if delivering a verdict.

I tell you what, he said. You get me to sleep by four AM, you have your worthless permission. But if I'm still awake, I get the rights to any books you have in print. You sign them over, the residuals.

It did not occur to me to respond.

Seeing that I was not joining the negotiation, the Great Man changed tack.

Or I throw you in the clink. How would that be, a week in solitary? I suffer with sleeplessness, why shouldn't you?

A minute later, he said, If anyone catches wind of your being here, you'll be off to Peru. You and your delicate relatives. Believe it. If you say a word about me, it will be over my dead body.

Once before, I have mentioned this tendency in the Great Man. Have others made note of it? He was a lover of words. He liked to choose one and roll it on his tongue.

Having landed on *Peru*, he repeated it. He did not think that I was so much of a Peruv as to cause him to deport me to Peru.

*Peru* was the Great Man's word for any impoverished or war-torn foreign country. *Peruvs*, short for *Peruvians*, was his term for feckless, ignorant slobs, people who were worth nothing. *Those Peruvs*, he would say, or, *That schmuck's a real Peruv*.

Soothed by the thought of ruining me and mine, he dropped off to sleep. I took out my phone, documented the event, and time-stamped the image.

I had given my spiel. I had been granted permission, if you think that confidentiality can be waived in that manner.

I did and still do. The Great Man dealt in negotiation and humiliation. Speaking in his dialect, he had said yes.

If you have made note of the expression the Great Man used, *over my dead body*, you may be wondering how much weight I give it. I had gotten lucky in the expression of his dismissal, but surely I know the difference between a turn of phrase and a contract? My patient had said *no* in a way that happens now to sound like *yes* in light of current circumstance—the presence of his corpse.

Point taken. But must we ignore *my dead body* entirely? Like all psychotherapists, I attend to the manner of self-expression, and to metaphor especially—not just for this utterance, but always. The Great Man was hiding from his own subjects or citizens. There were rumors of plots afoot, including plots involving his intimates. His death might be immanent. It was very much on his mind.

Is it far-fetched to speculate that he was thinking about his obituary and whether as an author I would suit its needs? He listed conditions under which I might write: exile, penury. His jibes presaged Maury's analysis: I could write if I would accept punishment.

Within days, the Great Man had turned my note taking into a running gag. When he let slip a revelation about his double dealing in business, he caught himself. *Take that down for your memoir…from Peru.* Similarly, for his early dealings with the Russians. He offered a fragmentary account and said, *Oh, the copies you'll sell!* He had tantalized his enemies with hints of frank treason—while managing always to keep concrete evidence beyond reach. He seemed to want me to continue that game.

As an acknowledgment of consent, do teasing and mockery suffice? Medical ethicists say that consent is not a moment but a process. The Great Man became ever more comfortable with the idea that I would memorialize him. He granted permission over time.

If I had worries about the Great Man's waiver of privilege, it was on different grounds. I wondered how much his ailment, call it what you will, influenced his choice. The Great Man considered himself a fine fellow—well, much more than that—and assumed that any fair-minded person who got to know him would too. That belief was grounded in his mental condition.

The therapeutic method may have enhanced the illusion. In the mirror, the Great Man saw a demigod. For the purposes of the therapy, I saw him as he saw himself. He was meant to be aware of my empathy, to feel understood.

A more complete account would say that I toggled between viewpoints. Sometimes, when he asked to be applauded, I remained neutral: *I see.* My hope was to have him realize how much he needed acknowledgment. At other times, when the Great Man was in the midst of a productive discussion, when I wanted not to get in his way, I became the admiring audience he demanded: I *see!* The second posture was as preliminary or experimental as the first, but it may have seduced him—made him think that I worshipped him as he worshipped himself, so that he would be celebrated in my writing.

That assumption arose from his grandiosity, which could push him in the opposite direction as well. No one appreciated him! I was just like the others—jealous! I wanted to tear him down.

How to balance the distortions—the certainty that I would honor him, the certainty that I would fail to give him his due?

Here's the embarrassing truth: I am relying on one more joking dismissal.

Once, in my sleep-doctor role, I asked the Great Man whether bowel problems were contributing to the insomnia. Should we review his diet? Might he be gluten or, more likely, lactose intolerant?

If I am, he said, it's your problem. To underscore his point, he took a swig of a milkshake.

He liked his bowels as they were. He let go a great fart. *Make note of that one*, he said, waving at my tablet. When he saw me scribbling on my pad, he demanded that I portray him *farts and all.* Again, I was being joshed and, I believe, encouraged. He did not mind being seen as simultaneously offensive and potent.

My prior therapeutic work influenced my understanding of the Great Man's ability to give consent. My guys make all sorts of decisions, social and legal. They marry and divorce. They sign business contracts. They wish and demand to be accepted as competent—certainly, competent to give or deny permission. Finding themselves in a book of mine, none of them felt ill used.

The Great Man did more harm in a day than any of my patients has done in a lifetime, but in terms of level of pathology, he was no worse off. To treat him as an ordinary patient required that I give him the spiel and equally that I accept his response, his partial waiver of doctor-patient privilege, as valid.

How broad was the license? I ask my patients to allow me to use their cases in my writing about psychotherapy. The proposal I gave to the Great Man was on these lines, and then he widened the scope. He imagined me writing about how he double-crossed legislators and how he punished rivals. The permission he gave was extensive. Often, he indicated that he expected me to do my worst. He would do his worst in return. If I wrote, it would be from a position of isolation, the position I am in now.

I did not always take advantage of the privilege he offered: Make note of this! The electronic pad was reserved for observations that might serve the therapy. In real time, with the Great Man, as with all of my patients, my writing was an afterthought and ongoing care the first consideration.

In writing about my patient, do I do him an injustice? I feel that way with every book. No sooner do I send off the final draft than I want to cry out to Meg Galliard, Let me pull it back!

Finally, I believe in the premise I opened with in my talk with the Great Man. For better and worse, in every minute, I'm a doctor-writer. Any wizardry, to use my patient's word, is in the amalgam.

A SIDE NOTE: YOU MAY ask why I ignored my patient's implicit antisemitism, his calling me by any random Jewish name. To inquire about his intent would have been to pick a fight. I don't fight with patients. I don't try to define myself. Patients treat me as they will. In time, I trust, we will come to understand what each of us about.

Some elements of the Great Man's makeup were evident from the start. He thought in categories: immigrants, foreigners, egg-heads, minorities. All were dismissible types, not his admirers. Few people existed for him as individuals.

Therapy must be for real—based attention to the patient's makeup, his current potential for insight. Only if I feigned ignorance could I engage the Great Man on antisemitism. The first task was to help him see other people at all.

I should add that I was inured. If you're Jewish and you choose to treat paranoid men, you will encounter causal antisemitism. I was never tempted to address it through making demands or adducing facts. My guys would taunt me early and apologize in time or simply come to address me with respect.

I had no fantasy that the Great Man would ever call me by my name, Weitz or Farber. Muscle, Ballbuster, Reaper—others existed through the functions they served or the feelings they aroused in him. If I came into focus, the Great Man would assign me a demeaning nickname, something less kindly than Wizard. For now, I remained inchoate, a vague figure, talented, untrustworthy, powerless, and perhaps useful, an amalgam united in his mind in the concept Jew. If I was to treat him, it would be from that position.

And now, as a writer, do I want my own back? I hope not. My goal is to say what I saw and felt, with no extra edge. I do, yes, know that I may fail—that I may have failed already.

◊ ◊ ◊ ◊ ◊

Look at you with your grin! You conniver! You prince! Maury said. You gave him the spiel!

Maury has a big man's laugh. He gets lost in it. Me too.

What I'd give to have been a fly on the wall! Promise you'll write about that conversation.

Immediately, Maury was laying out logistics.

I would provide him with a first-hand account of the events that had led to my disappearance and the goings-on that I had witnessed while away. The material would guide him in the preparation of my defense if I were ever charged or sued. The document would be protected by attorney-client privilege, the one legal protection that the Regime had strengthened. The Great Man was a huge fan of attorney-client privilege.

If some of what I sent was fictionalized—what client's reports are not? I could write as I pleased, without inhibition. Maury would publish selectively, withholding material that might weaken his negotiating position or expose a third party to harm. Maury would also omit passages that he found indiscreet, regarding my own thoughts or life. What escaped the red pencil would go up on a blog on an open publishing site on the web. Entries would post daily.

You'll act as my editor, I said.

When patients grant permission to write, they also grant me permission to consult editors.

Maury would discuss contingencies with Muscle. If publication proved difficult, there were online groups skilled at skirting restrictions, groups that took on politically critical projects.

Muscle popped in to say that we'd leave in an hour or two.

You'll want to eat, Maury said. He had a bachelor's larder. He set to gathering ingredients and puttering—slicing, chopping, and sautéing. He began with onions and leftover potatoes. He set out sweet peppers and slices of ham. I knew what was in the works, a scrambled-egg version of a peasant omelet.

There are limits, I said. There are limits to what the spiel makes possible and limits to my abilities.

Maury brought a plate to Muscle and returned to serve me from the pan.

It had been weeks since I'd had the pleasure of bachelor cooking. Ground black pepper, like love, covers a multitude of sins.

I miss her too, he said, meaning Miriam and her cooking.

No, really, delicious, I said.

He set out wine glasses, small, stubby ones, like in old French cafes.

I'd like to drink French wine again, Maury said. I'd like to drink it in Paris.

It's nothing like Chablis, Maury said, but I like seeing the name on the label.

Things are called what they are not, to mask a sad reality.

Seeing an opening, Maury asked whether I might, in my blogging, go easy on strangeness—the changed names and professions. What would work best, for the act of witness, for the mosaic tile, was straightforward reporting.

You don't understand what you have, Maury said. It's gold.

In the blog's concluding post, I would offer the definitive verdict on the Great Man's mental infirmity. That prospect would draw the reader along.

Had I witnessed palace intrigue? I could describe plots that the Great Man had set in motion. I knew times and dates, who had been at what meeting.

Did Maury see that I was looking uneasy?

In the first go-round, when the Resistance leaders—our Gandhis and Mandelas—called for mosaic tiles, did the cartoonists sing arias? Did the mezzo-sopranos write graphic novels?

Raising a glass of vinegary Chablis, I offered the familiar lines from Henry James: *We do what we can. We give what we have.*

Maury knew the content of the spiel.. He had formalized it. I was honor-bound to alter the Great Man's name, his identifying characteristics, and, where possible, his life circumstances.

Maury raised his glass in return.

To a brighter future!

I suggested that a modern toast might go, To the past!

The pre-Great-Man years, how we long for them!

Maury was still thinking through the blog. What will you call him?

I said.

But why? Maury asked. The name seemed almost respectful.

Here, I encountered another of my inhibitions. Even though Maury was my lawyer and, now, my editor, I was reluctant to speak with him about a man I thought of as my patient.

I had discussed pseudonyms with Meg Galliard, from the perspective of storytelling. *Rex* has a different effect than *Hubert*. But in conversation, I never offered Meg more about patients than what appeared on the page. If Meg requested elaboration, I replied by submitting a revised chapter.

To Maury, I said, Ask Muscle about nicknames.

WHEN MUSCLE JOINED US, HE waved off an offer of wine. He was on duty. He had updates. Pending an autopsy, the cause of the Great Man's death remained undetermined, but the state police were proceeding as if murder was at issue. They were making traffic stops.

The Providence Police wanted to contact me for questioning. A search was under way. City residents were requested to report sightings. The announcement featured the same author's headshot that the vigilantes were using. I was *wanted*—once more, in the guise of a kindly grandfather.

On Maury's laptop, Muscle had cued up video footage that he thought should interest me.

A reporter stood outside my office. She was an earnest-looking woman. Gonzalez-Mena, the name was.

Is that Patty Mena's niece? I asked Maury.

Patty is an internist. She and I had had patients in common. I seemed to recall a niece who had studied journalism.

The reporter said that it was known that I had returned to my office that morning. Prudence Street neighbors had been relieved to catch sight of me. They'd had concerns about my health.

The same neighbors spoke of visitors entering and leaving prior to my arrival. Nothing unusual. Often people showed while the doctor was absent.

The police had been knocking on doors. They wanted to know about those visitors. It was understood that I specialized in the treatment of paranoid men. For now, my patients were all considered persons of interest. Anyone who knew their identities or whereabouts was requested to contact authorities.

The segment ended with a clip that made me proud. An office neighbor, Mercy Goodenow, a jolly-faced woman, well-named, was asked what she had told the cops about the figures who frequented 190 Prudence.

Mercy scolded the reporter. Those men are patients, most of them. As patients, we all want our privacy, don't we?

The accent was harsh and local, the dismissal, crisp and definitive.

Mercy, God bless.

YOU HAVE TO UNDERSTAND, MUSCLE said, the fortress was a house of nicknames.

In response to Maury's question, Muscle launched into a detailed recitation.

The Great Man barely used proper names. No one existed for him except in relation to himself, how they struck him. Beelzebub was Moloch or the Reaper. Your buddy, Henry, was any Jew, Freud or Einstein, but also Portnoy or Rosengarten. Once, Darwin. Once, Galileo. For the Great Man, all scientists were Jewish.

Naomi was the Bitch or the Ballbuster.

I was Shadow or Pest. All the security guards were.

Among ourselves, we adopted the Great Man's practice, multiplying nicknames. The Great Man was Adonis or the Mastermind. Generally, the intent was a reversal, like a football team nicknaming a five-six scatback *Moose*—and then the joke was also that the Great Man really did consider himself handsome or clever.

The best names pointed in multiple directions. A guard who was Boston-born called the boss the Golden Golden—Bruins fans' name for Bobby Orr, the hockey god. The Great Man saw himself as a legend. Gold was always on his mind. He sported a blond fright wig.

And then there were his sexual proclivities. It had been rumored—famously—that he loved to watch women pee. That report had been debunked in the press. But then, one morning in the fortress, the boss emerged from a houri encounter—that's what we called them—in an especially upbeat mood, and the smell of fresh urine had come wafting from the boudoir. Who knows? Maybe he'd gotten excited and pissed himself. But it was fun to revive the story.

So, the Golden Golden it was, for a week or two.

To accord the Great Man dignity would be to give way to despair. He presented himself as a cartoon figure. It was as well to see him that way—to imagine ourselves in a sinister-comical dream from which we might yet awake.

Nicknames imitated the Great Man's speech. They participated in his modes of performance, vaudeville and burlesque. To the extent that they signaled disrespect, nicknames expressed our attitude toward the master we served.

Some nicknames went deep. The Great Man's wife called him Krishna, which was both straight-up and ironic. He was Death, the Destroyer of Worlds. He was far from what he imagined himself to be, an ideal lover.

Actually, she switched back and forth between Krishna and the Great Man. I believe that Henry got that name from her.

Maury looked at me. You and your medical ethics! You have me call in your pal Muscle so that he'll say things you can't or won't.

You know those science fiction stories that are built around rules? At the start we learn that robots must never let humans come to harm, and yet somehow, by the end, the villain is alone in space with an empty oxygen tank. Is that how medical ethics works for you? You find ways around the restrictions?

Perhaps medicine is like the law, I said. We need rules. We need ways of skirting rules.

Write as you must, was Maury's instruction. I should set off. He would await my contribution.

The hope was that once readers heard my voice, they would resist efforts to railroad me.

Maury's advice, to respect chronological order, was strategic. He would use the prospect of access to me as a bargaining chip. If the authorities wanted to know about the immediate lead-up to the Great Man' death, they would need to wait—or come to the table.

Maury lent me an old laptop that was still in working order. It would suffice as a word processor. If I stayed off the information grid—no news, no subpoenas—I would not need a current operating system.

Muscle set to configuring the laptop to encrypt text. I told Muscle that, to aid my memory when blogging, I would want access to my case notes from the time in the fortress and from recent sessions with my guys. The downloads were balky, but with his help, I got the job done.

The carry case contained a starter supply of thumb drives. When I was ready to send off a submission, I could copy it to a drive. Muscle would instruct his contacts about ways to deliver files safely.

It will be strange, he said, to be shut off from information.

Funny, how quickly we come to depend on what we acquire. For most of my life, there had been no internet.

I recalled the recent encouragement from Miriam. I was to put country before comfort. I was to make myself heard, for the sake of the Resistance and in the name of better days ahead.

◊ ◊ ◊ ◊ ◊

The parade had been endless—did people walk the route three times? Now was the moment, between the march gone by and the fireworks to come.

We would try to avoid checkpoints. We had one advantage. Muscle's presence at the scene of the death might not be known. The Great Man had intended to keep his visit to Providence secret even from allies in the fortress hideaway. To that end, sham assignments and itineraries had been generated for the security detail. In theory, Muscle had been in Washington, DC, reviewing protection requirements for the Great Man, should he need to meet with legislators.

When news of the Great Man's fate hit the Web, Muscle had contacted central command. He said that he was going into scramble mode—aborting his DC mission, heading to Rhode Island to be available as needed, and meanwhile, flying under the radar. In theory, then, if his higher-ups determined which car he was driving, they would consider it an active resource in their inventory, one not to be identified to law enforcement.

The free pass would last for only so long. Beelzebub knew that Muscle had been due in Providence by early morning. Once Beelzebub was debriefed, explanations would get complicated. But Beelzebub, too, had a false route on file. It might be some time before he was questioned.

My office neighbors were a concern. Mercy Goodenow's discretion notwithstanding, someone might well have described Muscle. His co-workers, any who collaborated in the investigation, would make the ID.

Muscle's Malibu was likely still anonymous, but Maury's old Jeep might serve us yet better. It was here, in the second spot in the garage, but mostly Maury had kept it at his lakeside camp in Maine. It would take time for the out-of-state registration to appear on anyone's radar. No one knew that we had visited Bristol.

The Malibu would stay parked where it was. If Muscle's agency, and the Feds with them, tried to track the car down, it would be off the streets.

WERE MUSCLE AND MAURY OVERLY prudent?

That sort of question arose often, didn't it, in the reign of the Great Man? Imagining that Regime agents might track our clicks on the web, we self-censored. When social media sites imploded, it was not only because misinformation had flooded every feed. No one wanted to leave trails for the authorities to follow.

At the same time, we wondered whether anyone in the Regime had enough technical know-how to light a match. Perhaps we feared a bogeyman.

I was uncertain that flight was necessary, but Muscle and Maury were my experts. They advised leaving now, and stealthily.

Muscle was disguised only by a five o'clock shadow and a Red Sox cap he had found on a peg in Maury's garage. At the wheel of the Jeep, he was meant to look like any working stiff heading homeward.

I lay on the floor behind the sedan's front seats. Maury had an ample supply of old quilts, obtained in lot sales at auctions when his interest was in a single fine specimen. He stacked quilts, folded neatly, on the rear seat, and then draped a couple loosely over me.

We set off on small roads.

◊ ◊ ◊ ◊ ◊

For the therapist, good news often comes in the form of bad. I have sketched the aftermath of the Great Man's birthday fete. He begged for admiration. He bemoaned the lack of warmth in his marriage. But an element was missing. He had not revealed or wondered why loving him was difficult.

When approaching their own lovability, often patients will begin by testing the therapist. The patient will display what he fears is his least likeable self and observe the response.

A patient may reveal a sexual perversion that he worries will provoke revulsion.

In childhood, he harmed small animals.

He betrayed a good friend or committed an act of violence—or both, an act of violence against a good friend.

Sharing the secret, the patient will express pride or shame. The implicit question is the same: Do I repel you? Can you still care?

Sometimes the revelation comes in stages. I abused my wife. I abused our daughter. I abused her this other way as well.

These moments are difficult, but psychiatrists arrive at them prepared. Although we may not know the specific source of shame, we will have noticed that the patient was avoiding certain topics. We will have heard similar confessions in other therapies.

Relief at progress in the treatment will counterbalance revulsion. How good to learn that we have earned trust! If we handle the challenge, we will earn more.

But some truths are unexpected and deeply unsettling. They strike home. We may show alarm or distaste. As therapists, we will fail.

FOR THE BETTER PART OF the first week in the fortress, well past the birthday party, I remained out of kilter.

I do poorly away from home. Because my first book had begun to sell well, Meg Galliard planned a publicity tour for the second one. I asked her to keep trips short—long weekends—in hopes that my absences would remain invisible to patients. Meg sent me on quick-turnaround visits to Seattle and Portland, San Francisco and LA, New York, and then Chicago, Milwaukee, and Minneapolis.

Out of town, I never got my feet under me. The orientation of the hotel room would be unfamiliar, with north light when the windows in our bedroom at home faced south and west. The HVAC system hummed. The phone and fire sensor indicators glowed intrusively. The windows were stuck shut. I suffered jet lag. I missed Miriam. I returned, only to head off to more book events and further disorientation.

The fortress was more alien yet. My room was narrow and low-ceilinged—coffin-like. The sheets were rough, the pillow thick and stiff. The plumbing clanked. And then there was the day-night reversal. I slept mornings. Afternoons, I was groggy. My stay had no fixed end. I did not know when I would leave or whether I would acclimate.

A service elevator ran near my bedroom, but I saw no housekeepers. They must have been notified of my absences, when the Great Man summoned me. The political and service staff were housed in separate wings. I was in a third category, call it emotional service. Perhaps there were no others like me.

I thought to take a walk around the grounds, but it was chilly in the mountains, and the bulk of my clothes order had not arrived—no boots or jacket. The exit door on my corridor was labeled *Emergency Use* and wired to trigger alarms. Was I confined to quarters? I found back stairs that led to a rear-facing fire-escape balcony overlooking a parking lot. I exercised by climbing up and down. Once I was winded, I sat on the balcony floor, looked out through the bars, and enjoyed the autumn air while I made further notes on the clinical sessions in the fortress and tried to think fresh thoughts about my patients back home.

On the fifth day, the Great Man summoned me by daylight. A buzz came on what I thought of as the Ezra phone, the one that Beelzebub had provided. An accompanying map directed me along a basement route, to prevent my being spotted. Automatically, doors opened before me. By service elevator, I ascended to the guest level of the hotel and a utility hallway that led to a media center and, farther along, a meeting room where the Great Man and his staff conducted the business of government.

Between the public rooms stood what the Great Man called his Retreat. I took it that he permitted himself to exit in mid-conference and take a nap or enjoy a drink in private. The Retreat was outfitted with a substantial bed, a well-stocked bar, flat-screen TVs, and portraits of the Great Man. In one, he was dressed in military regalia, as at a costume party. A photograph of Náomi staring upward was set off to the side and below, so that she appeared to be admiring her consort in his finery. Red velvet curtains added grandeur, although there were no windows.

Miriam would have gagged at the décor, but never mind. For me, the Retreat was a clinical workspace, one that spoke to me of my patient.

The Great Man sat in a throne-like chair. You see the setup? he asked. He pointed to the door to the media room. They can make me appear from anywhere. Why make my followers anxious?

The TV was tuned to the Regime Network. The screen displayed an impressive graph showing ever less immigration since the Great Man assumed power.

You'd think I'd get credit, he said.

Because the complaint was familiar, I invited elaboration: You get no credit?

What kind of quack are you? the Great Man asked.

He was right. The seemingly typical psychotherapeutic move, flipping a comment into a question, amounted to an expression of skepticism. Wasn't it the economic disaster and the failed response to plague that had slowed immigration?

Implicitly, I was challenging the Great Man on a second grounds as well. On screen, talking heads praised him to the skies. To accept my patient's premise—no acknowledgment—was to admit that the correspondents were his creatures, ventriloquist's dummies.

The Great Man pointed to a low stool, commanding me to sit.

You think these victories just happen, you and your people. Let me tell you about immigration. I did shut it down.

Do you remember that sob story in the bleeding-heart press, about *fillettes*? French history, some king, knew how to deal with upstarts. Kept them in cages too short for standing, too narrow for sitting. Brilliant! You don't cross a king like that.

The dunderhead press—they think that the image is original to them. We created the image. We put grown men in cages meant for young children.

How many cages? A handful? Dozens? Does it matter? Don't count the cripples, I say. Count the gang leaders. Count the drug traffickers.

These men act injured. Let them stay home. Who invited them? You cross the border, you're crossing me. There's a price to pay.

A reporter sneaks in to investigate. When she arrives, she finds only one small cage. A cage and a big fellow's coveralls.

Did we leave the cage behind by mistake, or did we want it discovered? You tell me, Eisenstadt.

We gave her the makings of myth.

She loves the words, our reporter. The Chinese speak of *squeeze cells*. The British like *Little Ease*. The French, *courbaril*—similar, look it up. Brutality that leaves no marks.

Our cages were never at that level. At most, a little hunching. Like curling up in bed.

Could have been worse. We discussed making smaller cages. We made some. Never mind.

We get the expected outcry. We love the outcry.

We deny. We demand evidence. We claim that we've been libeled. We sue. We put the press under our thumb. The more do-good pieces they write, the more we own them.

You think it's by chance that I'm unconvincing? My fans love denial that acts as confirmation. Nothing they love more than thin denial.

They love the denial, and they love the image of barbarity.

We're a tough nation. Don't mess with us.

We're having fun now, aren't we, Eli?

We love frustrating the haters. We love burying evidence.

The Regime investigates its own agent, the Reaper. Did he direct torture? Raises his profile, to be accused—higher fees, more kickbacks. The investigation results need to remain confidential.

More hubbub—all fuel for what? *The story*, Saul. You tell stories, no? But not like me. No one matches me. Born storyteller.

The story gets out and—*boom!*—no more migrants.

We create images that stick in the mind. No one likes a tiny cage.

Except my fans. They love the tiny cages.

Oh, Mimi.

Miriam had followed reports on the *fillettes* and insisted that I do the same.

It's your news, she said. Psychiatric news. News of psychosis and suicides.

I recalled how burdened I had been by the reports that Mimi forced on me.

Hearing the Great Man boast, hearing him cast torture as entertainment, thinking that the man with the clown face had been the origin of so much misery—I felt dragged down again.

I tried to set painful thoughts aside, tried to imagine acknowledging my patient for his acumen, but I was fixed on an image of a victim whimpering and screaming, cramped and alone in the desert sun.

As if reading my mind, the Great Man curled up in his throne-chair and did an imitation of a prisoner with his knees pushed up and his spine curled. He made desperate movements with his hands.

The Great Man said, *Take pity*!—at first as if sincerely, but then sarcastically. *Save me! I'm suffering!* He flapped his harms spastically.

In sensual tones, he repeated the French words for torture chambers: *fillette*, *oubliette*, *courbaril*, *bagnard*, *tombeau*, *crapaudine*. He got stuck on *crapaudine*. He emphasized the first syllable. He liked that it sounded like an English curse word and, better, an embarrassing bodily function.

Be a sport, Sammy. Put yourself in the *crapaudine*! Squat like a toad!

The Great Man sounded most serious when he gave directions that were demeaning.

Squat! he commanded. Join in the fun.

He turned threatening. Squat, or I'll make you do worse.

When the Great Man asked me to contort myself, I thought of my training in child psychiatry. I had a three-month placement. Most sessions were built around play therapy. I sat on the floor, surrounded by toys. Half of my hours were devoted to young delinquents referred by the courts. Threats were common. A child might demand more time with me. *If you try to leave, I'll throw this block at you.*

I would name the feeling. *It hurts to say goodbye to people we care about. We never know whether they'll be back.*

I will be back. Last time, I told you that I would be back, and here I am. I will be back on Thursday, two days from now, before lunchtime, and I will be happy to see you then. Besides, that block belongs on the castle wall. Do you want to add a block here? I will ask your nurse to stay with you while you finish the castle.

Often, I failed. The block flew at me. I was young and nimble.

Or the block hit me on the forehead and made a lump that swelled to look like half a ping-pong ball.

Why should I not suffer injuries, now and then? Doctors deal with illness. Doctors assume risk.

With the Great Man, what feeling should I name?

He coaxed me, Come!

The sadism was precise.

He had okayed Bub's plan to threaten my daughter-in-law—okayed it or devised it. Knowing about Kareena, he might easily have guessed that I would feel protective toward immigrants. My other investment in the safety of migrants, through Miriam, was incidental. He had stumbled upon it.

The Great Man built on his luck. He was quick to grasp other people's sensitivities—in his view, their weak points. What he did not know in advance, he picked up quickly.

Treating him, I would encounter cruelty that hits home. If I could not remain sympathetic, I ought not to attempt the job.

I judged it best not to name the sadism directly.

In psychotherapy training, I had been taught a technique called upward interpretation. The therapist casts complex matters in a favorable light.

A famous example: an inpatient declares that he is Jesus Christ. The therapist says, *We can use a good carpenter*, and sets the patient to repairing furniture, in the belief that purpose and routine are therapeutic.

I was never a fan of upward interpretation. My job is to let the patient tell me in what sense he is the Christ and to reflect that meaning back to him. I must not use his words to manipulate him, even if I believe that the result, engagement in productive work, might be beneficial.

Upward interpretation. Do we know which way is up? Is making a footstool more sublime than sitting at the right hand of God while He makes your enemies your footstool?

In the face of the demand to make light of torture, I thought that a variant of upward interpretation might offer a way forward. Might I deflect our attention from the awful behavior to my patient's self-image and, implicitly, his motivation?

I said, *Not a man to be trifled with!*

If I am not to be trifled with, why are you defying me?

The Great Man had intentionally misheard me. My exclamation was in his voice, as if he had been underscoring his own grandeur. Implicitly, I had been asking, Why make needless demonstrations of your power?

He chose to take the exclamation as affirmation. He brooked no opposition. Given that reality, why had I not yet joined him in mocking the unfortunate?

He was asking me to betray my late wife. He may not have known the first thing about Mimi. He did see that I hesitated to cross a line. It followed that I found his past behavior repugnant.

He loved to force people forsake their principles.

Any psychotherapy worth the name would need to explore that pleasure. Why was it important for him to lay virtue low or expose the hypocrisy it hides? That question is unsuitable for early sessions. I thought it best to refocus the discussion by emphasizing my own incapacities.

I'm arthritic. If I did what you ask, I'd spend a week recuperating. You want me here every night.

That's the point of the *crapaudine*, Finkelstein. You feel pain, and then you break.

I'm having enough trouble sitting on this stool, I said.

With a creak and a groan, I stood. I have to excuse myself. Crouching puts pressure on my bladder.

You'll stay here and sit while I talk, Ziggy, the Great Man said. You'll hold your water. It's healthy to stretch out that bladder.

My child patients had threatened violence because they felt helpless. The Great Man threatened violence because he could. I was content for the power relationship to be out in the open.

I chose another upward interpretation: You weren't always like this.

It was a mark on the canvas in a warm hue. The implication was that my patient's cruel behavior did not match up with his better self.

The Great Man might have protested, I'm a bully. What of it?

He might have come after me. What are you implying?

Instead, he took a detour into whining.

You need to understand..., the Great Man said.

I waited.

...how badly I've been wronged.

If he was in an ill humor, it was with reason. He had rescued the country, and yet he would be remembered as cruel and incompetent.

He was pained, and he was content for me to feel pain too. He believed that he needed to enforce empathy on me.

You and I, Doc, are practitioners of the narrative arts.

The difference was that I thought small. I wrote about saving Peruvs.

He began making the case for his greatness, as if to posterity.

To pay for the cages and the staffing that went with them, he had used funds earmarked for education. He was teaching the wetbacks a lesson.

Once I had mentioned my arthritis, once I had mentioned a full bladder, what could be more pleasing than the passage of time? The boasting about misdeeds continued at length.

After he was sued for misusing education funds, he corrupted the courts and gained monarchial powers for the executive branch, all in the service of this one move, claiming the right to misspend appropriations.

A trifecta-plus! he said.

He hijacked the budget, injured immigrants, and expanded the Regime's scope—while gladdening the EverGreats.

Once I can use education funds for torture, what can I not do?

You tell me, good doctor, am I underappreciated or not?

Repurposing the small cage was my inspiration. Mine! The Great Man's! Write that down!

The full bladder. Was my discomfort visible?

Squat like a toad, the Great Man said, returning to that theme. Squat just once, and I'll let you go.

Remembering Hans Lutz, I reached for the therapist's prerogative. The whole of a session can be colored by the choice of end point, the precise timing of the declaration, *Our time is up*.

We've done a day's work, I said. Why don't we both digest what we've discussed? If you have an opening, you may want to meet with me at this time tomorrow.

You know what I hate? the Great Man said. I hate when people tell me what I may want. You have to pee, you want to sleep nights, and suddenly, you're selling me something. Leave the selling to me, Oppenheimer.

If you need to pee, pee. Pee in your pants. Pee on the rug. Then squat like a toad.

And don't think about walking out on me. You make a move toward the door, and I'll throw you in a *crapaudine* for real.

I thought of past patients who had threatened me. One prisoner had demanded that I prescribe opiates for pain. If not, when he got out, he would come after me. Well, more than one prisoner.

I did not prescribe. I carried on in my role as therapist, trusting that if I kept my patient's interests at heart, he would come to respect me and the process of treatment. With the Great Man, I was following a similar line.

He was right that in trying to dictate his schedule, I had made a technical error. Everything done in session must serve the therapy.

I tried to return to basics—to act fully from within the clinical framework. The Great Man said *Pee*, and I asked myself: If I comply, will the act help or harm our work together?

I had heard that peeing stimulated the Great Man—watching the act. I was not so disconnected as to have missed that report. It had the quality of small-city gossip.

Too complicated, I thought, if I pee and he shows a sexual response.

If arousal was not at issue, if he was only out to humiliate me, might he feel safer once he had seen me wet myself with an old man's dribble? Safer, but also more contemptuous. We want patients to feel safe because the doctor is reliable, not because he is inferior.

Better to hold off. Better to hope that the Great Man would come to recognize the anxiety or grandiosity that made him demand that I pee.

But not yet. I would approach the need to humiliate when he was not in the process of trying to satisfy it. In therapy, if not in blacksmithing, often it is best to strike when the iron is cold.

I decided to try to regain control of time by admitting fault.

*For my own good*, I said, acknowledging that he was right on the earlier point, that I had been trying to sell him. I am ending the session for my own good.

For better or worse, I was out the door.

The Great Man had provided a sample of the news I had tried to avoid: he used torture of the most vulnerable to weaken democracy, consolidate his power, and indulge his sadistic and narcissistic drives. In session, he had wanted to give me a personal experience of the pain he caused and the dominance he enjoyed. In response, I had signaled that, yes, I hoped to be able to treat a man that horrid, that perverse.

I had been tested. I had not shown revulsion.

Had the interchange gone well enough? The Great Man did not end treatment, but neither did he schedule the daytime appointments I had suggested. Instead, he called for me that very night, to reset the terms of my service.

Outside the boudoir suite entrance, the ripped guard greeted me.

Seems you'll be close by.

Just beyond, inside the anteroom, someone had placed a shabby Barcalounger, faux-leather, foraged, I was guessing, from the old hotel's storage closet. The chair looked peculiarly uncomfortable. Strapped to one arm was a coaster-shaped restaurant waitlist buzzer, doubtless with a similar provenance.

I got the picture. I was to rest within hailing distance of the Great Man's bedside and appear when alerted.

On the drive to the fortress, Bub had made what I thought were passing remarks about insomnia. Did I know how noblemen dealt with it in the eighteenth century? They would hire a chess master or violinist to sit outside the bedroom door—at the ready, should the lord of manor need help passing the time.

Bub lingered on a story about the origin of the Goldberg Variations. One Count von Kaiserling had employed a young harpsichord prodigy, Johann Goldberg, as a sleep attendant and apprenticed the boy to Johann Sebastian Bach. He composed the Variations to serve as nighttime entertainment, to help the boy lighten the burden of insomnia for the Count.

Bub said, You're about to join a noble, or, more properly, a servile tradition.

I guessed that the Great Man had complained to Bub about my having left to pee. In response, Bub had shared the Goldberg story. I make that assumption because later, when the Great Man buzzed me to the bedside, he called me Goldberg.

In employing a sleep minder, the Great Man would be acting like royalty, commanding talent to provide quick distraction. If the Great Man could not make me squat like a *crapaudine* victim or hold my urine until my bladder burst—not without sabotaging the project he had hired me for—still he could make our relationship, master and servant, explicit and cause me discomfort in the process.

Resting in the lumpy reclining chair, I thought of an intellectually disabled woman who consulted me shortly after I established my private practice. Roberta would phone me at home in the middle of the night, waking me from sleep. Ostensibly, she needed to discuss worries, some delusional, about the health of her aging father, in whose house she lived. I made out a pattern. The calls peaked in the weeks after sessions that had been difficult for Roberta. Nights, she replayed them in her mind and built up resentments. She woke me because she found the phone contact soothing, but also (so she finally said) so that I might suffer as she did.

Incidentally, after that confession, Roberta stopped phoning—and I worried about her all the more. I increased the frequency of our meetings and gave her the first morning slot. On waking, I wanted Roberta to be able to look forward to sharing her fears.

Thinking of Roberta made me consider the fixity of the Great Man's impairments. I had hopes of inducing slow change, but some of his character traits might prove to be as set as Roberta's intellectual limitations. And his needs had as much acuity as hers. For him, the least one was urgent. Why should I rest in bed when my tossing and turning in a chair would save him minutes of unease? Like Roberta, the Great Man needed to know that I was always available.

When he buzzed me, at three, it was to initiate a brief and unremarkable therapy session. He complained about being misunderstood as a political leader. He shared an example of sadism toward an ex-wife who had it coming to her. The story had points in common with Bub's finger-smashing vignette. I had been right in thinking that Bub's narrative had been a provocative test, meant to assess my tolerance for tales of spousal abuse.

Satisfied and self-satisfied, the Great Man found sleep.

I took the performance as conciliatory. The Great Man reserved the right to misuse me, but he valued treatment.

When I left the bedside, I thought to step into the corridor and walk off the stench. I could hear the Great Man's rough snore. How likely was he to summon me again?

From outside the room came a woman's sobs, louder—closer—than before. I trundled farther down the hall. There she was.

◊ ◊ ◊ ◊ ◊

As before, she was turned away from me, gripping the balcony. She managed to catch her breath. She wept quietly.

Hearing my steps, she turned and gave a teary smile.

A first encounter with Náomi is not soon forgotten, even for a man of my age.

Her beauty is profound. Slumped, sniffling, slow of movement, Náomi evoked a special sort of feeling, call it lethargic desire, a deep and quiet longing. Tenderness was a feature, not lasciviousness, although of course, a man can fool himself on that score.

Náomi is an earth mother, a relaxed and generous presence. At rest, she has a frank and open face, expectant and accepting. She appears to wear little makeup. Her skin, lightly freckled, shows the marks of time. Naturalness in someone so lovely can be shocking. It is possible to be abashed at the nakedness of her cheek.

At our first meeting, her sadness predominated, downcast eyes and quivering lips. I thought of the Contessa in *The Marriage of Figaro*—of operatic dignity in the face of a husband's heinous acts.

Náomi motioned me to a darker part of the corridor, appointed with an upholstered sofa framed in wood carved with vine and leaf motifs.

Oh, that's restorative, she said, to sit with you.

I must warn you that I tend to vomit. It's become a chronic problem, nausea, when I know that my husband is near.

Oh, dear. You have a tonic effect. My goodness, that's helpful.

Having controlled her queasiness, she considered it analytically.

I wish my nausea were more sublime, she said.

As a student, she had been taken with Sartre's account of nausea, not in his novel of that name, but in *Being and Nothingness*. He was resigned to chronic nausea as a fit response to the contingency of our existence, to the infinitude of choice and the randomness of circumstance.

That sort of nausea would be bearable, Náomi said, because it reflects the human condition.

She saw one connection between that noble nausea and her own degraded variant. Both arose from the cooccurrence of futility and necessity. Her fate was existential in this sense. It was Sisyphean. She must try to rein in her husband, even as she failed endlessly.

Is it widely known that Náomi is an intellectual? If that word is inexact: she is smart, cultured, and well read. In college, she majored in English literature with a focus, since she was drawn to the stage, on dramaturgy. The Western canon, as it was in her college years, is her reference point in daily life.

Not that night, but later, I asked why the media had not captured that side of her.

She said that offstage, she requires privacy. Among actors, that temperament is not rare. Later, she avoided public appearances for another reason. She did not want to support her husband's career. His judgment was so flawed.

Before his ascension, Náomi allowed herself to be trotted out on occasion, to please him. His handlers had been instructed to underplay her attainments. To her husband's followers, a bimbo wife, more than an educated woman, was a gaudy indicator of wealth and power.

When the tabloids discussed Náomi's college years, the subject was men. She'd broken up marriages and run through sugar daddies. There was truth to the reports. Getting the tuition paid had been an issue.

Because of Náomi's off-Broadway roles, her college semesters had been spread out over time. Her classmates barely knew her. As for her good grades, the press attributed them to favoritism. She had not been beyond gratifying professors.

Náomi told me otherwise. She worked hard at acting and academics alike.

The mental discipline shows in her conversation. She is quick to size up any situation.

That first night, I was tongue-tied in her presence.

It's not because she is statuesque. *Ample* might be the word. As I have tried to suggest, hers is an all-too-human beauty. Hints of mortality are not absent.

Did she seduce or, at least, flatter me?

I must sit with you more often, she said.

She turned toward me, letting her robe fall open, slightly more open.

I righted myself.

Even at this distance, that snoring may set me off, she warned. And to think that he used to amuse me!

Now the tone was playful.

Oh, my gosh. I feel good.

She pulled a handkerchief from a pocket and dabbed her eyes.

May I call you Henry?

I said, You are Naomi.

She corrected me. *Náomi.*

I have always had it wrong, I said, the placement of the accent.

She said that she had changed the name, changed the pronunciation.

Privately, she said. In my own mind.

I want you to call me by the name I call myself.

If she had not approached me, she said, it was because she was an emotional wreck. She preferred to show composure in her first meeting with a psychiatrist.

Not that I want you to take me on, she said. It's important that you tend to my husband. But I want you to see me as I see myself—as Náomi.

She made reference to a phrase from Shakespeare, *like Níobe, all tears*. Níobe, with the accent on the first syllable.

Náomi said that it had occurred to her, since she wept incessantly, to adopt a parallel pronunciation, Náomi, as a reference to Níobe.

Skeptical readers will complain, We know her name. It's not Naomi. She can't have amended it in this simple fashion, through choosing which syllable to stress. Artistic license may have its place, but imaginative translation can go too far.

By way of partial answer: When I first met the Great Man's wife—alone, at night, in a hallway—I addressed her by her first name, and she corrected me, offering a private alternative, one that expressed her mental state, chronic sadness. Later, toward morning, when I had gone off duty, I fell into a half-sleep. In this reverie, she came to me, and so did the Náomi/Níobe conversation, as a substitute for the actual one. Ever since, when I imagined describing her, she was Náomi.

Soon, fact and fantasy met. Days after our first encounter, I chanced, in conversation with Náomi, to stumble and call her by the dream name. She asked why. I explained. She thought it was true that were she, like the mythical Níobe, to be turned to stone, she would continue weeping. There was no recovering from what she had seen.

She professed to be charmed by my translation and suggested that I address her as Náomi whenever we were alone together. She would adopt the name herself, again in private. To me, to herself, she's been Náomi ever since. The dreamt name became real, which is to say that in this writing, my use of the name represents both imaginative translation and unembellished reporting.

But I was describing our first meeting.

How does it work with shrinks? she asked. I talk, and you listen? How dull would that be? Let's try something different. I ask a question, and then it's your turn. Agreed?

She had that capacity, to shuttle from despair to playfulness, or perhaps it was an antic aspect of despair that I was seeing.

One rule: the questions must be related, she said. The subject matter can drift, but it can't take leaps.

I'll start, she said. How did you come to be here?

I must have looked like a man who would suffer inhibitions. By making conversation a game, she was giving me a break.

Came here? I'm not sure what I'm permitted to say.

As a doctor, I would not discuss the reasons a patient had asked to consult me. As a conscript, I was not free to describe Bub's means of coercion.

But it's the easiest question. How can we converse if you won't begin there?

Exhausted, far from home, there are worse things than being teased by a mercurial woman.

I'll tell *you*, she said. I wanted someone to treat my husband, someone who would be acceptable to him. I had happened to pick up Trude Nilsson's memoir, the one with the photo of your couch on the jacket. I had leafed through the book years ago—and now I thought, Ah, a brand-name therapist for insomnia.

Online, I read that you had written about the treatment of paranoia in men. I checked to see whether you were practicing.

If I had followed Miriam's advice, and Nina's, if I had announced my retirement, if my voicemail had said that I no longer saw patients, Náomi would not have identified me as a solution to her problem, Kareena would not have been threatened, and I would have remained in Providence but—having closed the practice—without my men's group.... Even seeing the trouble that I had caused, it was hard to decide which course would have been preferable.

I doubted that there would be two like you, Náomi said, a famous sleep doctor willing to address delusions. I took a chance. I played you up as a therapist to the stars, Hollywood's answer to *nuits blanches*. That was the pretext. But you know why you're here.

I had heard already, from the Great Man, that Náomi had recommended me, but I had not thought through the implications. She had put me and my family in danger.

My apologies, Náomi said.

Was it awful? she asked.

She was solicitous. She was contrite.

I sicced Beelzebub on you. In effect, I did.

I knew that once the Great Man wanted you, he would send a henchman.

What do they have on you? she asked.

Enough and plenty, I said.

They have that on everyone. They write laws that make everyone guilty. They enforce them capriciously. It's an old method. Everyone's convicted but most have not been arrested yet.

She seemed troubled, brittle.

Oh, my quiet Henry. You're right. Must I confess in words? I gave my husband your name, and he said, What is his vulnerability?

He said, Give me the package the way I like it, wrapped and tied with a bow.

He is like that. He demands complicity. He would consider bringing you in only if he had something on you. If he was to try to import a shrink, it must be one who would not talk if the effort failed.

I did the research through Regime sleuths as if I were the one needing secure access to treatment. I provided the leverage. I tied the bow.

She set to crying again. She spoke of her marriage. She spoke of the times we live in.

I wish that there had been some other way, she said.

Speak to me, she said.

The implication was that I was causing pain by not offering quick absolution.

Isn't there always another way?

That was the Kant in me. My thought was, You don't put a family in Bub's clutches based on vague hopes of transforming the Great Man. The benefit is speculative. The harm is certain.

Thank you, Náomi said. Men don't confront me often.

They don't.

It was mostly a question. Sitting beside Náomi, it was impossible not to wonder about the effect of beauty at her level, how men respond.

Some have abused me. Abuse has not been rare. Quiet contradiction is what I have missed out on.

Look, Náomi said. You have been conscripted. It's common when the country's need is great.

There is only one of you, she said. Only one, and you've been called to duty.

I considered her claim.

In Russia, the Tsar conscripted subjects, my ancestors among them. *You've been called to duty*, might mean, *Life's not fair. I use you as I will.* That's how Bub conscripted me, through the exercise of power.

That's not the usage we have in mind when we make the call to duty an example of a moral obligation. Appealing to conscription, as Náomi had, made sense in the context of a democracy. We sign on as citizens. We assume obligations.

The Great Man's was no longer a democratic government, and Náomi had not conscripted me to serve it. In summoning me to re-sculpt her husband's personality under the guise of treating his insomnia, she was asking me to defy or circumvent his orders. She was conscripting me into the service of a country that no longer existed except as an ideal. Effectively, she was conscripting me into the Resistance.

Or else, she was positing a nation that stood outside its government, our nation as an entity that survived and remained distinct from its recent political incarnation. To save that ideal, she had brought my daughter's family to the attention of a man known for his heartlessness, a man known for his willingness to send people like my daughter-in-law to their deaths.

Did a member of the Resistance, if that is how Náomi saw herself, have a right to expose us to that disaster? In accepting citizenship, had I agreed to be thrown in harm's way by a private person with a viewpoint?

Perhaps I had. Perhaps, if we love our country, we need to come to its defense when it is hijacked.

Náomi's goal was to temper tyranny, to make it more humane and less erratic.

Thinking of Náomi as a moral agent: Can there be a Kantian politics? One that, like psychotherapy, prioritizes the claims of the one individual before us over all other considerations? Perhaps that's what Kantian politics means. But then the phrase is an oxymoron. To do politics at all is to be willing to threaten one immigrant—Kareena—so that the nation as a whole sees less arbitrariness, less rule through pique.

Náomi continued to make her case. If no one can wake him, if no one can make him drop the reins or loosen them, to give the country a sporting chance—then we're all doomed anyway.

I'll try to make it as comfortable for you as I can, she said. I will try to make it come out right for you and yours.

And now she leaned in to kiss me on the temple, as a child would a beloved grandpa—only it was not a child, it was Náomi. I pulled away preemptively.

I felt—more with Náomi, who was not in treatment, than with her husband, who was—what I often feel at the beginning of a psychotherapy: awareness of being in the presence of emotional complexity. She was sensitive and fragile. She was hard as nails. She was Machiavellian. Or was it that she had an extraordinary capacity for compartmentalization and denial? Well, you would need defenses if you were to be married to the Great Man and survive.

Perhaps the complexity was within me. Loosely, we speak of ambivalence as if it were a matter of being lukewarm and indecisive. The technical term refers to something else, to strong forces or inclinations pointing in opposite directions. With Náomi, I felt attraction and repulsion, both intensely. Likewise for trust and suspicion. She had done something deeply immoral. She had done her best.

Was I sensing ambivalence in her as well? She wanted her husband cured. She wanted the treatment sabotaged.

I can't, I said, be kissed by a patient's wife, not even in jest. Not even in kindness.

Hasn't he told you he's not your patient?

That's how she had convinced the Great Man: take him on as a consultant. Let Bub do the hiring. He'll guarantee the guy's silence. Your image will remain intact.

I did not comment on what he had or had not told me.

You are as I had thought you would be—as you are in your books, Náomi said.

It seemed a balanced judgment. For better and for worse.

◊ ◊ ◊ ◊ ◊

At the kitchen table this morning, I found that I could not write. I knew why. I have mentioned my compulsion for disguise, but as an author, I have one for truth-telling as well. When unsatisfied, it, too, will stymie me.

How rare is this problem? Elizabeth Bishop, the poet, wrote of her *George Washington handicap*, the inability to tell a lie. If she described a dead hen, run over by a car, as white, she had to circle back and revise: now the hen was white and red, because of the blood.

Here's my confession: the meet-up with Náomi did not end with my receiving her mixed blessing. As we spoke, she discovered that she had another agenda, and she pursued it.

I cannot fathom why I chose to conceal that part of the conversation. Because it might cast Náomi in a bad light? Hadn't I done that already when I wrote that she had offered Kareena up to Bub?

Best to tell the story before examining my wish to suppress it.

When I had thought that our conversation was done, Náomi raised her hand with spread fingers. Wait! She had a question.

When you're with him nights, what does he speak about? His popularity? His high intelligence? His leadership abilities? Financial acumen? Sexual prowess? Skiing? Dear me, not that!

I had shown what I think of as my poker face, but I am not much of a bluffer. She saw that she had hit the target.

She grabbed my upper arm and, leaning forward, prepared to share a confidence. Her perfume, lightly applied, was grassy. I imagined that she was trying to reset our relationship, to bring it back to where it had been before she had confessed to endangering my family.

I'm concerned for your safety, she said, as if her husband's choice of topic, skiing, might lead me into danger.

You've met my security guard, Muscle? I will see whether I can detail him to tend to you, not just incidentally—as an assignment. These changes take time, but if what I have to say does not dissuade you, I will set the process in motion.

I have a half-dozen bodyguards, she said. Bodyguards are what we have most of in this godforsaken place.

Náomi gave what I later came to recognize as her too-clever-by-half smile.

It's the skiing, she said, that made me think of Muscle. Sit with me for another second, will you?

I'll tell you something about Muscle, something that allowed me to forgive his quirks. As you may imagine, we vet our security guards thoroughly. Well, we don't do anything thoroughly—but in this case, someone made an effort.

Before selecting my staff, I read the files on hires. I discovered that one of our recruits was known to me indirectly and distantly through the Great Man's father, Aldo. For Muscle, I had both the dossier and family lore to go on. I was able to build on that early knowledge through incidental chats with him in down time.

Our seemingly uncomplicated Muscle had an unusual upbringing, and its effects show in his behavior. Before you agree to be placed under his care, you need to hear what I have learned.

As I might for a patient, I objected. Can't he introduce himself?

But I was tired. I was hearing a story. I did not have it in me to pull away.

Náomi continued.

Muscle did not come to us through an agency. He had family connections. His father, Eidan, had worked with my father-in-law, Aldo, in the ski industry.

In his final years, Aldo fell into what Disraeli called anecdotage. He loved to sit beside me and tell tales. His favorite topic was piracy—how he earned his fortune as a businessman by cutting corners and skirting laws. Eidan was his lieutenant or, since we are speaking of buccaneers, first mate.

By the time that Muscle—Patrick—was seven or eight, his father had alienated so many state regulators that Aldo took him off domestic duty and posted him abroad.

Eidan began with an attempt to establish a resort in Patagonia on a mountain called Cerro Catedral. The project required political skill—silencing indigenous peoples, steamrollering locals—and Eidan failed. But while on the job, he met an Argentine Firecracker *avant la lettre*, a teenaged stripper named Lieselotte Schüller who also tended bar in Bariloche. Early in the last century, Austrians, Belgians, and other Europeans settled in the temperate parts of Patagonia. Lotty was the spirited daughter of a respectable Swiss-German couple. Eidan hired her as a nanny, ostensibly as a nanny, and brought her home to Forest Hills, in Queens.

The stunt threw his wife, a fragile woman, over the edge. Instead of tending to her, Eidan doubled down and had Lotty accompany him now to Chile, where he was negotiating to take over an old ski resort that had fallen on hard times. Our Patrick and his brother, Sean, were on summer break from school, and Eidan brought them along, in Chile's winter.

His intention was to teach the boys skiing, using his own harsh methods.

Eidan was certain that, as his sons, Patrick and Sean must be natural athletes. To ski like an Olympian, they had only to be plunked down at the top of a mountain and left to make their own way.

Sean was a daredevil, but the father's methods terrified young Patrick. Perhaps terrorized is the better word.

Lotty, who had taken charge of the boys, took pity on Patrick and got one of the locals to give him lessons daily, behind the father's back. The accomplice would follow Patrick up the mountain, ease him down, and teach him on shallow slopes.

Patrick progressed, but his skiing remained tentative. Sean was a hero. The father dismissed Patrick as unmanly.

Lotty felt compelled to comfort Patrick, and she had a limited sense of how that might be done. Whenever Eidan was away on business, Lotty invited Patrick into her bed. She held him close. When that approach partly succeeded, she let him nuzzle her breast while she played with his widdler. She was closer in age to Patrick, young as he was, than to Eidan.

When Eidan returned, Lotty turned her attention to him, and Patrick felt newly abandoned.

Náomi seemed lost in the narrative, intent on offering a detailed account of her bodyguard's childhood. Did I sense that something was *off*, that the telling was too insistent and the account unreliable? It is my job to listen to deceptive storytelling. I knew that the tale we would end up with was not the one that I was hearing, but I did not understand, not yet, how I was being hoodwinked.

I am describing a single summer, Náomi continued, but in haphazard fashion, this routine continued for years. Eidan had his wife institutionalized, and then he divorced her. Sean died young of drugs and alcohol. Lotty went in and out of Eidan's life, sometimes resuming the involvement with Patrick.

The back and forth destroyed the child's sexual functioning. For him, intimacy had become the realm of caring and abandonment, superiority and inferiority, sadism and masochism. It took ever more stunning women and ever more perverse sexual dramas to get a rise out of him.

Doubtless the Great Man will spin tall tales for you about his talents as an athlete. By his account, he needed no more training than being thrown into the deep end of the pool. About sex, he'll tell similar stories. In truth, they are all about Lotty.

When the Great Man brags that he entered the sexual arena young, the names of the women, and the women themselves, are invented. He was attached adoringly to the nanny who was an inconstant protector and, insofar as she put Aldo first, a constant betrayer.

Excuse me? I asked.

Náomi continued, undeterred—only now calling her husband *Krishna*.

She said, When Krishna's lying began to unsettle me, I made it my business to meet Lotty. I wanted to know whether what my husband told me could be relied on and whether, when I discovered that it could not, he would acknowledge the truth. You will be unable to duplicate the research, so I'm handing you my results.

Lotty was a tallish woman, well rounded, warm, and open. Her distinguishing feature in old age was thick, lustrous hair. You can guess: physically, she was me down the road, if I turn out to have good genes and moderate habits. Krishna did not marry his mother. By wife four—me—he was marrying his nursemaid.

Lotty did not know whether to be proud or ashamed of her ministrations. She had been out to save a fragile boy from a father who was at once neglectful and overbearing. On balance, she was inclined to forgive herself.

No one then, she said, used words like *abuse*.

If abuse was at issue, psychological abuse, it came from Aldo. She and Krishna had been two abused children clinging to one another for comfort.

Why shouldn't an older woman introduce a boy to sex? Her family was European. It was that way in Europe.

Dates and ages kept shifting as Lotty told her story.

Hadn't her intervention made Krishna what he was, a success? Like the father, but in her own way, Lotty had been ambitious for the boy.

What do we make of such a woman, good doctor? She died last year. I believe that she was at peace with the way she had used her sexuality.

I was not concerned about Lotty. I was focused on the switch of boys in Náomi's narrative, from Muscle/Patrick to Krishna—the Great Man.

Excuse me, I said, but did you change horses?

I said, That trick was not amusing.

Was it not? My apologies.

Náomi had been afraid that once I saw that she was outlining her husband's history, I would cut the conversation short. On the spot, in the corridor, she had decided to bypass my preferences or, as she saw them, inhibitions.

Náomi was right. I had been reluctant enough to hear her out when I thought that she was filling me in on Muscle.

I asked, Why recruit me if you mistrust my methods and inclinations?

There's no time, she said, no time to discover what the Great Man has no intention of revealing. I do trust you, as a partner in a collaborative enterprise. I look forward to our working together.

To treat him, you need a solid starting point. For my husband, lying is beyond being reflexive. He prefers to fabricate. He would rather lie than overcome his insomnia—rather lie than sleep. He wants you to cure him without disturbing his self-deception.

I protested. That preference is universal. We want to recover without abandoning what has sustained us: our habits, addictions, or delusions.

His is not an ordinary case. Ours are not ordinary circumstances. You need a head start, need to know what he hopes to keep hidden. It's relevant, isn't it, if he clings, against all evidence, to the belief that he is naturally competent?

His political leadership is like his early skiing. His abilities are unremarkable. He takes on too much and falls short. How will he be able to reconnect with reality? He has humbled the nation. He has proved his father right.

I was still adjusting to the conversation's new framework.

What about Muscle—Patrick? I asked.

Healthy American boyhood. Father died young. We have that in common. Muscle will fill you in. He's not secretive.

I can't believe you pulled that switch, I said.

I took it from you, she said. Don't you write about how you retell stories, changing names and so on?

To protect patients, I said, not to expose them.

Like you, Náomi said, I try to do what the crisis demands.

At the word *crisis*, she teared up again. I did not think that the display was for effect, although Náomi had already demonstrated that there were limits to my ability to interpret her intentions. By the looks of it, she was bearing an indescribable burden. She had allied with the devil. She was desperate to put things right.

I did not ask Náomi about her use of imaginative translation. Had she given the Great Man's history straight up, only substituting Eidan for Aldo, and so on? Hadn't the Great Man learned to ski near where he'd grown up, in New England? What mattered was the gist, the nanny who protected and betrayed, the early sexual stimulation, the sharing of a partner between a demanding father and an insecure child.

There was no unlearning that history. I would enter the next session understanding the Great Man differently. I would listen for hints of impotence. I would question my patient's accounts of his natural abilities and superior competence.

You have created complications for me, I said.

Privately, I wondered whether I was obliged to report this conversation to the Great Man.

I take that tack. In the course of a referral, a department head confides that my prospective patient is a difficult employee. When we meet, I will say, Heather mentioned that your colleagues find you hard to work with. I want my patient to be aware of what I have heard.

There can be tough choices. Say that I happen to see my patient's wife walk out of a divorce lawyer's office. She may spot me and look flustered.

Imagine that the wife approaches and says, I'm set on ending the marriage. I'm considering the timing. When I decide, I'll want to be the one to tell Larry.

What if I hold my tongue and, down the road, the wife says, Your doctor won't be surprised—I ran into him two months ago and explained that I was on my way out?

Can psychotherapy survive that breach of trust?

Secrecy is bad faith.

Náomi's news, if accurate, was not unknown to my patient, but my awareness of it was. If he learned of my conversation with his wife, he would feel betrayed, by me as much as by her.

Náomi counseled discretion. If my husband learns of our talk, he will punish me for what I have revealed and you for what you have heard.

I weighed outcomes.

I hold silent, and my patient later discovers that I have secret knowledge about him.

I speak, and my patient feels stripped naked—humiliated. He responds with lies, delusions, and punishments.

Náomi said, I created a crisis for you when I had you recruited. That crisis is part of the larger one that we all face. In the vicinity of the Great Man, there is nothing but crisis. The time of the

Great Man is a time of crisis. Your new awareness is not the crisis. The crisis is the crisis.

◊ ◊ ◊ ◊ ◊

The Great Man began our next session in unexpected fashion. He said, I've got a fantastic story for you. You'll want to write this one down.

I wondered whether he knew that Náomi had spoken with me. He seemed intent on capturing my interest and, perhaps, my loyalty.

Did I fail to perk up sufficiently? The Great Man said, It's a story that I have never told anyone else.

The never-before-told tale.

I have heard many. Typically, a patient will apologize. There's something I should have mentioned long ago. It's hard to talk about. I'm sure that I've never told anyone. I've been reluctant to burden you. I can't judge the importance of the memory.... I'm summoning my courage....

The gradual lead-up is appealing, the courtesy and doubt. I will want to be receptive but unhurried. The patient may share the tale now or later. I will trust that the telling is difficult and consequential.

The proudly announced untold tale is of less interest. When the shiny paper has been unwrapped, it will be found to contain an old chestnut. Often the supposed revelation constitutes branding, a definition of self. *See me this way*.

Responding is delicate. The patient demands congratulations for his new openness. The therapist wants to appear neither dismissive nor credulous.

The Great Man began, Earlier tonight, trying to sleep, I thought about my father.

The introduction sounded conventional, even poetic (Last night I dreamt I went to Manderley again), but the Great Man was not capable of sustaining that sort of presentation. He detoured, boasting of his brilliance, taking swipes at perceived enemies. He was no stranger to racist tropes. He revisited old themes—his achievements and the efforts, by the intelligentsia, to withhold credit. The narrative I will present contains only the through line.

You don't, Goldberg, since you're too pure to follow the news, but everyone else knows that my father made his money in the ski industry. Not the immense fortune. That took my boldness. But he started us off, and skiing was his game.

He came to it in middle age. He was an athlete. He took mountains top to bottom, fast, in all conditions—ice, whiteout, pouring rain. In those days, the knees were held tight together—true parallel carving, lots of jump turns. We're talking the old skis, straight planks, in the days before trails were groomed for duffers.

When he looked at mountains, Dad saw opportunity. But he wondered, would others love what he did? As part of his market research, he brought me to the slopes.

I'm maybe six years old, and he takes me to Behemoth. Enormous mountain. First lift only takes you halfway up, to a plateau. I make my way off the chair—my father was never one to give instructions—he knows I'm a natural—and I look across the valley to the hills beyond and I gasp. It's not fear. I'm overwhelmed at the scale of the Rockies—the scale of the world we live in.

You sniffle now, my father says, you'll be bawling in a moment.

He hustles me onto the second lift, the one to the top. A doughnut-shaped cloud is stuck on the peak. We enter it, and the visible world becomes cozy, just Dad and me. But I know what lies below—know how tiny we are on the immense slope.

We slide from the lift. We pull away on a traverse and then turn to point our skis down the hill.

Go, he orders me.

He disappears into the mist. What the hell, I figure. I follow. I master the sport on the spot. I cruise through whiteout. Because I can ski at age six, my father imagines that others—adults—will pick up the sport readily, and so he starts to invest.

Write that down, the Great Man said. No one knows the role I played in starting the family on the road to fortune.

The Great Man gave me a proud look. I was meant to admire him.

THE GREAT MAN HAD INTRODUCED the anecdote with a promise of new levels of intimacy, but the gist was tediously predictable. He was even more self-made than previously reported.

There was a poignant touch: the child's sense of smallness in the vast world. The telling contained gifts for me, more hints of a capacity for self-awareness.

Still, the main thrust made no sense. If the kid was a natural, why would his skiing well encourage the father? But then, who would set a klutz on the top of a mountain and say, *Good luck, son! You're on your own*?

I have said that outside knowledge is unavoidable. Because of my own experiences on the slopes, I had read about ski instruction. In the 1950s, the industry was hampered by the sport's difficulty. Innovation was needed. The graduated length method. Standardization of teaching. And then engineering. Snowmaking. Better grooming. Safer lifts. More comfortable boots. Skis that were easier to decamber. It would take years of technical development to make alpine skiing popular and profitable. The Aldo Company's early difficulties were legendary.

Aldo got into the business at the wrong time, teetered near bankruptcy, and finally cheated his way into solvency—stealing from partners, stiffing contractors, lying on loan applications, and paying off state regulators. When the Great Man entered politics, hadn't he needed to explain away his father's misdeeds?

Náomi's head's-up was proving burdensome. It caused me to reimagine the skiing anecdote in a way that gave it a somber cast. The father considered his younger son unathletic. A nanny's ruse had helped him ski well enough. The unexpected pace of the boy's progress caused his father to enter the business mistakenly, after which Aldo was desperate at work and bitter at home for the whole of the Great Man's childhood. By cruising down some slope—if not at Behemoth, then elsewhere, and if not at age six, then later—the Great Man had turned the father against him and so given rise to his own bad character.

I thought of Hitler, the passage that Mimi had me read, about the near miss—for history—when young Adolf hesitated at the art school threshold. If Lotty had not provided secret lessons, the Great Man would not have inadvertently nudged his father into risky investments. The father would not have resented the son. Krishna would not have grown up feeling rejected. Untold thousands of plague victims would have been spared. Our democracy would have limped along.

Unable to listen innocently, I said, You shaped your family's business life.

And then, No one appreciates how much.

My unease must have worked in the therapy's favor, because the Great Man took another shot at self-revelation.

He had been testing me, to see how I would respond. Good for me—I had known that there was more to tell.

He began again.

Another day: we're in whiteout. My father puts me on a narrow run, a steep couloir banked by large trees. He knows I'm a prodigy.

Go ahead, he says.

I'm facing straight down, seeing ice, stiff with cold, uncertain what's below.

I hesitate.

Here's the thing about my dad. For him, there's no such thing as impossible.

Super dad. You can see where I get my character from.

He gives me a shove and skis past.

I'm sliding. My edges won't grip. I'm hurtling down the trail.

I know that my dad has faith in me. I figure I'll be fine.

The Great Man has my attention. I'm horrified.

I get the feel of it, I can tell you that, he says. I see the point of skiing—speed and weightlessness. I might have made it down if I hadn't clipped a tree with my arm.

I'm on my back but still sliding, trying to brake with the skis. Bushes catch me. My face is scratched up.

I'm in pain. I know the arm is broken.

Luckily, a ski patroller with a walkie-talkie is testing out the trail. He finds it too icy. Before deciding to shut it, he takes a few more turns. He finds me and calls for rescue. A team arrives with a sled and warming blankets. Even the pros have trouble making their way down.

There's no on-mountain infirmary, but the resort lets a nurse ski for free so long as she monitors emergencies on her walkie-talkie. She meets us at the lodge.

It turns out not to be a full break, more what you call a greenstick. You learned about those in med school, Doc, greenstick fractures in children? I'll never forget that word.

The Great Man gets stuck on it. *Greenstick.*

In front of the nurse, my father acts the concerned parent. I know to play along.

*I should never have wandered off. I should have known my limits.*

Later, when we're alone, my father says, Next time, don't hesitate.

I never have since. My father made me who I am. He knew how to build a champion.

I have given this story more coherence than it had in the boudoir, but the core events are there. An adult sends a child down a narrow, steep, and icy trail alone and avoids blame for the injury that follows. The vignette contained internal tension. The Great Man had put his father's flaws on display without acknowledging them.

The two memories represented separate events—two instances of the child's being left to fend for himself.

Of the second story, I was hearing an early, sanitized version.

In later tellings, I imagined, the father would be enraged at his son's slow progress on the slopes. The injury would be severe—no greenstick, a compound fracture—and the parental behavior would be yet more egregious.

Late for an illicit rendezvous, Aldo had sped off and left his kid in the lurch. Ski rescue could not find the father on the mountain. He beat the child for embarrassing him—and for needing protection and instruction and encouragement and whatever else children do need when acquiring skills. In the hospital, Aldo made a play for the nurse—felt her up in the room when his son was supposedly asleep. Or more and worse.

It wasn't just that the Great Man had to lie a few times before approaching the truth. Truth made him uneasy. Truth was barely a category for him. Perhaps this traumatic episode was partly responsible. The father had demanded that he deny reality, that he recall events in complicit ways.

Had Náomi's interference hurt or helped my ability to listen? Hard to say.

The damning portrait of the father was implicit in the Great Man's ostensibly heroic tale. Speaking in code, he had let me know that he had suffered from bad—destructive—parenting.

I said, Some story!

I did a fantastic job, didn't I, Doc? You're stingy with the compliments, but I see it on your face.

The Great Man was pleased with himself. He had taken a step toward self-examination. Few would have thought him capable.

If this session had occurred in a normal psychotherapy, he would have prepared to leave my office. As he did, I would have warned him that early exploration can prove unsettling. At our next meeting, he would have a chance to share responses to his own effort—and so on. But my patient was going nowhere, except to sleep.

We're done, he said.

The Great Man plumped his pillows. He yawned. He snored.

◊ ◊ ◊ ◊ ◊

Taking my dismissal as absolute, I bypassed the Goldberg lounger and headed for my tiny bedroom.

From behind me, I heard sobs.

Náomi was closer than usual, down the hall, grasping a railing. I approached and found her wearing a shorty robe. Her right leg looked strange. I saw reddish-purple marks and a raised area, as if she had been taken a bad spill or been beaten just above the knee.

Hearing my footfall, Náomi turned. She gave a forbidding look. I was to let her be.

Was she drunk? Her eyes were unfocused. Her gestures were overly broad.

She shook her head and swept the air with her arms. As she did, the robe opened slightly, and I saw bruising on her right breast as well.

She shooed me away. Once more, I accepted dismissal.

I WOKE THE NEXT MORNING to sirens and alarms. A fist banged on the door. A basso voice shouted, *Code Scarlet*, *Code Scarlet.* I rushed to the corridor outside the sleeping quarters, but my Paul Revere had moved on. I was none the wiser about the emergency or my proper response.

Opting for upward interpretation, I took the alarm as a call to exit the building.

We had entered an Indian Summer. Even so, I dressed as warmly as the wardrobe allowed—an old man's habit. I grabbed the Ezra phone, in case I should be needed, and my tablet, in case I would have time to review patient notes. I pushed open an alarmed door.

I had glimpsed the scenery through windows at odd hours, but how much better it was to be in it. What is that Iris Murdoch quote, about how flowers would make us mad with joy if we were seeing them for the first time? Birds, too, and trees and mountains and mountain paths. I had been starved for nature.

I squinted at the fortress roof to see whether snipers were in position. Spotting none, I ventured across a small lawn to a point where the forest verged on the circuit road. An ill-tended path brought me up a rise to a broad-trunked beech girdled by a curving bench, one of those features in nature that the old hotel must have built for guests.

In the near distance, up the hill, I made out what looked to be the remnants of a small cemetery fallen into disarray. Had there once been a village nearby? Perhaps the hotel complex had been built on its ruins.

The rest of the park, if park it was, had been neglected for years. Even with some leaves fallen, the undergrowth, trees, and vines obscured what had once been a scenic vista. On the plus side, I was screened from the ugly fortress.

To the west, where the ground dropped off steeply, spotty distant views remained. We were in hawk country. Seeing great birds in their freedom made me realize that I had been in prison, more or less in prison since I had left home.

I wondered whether a walk up the hill would open out the view. Before I stood to move, a thought struck me. Might I be responsible for the state of high alert? The Great Man had shown his late father in a bad light. Such revelations are often followed by setbacks—worsening paranoia. Presumably, the delusion took the form of a belief that Resistance militias were approaching the fortress.

More plausibly, through spying or intuition the Great Man had gathered that Náomi had taken me aside and filled me in on—something. He had become enraged. He had beaten her. She responded in some way that pushed him over the edge.

Or else, I was the one experiencing paranoia. Náomi had tripped and fallen after taking a glass too many of wine. The Great Man was making progress in treatment. Code Scarlet was a preparedness drill, like a fire alarm.

Looking at distant mountainsides, fretting about my incompetence and my ignorance, I worked at conjuring Miriam, as if a visit from her might settle me. People prone to headaches can sometimes ward them off by relaxing into a pre-hypnotic state. My method for summoning Miriam is similar. I emptied my mind, and shortly I heard footsteps and the rustling of brush.

Wordsworth is right. Leaping is what the heart does—except that in old age, that sensation, the quick errant beat, is accompanied by intimations of one's own impending mortality.

My heart leapt, and then—disappointment. It was Náomi. She was dressed casually, as if for summer, in a colorful loose dress, a muumuu, if that is still a word, but draped from below the collarbone and with large pockets sewn onto the skirt. As if for modesty, she had a light shawl wrapped around her shoulders.

How many men can claim this distinction, that they looked up, saw Náomi approach, and felt disappointment?

*Mr. Weitz, the consultant?*

The twinkle in her eye suggested that she thought that ruse—Bub's having assigned me a pseudonym—gave her leeway. If her husband denied that I was her doctor, wasn't she free to be playful with me?

She said, I imagined I might find you here, in our plot of beechen green and shadows numberless.

The beech leaves had yellowed, but never mind. Náomi has that habit of speech, quoting poems or plays, lightly or conspiratorially, as if she and I held that knowledge in common.

In the fortress, when I had opened the alarmed door, a sensor and a video camera had alerted her security force.

Not pleased to see me? Or is it that you had a draining night? You poor thing—you look half-dead.

It's you who had a draining night, I said.

The muumuu worried me. It covered the bruises.

All better!

Are you?

*Later*, she said.

That one word held me in place.

Doctoring begins with devotion to a patient. But if that patient threatens to kill his boss, we advise the potential target. If a patient contracts HIV, we require him to inform his partners. We have duties to those our patients might injure.

If I let the conversation proceed, Náomi might share the facts of the assault, if there had been one. As my work with her husband progressed, I would determine whether he was violent on the basis of mental illness and whether she was at special risk. If so, I would be obliged to inform her, to advise her to leave or find protection, beyond whatever she relied on already.

In retrospect, I see how crazy that line of thought is. In that evil funhouse of a fortress, everyone felt threatened. But I was set on proceeding there as I would anywhere, assessing my patient indirectly and acting on my conclusions.

When I informed the Great Man that I would speak with his wife, I was imagining this circumstance. I had taken Bub's story about the keyboard lid as preview. Assessing violence the marriage was part of my brief.

Had Náomi anticipated or picked up on this train of thought? It occurred to me that she was aware of the constraints I acted under.

She sat facing me, with her legs tucked under and to the side.

Are we all right here? I asked. What is Code Scarlet?

A boy playing with soldiers, she said. This is the best spot in the domain. I come here often. The cameras can't pick us up. Regularly, I have my techs sweep the park for listening devices. Funny what a girl needs to do to find privacy.

He's intrusive, she said. I can't imagine how you work with the types you work with.

You must get that all the time. *How can you stand it?* You don't just stand it, do you? You revel in my husband's bad tendencies.

What would you have been like if psychotherapy did not exist?

You have a quirky mind, so you say in your books. *An admittedly quirky mind*. You write: *A man is lucky when he finds a profession that employs his quirks productively.*

I understood that my conjuring had succeeded, if in unexpected fashion. Miriam had arrived in the guise of Náomi, or Náomi was channeling Miriam, acknowledging and belittling me.

If we were engaged in a flirtation, I wanted to interrupt it.

I said, Last night, I saw something unsettling.

What happened? I asked.

Náomi began a monologue that might or might not have been meant to address my question.

IF I SAID THAT FAILURE has made my husband a different person, I would be telling a half-truth. He was always self-absorbed. He could always be cruel. But the Great Collapse, as I call it, has made him desperate. He denies that he's caused disaster, but his behavior betrays awareness. He's more erratic.

His claim to genius—atypical genius, madcap genius—was always false, but it was saleable. No longer. He has nothing to sell and no buyers beyond that shrinking band of diehards.

He's a comic who has lost his timing. Everything that he says or does falls flat.

He was boastful-funny, and now he's a pathetic blowhard. He was funny-mean, and now he's simply cruel.

That's why I brought you in, to see what can be done with a grandiose man who stands stripped naked before the world.

It occurred to me that since I could not dismiss Náomi, I should turn the conversation toward her—to have her say how it was to be his wife.

How have you dealt with his downfall?

She said, I prefer to begin at the beginning—to tell you who the Great Man was when we first met.

You know, in silent movies, the mustachioed villain who buys the mortgage in hopes of getting his hands on the farmer's daughter? He played that role. He wooed through coercion.

Náomi told her tale, starting with what is public knowledge.

She had been an aspiring stage actor with a difficult career arc, precocious success, a failure, another, and then a detour to experimental theater. The Great Man saw her in an ingénue role and become infatuated.

He tracked Náomi down at the midtown restaurant where she waitressed. He chatted her up, proposed a rendezvous, and was rebuffed.

He was old and uncouth. She was a young aspiring artist, proud of having cobbled together a college degree.

He boasted of his education in the school of hard knocks.

What hard knocks? she had asked.

He told a tale about skiing. The father sets an unreasonable challenge. The son excels.

Oh, she said. Your father was mean to you.

She had grown up without a father.

The Great Man became obsessed. He hosted parties for producers, arranging for them to extend invitations she could not refuse. He displayed wealth and reach. She was flattered. She was repulsed by his body and his bad character. She was amused.

In her presence, men could not help themselves. Amusement was her default response.

He was the same man then, Náomi said, but also a better man. He was greedy, vain, and possessive, but—despite his age—in a boyish way. She had seen him smile spontaneously, more than once. A smile, not a leer.

He could be almost gracious, too—if not naturally, then with assistance.

When I opened at a small theater, he showed up with one of my former acting teachers. Krishna was paying the guy to list my performance's strong points and feed him observations, to allow him to sound insightful and appreciative. He pulled the presentation off so mechanically that I found him out, but I made note of the effort. It's not one he would make now.

You may hear him signal approval of a fellow despot, but without specificity: *Terrific leader*. Even with coaching, my husband cannot bother to attend to any virtues but his own. When he looks at other people, it's to identify their weaknesses. He can still demean and belittle, although I wonder whether he's as precise as he once was.

I thought of Gretchen's lemon verbena tea and that last meeting with Hans Lutz, how he had retained hints of a therapist's ability to identify affect and reflect it back. What went deep with the Great Man evidently, what might persist were he to become demented, or more severely demented, if he had lost capacity already, was the instinct for the jugular.

Náomi hoped that I might assess the change, the thinning of his personality. Was there an organic basis for the slippage? Something major, anatomical, neurological?

Skiing, he fell often. Had he sustained concussions?

Perhaps the plague had changed him. He had scorned it, as if it were an upstart opponent. As if to bait or challenge the disease, he had exposed himself repeatedly. Had the infection affected his brain and mind?

Perhaps what she was seeing was only increased rigidity in old age.

Náomi was being helpful and also demanding. She wanted what the public was said to want, a clear diagnosis by a psychiatrist.

We were speaking of you, I said.

She said that she was defining herself. She would never have accepted the Great Man as he is now.

As it was, she had made a show of resistance, but declining his offer had never been in the cards.

Náomi's stepfather had been a compulsive gambler. When he died, he had left debts on a scale that was hard to fathom. Collectors sent the mother ultimatums. Huge men showed up at the house, men who might do anything.

They said, If we visit again, there will be no conversation. We will smash your right hand in the door.

Náomi had been threatened, and her young stepsister. *We ruin people's faces.*

How the Great Man knew what was at stake emerged only later. He had hired detectives to find a means of exerting pressure on Náomi. They discovered the mess left by the stepfather. The men who held his IOUs were themselves in debt. The Great Man bought up both sets of paper and put the lenders' feet to the fire. He demanded that the lenders send enforcers. Then, the Great Man had stepped in, seemingly in kindly fashion.

Why would Náomi choose continued danger when she could have a life of plenty, in the company of a man of talent and accomplishment?

He approached the mother. Could she make her daughter see reason?

In Náomi's presence, most men felt inadequate. Bargaining dominated their courtship. They offered luxury. They offered artistic genius. They did foolish things.

She had put the Great Man's deal-making in this category. It was so ludicrous as to be forgivable.

He was saving the family. Might she not be grateful?

The prenup was stingy, though. Only so long as the marriage lasted could she keep her mother afloat. The document anticipated that Náomi would want to flee.

It was at the wedding reception that she learned that her husband had created the crisis that he had pretended resolve. A loan shark said, *I can't believe you fell for that con artist.* The moneylenders, when they held the stepdad's chits, had made do without strong-arm tactics. Once the Great Man gained leverage, he made the debt collectors send goons.

The Great Man had specified the tactics. He liked threats that had specificity.

Say you'll crush her right hand. Or show how you'll break a finger.

He had a thing for fingers. A huge man grasping a finger is convincing. Anyone can imagine the quick snap.

By the time the top tier of wedding cake was boxed for freezing, I had a new understanding of my husband, Náomi said. I had thoughts about what I might and might not do. But first I had to control my nausea.

On the wedding night, when the Great Man approached her, she vomited.

She apologized. She'd had too much to drink. She locked herself in the bathroom.

On the honeymoon, she was fine on the beach. At table, over dinner, she did her new husband proud. But in the bedroom, when he approached, she felt sick again.

He insisted that she see a gastroenterologist. The doctor diagnosed sexual bulimia.

Is it really a thing? Náomi asked me. Sex-induced bulimia?

A butterfly—small, orange, with black spots—fluttered near Náomi's right shoulder and alighted on the muumuu's neckline. The resulting image was cartoonish—like Snow White and the bluebird.

I had treated a man who suffered tinnitus when his wife approached.

Some wives are allergic to their husbands' sperm.

Bub developed a tin ear for his pianist-wife's music—at least, he did in the story he told.

Marriage can have strange effects, I said.

You're a man of words, Náomi said. In his presence, my mind said *putrefaction*.

Imagine being thrown in bed with a rotting corpse.

In the City, Náomi said, there's an expert for everything. I was referred to the sexual bulimia guru.

The Great Man demanded that I go, but he did not want me seen entering the clinic. He made me wear wigs. A limo with smoked-glass windows delivered me via the parking garage. The service elevator took me to the guru's back door.

The guru was a fussy man with a long, narrow nose and thinning razor-cut hair. He dressed in a cashmere blue blazer, flannel slacks, and loafers with colorful socks. You may know him, another doctor-writer. He had a superior manner, as if my problems amused him.

I supposed that he mostly saw blushing brides who were astonished and embarrassed by their incapacity. They loved their husbands! He would explain about the powers of the unconscious mind and ask the delicate women to share childhood memories. Had they, at too young an age, seen their parents in action?

My predicament was different. I was no virgin. I found sex appealing.

I had no objection to the hypothesis that unconscious thoughts triggered my nausea. The vomiting arose spontaneously. But I had clear, conscious reasons for finding my husband offensive. He was a *senex amans*, the foolish old lecher common in theater since the days of ancient Rome. He had made himself out as my and my mother's savior when he had been our tormentor.

No one likes the teenager who holds a child out the window, pulls him back in, and cries, *Saved your life!* But at least there, the endangerment is out in the open. That's what makes the sequence a joke. Saving someone from a threat you create is a funny kind of heroism, not one we admire.

The Great Man wanted it all. Sadistic pleasure up front and credit and rewards after.

If the therapy made me aware of some other, unconscious, cause for disgust, one that would lose its effect once named—wouldn't my gorge still rise when my husband approached?

I asked the guru, What is the goal of the therapy? To extinguish the symptom?

Nausea protected me. I did not wish to have sex with my husband—did not wish for him to *take* me or *have* me. If stomach acid was going to etch my tooth enamel, I wanted protection. But you only need to barf on your husband a few times to keep him at bay. As a turn-off, a little odor of vomit in the mouth goes a long way.

Krishna only pretends to have high testosterone. Sex mattered less to him than possession and display. He wanted me on his arm.

I showed up for sessions, to maintain the impression of my *working on the marriage*. I was open to self-exploration—as open as the next young woman who grew up caring about the arts. Psychotherapy was self-improvement.

But if the guru was going to relieve me of sexual bulimia, he had better, teach me how else to ward off Krishna. A successful treatment—do you agree?—would have been one that put the nausea under conscious control, so that I could hurl at will. In the meanwhile, spontaneous barfing had the advantage of surprise and authenticity. What I offered my husband came from the heart as much as the gut.

I still had heard nothing about the night before, in the fortress—physical violence, yea or nay. Náomi was circling around the topic.

Did she treat our conversation like psychotherapy? She ventured back into an account of her girlhood.

Twice, she said, I was abused. Only a woman abused in childhood would tolerate Krishna.

After two unpleasant incidents with men in my pre-teen years, I turned chubby. The extra pounds conferred protection. I had two quiet years—a blessing. Any stability I have managed in adulthood dates to that respite. Then, my legs lengthened, and my figure declared itself. Men seemed to fear me, to stand in awe.

They gazed and then offered what they hoped would appeal. Often, they resorted to begging.

These appeals did not repel me. I took the social world as it was. I would be desired. To insist otherwise would have been disingenuous.

I have mentioned my talent for tolerance. Only rarely am I put off by men's superficially unattractive aspects, their age and appearance and level of desperation. Krishna's beer gut and pomposity amused me. Even his buffoonish lasciviousness, his playing at masculinity, was not off-putting.

With the talent came a limitation. I am not inclined to excitation. My tastes are ecumenical but muted. Perhaps complaisance is a word I am looking for.

Bullying is different from begging. Anyway, the nausea began on the wedding night. It recurred in response to any sexual approach by my husband. Lately, it has generalized. When I think of what he has done to us all, I retch.

◊ ◊ ◊ ◊ ◊

I told myself that the review served the therapy. I understood better why the Great Man was frustrated in the marriage. But what would progress look like? His ending the violence, if indeed he had beaten his wife. But did I hope that she would reconcile with him?

You must be wondering, Náomi said, why I stayed married. Money played a role. When it comes to Krishna, intimacy is always intertwined with money.

My stepfather's debt had not vanished. Krishna paid it off slowly and partially. My mother and sister might still be put out of their home. I wanted to set them up in comfort.

I had a wish to make something of my life—to be of use. I was convinced that my husband was a man of destiny. He was already moving beyond the ski industry to participation in civic life. I imagined him as Mayor or as an influencer, a backer of politicians, a businessman-advisor.

My marriage, my maintaining it, had an element of altruism. I might do good through him, or prevent evil.

I saw my husband as ruthless and conniving, but I did not foresee his wanton destructiveness.

I imagined his gaining political influence, working in the public interest, and enjoying acclaim. He had a weakness for me. I hoped to guide or restrain him. I failed. I failed repeatedly. I'm failing now.

I am misrepresenting what I foresaw. I knew what he was.

I was like one of those science-fiction characters who gets a premonition of a horrific scenario and sets out to avert it. Sadly, we're still in the part of the story where she falls short and the terrifying plot continues to unfold. That's the drama I've pulled you into.

NÁOMI WONDERED WHEN SHE HAD become complicit.

The Great Man valued her as part of his public image, as a marker of his virility and overall worth. Seemingly, he could attract and satisfy this woman.

After he had entered the political arena, she had begun bargaining with him—appearances in exchange for concessions. He would promise to pull back from a depraved policy position. She would stand beside him.

She achieved few successes. No one could match him for breaking promises.

The Great Man relied on her implicit support when he wanted to appear to champion women's issues—before making an outrageous move that degraded civil liberties in general. She was most ashamed of that sequence.

Any promise to defend freedoms was a prelude to eliminating them.

Should she give up? Each time she had resolved to jump ship, his career had advanced, and then it had seemed wrong—immoral—to leave, if there was any chance of reining him in.

Nothing worked? I asked.

She named minor accomplishments. When he deregulated of the use of methane, she had gotten him to insert a minor exception.

I was not taking notes.

What I recall was the dance they led each other on.

Public appearances were not the only token of exchange. The Great Man promised to act better in the public sphere if Náomi would provide sexual access.

She was embarrassed to admit that she had, up to a point.

She said, He has been celibate in the years of the marriage—celibate if, as others have suggested, *having sex* refers to vaginal intercourse. Intromission is not in his repertory. He has a fear of the vagina, a fear of entering it, a deep disgust that is, in its way, a counterpart to my bulimia.

He's focused on cleanliness, worried about what he calls *contamination*. Strange in a man who courts viral infection. But for him, sex is its own category.

He has a horror of contaminating me as well. It's as if he were aware of what I sense, the putrefaction. He considers himself dirty—unless that admission is a cover for his real concern: he can't face the shame of wilting.

I wondered what use I would make of this information or assertion. When the Great Man boasted of his sexual exploits, I would listen for deep self-disgust. But I doubted that the Great Man wanted me to know that he was flaccid.

Speaking of her husband now, Náomi said, He has his houris. Has he spoken of them?

Beelzebub provides young women—girls, really, undocumented girls, girls whose parents he can threaten. Daughters of kitchen and cleaning staff, big girls by preference, full-breasted and slightly overweight. Bub promises to return the girls virgo intacta.

Stop, please, I said.

The Great Man uses them to reenact the Lotty drama.

First, he asks them to shower. While they scrub themselves, he opens the bathroom door, peeks, and tries to arouse himself. When they notice, he crawls in and grasps their ankles—with the water still running—and begs.

They are to deny him and at last relent. They turn off the water, lift him to themselves, and let him lick their wet body. At last, they are to wrap themselves in a towel and take him to bed where they will lie beside him and pet his slack member while he bawls and sniffles.

PLEASE EXCUSE THAT FAILED PASSAGE. I have tried to enter a trance and transform Náomi's account. I lack the imagination.

Perhaps it's that I've had too much imagining done for me. So many patients are eager to confess! My own shortcomings extend to the conduct of the therapy. Accounts of kinky sex rarely fascinate me. Too fast, I turn to affect: *You are ashamed.*

Some are, and some aren't, but all offer details. The result, for me, is a burdensome mental library stocked with minidramas built around passivity, aggression, and basic bodily functions.

About the Great Man: say only that Náomi depicted a performance built around symbolic humiliations, one that may have left mental scars on any women he recruited to participate.

NÁOMI SAID, I THINK OF the women whose lives he ruined, women denied abortions, women shot by gun-toting husbands, immigrant women separated from their infant children, women dead of plague.

What can it matter if he blights a few lives more? And yet, I cannot bear to see them, the poor, dear houris.

Hearing Náomi catalogue the broad harm and then focus on individual instances of suffering, it seemed to me again that she was channeling Miriam.

AT THIS POINT, NÁOMI BEGAN describing her husband's pleas to her. The list of requested acts was long. Náomi can reproduce it in her own memoir, if ever she writes one. I did not take the inventory at face value. Náomi was out to shock. My fictive powers are no match for Náomi's—hers or the Great Man's, if it was he who had suggested the entertainments.

Now and then, Náomi would accede to one of her husband's demands. She allowed him to look at her, nude, and fantasize. He could grovel. He insisted on groveling. He was set on self-abasement. He got on his vast belly and slithered toward her, pleading for a taste or a feel.

Náomi added, He has the floor scrubbed in advance, and then he rolls out a special mat that only he touches, a red carpet for groveling.

He loved the sight of Náomi. Looking kept him living in hope.

Perhaps he preferred unconsummated desire.

The Great Man and Náomi came to an accommodation. He gazed. She withheld. He had to offer a small concession before she let him gaze.

◊ ◊ ◊ ◊ ◊

We seemed done for the day, almost done, because Náomi stood and stepped away from me.

She lifted the back of the muumuu, as if to pull the whole over her shoulders.

No! I said.

I understood the impulse, to punish her husband by giving me freely what he received only through bargaining. I could not be a party to that betrayal.

It's this strap, she said. It's cutting into my shoulder.

You are a good man, she said.

From under the dress, she managed to remove her bra. Had the bruises made the bra uncomfortable?

Náomi stuffed it into a pocket and re-draped her scarf.

I did not understand what had just happened. The thought that she might have undressed before me—was it my fantasy only? If not, perhaps the intent was to expose the bruising.

Náomi had my attention, but then, hadn't she, all along?

Of late, Náomi said, something has changed.

Music to a therapist's ears. What changed, and when, and why then?

I hoped to learn what caused the bruising, but Náomi had a prior tale to tell.

For many years, my nausea remained stable. It was in good enough control that it permitted displays of the sort—the sort that you feared I was offering you.

One day, lately, I found that it was all beyond me—or behind me, in my past. I am an actor by training, capable of feigning passion with distasteful fellow actors. I lost that ability. I could no longer perform.

When I looked at my husband, I saw corpses.

Sometimes, I retched until I had to be medicated with drugs ordinarily given for psychosis. Once my stomach had been calmed, the weeping began.

My time here on earth had been for naught and less than naught.

I had developed an inner prohibition against parading before my husband. It had the force of a religious edict in a harsh sect. *Thou must not.* If I satisfied Krishna's lust, I would be smitten with boils or I would puke until the lining of my esophagus gave way.

I cut off his opportunities for self-abasement.

To say why I arranged to have you summoned even knowing that Beelzebub would be the instrument: I could no longer play my modest role, could no longer bear to do what was needed to contain my husband.

And the bruises? I asked.

She brushed aside the change of topic.

She said, A story for another day.

She was Scheherazade, leaving every tale half-told.

Our interview was over.

I ASKED MYSELF, WHAT, IN this encounter, had been of use for my patient?

Náomi had familiarized me with her husband's sexual leanings and limitations. How Freud would have loved to investigate them! For classical psychoanalysis, fear of the vagina, or disgust with it, is a gold mine. Similarly for scoptophilia and obsessions with urine or feces.

Modern psychotherapy—anyway, the one I practice—is not overly focused on the sources of perversion, not optimistic about locating them, not entirely happy with perversion as a category. Nor do therapists have much investment in traditional notions of masculinity—doing in preference to watching, dominance in preference to submission. But I suspected that the Great Man judged himself for his leanings. If he was curious about how he arrived at his preferences, I would help him explore.

Although sex is a delicate topic, often it is a manageable one. People consider their sexual selves to be off to the side. For the Great Man in particular: how much easier to think about, say, golden rain—the embarrassment associated with that form of arousal—than his failures as a leader. Perversion might provide a starting point for learning about shame and how to bear or mitigate it. When it came to the form of his desires, it was at least possible that I could be more on the Great Man's side than he was.

As against this opportunity, there was the burden of specific harm. I did not take Náomi's testimony at face value, but I did not dismiss it either. If the Great Man was importing young women, he would need to stop. And if he was beating Náomi....

I had never walked away from a patient because of past criminal, immoral, or violent behavior. But then, my patients had tended to listen to me or to one another.

In the fortress, what would walking away mean?

◊ ◊ ◊ ◊ ◊

Ginnie arrived at dawn today. Through the kitchen window, she had seen me pottering about. She brought eggs warm from the hens.

I have only a minute, she said.

She was meant to be at the coops, and that task took only so long.

All the same, she lingered, as if she had something to say. I thought of Chet and his hesitancy. I was about to invite Ginnie to sit when she reddened, turned, and fled.

Taking a second look at the basket, I saw that she had included a purple scallion and, bless her, a perfect egg-like potato. How considerate! The blog posts had gone up and, somewhere, she had read them, read how I had taken comfort in these shapes, and so she provided more. The delivery suggests that I have Ginnie's permission, implicit permission, to continue to say how things are for me, out in the woods. Or else the small composition suggests a breakfast or luncheon dish, a country omelet, along the lines of Maury's bachelor egg scramble. That thought seems kindly too.

◊ ◊ ◊ ◊ ◊

In the evening that followed my encounter with Náomi, my summons to the anteroom came early. I headed to the Goldberg perch with a bounce in my step. I had spent time out of doors. I had made indirect contact with Miriam. I had settled on a promising topic to listen for in session, although it occurred to me that another subject remained unexplored: except for implausible boasts, the Great Man had not discussed what he claimed to value most, his public career.

When a patient avoids a topic, we are bound to wonder about resistance. Freud treated resistance like an x-mark on a treasure map: dig here. But I had worked with mob-connected patients without pressing them about *business*. They discussed friendships and parenting and romantic relationships. Once my patients trusted me, they began telling scary stories. We had made progress all along. It wasn't as if the therapy stood still until job concerns emerged.

Two topics, then: love and work. I was prepared for either.

WOULD THE GREAT MAN HAVE gone easier on me if he had found me rattled? He seemed intent on belittling me. At the bedside, the small chair had been replaced by a stool, perhaps moved to the boudoir from the Retreat. He motioned me to it. He was talking on the phone, handset to ear, while eating chicken tacos from a plate balanced on his thighs.

Nobody, he said to the caller. A nonentity. A Peruv. No worries.

He had arranged for me to enter while he was on a political call, to signal how slight his regard was for me.

Believe me, no one will hear from anyone.

You hear nothing, right, Einstein?

If Einstein here spills the beans, it means we're long dead anyway.

Besides, if they think we control the machines, it'll make them stay home. The machines—the ballot boxes!

He wiped his fingers and mouth on the sheets.

You *can't* go overboard. The more lopsided the result, the more we discourage the opposition.

You know what I love about false voting totals? The despair they induce. The soft-hearted goo-goos! They are so certain—and then...nothing. *They* trust in process. *They* vow to support laws, rules, customs.

Ha, ha, ha.

The Great Man did not laugh. He repeated the syllable, *ha*, to indicate that he was enjoying himself at his opponents' expense.

You made that point. A close contest to spark interest. You say, We make it exciting in the lead-up, and then we dash their hopes.

They're on the march with grenade launchers. We don't want interest. We don't want hopes.

Nah, not 60/40. What does 60/40 mean? No one understands 60/40. Crush 'em. When the results are reported, I want to hear a *crushing* sound.

I have my consultant here, Albert Einstein. Albert, what say you? We've dismissed a raft of legislators. Terrible charges against them. Embezzlement, treason. Bad people. We put together a nice package of indictments. Terrific replacements coming in. We're about to elect them.

Elect had air quotes around it.

Einstein, what's best for our followers' morale, a squeaker or a crushing blow?

Hate the sound of *squeak*. Love *crush*.

Einstein here is mute. Not a political genius, our genius.

We get all the votes, we destroy the thought of fraudulence. The show of power means it's dangerous for anyone to *think* fraudulence.

He ended the call but continued the monologue.

If they want to come after us, let it be with guns. Love to have it out with firepower. Getting ready to give the word. Getting ready to mow down the boo-birds.

Crush 'em at the ballot box, crush 'em on the ground.

All coming soon. Blood in the fields, blood in the streets. Mutilated bodies. Piles of them. Make the plague look like a picnic.

Whether or not there really were militia on the move, it was a frightful image. When he saw me startle, the Great Man doubled down.

Best thing that ever happened to this country—the plague. Thinned out the weaklings. Thinned out the doctors and nurses. Nothing worse than a weakling doctor.

Can't count on numbers. Anybody can make up numbers. I make up numbers.

If I have trouble presenting the content of the Great Man's monologue, it is partly because as a therapist I found him hard to listen to. In my reconstruction, the tirade progresses from voting fraud to crushing the opposition to massacre. The train of thought was never that linear. You need to imagine a sprinkling of references to the Chinese, liberals, minorities, experts, journalists, immigrants, and other enemies. The asides were at once stereotyped and illogical.

Rather than succumb to the confusion, I listened for a theme. He was putting his barbarism on display.

From the soup of words, I picked a single one: *crush*.

Crushing, I said, appeals to you.

Answering in action, he crushed a chicken taco and tossed it past me. When I ducked, he caught the back of my sweater and wiped his hands on it.

I'm thinking that you may be a fraud, Goldberg. I didn't sleep last night. I dozed, but I woke tired. I called for you this morning. I wanted to ask you to explain your failure. You were nowhere to be found.

He gave a cruel smile, like a cartoon cat who has cornered a mouse.

◊ ◊ ◊ ◊ ◊

I understood that smile.

The Great Man believed that I had spent time with his wife. We had betrayed him.

Monitors in the lair may have picked up any number of details: the door alarm signaling my exit, the briefing for Náomi by her staff, her subsequent quick departure. The Regime was famously incompetent when it came to important matters, but the Great Man's local obsessions were a different matter. Junior spooks intent on advancement would have been assiduous at gathering and assembling clues.

A sharp-eyed underling might have reported, She left with her bra on. When she returned, its strap was hanging out of the floppy pocket of her shift.

If the intelligence reports flowed through Bub, might he not have acted as Iago to the Great Man's Othello? *The brassiere, my lord!* Bub might well have had his eye on Náomi with a view to diminishing her influence.

Were my thoughts paranoid? In a sense, therapists are more paranoid yet. We believe that, within marriage, most secrets simply become known.

I AM THINKING OF A sequence that plays out frequently.

A husband—my patient—begins an extra-marital affair. His wife turns quarrelsome. He feels justified in his infidelity. See what I have to put up with!

But what if the wife's annoyance arises from insecurity? The husband has become inattentive. She feels abandoned. The husband decides to leave the wife because she is petulant, but the irritability arises from her near-awareness of the betrayal. He may make a choice that he later regrets.

Why assume that the Great Man did not know Náomi? I thought it best to understand his bluster as a resulting from spousal injury. He experienced the marriage as hurtful.

I said, You are disappointed.

You were not at your post, he said. Perhaps you need time to yourself.

The sentence came from out of the blue, as did the idea that the Great Man would consider another person's needs.

Do you need time to yourself? he asked.

It was a threat.

I ventured, You have thoughts about how I spend my time.

You will come to know my thoughts, the Great Man said. Spare yourself worry on that front. I express my thoughts through action.

When we first met, he said, you asked whether I had my own explanation for my insomnia.

Since you seem to have no notion, I will guide you. I am a sexually driven man. My testosterone level is sky-high.

I'm also a loyal man. Loyal and patient.

I could get sex anywhere. Even here, in the wilderness, when I go out for a walk, women throw themselves in my path. In the lair, in meetings, aides proposition me—female aides.

I ignore them. It's all about my wife, and she won't satisfy me. Won't or can't.

She's smitten with me. Always has been. She's all over me. A little too close.

Gratitude has something to do with it. When we first met, she was in trouble, she and her mother and sister.

I got them out of a jam. She can't thank me enough. Very, very grateful. Can't say enough about me. My most ardent admirer, our Naomi. If you've met her, you know. First thing she says in any conversation, how she thinks the world of me.

You'll put that in your book, the one you'll never write. How the Great Man is beloved by a devoted wife.

You're waiting to hear the problem. I see that you are. Best thing about you, Goldberg—your patience. Best and worst thing. You could move the conversation along. Pitch in.

He tossed another half-eaten taco past me. He might be subject, I thought, to concreteness when it came to words. When he said *pitch*, he threw something, just as when he spoke of *crushing* adversaries he had crushed food in his hand.

Here's the gist. She won't have sex with me. Won't fuck.

Don't give me that questioning look, Steinberg. I'm talking pussy. May need a little estrogen locally—you know what I'm saying. *In the area.*

He used a Yiddish accent, as if *in the area* were an element of a joke. It may well have been, because that joke, if there was one, made him think of another.

You know that old line, the Great Man asked, Suck! Suck! Suck! Doesn't anyone fuck around here?

Famous joke, the Great Man said, as if I were a moron not to know it.

Wants to cuddle with me, snuggle up, offer me a chance to see and feel that magnificent body. She loves to watch my member rise—enormous member—mesmerizes her. But when I'm aroused, all she'll do is suck. She's addicted. Can't swallow enough.

But she won't open up for me. Says I'm too big. She gets overwhelmed.

Houris! You've heard of them, genius? The wife recruits local talent, country lasses, for threesomes. Her preference, not mine.

Very dicey. Would be bad if the news got out, about my wife and houris.

No need to involve houris, the Great Man said. I'd settle for my wife as she once was. Missionary style would do. She's an actress, sure, but I don't need play-acting. Really not.

When we were doing it regularly, she was always happy. I satisfy women quickly. Many orgasms for her every night—many, many. A workout for me, I can tell you. Ha. Ha. Never mind your sessions. I slept well after sessions with Naomi.

The Great Man continued in this vein—feats accomplished in the marital bed. By his account Náomi was loose, submissive, erratic, and neurotic, but also inexplicably withholding. He was potent, attractive, desirable, and ill-used.

I gathered that the Great Man did not think that Náomi and I had engaged in intercourse, no matter the suspicions that Bub (I was imagining) had tried to implant. The Great Man won every competition. It followed that whatever I had been offered was less than what he claimed for himself. But I was being warned off. You worm! You dare to think about my wife! I do this and that with her. I can do more and worse!

The Great Man was also trying to create a new reality. I had been in or near the boudoir for nights. I had heard the Great Man's snores. I knew perfectly well, and he knew that I knew, that nothing sexual had gone on between him and his wife, not on my watch.

The list of sexual exploits contained a schoolboy taunt. Whom would I believe? The Great Man, or my lying ears and eyes?

The Great Man was demanding submission. He was also offering me a sample of his relationship to truth in intimate settings. In private, as in public, he fabricated without regard for plausibility.

But he had framed a real concern: his wife rejected him.

He was proposing a hypothesis related to his chief complaint. Because his wife denied him full satisfaction, he did not sleep.

The Great Man was approaching promising topics, albeit through cock-and-bull stories. The explicit message was his grandeur. The unspoken themes were: he felt inadequate. He felt unloved.

◊ ◊ ◊ ◊ ◊

I listened sympathetically. My patient's upset was not unjustified. If he had been a fly on the broad-trunked beech, he would not have liked what he saw. His wife looked sprightly and engaged. She teased me. She shared confidences.

For all that the Great Man boasted about his prowess, it was clear that he got no comfort from his wife. As he complained about her, I saw an upwelling of tears. The Great Man was a lorn creature, abandoned by the woman he loved, betrayed by the doctor he had hoped to rely on.

I thought of Náomi's account of the childhood fiasco with Lotty. She had been caring, she had presented her body to the child, but she had given herself fully only to his father.

In response to my patient's tears, I felt sadness. Mine drew on my private grief, for Miriam. Still, I was united with my patient through fellow feeling.

The Great Man began bawling. When had someone last acknowledged his despair?

In *Must We Be as We Are?*, I write about critical moments in the engagement phase of treatment. For weeks, a patient will be walled off, elusive, seemingly unlikeable, and then, suddenly, the therapist resonates with the patient. The patient experiences that joining, that solidarity.

Despite my missteps, the case had taken a favorable turn—or so I thought.

That was pleasant, the Great Man said, but we've talked enough. Talking does no good.

You need to rethink this treatment.

Your job is to find me sleep, which means getting my wife back on task.

How is your own marriage? the Great Man asked. You're settling, aren't you, with your tubby wife?

A man shouldn't settle. I don't settle. I need what I need.

Attend to my needs, Goldberg.

You're frustrated, I said again, leaving open whether with me or his marriage.

You need time to yourself, the Great Man said. He waved his hands to dismiss me. For the first time, I was permitted to leave the boudoir while he was still awake.

*Look to your own marriage!* the Great Man said as a parting shot.

In the corridor, I was intercepted by a guard I had not seen before. She was an imposing woman, broad-shouldered, with a dark-skinned face whose shape struck me as Slavic. She carried a side arm and taser and wore a uniform of a sort I had seen only rarely in the fortress, olive drab with an ominous lightning bolt logo on the chest and at the shoulder.

Was the reference to fascism intended? In the weeks before she died, Miriam had asked that question about the apparent symbolism in a series of the Great Man's public acts. She believed that the implicit references to fascism were strategic. People feared that those who spoke up would be punished once the Regime turned that corner. The threat was enough to silence objectors.

In the fortress, I guessed that the lightning-bolt security detail was used for internal discipline. Perhaps it reported to Bub. Was he taking me in hand? I had not yet paid the price for seeing him disrespected—by the entry gate guard, by the Great Man.

Sir! the guard with the lightning bolt logo barked as I made to walk past. I was to halt and await instruction.

Weitz!

Not having heard the name often, I failed to snap to.

She gave me a look. *You're not going to be one of those, are you?*

Without pausing to introduce herself, my guard pivoted in military fashion. She led me down a staircase and along a corridor to a wing I did not know existed. When the resort was in business, it may have served housekeeping functions. Sinks lined the hallway and, beside them, metal carts, dusty from lack of use.

My chaperone confiscated my phone, e-tablet, watch, and belt. She opened the door to a cell, half of which had been a utility bathroom. It retained a sink and toilet, along with small black-and-white hexagonal ceramic tiles on the floor. The remaining floor was bare cement. A single cot took up a third of the total square footage. The door had been refitted to lock from the outside.

The room was mostly below grade. High up, a thin horizontal window let through enough light for me to guess that the moon was out. A cloud intervened, and I was alone in the near-dark.

I understood my confinement as punishment. The Great Man was demonstrating his power over me, the power to make me suffer. Uncertainty was part of the cruelty. I did not know the term of my sentence, the structure of my day, or the nature of my company, if I was to have any. Perhaps the Great Man would ignore me altogether. When he spoke of torture, he had used the word oubliette, a chamber in which the prisoner is forgotten.

Best to assume the worst. *Oubliette* is the name that I gave my basement cell.

Immediately, a strange thought came to me. I had asked to come here. When Kareena was faced with deportation, hadn't I pleaded with the universe to let me take her place?

However irrational, the notion of trading places calmed me.

We undervalue irrationality, I believe. It can protect us in hostile settings.

I was not facing the maltreatment that I had imagined for Kareena in exile, but my discomfort was substantial. The cell was cold and damp. In my fingers and toes, arthritis flared. The saggy cot did nothing for my bad back. Thoughts of rodents and roaches kept me from moving the mattress to the floor.

Since sleep did not come, I thought about the psychotherapy. The Great Man and I might be in communication still. The duration of my stay would say something about how upset he was. If my demeanor or behavior was reported to him, I would be conveying a response. I had not previously engaged in a therapy of this sort, in which the patient takes almost full command.

PSYCHOTHERAPY IS ASYMMETRIC. WHEN A patient shares his perspective, I examine it and reflect it back or even inhabit it without revealing my own. Ultimately, both patient and doctor will become known to each other, but inevitably, the patient feels more exposed.

A patient can try to hide by telling tall tales, as the Great Man did, but that choice is revealing, too—showing him to be avoidant or deceitful.

Even the therapist's patience can signal an imbalance of power.

Nor is therapy painless. I had erred through offering the Great Man sympathy that implied awareness of his isolation. My discourtesy had made the shame—failed marriage, no true friends—yet less bearable.

It seemed just that he should impose retribution. I don't doubt that other patients would have exercised this option had it been open to them. Early in treatment, before the method had demonstrated its worth, mightn't one or another of my guys have been tempted to cast me into darkness?

Think how much more careful and courteous therapists would be if ruptures led to punishment. Would that threat be crippling to the treatment? As therapists, we want the freedom to act spontaneously, to take chances, to go astray. But at what risk to our patients?

As for patients' spontaneity: imagine how much easier it would be to reveal shameful truths if whenever the shrink offers an insensitive response, you can throw him in the hoosegow.

Hans Lutz considered therapy, the discipline, to be hardy. It could flourish almost anywhere. In prison, I had worked with men who were motivated to snow me, in hopes of earning a good word from the doc. We'd managed nonetheless to find our way forward. Was a treatment that requires a therapist to walk on eggshells out of the question?

I saw the downside. Solitary confinement is torture. If patients could torture doctors, who would treat sadism, sociopathy, narcissism, paranoia, or impulsivity?

But then, who does now? Only in the depths of the Greater Depression, when doctors entered the ranks of the working poor, had it become easy to find colleagues willing to treat delusional patients.

Foolish questions occurred to me. When doctors go to jail, who manages their remaining caseload? Will doctors bill for time behind bars when it serves the treatment?

If, finally, therapy à la Great Man was impractical, still I was engaged in it and bound to do my best. I took it as a given that he and I were discussing intimacy. He was underscoring his deprivation. If you make me feel lonely, I will make you feel lonely.

Who sends an old man off to sleep in dirty clothes in a clammy basement? Someone who wants to correct an imbalance.

HAD I FAILED TO GIVE the Great Man his due? As a citizen—prior to our first meeting—I had viewed him with alarm. Then he had put my family under threat. In the fortress, I had considered it an accomplishment to overcome my aversion and stay in role as the attentive doctor. But why be proud of achieving a neutral stance? Wouldn't true attunement, seeing the Great Man as he thought he should be seen, require reverence—holding him in awe? He was insatiable, but mightn't I, with some other narcissistic or delusional patient, have moved farther in the desired direction?

Even now, in the damp cell, I felt uplift at being relieved of certain duties. Sleeping here might be difficult, but I was not on call, not required to push myself to stay alert at three AM. I did not need to duck chicken tacos or craft responses to the Great Man's boasting. The level of relief suggested that in my work with him, I had not managed to embrace my role.

I am tempted to add, Or else, I had managed, up to a point.

Can one practice existential psychotherapy that way, *up to a point*?

On the plus side, my patient and I had connected, if briefly, on an emotional level. He had expressed pain that elicited a complementary response from me—awareness of my bereavement. I took my incarceration to be a continuation of that conversation about deprivation. We were in session still.

As is my custom when a patient is silent, I inventoried my own affective state.

I was far from home. I felt strangely at home.

I could not find a comfortable position. I felt deeply comfortable.

Regarding comfort: in my practice, paradoxical responses to catastrophic events were not uncommon.

In the wake of 9/11, two of my depressed patients reported a lightening in mood. In its bleakness, the external world corresponded to their inner world. The human condition was as degraded as they had imagined. They were in tune with circumstance. One patient, a psychologist, used the term *rightness of fit.*

In the plague years, my guys were amused to see their neighbors regulate their behavior in the face of an invisible foe. Welcome to my life! My guys were old hands at social distancing.

In the makeshift dungeon, I had a complementary sensation. I thought of prisons, how overused they were. Black men, drug addicts, protesters, immigrants, and the gravely mentally ill—so many around us found themselves behind bars. I was getting my personal dose, a mild one, of the general disaster.

Is *moral rightness of fit* a concept? Working closely with the Great Man, should I not feel the burdens he imposes on his countrymen? The farts and flung tacos had been unpleasant, but they were also childish and foolish, when the damage he did elsewhere was substantial and serious.

I realized how wrong it would have been to conduct the whole of a therapy without feeling solidarity with the oppressed.

The Great Man had not meant to afford me relief. Even upward interpretation did not allow me to entertain that belief. But he may have intended to put our relationship on a frank footing. He owned his identity. *I subject people to misfortune.*

Surely, I had erred in the treatment. I thought of Náomi's bruises. If the Great Man had caused them and knew that I had seen them, he may well have imagined that I had lost all sympathy. How had I failed to anticipate and counter that impression? In arranging for my incarceration, he was saying, *You hate me? I'll give you reason to hate me!*

The Great Man was forbidding me to know him in any external way, to know, for example, that he had bankrupted the nation. *See me afresh!* was the command. I was to set aside politics—all those years of news—and rely only on his presentation of self and his elaborate lies and, now, this banishment to the oubliette.

I would need to take his cruelty as a given, discount it, and see him as a sufferer.

My imprisonment could serve that end. For the Great Man, the fortress was a prison, one he had been forced into by marauders. Equally, he may have believed that if he ever he left office, he would find himself in prison. There was no way out.

My patient was forcing empathy upon me, making me feel what he felt.

I let the new form of uplift, at finding myself still in dialogue with my patient, displace the initial one, at no longer ducking tossed tacos.

I am made for patient care.

I was confident that I was conducting an ongoing treatment. We would meet face to face again.

Patients subject to paranoia are fragile. I had been fired often. But Hans's method has an addictive quality. In my practice, almost always, patients got past their upset and returned. The sequence, quitting and rejoining, had a cleansing effect. Resentments were set aside. We continued as old friends.

Back when I had paper charts, I kept two sets, active and inactive. Active folders sat in wooden file drawers next to my desk. Inactive ones, for patients who had left town, finished treatment, been transferred, or died, were consigned to metal file cabinets in the back room. When patients stalked off in anger, I kept their charts within arm's reach.

My mental bookkeeping ran on similar lines. I remained engaged with these patients, as, in the oubliette, I remained engaged with the Great Man. If I had made errors, in permitting the teasing byplay with Náomi or in expressing sympathy for the Great Man's pain, they were counterbalanced by the punishment he was imposing. He had saved face. When the time came, I could resume his care on the assumption that we were quits.

Insomnia was part of my punishment. I was meant not to sleep. Not sleeping would help to further fulfill the requirement to feel what my patient felt. I must reconcile myself to sleeplessness.

In the midst of musings such as these, I drifted off.

◊ ◊ ◊ ◊ ◊

The upbeat thoughts that had sustained me did not last. In the dark of my second night, I woke in despair.

I do not want to understate the unpleasantness of my confinement. With the sudden stoppage of blood pressure pills, my head ached, and I foresaw worse—migraine—to come. After washing up as best I could, I set to exercising. I paced, four steps forward and four back. My joints would not loosen.

I missed the benefits of civilian life, walking in the city, reviewing case notes in my office. But why could I not have those pleasures, even here?

Psychiatrists of my generation learned hypnosis as a clinical tool, and the instruction included training in self-hypnosis. At the dentist's office, I almost never accept anesthesia. I *take myself to an enjoyable place*—a Cape Cod beach, with Miriam—and ignore the whir of the drill. Trance provides an interval of absence.

Needing that relief now, I turned to self-hypnosis and to yoga, to poses that Miriam had taught me.

In her final months, confined to our house, I did yoga to stay in shape. I wanted to be limber so that I could help Mimi to the bathroom or flip the mattress. She laughed at my routine, consistent and repetitive. I was content to provide diversion.

Now, facing downward in the frog pose, with back sagging, I transported myself to my desk at home. At first, I heard sounds local to the oubliette, whisking and scraping, as if the hall were being swept, and scratching, too distinct, perhaps, to be mice scrabbling by. But soon I was back in the office on Prudence Street. Sun streamed through the window and warmed my face.

IN THE COURSE OF THERAPY, when I am at an impasse with a patient, as I was then with the Great Man, it is my practice to let past cases drift into mind. I do not select them because they present similar difficulties. I do not select them at all. Memories filter up.

I found myself reviewing a case from long ago that I have considered including in my book-in-progress about error. During residency training, in the low-fee outpatient clinic, I had treated a young man named Graham. Ostensibly, he needed help with anxiety, but what he most wanted was for me to side with him against his girlfriend, Jody. She teased him about his relationship to money. She called him a miser.

How could that be? Graham asked. He was a graduate student living on a stipend. He had been raised in poverty. Attending college had put him in debt. By the end of each month, his wallet was empty. Some money would have gone to indulgences for Jody, a new frock or dinner out. If in restaurants he calculated tips down to the penny, it was so that he could deposit the remaining change in a jelly jar—savings meant for small gifts for Jody. She complained that he took excessive pride in his ability to stretch a dollar. He wished that she would appreciate the effort he put into spoiling her.

Graham turned to me as an arbiter. Can any man who spends down to his last cent justly be called cheap?

The protestations of many a neurotic will contain elements of farce, and yet the injury sustained is painful. Graham gave until it hurt. Would he never be loved for who he was?

The resolution was unexpected. I had been waiting for Graham to acknowledge the justice, partial justice, of Jody's critique. He did not move in that direction, toward awareness of how tight-fistedness can show through in the performance of generous acts. Instead, he thanked me. My quiet listening had validated his original understanding and, so, cured him of anxiety. A man cannot spend all he has and be miserly. Case closed. What Graham had overlooked—what speaking aloud had revealed to him—was his good fortune. Jody had chosen to attack him on a front where he was invulnerable.

Graham was making progress in his academic career. As an aspiring journalist, Jody was floundering. He could see why she might want to cut him down to size. When prior girlfriends had tried to undermine his confidence, they had complained about traits like social awkwardness that were real enough and hard to change. Jody had done him the favor of grousing about behaviors for which he could not be faulted.

Graham credited the therapy with correcting his emotional response to Jody's sniping. In the past, he had experienced it as a challenge to his worth. Now, he felt appreciated. She was showing that she saw nothing substantive to carp about. He was involved with a wonderful woman. The cost to him, putting up with irrelevancies, was trivial.

I counted Graham's case as a failure for my method. Inadvertently, I had instructed Graham in the use, or misuse, of inappropriate affect. He had managed to experience Jody's criticism as praise. As for the stance I had adopted from Hans, non-judgmental curiosity, it had left me on the sidelines, observing, as Graham sidestepped self-understanding and headed straight toward self-congratulation.

Graham proposed marriage. Jody accepted. He credited the therapy for the happy result.

As a teacher, Hans asked trainees to think about two treatment outcomes: The patient stops picking his nose. The patient comes to enjoy nose-picking fully and sensually. In the second circumstance, we feel disappointment, but do we have the right? To embrace Hans's method is to remain agnostic about the desirability of results that patients value.

Nonetheless, I blamed myself. Graham had stopped taking Jody's complaint too much to heart, but he had also stopped seeing her as a fit observer. He continued to adore Jody, but with condescension.

I heard from Graham twenty-five years on. His marriage was collapsing. Could I refer him to a good therapist in southwestern Ohio? He and Jody had raised a family there.

A trainee of mine had settled in Cincinnati. I offered the name.

Is a quarter-century marriage a good outcome? The kind of match that Graham had been describing toward the end of treatment, the critical wife and the imperturbable husband, may be especially stable, but I might not congratulate myself for having steered a patient into it.

We wish for patients to gain awareness even though its consequences are unpredictable. If Graham had come to believe that Jody had his number, he might have proposed with more insecurity or not at all. Perhaps his cluelessness appealed to Jody—if she was insecure herself and uneasy in the company of insightful men.

For all I knew, down the road, Graham had become more perceptive, only to see Jody withdraw out of discomfort with this more fully present husband and then start an affair with another emotionally inaccessible man.

All that I could reliably assess was what Graham had achieved in the therapy. I had not been happy with the result.

In the oubliette—on all fours, letting my back sag—I wondered why, of all cases, Graham's had bubbled up.

I guessed that I was worried about a comparable outcome for the Great Man. If, in therapy, he became more fully satisfied with his character and behavior, if he felt all the more justified in his egotism—what a nightmare! The Great Man had already shown a tendency to use therapy in that way—telling distorted stories about his childhood, patting himself on the back, and dropping contentedly off to sleep. Mostly, Hans's methods lead to radical reassessments of the self, but there it was before me, the example of Graham.

◊ ◊ ◊ ◊ ◊

Did I nap? I found myself on the cot, with a different idea about why Graham's case had come to mind. As a trainee, I had indulged in the bad habit of contrasting patients' lives to my own.

While treating Graham, how lucky I had felt! As a psychiatry resident, I, too, had been living on a stipend. I earned ten thousand dollars a year, which I thought a princely sum. With that income and the little that Miriam was paid as an apprentice in an interior design firm, we managed to rent a converted carriage house on the grounds of a College Hill mansion. We watched our money, but not vigilantly.

For a week's vacation in August, Mimi found another tiny house, a two-room cottage in East Dennis, on Cape Cod, that overlooked a marsh and, farther off, Sesuit Creek. Mimi loved the small bayside beaches and the little town. On gray days, she visited a local auction house and placed low bids on elegant items.

There was a contrast with Graham! I trusted Mimi to spend our money as she pleased.

Once, she returned from an auction with a hand-decorated porcelain dinner service. To celebrate, I picked mussels from rocks in the bay and prepared them with white wine, garlic, parsley, and a special linguica that I had brought up for the purpose from a Portuguese market in Providence.

I cooked the dish and set to serve it on dinner plates from the antique china set. Meanwhile, Mimi showered. Designers were in a Provence phase. She used lavender soap and shampoo from samples sent her way, and the fragrance filled the cottage.

She emerged with just a bath towel wrapped around her. She knew how fetching she looked, with the length of her legs exposed and the hint of décolletage above white terrycloth. She asked, Do I have time to change for dinner?

She was perfect as she was.

We ate outside under a clear evening sky. We sat on the cottage deck, at a table with a round, rough-hewn wooden top set on a mechanical sewing machine base complete with treadle. We had worried about mosquitoes, but instead we were treated to an efflorescence of dragonflies, replaced after dark by lightning bugs.

For as long as I could, in the dark of the oubliette, I lingered on the marsh side with the fragrance of garlic and Mimi's just-cleaned skin.

In the hypnotic state, you see small objects up close. We had picked blackberries, and Mimi had arranged them like a wreath around the edge of our new fruit plates, leaving the image at the center exposed. The artist had painted common wildflowers. The wood violet had faded to light blue, the heart-shaped leaves an almost transparent green. Mimi leaned forward to pick up a berry with her fingers. As she moved, the low sun gave her freckled forearm a rosy blush. Her red hair, not yet dry, was cut in a no-fuss bob. Getting chilly, she said.

In the oubliette, I could not quite see her stand and let the towel drop.

Those early years of the marriage seem fabulous. How quickly did the mussel beds disappear? No need for global warming. Overharvesting and pollution did the trick. The untended woodlots whose margins teemed with blackberry canes were soon built on. East Dennis turned suburban. The two-room cottage was a thing of the past. How pleasant, though, to have the oubliette become a setting where I might visit an Eden that is no more.

Was my random-thoughts method working? Graham's case had led me to worry over therapies that succeed from the patient's vantage but leave the therapist unsatisfied. And now I seemed to be obeying the Great Man's edict to look to my marriage.

◊ ◊ ◊ ◊ ◊

I must not normalize the oubliette. In it, another factor was always at play, the Great Man's malign influence. He was a cynic, and at a penetrating level. Come, come, he said, you're just like me, a less bold version. *Like me* meant mistrusting, dishonest, and misogynistic. After time in his company, I saw those traits in myself.

Forget dragonflies and blackberries. It was not reassurance, I now thought, but self-doubt that had led me to think of Graham. On a quite different occasion, far from Sesuit Creek, I had done to Miriam what Graham had done to Jody.

My memory drifted to the year when *Rest for the Weary* was the talk of the town and the limelight shined on me. The success of my writing threatened to throw our marriage out of kilter.

Miriam had left a design firm job and struck out on her own. Her work on a liquor store in Boston brought her recognition. She redid a laundromat in Providence, to amusing effect. She was hip. Her services were in demand. Meanwhile, my private practice had been growing. We were giddy in our love for one another. Well, I was giddy. Miriam was happy and fun to be with.

Then my first book, in paperback, began flying off the shelves. I was on Fresh Air and Charlie Rose. In Providence, readers stopped me in the street. Couples who had ignored us phoned with dinner invitations and switched dates so that we could attend. When the conversation turned to Miriam's career, the questions were about her work on the furnishings for my office. I had described them in a magazine article and later cannibalized the material for my second book.

Until then, Miriam had been the creative genius and I, a nerdy technician. An artist, elegant in taste and person, she had bestowed her favors on a socially awkward man. I provided stability and she, flair.

As my star rose, she came to look like a trophy wife.

I don't know that Miriam had often thought of leaving me, but suddenly, the marriage—the commitment—seemed confining. Who abandons a best-selling author as he comes into his own, much less one who serves the needy? Every clinical hour was a mitzvah performed by me, and so, in a sense, was every case vignette and every media appearance where I talked up therapies for mental illness.

I imagine that Mimi was confused by her own response. I was realizing the potential that she had seen in me. Why wasn't she delighted? How could she feel a loss of autonomy? She had made the choice to marry for good and all.

As if to prevent my getting a swelled head, Miriam began to belittle me. She started with particulars and leapt quickly to questions of character. I'd left a pair of sneakers in the back hall where she might trip over them. It was *just like me* to overlook details. I was a *luftmensch*, hopelessly impractical.

She despaired. Could she manage to set me straight when I was being celebrated for my attachment to mystical theories?

By my lights, Mimi's take on me was wrong. Granted, I used clinical methods that sounded implausible. But, for the rest—I was no bumbler.

Playing basketball, I had been that young point guard, quick and accurate, aware of teammates' movement and their likely next location. Passing and shooting and gathering rebounds, my mind or body integrated the effects of gravity, velocity, spin, and angles of incidence and reflection. I sprang traps that took opponents by surprise. I drew on the playbook. I improvised. The talents that I later brought to group psychotherapy—anticipation and fast reaction—they ran deep.

Do we hear Graham in this defensive litany? Perhaps all marital arguments bear a family resemblance, and all attempts at self-justification.

Like Mimi, I was genuinely confused. Early athletic success convinces you of your own competence. So does training in a profession. In med school and internship, I had drawn arterial blood, biopsied bone marrow, stanched head wounds, talked down alcoholics, delivered babies, performed autopsies, and supplied the breath of life. Through thin surgical gloves, I had held a beating heart. It's hard to convince a doctor that he's ungrounded.

My job involved listening for false notes in patients' narratives. It hardly seemed that I could be a babe in the woods. I had treated prosecutors and mafiosi, bankers and used car salesmen. As for how the world works—my patients filled me in.

Even as a writer, I turned airy concepts into homey stories that everyone could understand. In what sense did I lack the common touch?

Like Graham in the face of Jody's complaint, I found Mimi's criticisms wrongheaded. Instead of trying to see matters as she did, I dismissed her silently and relied on simple obedience—care with sneakers—and the externals—my success—to hold her in the marriage. But in truth, the proofs of competence that I brought to bear in my own mind—athlete, doctor, storyteller—were of less relevance than the state of Graham's bank account.

Deep down, I understood that Miriam was right. *There was something about me*. Naming it was difficult. That was part of what frustrated her. She might be wrong on every point, and still the core complaint was valid. The media and my readers gave me credit for wisdom and practicality that, if I had them, did not extend to our domestic life. Miriam was constantly having to put up with foolishness.

DURING MY STAY IN THE oubliette, a handful of cases thematically related to Graham's rose into my consciousness. A man faces the suggestion that he has some essential defect. He dismisses the attribution or takes pride in it. The consulting room serves as a space for reassessment.

In consigning me to the oubliette, the Great Man had provided me with just such a refuge. I wondered about my marriage's imperfections and my own shortcomings.

The sequential case review also seemed directed at my therapy with the Great Man. In time, might I be able to link his grandiosity to an as-yet unacknowledged sense of defect, perhaps a conviction that he was terminally unlovable?

The therapy would be arduous—I seemed to have failed with Graham—but in principle, progress was possible. This thought sustained me during hours of despair. Yes, the Great Man might behave like a sociopath, locking men in cages and sending thugs to terrorize a poor widow. But if I could exercise patience, in time his behavior might prove psychologically explicable, through being tied to anxiety about his worth.

◊ ◊ ◊ ◊ ◊

I dropped the thumb drive in the milk box, made tea, and felt a pang of conscience. I worried that, however accurate, the current blog post, with its breezy mention of thematically related cases, shows bad faith through omission. I have shied away from sharing thoughts that had floated into consciousness and unsettled me deeply.

I headed out to retrieve the drive. When I opened the cottage door, there on the porch sat a winter squash. It had the form of a squat pumpkin, but the skin was a dusty gray green.

Ginnie must have just come by. I did not chase after. Let the file find its way to Maury.

I set the squash on the kitchen table beside the laptop. Today, when I take breaks, I run my hand over the skin. It is nubby, like rustic pottery with a matte glaze. What an artist Chet is! Or else it is Ginnie, in her role as curator, who has the fine sensibility. She has never brought me a vegetable that is without charm.

I, too, have standards. I need to represent memory as I experience it. In that last entry, I held back.

It would surprise me if what I am about to set down finds its way onto the blog. If Maury has not stockpiled material, we will go dark for a day or two. He can apologize on my behalf.

As a writer, I'm back to that paradox: When we obey inner compulsions, do we act freely?

ON A COLD NIGHT IN the basement cell, I found myself thinking about Miriam's vague but damning core complaint and my own deception in the marriage. In imagination, I was back in that difficult stage of family life when a daughter reaches her middle teens. Nina was often unhappy. A father keener to diagnose might have called her depressed. The leading symptom was intolerance for her mother. Nina criticized Miriam without regard for plausibility.

*You made me overeat* was a favorite accusation. Nina could make it when phoning home from a high school class retreat, when she had not seen Mimi for days.

Bickering became the norm, with back-and-forth accusations about clothes, piercings, mannerisms, and tone of voice. *Ninarchy* was Mimi's name for the state of our home life. Nina ruled, and the result was chaos.

In contrast, I was Nina's Pooh-bear dad, beloved in his daftness. When Nina registered complaints, I would express interest and ask for details. Nina would dismiss me with a kiss on the forehead and return to attacking her mother.

So unequal was the distribution of ill treatment that Miriam sat me down for a chat. I must commit to supporting her in all circumstances. No nodding my head in understanding. I had to act as what Mimi called a fact witness. *Your mother did not make you buy that outfit. Far from it. She predicted that you would never wear it. We were on the escalator in the mall. When you reached the top, you stomped off.*

I had never addressed my daughter, or perhaps anyone, in that manner. Still, I understood the requirement. *No half measures* was Mimi's demand. In return, she vowed to shield me from retribution and to stand up for me should Nina ever redirect her criticism.

Family therapy is of two minds about these arrangements. Should parents present a united front, or should they be honest about their opinions when they differ?

I accepted that individual judgment was a luxury I could not afford. Mimi was beleaguered.

Mid-morning on a Sunday, after a sleepover at our house, Nina made a bitter complaint: Mimi had insisted that she include a classmate, Jenna. What a mistake! When Jenna wasn't sulking, she was insulting other girls. Jenna ruined everything! Mom had ruined everything.

I said, Mom warned you that Jenna could be difficult.

To my surprise, I had retained a salient detail: Mom reminded you that the last time Jenna visited, you thought she had swiped your earrings.

Nina told me to stop yelling.

Miriam's defense was less than full-throated. *Your father was whispering, in his infinite-toleration voice.*

Mimi needed respite. If defending her made me Nina's target, I would absorb the blows. I had said as much in advance—but had I signed on to become Mimi's punching bag as well?

I preferred not to think ill of Mimi.

I decided that she was right. When I stood up for her, the tone had been off.

THOSE WERE GOOD YEARS, WEREN'T they? The years of bickering?

In the oubliette, I thought, What I would give to return to that Sunday!

◊ ◊ ◊ ◊ ◊

Are all therapies mutual? The best are, I believe. Contact with patients' avoidance or self-deception makes me attend to my own.

Ordinarily, the process plays out over time. I will see a patient weekly. Three months in, a detail from an early session will return to me. I will find that the memory relates to my own inadequacy—say, a lack of courage in a family crisis where I could have dug deeper and offered more. And then I will wonder whether I can give the patient more, whether I have been too quick to mute his anger and disappointment—whether I have colluded with him to duck a topic that needs exploration. I will be more sympathetic, too, having found weaknesses in my own character that correspond to traits I have noted in the patient. The continual shifts in focus—from the patient's flaws to mine and the therapy's and back—give the treatment life.

In my work with the Great Man, this process was condensed. We'd had a short time together, weeks, not months, and his form of communication, locking me in a basement cell, was extreme. So was his level of deception and self-deception.

My response may sound strange, but I found the depth of his inner corruption moving. The journey back would be long. The project's difficulty made me feel tender toward him.

Repeatedly in my training, supervisors called me pollyannaish. All but Hans Lutz did. He said, We owe patients hope. If we do not provide it, who will?

I intend for my responses to patients to contain enough realism to maintain that other quality we value in therapists, honesty. I offered the Great Man hope but for an undertaking that may have struck him as hopeless. At some level, he understood—I believe he did—how nearly interminable our trek together would be. Perhaps it was that awareness that caused him to cast me into the oubliette.

There, I resonated with his despair—and also with what I have called his sociopathic behavior. I called myself out on my own dishonesty.

THE *INFINITE-TOLERATION* MEMORY WAS A screen.

Soon, I found myself reviewing—reliving—the events of an especially difficult evening.

I was scheduled to keynote a mental health fundraiser sponsored by a family foundation. I spoke at many such events. Mimi and Nina tried to avoid them, but this one celebrated the life of a child, Adam Hastreiter, with whose family we had numerous connections.

In adolescence, Adam had begun behaving erratically. He stole from the liquor cabinet. He bunked school. He cut his wrists. Finally, on a Memorial Day weekend, when the family gathered at their summer home on the Connecticut border, he disappeared. Hours later, he was found in the hayloft of a neighbor's barn. Adam had climbed a ladder and hung himself from a ceiling joist.

In grade school, in a weekend art class, Nina had made friends with Adam's younger sister, Ruth, although the girls were now on the outs. Adam and Ruth's mom, Roni, was a departmental administrator at RISD. She had helped hire Mimi to decorate new studio space for undergrads. Mimi and Nina would need to attend the event.

Nina set one condition. She would dine at the head table with her mother and me. The thought of sitting with agemates while her dad droned on was more than she could bear. Besides, the other families would bring weird children—that was who attended fundraisers for mental health causes.

That afternoon, just hours before the event, a patient arrived at my office agitated, delusional, and suicidal. He owned rifles. His medicine cabinet was full of pills.

Reluctant to involve the police, I sat with my patient and helped him arrive at a safe decision. With permission, I contacted his partner and had him drive my patient directly to Butler Hospital, our leading inpatient psychiatric facility. I followed, to expedite an admission. I arranged for the partner to dispose of the pills and secure the firearms at a rod and gun club.

I knew what resources were available because I had done this work before. Each time, it must be brought to completion attentively. There's no skipping steps.

Late and frazzled, I arrived at the dinner and made my way toward a seat on the dais beside Miriam and Nina. Before I took my place, Nina left to join her agemates after all.

She sat at the back of the room next to a heavily made-up girl who gesticulated dramatically. The girl scrunched up her face and burst into a surprised look, perhaps reinforcing a punch line. She could use tending to, I thought. I wondered how Nina was faring.

Meanwhile, the bereaved father, Aaron Hastreiter, introduced me, making much of my delayed arrival—on the front lines, putting patients first. I thanked him. I acknowledged donors and organizers. We were one large family. We had all suffered loss.

I shared a memory of Adam. On a ski trip organized by the Jewish Community Center, we had chanced to take a run together. Adam must have been all of twelve. We came upon an inexperienced skier, paralyzed by fear, stuck two turns down a headwall. How like a therapist Adam had been, letting the panicked young woman give voice to her terror before offering direction. He had a way with her, getting her started, telling her where and when to turn. I remember his voice as he said *Now!* He was firm. He was respectful. He was effective. How lucky we were to have known Adam in his brief passage here.

In the banquet hall, we observed a moment of silence.

Delivering the body of the talk, I used the ski mountain as a metaphor. Was it the recent patient encounter that made me sappy?

How fragile humans are! How easy it is for people to start down a headwall only to find themselves stuck. From us, they need patience, caring, and guidance. Often professional help is of use, but there is no substitute for kindness. As friends, we must be alert and available. Despite our best efforts, we can fail. The terrain is treacherous, the trail, challenging, the visibility, poor, our preparation, inadequate or incomplete, the way ahead, unknown to us.

Was the analogy getting away from me? I looked to see if I was losing the high schoolers in the back of the room. Seeing Nina, I thought of her confusion about many things. I found myself moved, too deeply.

To regain composure, I turned to practical matters: funding, legislation, education, and political organizing. I closed the full circle, expressing gratitude to the couple who were turning their terrible loss, of Adam, into inspiration and help for others.

I was wrung out. People gave me space—except for Nina, who resumed her place at the head table. She berated me. Why had I encouraged her to sit with Adam's unfortunate cousin, the dramatic young woman?

I reached for the water glass, to buy time.

I did not say that I appreciated Nina's having befriended a fragile girl, that in her considerateness Nina had anticipated my talk, that I was proud of her. None of that. Even from a distance, the pairing had seemed wrong to me—burdensome for Nina.

I was sorry, I said, that the dinner had not gone well. I asked Nina whether she could say more about how I had upset her. Meanwhile, I elbowed Miriam and gave a quiet cough that meant *time to step in.*

To my astonishment, Mimi turned on me. *Nina said she'd prefer to sit with us. You should have left well enough alone.*

I gave a longer cough.

Adam's mother, Roni, approached, uncertain whether to intervene.

From Nina, I expected an argument about how my absence, due to the exigencies of patient care, had constituted implicit pressure, as if my devotion to work demanded sacrifice from her. But, no—Nina was concrete. She insisted that I had suggested that she join Carlotta—a name that I believed I was hearing for the first time right then.

Would Mimi say the obvious to Nina? *You left the head table just as Dad got here.* Instead, Mimi admonished me. *You ask a lot of her.*

Excuse me, Roni said. I couldn't help overhearing....

But before Roni could offer a correction, Nina put her hand to her neck. Her face turned red. When I moved to smack her upper back, she spat up noisily, wetting the tablecloth. She set to gasping while trying to yell about the harm I had done her. Roni took Nina aside and wiped her face and clothes.

Other rescuers appeared. All had a disturbed child in the family. They understood this scene or thought they did.

*You must be proud of your husband*, someone said to Miriam—naming the demand that had energized the contretemps.

In the days that followed, attendees wrote to express sympathy. They assumed that it was because I had an unstable daughter that I had accepted the invitation to speak.

The Hastreiters had commissioned a recording of the event, with clips to be used in a fundraising video. They sent me a VHS tape containing raw footage.

When I found myself alone at home, I threw the cassette into the player.

The recording shows Nina consulting with her mother, who gestures toward the young people's area. *Do you know that girl—Carlotta—at table nine?* Mimi asks. *She looks like she could use company.*

Mimi invokes my preferences. *Your father would want you to be supportive.*

I make my way to the head table. Aaron H rises to introduce me. At the edge of the frame, you see the tines of my fork as I play with my salad.

I stand at the podium. I speak—yet more awkwardly than I had imagined. Finally, the camera and its mic capture the argument and Roni's abortive intervention.

I said nothing to Miriam. I took the cassette to my office and hid it on a shelf in the back room. The tape offered certainty. Mimi was willing to lie or misremember to put me in the wrong.

These days, when every passing word or deed is archived on social media—or on body cameras or surveillance video—it is hard to recall how rare it once was to find hard documentation of informal aspects of daily life. Most marriages ran their course without a single example of this sort, a partner caught dead to rights, with every aspect of the deception on display, the exasperation, the disdainful look, the dismissive tone of voice. *You should have left well enough alone.*

Months later, arguing with Mimi, Nina said, By the way, Mom, at that sob-story dinner, you were the one who insisted that I join the teen crazies. Dad was off locking up sickos in the loony bin.

THE TAPE. HAVE FEDERAL AGENTS pored over it, in search of clues? If so, they have spent more time with it than I ever did. I viewed it just the once. But I did hold on to it. To what end?

Wrists under shoulders, knees under hips, shifting between the cat and cow poses, letting my back rise and sag, in the oubliette, I judged myself.

Mimi had hated the public evenings with their mix of upbeat promises and frightful memories. Oh, the unspeakable husbands pairing expensive suits with colorful socks and fat, bright bow-ties, like pinned butterflies under the chin—as if jokey, mock-aristocratic outfits could deny death. The ill-designed rooms made Mimi uncomfortable, as did the awkward encounters with strangers who *just had to tell her* how her husband had saved the day with their beloved aunt.

I was the problem, donning the guru's mantle, arriving late, leaving Mimi exposed.

Her lie served a larger truth, assigning me blame.

I could have called an ambulance, handed my patient off to the EMT, phoned the admitting doctor, and let standard procedures kick in. I had put the final details of clinical care before my family's needs. Enacting a lesson about scrupulousness, had I not been looking for a pat on the back?

I am focusing too narrowly. Mimi's point was that she was due moments of connection with her daughter. I had pledged to help provide them—and then I had put the two in a position where misunderstandings were bound to occur.

It had been time to take me down a peg. What better occasion than an event, built on suffering, that somehow celebrated me?

In the oubliette I found myself laughing.

That speech! What a horror!

Small-city sentimentality. Metaphors burdened with endless predicates. Clichés. Coziness. Complicit self-satisfaction.

I had lost touch with Adam as he had been, pimply and tortured and utterly peculiar. In conjuring a noble pre-teen on the slopes, I had not reimagined him. I had erased him.

It is no wonder that I never viewed that tape a second time. Oh, I deserved to be punished for that speech and, more, for holding on to the recording of it, for squirreling away evidence that allowed me to downplay my wife's complaints.

Honestly, Mimi, tie me up and horsewhip me. Throw me in a small, dank cell.

I was where I belonged.

◊ ◊ ◊ ◊ ◊

The medication withdrawal came, not as a headache but as a visual disruption. Between me and the world, I saw flames flickering, and then I felt depleted. Ocular migraine. I slept, which was a mercy.

When I woke, I thought again about the flow of memory, the series of cases. I had put them to work in the service of my patient's admonition to examine my marriage. But perhaps the sequence that led me to recall the Hastreiter dinner had another impetus, to inform the therapy. In effect, I was wrestling with the question that Muscle had posed amidst the chinoiserie: Was the Great Man deluded or delusional?

It had never occurred to me that Miriam was either. She had no mental disorder. Her lying only showed how deep her frustration ran.

Better, by putting me in the wrong, she was redecorating in the marriage, rearranging elements or putting them back in place. Surely, some of Nina's anger should be directed at me.

As for Nina, if a normal teenager distorts reality when complaining about her father, we would be crazy ourselves if we asked whether she is deceptive or deluded.

I was advising myself to look past that dichotomy.

When Mimi gave voice to a complaint that she half-knew to be false, she was expressing important truths: the marriage was failing her. I had failed her.

Surface honesty can be overrated. Yes, I had proof, on videotape: to put me in the wrong, Mimi and Nina had misrepresented events. My love for them was undiminished.

The Great Man lied endlessly, about his childhood, his marriage, his athleticism and sexual potency, and the state of the nation. Could I care for him nonetheless? I had better.

◊ ◊ ◊ ◊ ◊

I have said that as a small-city psychiatrist, I may know a good deal about patients before I meet them. To make the Great Man more truly one of mine—to relieve him of VIP status—in the oubliette, I took myself back to the hours in the balaclava. What had been my advance impression of the Great Man and his lies?

My patients, who admittedly were prone to see purpose where others might not, considered the Great Man's public, political falsehoods strategic. Lying was his brand. He was too bold to bother with accuracy and too visionary to be held accountable in small matters. Lies served as virtue signaling—the virtue of those who disdain experts, science, stability, and convention. The disdain brought him devoted followers, often men for whom facts were unfriendly, men to whom fantasy brought comfort.

Was the lying for, public consumption only? Treating the Great Man, I had heard lies told in private, where no strategic considerations came into play.

I imagined my patient in his boyhood, acting up at school and being shielded by his father's influence. Misbehaving and getting caught was a way of eliciting what felt like love from an otherwise distant or rejecting parent. Something similar may have held for lying. As a child, the Great Man lied as children do, and then he lied as an expression of family values.

The ability or even the tendency to lie served as what psychologists call an ego strength—an inner resource. Lying informed identity. Lying brought success.

This reconstruction skirted questions of delusion, sociopathy, and the rest. The relative contributions of inheritance and environment remained unspecified, as did the proportions of cunning and reflexive behavior in the Great Man's practice of lying. In youth and after, his lying was reinforced in Pavlovian fashion. His lying worked for him and, so, continued apace.

But what was his inner experience?

When I tell a lie, my mind labels it as such. The sentence is typed in italic, or it's tagged with an asterisk. In the moment, I may half-convince myself, but a hint of awareness will remain. I will blush or wince immediately—or else later, remembering the telling.

Not so with imaginative translation. While writing, I embrace the resulting fictions fully. I see Priscilla and relate her history—with no guilt and scant conscious awareness of Raymond. My guess was that the Great Man's lies had that quality for him, full reality. He had won the election. His wife desired him.

But, no. He was especially insistent about lies, especially enraged if they were contradicted. Perhaps his mind labeled them as hyper-truths. The Darwinian adaptation involved a special, enhanced attachment to falsehood.

Once we develop ego strengths, we expand their range. For the Great Man, lying became a multipurpose tool. He might lie to deceive or confuse or stonewall.

Lying was a form of self-expression. Lightly, we speak of *bullshit artists*. The Great Man was the real, the non-metaphorical thing. He was a lying virtuoso.

In lies, he captured other people's character weaknesses in memorable fashion.

Lies were weapons.

These functions were evident in our sessions. He used lies to convince. He used lies to confuse.

He dealt in improv. If I found one of his lies intriguing or appealing, he noticed and riffed on it.

He dealt in insult comedy—in unpleasantness. If I seemed to dislike a lie, I would hear more lies like it.

He performed theater of the absurd. He told laughable lies.

No, the distinction between public and private lies could not be maintained. Some private lies were strategic, and some were not. Even the seemingly non-strategic ones served a broad purpose, claiming a zone of autonomy. He was free to lie.

His childish lying gave him skills that served him in business and politics. He then reimported these skills into intimate settings.

For me, fictive translation seeped out from my writing into the everyday. The Great Man was like me in that way. For each of us, invention that led to professional success served us in our private lives.

Always, there was the other side of the coin. Inventing stories to better understand a neighbor is unlike lying to undermine democracy. I did not want to propose false moral equivalences.

But the structural similarities were evident. Like Miriam and Nina, the Great Man could lie without being deluded or delusional. Like me and like certain of my patients, he put his strangeness to use. Perhaps these parallels would help me to see the Great Man as an ordinarily flawed human being.

THE GREAT MAN HAD COMMANDED me to look inward. I had discovered obstinacy, my wife's and, more, my own. I have called the Great Man's influence malign, but at times, I experienced it merely as exigent. He had helped me add a dimension to memory. What could be more precious than the truth of my marriage?

I wanted Miriam to appear. I needed to beg forgiveness for my having preserved the VHS tape, that ace in the hole. If she wanted to keep me in doubt and off balance, hadn't she earned the right?

I had those thoughts, and suddenly, here she is, in the doorway. She smiles a wicked smile. Is she a fuller Miriam, more fleshed out? I sense her separateness, her resistance to my adoration. She is harsh and comical, dismissive and forgiving, misguided and precise in judgment.

The hour is late. Mimi is tired. She is just back from an out-of-town meeting. The flight home was delayed. She is carrying the small glove-leather duffle bag that she takes on short trips. She slings it onto the window seat and slides out of her coat.

Her mascara is clumped. A minuscule black ball hangs at the end of an eyelash. There's another smudge of black at the outer canthus of the eye. It gives her face asymmetry. What a fetching look.

She has on earrings I gave her, nothing special, thick sterling silver hoops, Mexican. They were lost long ago, but she wears them now. How wonderful to see a wife in the earrings that you thought to pick out. And the sterling silver necklace, too, a simple band.

Jeezus! You don't know to put the utensils away?

We are in the oubliette and, simultaneously, in the kitchen on Beneficent Street, and she is lecturing me about neatness and disorder.

You and your writing! Clear the counter first, then wipe it down!

It's true, I had set a lined yellow pad down near the sink. There are crumbs beside it.

She complains, Why did I marry a *Luftmensch*?

Not so loud. Nina's dozed off.

I asked you to keep her awake until I arrived!

Nina has a cold coming on. Her throat hurt. She refused dessert.

She chose *First Tomato* as her night-night story. In the middle, she started crying.

The pajamas were itchy.

I just now got her to settle down, long past her bedtime.

Mimi says only, I'm at it all day—and the mess you leave me!

I move to serve Miriam the dinner I saved for her, but she waves me off. Has she been drinking? She does drink sometimes, on planes, to help her unwind from the stress of a conference. Miriam handles liquor poorly.

She is close to me, threatening. She hisses, to communicate rage, but rage tempered by the requirements of the moment. She won't rouse Nina.

Clean it up, will you!

She heads for Nina's bedroom.

There's not much to put away. I clang knives together, not loudly, but with the sound of fuss, to signal that I'm the obedient househusband.

I had a productive writer's morning before I saw patients. This evening, once Nina dropped off, I jotted down new ideas. I'm hard to perturb once the book work's gone well.

How good to have Miriam back—upstairs, in a bed where I will join her, after my productive day, after my time with little Nina, all in the middle of life.

I climb the stairs.

I didn't bathe, she warns me. Too exhausted. I smell awful.

I think, Don't you dare shower. Give it all to me. You can trust me as I trust you, fully, finally, despite the charade you have subjected me to, the phony anger over the state of that pretty-clean kitchen, despite it and because of it.

Miriam has me wrong. I do not reside in the air or in my mind. I live in the world. I am aware, as she is, of the state of each room I pass through. I am that point guard who knows space in all its dimensions. I live in the body. I love sex and the flesh, the taste and the tang, the rough and the smooth, the sharp and the sour of it. The preparation and the consummation. Attentiveness and distraction, pleasure and hunger, merger and separation. Textures, transitions, sensations. Oh, the pain I feel, the pain of loss, even as she is wrapped around me.

We have ecstatic sex, the best sex since her death. She reprises the wicked smile.

See, she says, you are a *Luftmensch*.

She means here in the oubliette, where I have conjured her.

Oh, have the last word.

◊ ◊ ◊ ◊ ◊

Maury, it is time to bring me home.

I can't know where you are in your negotiations or how things stand in Providence or the nation. I have no idea how to make an exit—how it's done from your end.

I have asked Ginnie to make inquiries. She has declined. She counsels patience.

I am signaling my preference and awaiting your judgment. If you have any inclination to end my exile, please do.

I'm also giving a head's up: I'm not sure that I'll be welcome here much longer. The signals are contradictory.

YOU WON'T PUBLISH WHAT I'M about to write, but it's what I feel impelled to set down.

Just now, Ginnie dropped off a slice of a Hubbard squash pie. She'd been baking, and she'd made more than she and Chet could eat. The dessert had a Thanksgiving smell, aromatic spices.

Normally, when she offers a gift, Ginnie scurries off. Today, she asked if she might she join me. Without waiting for an answer, she took the wingback chair.

The entry, the quick move to sit down, had the feel of therapy.

Ginnie said that, in her visits, she had been avoiding a certain discussion. She was rethinking the marriage. She despaired of it.

Her husband had changed.

In the evening, when the outdoor work was done, Chet would offer to sit and chat. He never had before.

He asked what she was reading and listened as she talked about books.

The new Chet is the husband she had long wanted, patient and considerate.

Ginnie said, I hated it when Chet would not speak. Now, he seeks me out, and I feel rage at the wasted years. But why? He bores me. I can't wait for the conversation to end. The closeness I longed for? I needn't have.

I have a friend, Ginnie says, who speaks of the damned-if-he-does problem. If your husband annoys you and then he reverses course and annoys you again, the marriage is in trouble. You learn that the problem never was the behavior, or not that only. The problem was who he is.

I had imagined that Chet and Ginnie were well matched. I saw now that this belief was grounded mostly in the thought that their situation, rural and isolated, suited each of them.

I asked Ginnie whether I might take a minute to consider what she had said.

I worry about psychotherapy's potential to perturb marriages. The problem is worst in people who seem well suited to treatment, the contemplative, those avid for intimacy. Therapy may provide what a wife lacks and craves elsewhere. She will wish that her husband were more like the doctor.

The husband may adjust. He will pull away, believing that he no longer needs to offer support. Or he will mimic the therapist, or his image of a therapist, but clumsily and with effort and resentment.

I wondered whether my merely being nearby might have similar effects. I was an alter ego for Ginnie, reading what she read, valuing food items as she did, listening attentively and trying to reply with precision.

Or rather: I'm a peculiar person. I have peculiar effects.

Against that thought: Ginnie has been with me rarely and briefly, and she has been critical of the way that I go about my work, the work that she has taken risks to support.

I entertained a more mystical hypothesis. My presence and my blog posts have cast the shadow of Great Man over the North Maine Woods.

Off the grid and away from the VFW, Ginnie and Chet had known the Great Man as a malign force, someone for patriots to oppose in action. But on a personal level, they had been shielded, partly shielded, from him. Now, after death, he is in their lives.

He makes us devalue people unlike ourselves.

In the fortress and the oubliette, how flawed my own marriage had seemed! In the end, the foray had strengthened my attachment to Miriam, but perhaps only because my talent for emotional reversal saved the day.

Oh, to be quit of the Great Man!

When I looked up, Ginnie was reading—re-reading, likely—the volume that I had left on the side table.

He was not much of a husband either, Ginnie said.

Thinking not of Knausgård but my friends, neighbors, and patients, I said, We are all damned, however we act, don't you think? We are one way, and that way has its limitations. If we try to change, the other way has its downside, too, and we pull it off poorly.

If we are messy and inattentive and perhaps charming in our laxness, when at last we scrub the counter, we will do it angrily or calmly, daintily or cloddishly, systematically or haphazardly, fast or slow, garrulously or in silence, drunk or sober, in a manner that reflects or tries to deny our character. There is no escaping particularity.

My fiddling with words seemed damaging to Chet's case—he does not love language as I do and as Ginnie does. I changed direction.

You have been brave, sheltering resisters....

I don't know what's going on out there—don't want to—shouldn't, while I complete the work that you are allowing me to do. I'm guessing that there's a transition. The danger is less, or there's room for hope that it will be.

It's natural that you should rethink the marriage. The Great Man aroused our capacity for contempt.

He also pushed us toward one another. We clung to the safe and familiar.

Perhaps the malign influence does not wane uniformly. The need for one another fades before the disdain does.

Give the marriage time, I said.

You and Chet were comrades in arms, guerilla warriors. You may yet—once more—admire him for his courage and, equally, his vision, knowing what mattered.

I could see that I was rooting for the marriage, rooting for Chet, a stance that might do Ginnie a disservice.

I shifted gears. If I were working with you, I would ask you what you want. Not what you want from him. What life is right?

Later, you can consider whether he contributes or interferes.

I will leave, I said. Is there a safety valve after all, someone you can contact? Tell Maury that I'm close to finishing the writing project, or close to abandoning it. I have loved your hospitality, but I am ready to go home, to take my chances out in the open.

I thought of the Great Man, his impulse to leave the safety of the fortress. Was I paying myself back for not having hindered him? Never mind. I was set.

Ginnie said, I like having you nearby. We do. Chet says that he's grateful that you're here.

Yes, and he says that he wants deep conversations.

Be honest, Ginnie says. Should I leave him?

She is bolder with me, franker, less hesitant than at first meeting.

Not just with Chet and Ginnie, but in most cases, the ones where abuse is not at issue, my bias is toward staying. When I meet couples, they make sense to me. I see how each member complements the other. But not everything that makes sense is for the best.

Here's advice, I said. Go slow. I will leave. You will have time alone together.

Wait until late winter or early spring, when you set onion seeds under lights or plant lettuce in the bulkhead greenhouse, or when the soil is dry enough for peas and spinach.

See whether you want to garden together.

Noting down this conversation, I see that the damned-if-he-does part relates to my own marriage. Often, I tried to please Mimi and ended up repelling her. It did not matter what I did. The problem was me or something in me, a central flaw.

SHOULD I WORRY ABOUT DAYS when the blog goes silent?

Gaps were once common in literature. In eighteenth-century novels, the missing bits, signaled with clusters of asterisks, were called lacunae. The texts were *lacunose*. I read the word freshman year in college, and it stuck with me.

Jonathan Swift peppered his fiction with lacunae. Lawrence Sterne and Henry Fielding followed suit. The conceit was that a scholar had come upon a diary or collection of letters, but one that had been damaged, with sections missing. The device whisked readers past parts of the story that were routine or risqué, domestic interludes or sex scenes.

I am guessing that the paragraphs that Maury chooses to omit from this account will be of both sorts.

One missing fragment—present in these notes, but absent, so I speculate, in the blog—has to do with my stay in Maine. It is coming to an end. Another concerns the final hours of solitary confinement during my time in the oubliette. The gist is that I managed to keep my spirits up.

◊ ◊ ◊ ◊ ◊

After days of isolation in the oubliette, I woke to a sharp rap.

Yes, I said softly. I patted my clothes, as if I were welcoming company. I made a half-move to open the door, as if I could, as if I were a host inviting in an overeager guest, early to a gathering.

Did you not know to stand back? my guard asked—the one in the olive drab uniform.

I thought that I was being upbraided, but she grasped my elbow gently, as if she judged me to be unsteady on my feet.

I let my eyes accommodate to the brightness. How welcome the basement hallway was! Paint was flaking off exposed pipes. The cement floors were dusty enough to show the traces of a straw broom. My eyes misted with sentiment, as if I were nostalgic for the world.

Come, my guard said in a near whisper. She ushered me across the hall and into a room the same size as my cell. Lacking a window, it was lit by a single naked bulb. The room's sole furnishing was a pair of molded-plastic chairs, borrowed from a cafeteria, perhaps. Was I to be interrogated?

I was wondering, my guard said, whether there is anything you need.

The question was the strangest I had ever heard. What might an unwashed man in solitary confinement need?

There is, I believe, a Sholem Aleichem story about a simple and virtuous shtetl dweller. On his death, he arrives in heaven where he is invited to ask for anything he wants. He wonders, might he have a crust of bread?

What should I have named? A warm shower? A crisp apple? A glimpse of the outdoors? My freedom?

My guard had changed. Her chiseled facial planes remained commanding, but her gaze was warm.

Is there nothing I can offer? she asked. I may want something from you.

I could not think what that something might be, beyond listening. I gathered that the Ezra Weitz strategy had failed. My identity and profession were known.

I moved a chair to form the canonical angle.

Please. It will be good to sit with someone, I said, as if the wish for conversation were mine.

She closed the door and sat down.

I have not slept for nights, she said. Rumor has it that you can help.

Can you imagine fetching a man from solitary confinement and complaining about *your* sleep? Good, good. My jailer was one of mine, anxious and self-absorbed.

You have your own thoughts, perhaps, about what might be the matter?

I hate that I had to bring you here, to that room. If you repeat that statement, I will deny it, but it's true. If other employment or another assignment had been available, I would have taken it.

Well, you can imagine, she added.

I assumed that she was referring to her race or her ethnic origin. I guessed at it. Mixtures of Native and African American are common. I was open to a less familiar answer, say, Russian with Pakistani.

Hard to for a Black woman to put her life on the line for a white supremacist. Hard for a Muslim woman to die for an Islamophobe. Hard for a Russian émigré to stomach a leader who kowtows to dictators. Sexism cast a shadow. In truth, there were few groups that the Great Man had not injured or betrayed.

For some reason—or none—I gave my jailer the name Marya.

She had, I thought, a slight laxness at the waistline.

You are supporting an infant, I said, tentatively.

I knew no such thing. I meant only to indicate that our work together might require self-revelation.

Marya said, An infant or a child. Or a lover. Or an aging parent, or a family stranded abroad. Or else, I'm under the gun for debts. The less you know, the better.

Can you do that? she asked. Perform psychotherapy without having access to salient details?

In the small room, *psychotherapy* seemed a big word.

I will imagine the details, I said, as I just imagined that child.

It's in your skill set, I suppose, imagining. Can you imagine what my job calls for? I don't like confining an old man, but I have done worse—what the times have required. I tell myself that the evil is of a sort that will occur anyway. If I am not the instrument, another will be. I spare some poor soul that burden.

I said, The reasoning brings comfort.

You are kind to suggest that it may not. I seem scarcely troubled by the cruel assignments. I doubt that it's guilt that causes me lost sleep.

She took a moment to consider whether she believed herself. Perhaps she was relieved to discover that she did not. She still had a conscience, a remnant of one.

How good it is to talk to you! she said.

It is not only therapists who rely on exclamations. I find that Hans's method causes patients to express emotion with force and concision.

I might make efforts to save you, she said, if I thought I could. There's no saving you.

I did not take the verdict for gospel. Marya had no way of knowing how often my patients call me back into service. The Great Man might summon me yet. But talking with Marya, I thought it best, for the sake of the therapy, to adopt her pessimism. If there was no way out for me, I was a fit repository for secrets.

You have no one to confide in, I said.

My problem is delicate—delicate and consequential.

Had the Great Man approached her sexually, I wondered?

I have been asked to prepare for change, she said.

Things may go from bad to worse.

I have been invited to train for a contingency. It has a code name, a technical name. I will call it TOP-OPS.

TOP-OPS brings uncertainty.

Today, technically, my unit reports to the Great Man, although it is run by…a second-in-command. TOP-OPS will report to the subordinate exclusively. He promises glory for followers. Do you understand me?

I took it that Bub was preparing to make a move against the Great Man. I found myself feeling protective of Marya. Is it strange that the doctor-patient relationship should predominate over that between prisoner and jailer?

Your boss would not make his move unless the structure was crumbling.

Unless he believed that he could make it collapse. I am being asked to commit to a gamble without being certain what it is.

You can guess, I said.

My guess is that I do not want to be on the wrong side of the bet.

Where to place your chips!

I want safety for that imaginary infant.

How to decide?

I think about character. One of the principals plays the buffoon. One plays the martinet. The buffoon seems the weaker of the two, but those who bet against him have always lost.

You will decline the offer, to join TOP-OPS?

If I decline, will I not have to reveal it as well—to make the buffoon aware of the martinet's plot? What if the buffoon knows already?

Most people would say that it's no wonder you toss and turn. But you believe that there is more—some mystery about what keeps you awake.

You don't know me, Marya said. I am fearless.

Psychotherapists have trouble with absolute claims about identity. We believe that people choose to ignore difficult truths. Personality contains contradictions. A woman who is fearless in battle may lose sleep when her child's wellbeing is threatened.

I saw an obstacle or paradox. If Marya believed that she *simply was* a certain way—brave—then the effort I make, to question absolutes, would put me at odds with her. To be empathetic would be to remain blind to any nuanced account of her makeup.

I sought a compromise position.

It is a privilege to work with you, I said.

Although sincere, the compliment was cryptic. Marya puzzled over it. Was I honored to work with someone fearless, or was I gratified that she had begun the project of self-examination?

I see, Marya said. I do feel shame. Shame that I am plagued by uncertainty about whom to offer my allegiance, when the choice is between two vile men.

Vile and traitorous, I think she said. I am not certain about that final word. I may be inserting it, based on information I learned later.

Marya thought aloud about her predicament. It was not only that she needed to bet right, but also that she needed to root for an outcome she detested.

The Great Man damaged everything he touched. Deposing him was simple justice. But what could be less palatable than the prospect of ceding power to his amoral rival?

When I speak to groups, sometimes I am asked how a therapist can ever hope to know enough about practical matters. When a car salesman describes the shortcuts he takes, how can I tell whether they are over the line or par for the course? I can't—just as here I had no special experience to bring to bear on Marya's dilemma. What I hope to offer is a good ear. I have a sense of when a patient is conning me or filibustering herself, when she is avoiding a salient issue.

Nothing less palatable, I said.

It struck me that Marya had not made a full confession of the demands on her. Siding with the buffoon might require unmasking the martinet—and then what would be his fate? Throwing her lot in with the martinet had its own implicit consequences. In a coup, there can be no holding back. Would Marya be willing to set her hand against the Great Man?

Until now, I had put little stock in the threat of armed insurrection. Was the Great Man in imminent danger? I must have been tracking Marya's train of thought because she said, Except in combat, I have never had cause to kill a man.

Can you excuse me? she said. I feel nauseated.

Excusing Marya in the usual sense, allowing her to head off briefly, was out of the question, as she could not leave me alone and at liberty. She grabbed my elbow, guiding me back into my cell and past my cot. She proceeded to vomit into the toilet.

I made note of a theme. For those whose lives the Great Man touched, vomiting might signal awareness and self-awareness.

Perhaps it was not coincidence that just lately I had recalled that scene at the Hastreiter dinner in which spitting up played a role—spitting up that, if Mimi was right, represented my daughter's response to my self-absorption. Therapy is often eerie in this way. Drifting, the mind lights on themes that will appear in sessions to come.

Theme or no theme, I was pleased to have made quick early progress with Marya and looked forward to what I imagined would be repeated contacts in the course of my imprisonment.

She made the same assumption. Her face still dripping—she had rinsed in the sink, and there was no towel—she turned to thank me and apologize. I would be left alone again. She would re-consult me when circumstances allowed.

Before she locked the door, I had the presence of mind to say, Do you know a guard who goes by the nickname Muscle? As the favor you said I might ask, will you let him know my whereabouts?

We need human contact. Back in the cell, after the visit with Marya, I found that my sore joints hurt less.

How pleasant my short visit with her had been. Often, therapy addresses problems that are vague, longstanding, or apparently interminable. Marya had presented a circumscribed challenge. Within days or hours, she would cast her lot with one faction or another. As she approached the decision, the whole of her psychology would come into play. What in her makeup might interfere with her choosing wisely?

I saw how dependent I am on permission to exercise my competence. I don't claim to have brought Marya to a clear resolution, but she had achieved nausea, that is to say, acute awareness of the dilemma facing her and the employers who had forced it on her.

In the lockup, I had remained intent on the Great Man's treatment, but the work had been contemplative. It's face-to-face therapy that is like skiing, requiring minute adjustments at high speed. I had been brought out of myself. I was refreshed.

The prospect of further work with Marya made the oubliette stay more tolerable. I nodded off to sweet dreams and woke to the sound of my name being called, the real one—Farber. As I answered, the door opened, and a body filled the frame.

I've come on Náomi's behalf.

To me, the red hair was the rising sun.

I'm relieved to have found you, Muscle said. I'm sorry for what you've been through.

He asked what shape I was in.

Better, now that I see you.

He asked again about fragility in mind or body.

I said that I'd know more after a shower and a shave.

There is a risk, Muscle said, in your walking out, and also risk in remaining.

I chose escape. Not wanting to be treated as an invalid, I said nothing about my heart medicines, but that consideration alone, the prospect of resuming them, trumped any concerns about the downside of going AWOL.

We should leave now, then, Muscle said.

I asked about the risk that Marya—my guard—was taking.

She will attribute your release to Náomi. She requires your services.

I was surprised to hear the private name. Evidently, Náomi had shared it with Muscle.

Her word suffices?

Muscle's did, on the spot. Which was not to say that Marya might not pay a price.

The countervailing forces were balanced. Muscle had enough immediate authority to secure my release, and Beelzebub had enough to keep me under lock and key. We made haste so as not to try the contest.

Muscle had brought a gray plastic wheeled cart of the sort used to transport soiled linens. Off I rolled, covered by clean uniforms. When we reached Muscle's barracks room, he had me stand and put my arms on his shoulders, so that he could lift me back out.

I apologized for the way I smelled.

Muscle was ex-military. He'd been exposed to worse.

I was too light, he said. I would need to regain weight—to eat and to exercise.

He had set out a box of cereal and a tub of yogurt. I was happy to see them and happier to find that Muscle had provided dental floss and a toothbrush and paste. He must have known that I would choose freedom.

I cleaned my teeth and tucked into breakfast. Muscle ran a lukewarm bath. The worry was that I might faint in a hot shower.

I began in the tub, drained the water, and showered for good measure.

It occurred to me that a hot shower is like the exercise of competence. Both bring us back to ourselves.

While I bathed, Muscle fetched medicines from my room, along with socks, underwear, and hiking boots. From the laundry cart, he had selected a uniform that resembled his own. My cap and winter coat had arrived at last. Muscle would carry them in a knapsack and produce them for me to wear when we were far from the fortress. I would exit as a guard.

Muscle set to texting—about his having located me, I supposed.

In the bathroom mirror, I looked ancient for a guard, but the shirt and tunic fit.

Muscle recommended our heading outside now, if I could manage it. He wanted me elsewhere while Náomi negotiated on my behalf. Why didn't we exit through the basement? He would observe, to see what shape I was in.

Pacing in the cell had preserved me, I told Muscle—pacing and yoga.

Muscle apologized on Náomi's behalf. She should not have tried to meddle in her husband's therapy.

The Great Man had misled Náomi as to my whereabouts. He said that he had sent Beelzebub on a political errand that promised to bring him through Providence. Thinking that I might enjoy a visit, the Great Man had arranged for me to accompany Beelzebub. Once I had spent a night in my own bed, I had been so reluctant to return that the Great Man had granted me my release, on condition that I keep a low profile and avoid contact with anyone in the fortress. The Great Man was glad to see the back of me. How had anyone imagined that a small-city doctor could keep pace with someone at his level of intelligence?

Through army buddies, Muscle had tried to verify the truth of any piece of that narrative. Beelzebub had indeed been on a reconnaissance mission that had brought him to New England. There had been activity at my clinical office on a Tuesday morning, men leaving and arriving, but no direct sighting of me. My home appeared unoccupied.

Meanwhile, Muscle had checked my bedroom in the fortress. My clothes and gym bag were still there. The odds were overwhelming that the Great Man was lying on every important count. When were they not?

One thought gave Náomi comfort. If her husband had harmed me, he would have told her, to make her suffer secondarily. Still, she was aware that he and Bub were great banishers. One of their first moves, on relocating to the lair, was to build out prison cells. Their existence put employees under threat. Any offender would remain local, with no chance to disclose the fortress's location.

The lockup was in its own wing. Muscle had polled contacts there, to be certain that I was not among the detainees. He'd had no hint that Beelzebub had opened new quarters just for me.

The therapist is always a special case.

And then someone you may know intervened, Muscle said, convincing me to renew my search.

Someone I know.

Here is not the place for the discussion—but yes, someone who claims to know you.

Stand tall, Muscle said. I was to march beside him as best I could.

I chugged along, high on whatever brain chemicals kick in when you see the out of doors after internment.

How many days was I gone? I asked.

Eight or nine. They blended in memory.

I did not feel debilitated.

We're resilient, I said, in our musculature.

I had read articles to this effect, that regular exercisers lose fitness less quickly than they imagine.

I'm a walker, I offered.

Náomi says that your books feature strolls in the city. How are you on uneven ground?

Providence has its hills.

No heroics, Muscle said. Tell me when you near your limit.

He took us on what Maury, in cyclist mode, calls a *faux plat montant*, an uphill slope gentle enough to appear flat.

We're meant to stay on the reservation, Muscle said, but beyond that drop-off, the cameras no longer function.

The Regime is the same through and through: authoritarian and sloppy.

On the far side of the rise, we walked downhill before climbing, on steeper trails now, toward a ridge. Strange season. The trees were past peak, but few were bare.

At the side of the path, I saw a small maple leaf, red with black blotches. I thought of Tamara's hands and then, strangely, of her skin when she had a bad case of poison ivy, the contrast between smooth and rough.

Muscle was ruminating aloud about the Great Man. When he locked staff up, soon the sadistic pleasure faded, and they passed out of his mind. That was a danger, imprisonment with no fixed term and a forgetful jailer.

He might not be surprised to find me out and about. If he was surprised, still, with his wife's encouragement, he might come to accept the result as the one he had chosen.

The Great Man was a great re-definer. As the Greater Depression spread, continually he had called disasters victories. Tariffs, trade wars, tax cuts, desultory measures against plague—all failures he celebrated. How hard would it be to declare my incarceration a success? He would conclude that I had learned my lesson.

A steep downhill now, Muscle said, but you can set your hand on the top of the boulders as we descend.

We were on a ridge, or just below one, so we remained high above the valley floor. When we reached a plateau, Muscle broke out my coat and cap and suggested that we pause while he trimmed a branch for me to use as a walking stick.

I protested. I was fine as I was. I found a place to sit, knees to chest, my back against the trunk of an old oak.

We need an exit strategy, Muscle said. For you. For the Great Man. For the nation. But I am thinking about you.

The oubliette stay must have exhausted me, because at that critical point in the conversation, I fell asleep.

I dreamt. I am not much for reading about other people's dreams, not in psychiatry monographs and not in autofiction. I recount my own dream here only because its meaning is crystal clear and was to me at the time.

Beelzebub stands before a bonfire, looking every bit a devil. In his hand, he has a branding iron whose small tip, in the form of a capital letter G, is so hot that it glows red against a black and starless sky. He stands over the Great Man, who is naked and supine, his body visibly vulnerable in its flabbiness. Feeling the poker approach, the Great Man whimpers. Beelzebub does what the Great Man fears most. He kicks the Great Man onto his side and sticks the poker up his ass.

I hear the sizzle and smell burnt flesh.

The Great Man writhes in pain and in ecstasy.

In the dream, I am aware of the homophobia implicit in the Great Man's consciousness. It is not just that in his hell he is being seared with a red-hot brand. He is being reamed up the ass, which entails humiliation, and all the more if the torture also gives pleasure, so that there is no way for the Great Man to deny his submissive and masochistic leanings.

Beelzebub holds the poker in place until the stimulation gives way to pure suffering and then death, although the nature of death in the afterlife is ill defined.

Reviving, the Great Man grabs the poker by the handle, extracts the working end—implausibly, it is still glowing and also dripping with excrement—and threatens Beelzebub, who puts his hands before his face. They afford no protection. With glee, the Great Man applies the brand to Beelzebub's forehead, searing it with the mark of Cain, which is also the mark of ownership by the Great Man.

It is Beelzebub's turn to writhe. He drops to his knees, begs, confesses, and pleads loyalty. He blubbers, weeps, and wails—until he manages, craftily, to wrest away the poker. Immediately, the sequence repeats, with Beelzebub heating the working end in a flame while the Great Man cowers.

If Maury publishes my account of the dream, some readers will wonder about the images. Can a doctor think of a patient in those terms?

In contrast, colleagues of my generation will find the content stereotypical. In the Freudian era, we were taught that dreams reveal repressed thoughts and impulses, centering on sex and violence, as outgrowths of the Oedipus Complex. Sons wish to murder their fathers, and fathers threaten to castrate their sons. These dynamics play out in therapy, in the unconscious of either participant, often with the therapist assigned the role of a torturer father. If the patient does not report a dream like the one that I have just transcribed, or if the therapist does not waken to one in the course of treatment, we will presume that the analysis is incomplete.

All very well—but the dream was not typical for me. Like my imagined readers, I was shocked at what my mind had produced.

I kept my eyes shut and felt the roughness of oak bark against the back of my head. What more could I understand? I ran through considerations.

I had been more sleep deprived than I had realized. The vivid images suggested REM rebound.

Nightmares are a common response to the Regime. Numerous articles in the psychoanalytic literature say as much.

Had the ocular migraine set the scene? The flames of hell had flickered before my eyes.

The theme of torture was timely. I had just been released from the oubliette. That word was linked to the crapaudine and the Great Man's boasts about his cruelty.

Bub and the Great Man had told me stories in which they took pleasure in causing pain.

These associations were right on the surface.

The dream's central object was the red-hot poker. A Providence mayor—also narcissistic, also criminal, also a breezy liar—had threatened a romantic rival with one. I had borrowed that image. It suggested an ominous precedent. The mayor had pleaded no contest to assault charges, left office—and won reelection.

Perhaps endlessness was the dream's core theme. Was I telling myself that there is *no exit*, that we are in hell for eternity? The dream bore the mark of my imprisonment, whose signal feature had been its uncertain limit.

Or, say: the dream merged Muscle's talk of an *exit* with Marya's disclosure that Beelzebub was planning a coup that might include regicide, if that is the word. If I was maligning my patient by consigning him to hell, I was also alerting myself to a worry on his behalf. Perhaps we needed to think together about his relationship to Bub and what would come of it.

Say also, I had been attempting a little joke—working a variation, giving the Great Man the climax appropriate to him. There was no avoiding the obvious understanding, *I'll see you in hell!*

I had tried to maintain equanimity, approaching the Great Man as I would any patient with mild-to-moderate paranoia—and then tried considering time in the oubliette as a continuation of treatment. Apparently, I had not escaped free of revenge fantasies. There were leanings that I would need to bring under control, to prevent their impeding treatment.

It felt good to have done that piece of work there on the mountain path—to have done it while refreshing myself with sleep.

Fantastic. I had started the day confined in a cell. Now, I was in excellent company, in the great outdoors, getting ready to stretch my legs again.

I opened my eyes to see a hawk circling overhead.

You must have been exhausted, Muscle said.

I was ready to hear about exit strategies. What might one look like?

Let me orient you, Muscle said.

Náomi had told him that I was not well informed about our situation. Might he fill me in on the most general level? He was glad that I had napped. We might have a hike ahead of us, if I was game and able.

In truth, I had felt a slight tightness in my chest. I slipped a nitroglycerin tablet under my tongue.

Here's what has us worried, Muscle said. When we go online, we see that the truth is filtering out, truth about the present and, more, the recent past. On public radio, too—public radio, which had become a duplicate of Regime Radio—we now hear occasional accurate reporting, acknowledgment of unemployment and crime rates.

That's worrisome? I asked.

It would seem to signify a shift in policy or a power struggle.

How much do you know about the press? Muscle asked me.

He launched into a lecture about the Great Man, his proxies, his foreign allies, and the media. Much of what Muscle said went over my head.

I gathered that the Great Man, abetted by EverGreat judges, had managed to gut the first amendment and then, through libel lawsuits, bankrupt or intimidate media companies large and small. His cynical grand gesture was using climate change—harm to trees—as a pretext to ban printed newspapers and magazines.

Once the press was web-only, the Regime subverted news and social media sites, inserting stories meant to sow confusion. The same went for private email groups and listservs. The infiltration was pervasive enough to make most information sources unreliable. Resistance publishers faced a difficult decision, whether to soldier on despite the Regime-induced distortions in the finished product.

That's why the truth about the uprising, if any, remained unknown. Every good-faith posting was matched by thousands of false ones.

But rumor had it that the Great Man would be on the move soon. While I was in seclusion, he had promised to grace an EverGreat rally with an appearance. The Regime had blanketed the airwaves with images of adulation. People tossed caps in the air, revealing curly golden fright wigs below. The stadium distributed chicken tacos to all. Attendees held them high.

The Great Man did not show, except by video, but expectations had been raised. Surely, the next rally would bring him out.

In the meanwhile, here and there, news was being normalized, despite the fact that truth was not the Great Man's friend. Perhaps the kleptocrats were turning on him. Perhaps Beelzebub was setting the groundwork for a coup—one that would be followed, in short order, by more clamping down and propaganda.

Did Vera speak with you? Muscle asked.

Vera.

Your jailer—with the chiseled features. She's a catastrophizer, but not without cause. Her boss, Beelzebub, likes springing tests of loyalty on her. She believes that he is grooming her for an extreme act—now, in the coming days.

I said nothing. I considered Vera/Marya to be a sort of patient.

You owe your freedom to Vera. She's the one who dropped a reference to the new lockup, where you were being held.

Fortunate, for me.

How are we doing? Muscle asked, and, Do you have something left?

We worked our way up a goat path to the top of a wooded hill. When Muscle was not looking, I slipped another heart pill under my tongue and was rewarded with a sense of ease.

When the trail peaked, the tree cover thinned, and views opened to the southwest. Muscle suggested we sit on a pair of rocks and absorb the sunlight.

He asked, Do you know a fellow named Duncan?

Duncan?

From Providence, he says. Awkward. Urgent, insistent, earnest, jumpy.

Duncan, I said, as if searching the memory file.

Muscle said, I'm an early riser. Some mornings, when I'm not yet on duty, I drop into the town diner for French toast. Yesterday, I was there at opening time, 5:30 AM. I parked my car outside—a security company car. That's what made this Duncan approach me, I'm guessing. That and my size and the sidearm.

Duncan stood close. He whispered. He asked whether I worked for the Feds.

He said that he'd heard rumors, ones that he was tempted to post on a listserv he subscribed to.

He was tech-savvy. He could multiply his messages as well as any Regime flack.

He used the word *houri*. From what he'd heard, the locals had concerns about wayward young women who vanished from neighboring towns. A few girls had reappeared with more drugs than they knew how to handle.

Duncan began with wink-and-nod hints—but I sensed that he wanted to speak his mind.

Seeing that I denied nothing, Duncan turned to the topic that had set him to snooping in this neck of the woods.

Word had it that the Great Man was undergoing psychotherapy. A doctor had been kidnapped to conduct the treatment.

Duncan wondered whether I was interested in hearing more.

When I said that I might be, he ordered tea and sat across from me.

He asked whether I'd seen the psychiatrist. When was the last time?

I asked Duncan what he knew.

He became agitated. He was concerned for the psychiatrist's safety.

Duncan was roundabout in his speech. Reading between the lines, I gathered that he'd been tracking a mobile device and had noticed that it had stopped moving.

I told Duncan that he had found the right man. I shared his worries. I was on the job. I'd get back to him. Until I'd had a chance to investigate, he should hold off on any revelations. If he went public, he might do more harm than good.

Duncan gave me twenty-four hours, thirty-six at the outside.

I left and phoned Náomi. I can't tell you how upset she became. I hurried back and made the rounds, interviewing my fellow guards, conveying a sense of urgency. No dice. And then this very morning, early, at the staff canteen, Vera let slip—something.

Did you make an arrangement with Duncan, so that he could locate you?

Is that a bunting? I asked. I'd seen a bird on a naked branch and then a shimmer of blue.

If you're carrying the device and if we're in range, our walk is relieving Duncan's worries.

Is it late for buntings here?

Must you always talk politics! Muscle said.

He explained his own joke: those anomalies used to please us, birds slow to fly south. We'd notice an indigo bunting in October and think ourselves lucky to have caught sight of it. Now we worry that the planet's gone awry.

Scarcely a sentence passes our lips that's not political. No corner of our lives but the Great Man has blighted it.

Seriously, Muscle said, how is Duncan following your progress?

I said that sometimes it struck me that not providing help was at the core of my profession. I did seem to be receiving help. I owed this Duncan a debt of gratitude. You, Duncan, and Vera, I said to Muscle.

And Náomi.

In my experience, she is a complicated case.

Can you manage more? Muscle asked.

I wanted to see the day's adventure to its end.

◊ ◊ ◊ ◊ ◊

It speaks of simpler times, Muscle said. He meant the grand vista before us.

It makes you want to return to them.

Except that the Great Man destroyed that illusion.

Race and class divisions, power imbalances, anti-intellectualism, anti-democratic leanings, and widespread poverty—not to mention Ponzi schemes—once we saw them as glitches in a country built on high ideals.

The Great Man showed us otherwise. The flaws we had called incidental were underpinnings. They composed a grand tradition, present always.

He's in your line of work, Doc, Muscle said.

He's made us face ourselves.

Only it's a strange kind of therapy that makes us see the worst in everyone.

MUSCLE LAUNCHED INTO A RECITATION that resembled ones I had heard from Miriam.

Never had a leader of any stripe waged so destructive an attack on our security, laws, values, and wellbeing.

The Great Man had squandered our stock of goodwill in the community of nations.

When the rule of law disappeared, so did foreign investors and trading partners.

The ruined economy served the political philosophy, governance through fear.

Muscle's goal, I guessed, was not to improve my clinical work.

He was like a patient's wife hoping to pull me over to her side and cause me to act against my patient's interests in a contested divorce. Muscle was recruiting me as a co-conspirator in an effort to hasten the end.

He said that we were so focused on the Great Man's egotism that we dismissed the notion that—beyond petty motives, beyond the quest for profit and self-aggrandizement—he was capable of intentionality. We bypassed an obvious likelihood, that the Great Man was a traitor.

We had reached an overlook, nothing before us but wooded hills and mountains. We saw stretches of evergreens, but around us were occasional birches, many still with leaves, enough to dapple the light.

Muscle found a spot to sit. He continued, It occurs to me that I have questions for you, Doc—professional ones. I have companions who have been investigating that possibility, treason. Are they paranoid? If I am inclined to believe them, what does that say about me?

◊ ◊ ◊ ◊ ◊

Can you take coffee? Muscle asked.

From the knapsack that had held my coat, he pulled a compact thermos jug and served us. We had nut bars as well, military surplus, with unsulfured dried fruit, dusty brown, with a metallic tang. The taste brought back Boy Scout hikes, when we drank water from flat round canteens that gave it a metallic taste, refreshing on a summer day.

Are you comfortable? Muscle asked.

During my nap, he had confirmed arrangements with Duncan. He and I would be meeting, but late in the day. Muscle and I had time to kill, and surely I could use a rest.

Muscle hoped that he was not taking advantage of me. He wanted my opinion about information that he had received, information or rumors. He had a story to tell that involved spy craft.

Muscle turned intent and conspiratorial. He was displaying a side of himself I had not seen before.

As always, I heard music more than words. Vaguely, then, I gather that in the leadup to the election, a certain few of the Great Man's current and former guards, largely ex-military, became concerned about his behavior. They worried that he and, by extension, they might be on the wrong side of a plot to betray the country.

They had reconciled themselves to protecting a democratic leader who happened to be destructive. Protecting a traitor was another matter.

To investigate, they formed a small study group and called themselves the Persians. The members took as their model Persian rug makers. During the Iranian revolution, when our diplomats abandoned the embassy in Tehran, they shredded reams of paper files. The mullahs recruited carpet weavers, with keen eyes for patterns and the dexterity to tie hundreds of knots per square inch, to sort the thin strips and reconstruct sensitive documents by hand.

The study group would attempt something comparable. Participants shared snippets of overheard conversations. Members who were veterans of the intelligence services worked at integrating the fragments. That was their version of de-shredding.

Here's what had first caught the Persians' attention. In various private meetings, the Great Man had made quick mention of numbers that had an easily remembered form: 321123 or 76543. When alone, sometimes the Great Man sang digit sequences to himself. He favored the opening to "The Song of the Volga Boatmen": 8-6-4-2, 8-6-4-2....

What might the number strings signify?

The path to an answer was circuitous. Evidently, the numbers represented electronic ballot box counts. When a legislator dared to cross the Regime, an intermediary would approach him and provide the figure—say, 23432. A few days later, in an incidental special election for a minor office in a far-off state, the losing candidate would be credited with precisely 23,432 votes.

The demonstration that the Regime could rig vote counts would help nudge the straying party member back into line.

Generally, the number sequence was not offered in isolation. If the legislator had slept with his wife's sister, evidence of that compromising behavior would be offered as well.

What was the source of the information? The Persians went outside their ranks to interview guards who had been retired and, finally, one who was in jail. The conclusions were not firm, but they pointed, yes, to treason. The Great Man had made a deal with a foreign despot, the Smiling Gnome: land for votes. The Gnome got a go-ahead to annex territory, attack neighboring nations, and take control of oil fields and deep-water access. In exchange, the Gnome's intelligence forces provided access to their *kompromat* files, along with the hacking needed to set certain election results and, ultimately, prevent a landslide loss in the general campaign.

What I recall best from Muscle's narrative is a recreation of a private conversation, in the leadup to the election, in which the

Great Man voiced his fears to Beelzebub. The Regime would lose. In the transition to a new government, damning documents would come to light.

The Great Man was agitated. Can you picture me in a six-by-eight cell, living on bread and water? I'm locked up already, in my mind.

Me! In prison! Every night!

I gave a psychiatrist's grunt, to signal to Muscle that I saw the parallel.

As I had surmised, my consignment to the oubliette had been part of the therapy. The Great Man had banished me to a small cell because he had envisaged himself in one. He had wanted to subject me to what he had felt through apprehension, that specific discomfort.

In response to his fears, the Great Man had given Beelzebub the go-ahead to close a deal with the Gnome.

The Persians had tapes and texts and interview summaries. They saw signs in the election returns as well. The vote totals were *lumpy*. In localities where electronic ballot stuffing had proved impossible, the Great Man lost big. Elsewhere, he won by lopsided margins.

The Regime analyzed the pattern in reverse fashion. They claimed that where the Great Man had performed poorly, results had been rigged. They opened investigations into state and local authorities. The Gnome's minions swamped the web with comments amplifying the electoral complaints, lending plausibility to the fiction that the Great Man had once more defied the polls and swept the contest.

What I've just written is approximate and abbreviated. And I have the impression that Muscle, or the Persians who briefed him, had done some imaginative translation. But I had gotten the gist. To their own satisfaction, obsessed intelligence experts had proved the Great Man's perfidy.

When Mimi lay awake nights, she fantasized about the Great Man's death. When those images grew stale, she saw herself amassing incriminating evidence so irrefutable that even loyalists could not ignore it.

I told Muscle that I seemed to be hearing a daydream.

How would the Persians' evidence fare in court or before a jury of legislators? A disgruntled guard heard a number sequence. An imprisoned criminal broke confidentiality to help the group reconstruct a conversation conducted in code. As for the Great Man's kowtowing to a despot—what else was new?

I said that I would love to meet the Persians.

Muscle said that I knew one. My guard, Vera, was a Persian, although she had joined the group late on.

I had meant, I would love to sit in on their meetings.

In Muscle's account of the investigations, I had heard echoes of sessions from my paranoid men's group. Members gather, scour their memories, amass collateral information, fill in missing elements, let the ideas bounce around an echo chamber, and discover a consequential plot that has led to disaster, with more imminent.

Which is not to say that the Persians were mistaken.

At my feet, a tiny gray lizard struggled to cross a row of pebbles. Was he a doomed creature? As with the bunting—I did not recall having seen lizards so late in the season, not even in Providence. Across the valley, the peaks seemed to have multiplied. The contrast in scale, lizard and mountains struck me as improbable.

Improbable. The word had escaped from my mouth.

The Great Man seemed to lack concentration. Could he remember six-digit figures? Could he find the slip of paper he had written them down on?

I said, To answer your question, the story has a familiar form. The form of paranoia.

Don't get me wrong, I said. I have warm feelings for paranoia.

And the content?

Muscle knew that I could not say whether, based on my contact with my patient, it struck me as plausible that he had made concessions to a dictator.

Privately, look: the Great Man had humbled our nation. Behave as he did with intent, and you were a traitor. I had known as much going in, but I had an advantage over the Persians. Doctors treat everyone.

As for the Persians' revelations, I would welcome them as I welcome other testimony from collateral sources, gratefully and conditionally. I wanted not to find any ancillary perspective too convincing, lest it interfere with my ability to listen to my patient with an open and generous mind.

Certainly, I was curious whether my patient believed that he had committed treason or might be punished for it. I could see where either thought might contribute to insomnia.

I did wonder about Muscle's motivation. Why had he chosen to fill me in?

You're a quaint creature, Muscle said.

He had expected more from me, given my time in the oubliette—more outrage or pleasure in response to the Persians' discoveries.

◊ ◊ ◊ ◊ ◊

Muscle turned to the concerns that Vera/Marya had raised. There was talk that Beelzebub was preparing to make a move.

If the Persians preempted Beelzebub, if they took matters in hand, would that choice enact or subvert ideals of loyalty to democracy?

Muscle was asking me to imagine circumstances when I might not put my patient's interests first.

Did Muscle consider saying more? Perhaps, like a therapist, he imagined that his interventions, rejected for now, would do their work over time.

We stood and brushed pine needles off our pants.

And now, Muscle said, our paths will diverge. He pointed to a continuation of the trail we were on. It took a gentle downhill course. Within two miles, I would come upon a rustic campground.

Muscle hoped, he trusted, that I would be fine. For his part, he would follow a steep path down to the valley floor and an old logging road with a gate through the fencing that controlled entry to the fortress domain. Duncan would be waiting there. Muscle would let him through. Duncan had demanded a face-to-face with me, alone and unobserved.

Watching Muscle jog off, I realized how deliberate my pace had become.

◊ ◊ ◊ ◊ ◊

I must have walked quietly because Duncan did not hear me approach. I first saw him from above and behind. Sketchpad in hand, he was slouched in a web-backed folding chair placed at the edge of a grove of maples. He was shading in a pencil drawing of the scene before him, a field, filled with milkweed and blackberry bramble, that had attracted, in the distance, a family of white-tailed deer.

I like coming upon patients unnoticed. There's nothing better than entering my office, finding the group in session, and lingering at the door as the men go about their business unselfconsciously.

Oh, Duncan! How remarkable, after days alone in the dark, to see one of my guys in the out-of-doors on a sunny afternoon.

Duncan stood, turned, and beamed—and hesitated. Mine was not a practice in which hugs or even handshakes occurred.

We were worried, Duncan said.

He must have hiked in with a pair of folding chairs strapped to his backpack, identical seating for doctor and patient, following Miriam's esthetic.

Duncan had brought my favorite mug from the office. He filled it with water and set in the holder on arm of the chair meant for me.

You've lost weight, he said.

I felt small in the chair, small and contented. A makeshift office at the edge of a grove of striped and sugar maples. Noisy jays overhead. A leaf-quilt carpet. An anxious client.

It's a relief to see you, Duncan said.

He did not look relieved. He stood.

New clothes? he asked. Did I mind if he checked for bugs? From his backpack, he extracted an electronic wand. Like an airport security screener, he gave me the once-over.

When it comes to deer ticks, he said, you're on your own.

I was glad for the little joke, glad that Duncan could employ social skills, if clumsily.

About my devices: in an excess of caution, he and Jamal had readied a belt buckle and so on, for contingencies. Beyond acting as a charger, the shaving kit served as a booster and bypass that would let the group stay in touch even in conditions like the those that prevailed in the fortress, where an intranet controlled communications.

And then, nothing moved, not the credit card, not the belt buckle. I had not passed near the shave kit.

Sorry for the scare, I said.

I know you think we overdo, Duncan said. But we're right this time, aren't we? The Great Man and his henchman mean you harm.

We thought it best to send an emissary, one of our number, to approach the fortress and linger, to scope things out. We had what the rest of the country lacked, certainty about the Great Man's whereabouts. We'd followed your movements. We knew that you'd been taken to him.

Jamal had been right, Duncan confessed—half right. Duncan had bugged the landline. He had listened in on calls, so he had known that Beezelbub would be by and that my daughter had been threatened.

How many confidential conversations had Duncan monitored?

He had been out to protect me, imagining that I, like much else that was precious to him, might be in danger.

Whatever you've done to the office phone, I said, you'll need to undo it.

Duncan apologized. He would remove the tap. But the course of events had made him believe that he had done well to keep tabs on me. Aren't we all meant to look out for one another?

I suppose that with my emphasis on equality, I had encouraged that sort of reasoning. If I was there to help Duncan, ought he not to help me in return?

WANTING TO NORMALIZE THE CONVERSATION, I asked after the group.

That's why Duncan was here. After I disappeared, resentment of the Great Man ran high. At one remove, Miguel had done especially poorly. He took to cutting himself. He spoke of resolving my problems, of coming after the Great Man.

The group added extra sessions to help Jamal respond to Miguel. Arthur stood in for me. He said that empathy with the oppressed would have meant wanting to kill the Great Man every day, for years, for a dozen reasons. If the guys had not sought revenge then, they should not seek it now over their local misfortune.

Arthur spoke of epistemic modesty.

I was astonished. Did he?

Once, in a weak moment, I had introduced the group to that argument.

At Brown, I had studied with a philosopher who wrote about self-doubt as a virtue. When should we set aside our own opinion and defer to someone else's different reasoning? That choice must be right occasionally or even often.

Epistemic modesty is a logical outcome of pessimistic induction. Because I have been mistaken in the past, I know that I may be mistaken now. This logic is hard for philosophers to embrace. They are trained to reason precisely, to argue and make their case. But what of others who arrive at different conclusions? Epistemic modesty speaks against haste in committing irreversible acts.

The group fortified Jamal with helpful perspectives, and Jamal worked with Miguel, but then Jamal noticed that my devices had stopped moving. Had I been locked up—or worse?

Jamal and Duncan knew my location. They honed in on social media threads from nearby towns. A carpenter's post hinted at work, in a hotel basement, on a makeshift jail cell. Jamal and Duncan worried, What might the Great Man not do?

Miguel overheard Jamal's end of the call. Jamal assured Miguel that the group would take steps, that they would find a way to make contact. Miguel seemed satisfied, but some days later, he disappeared along with guns from the locker that the group had set up for Charlie.

Jamal was sure that Miguel would be captured or shot. What is the Regime, finally, but a machine for killing men like him: dark-skinned, undocumented, mentally ill, and gay to boot?

Jamal logged onto Miguel's computer and saw that he had hacked into Regime files to see how defense forces were arrayed around the fortress. The guys tapped Duncan to come in pursuit. He followed the route that Miguel had outlined for himself.

After Duncan set out, Jamal had found Miguel at a cousin's house in Wanskuck, near Providence College. Miguel is all but agoraphobic. Duncan was embarrassed that he had ever believed that Miguel would make his way here. Miguel is back home. The guns are back in the locker, with Ahmed in charge.

Duncan was in the mountains already. He figured that he was in for a nickel, so he set up shop and talked with people. That's how he met Muscle.

I thanked Duncan for his efforts. And how wonderful to hear how the guys were looking out for one another.

I said, As you see, I am fine.

Duncan was kind enough not to say otherwise. Instead, he asked for news from my end. Why had the devices gone silent?

I considered the imprisonment to be part of my therapy with the Great Man. I was not free to explain.

Without forethought, I said: I will come home—to the office. I will do my best to return by the end of the year. I appreciate what you all have done in my absence.

I am getting older. Shortly, you will go on without me, for good.

I wanted the guys to see the current brief absence as a preparation for that longer one. On my return to Providence, I would do bridging work—termination—in preparation for their continuing to meet on their own.

Back on Prudence Street, might Duncan join Arthur in representing me to the group? Modesty was the watchword. I would make it home. I wanted the guys there, in session and not in the clink.

I needed time to do the task I had left town for. I would be fine.

Suddenly, the talk took an unexpected direction.

Duncan had something to report. When my devices went quiet, Charlie had contacted my lawyer and asked whether I had checked in. Was there news? Had I been hospitalized?

Charlie let Maury know that I was serving the Great Man or had been until recently.

Maury seemed unsurprised. He had not heard from me, Maury said. He had his own request. If one of the group members managed to reach me, would the guy deliver a message? A certain person had been served with papers, as a preliminary step in what appeared to be an attempt to bypass the agreement, presented as ironclad, that had arrived as I disappeared.

That was another reason that Duncan had persisted in his mountain visit. He had wanted to deliver the update from Maury.

Duncan had listened in on the speak-to-your-daughter phone call. He must have had an inkling of what Maury's message meant.

In therapy, the core principle is: focus on the patient.

What response to the news about Kareena would serve Duncan best?

Should I show upset, as a way of modeling openness? I did not want to arouse anger toward the Great Man.

I chose to acknowledge a feeling, but in a way that referenced Duncan. You have moved me.

I meant by coming all this way, by persisting in order to update me on my family life.

I did not want Duncan distracted from the main point.

He assured me. He would tell the guys. The exercise of discretion would constitute a vote of confidence in the Doc.

We seemed at a point of rest, so I struggled to my feet.

I pulled off my belt. Would Duncan swap with me? I did not want the group obsessed by my every move. I would toss the false credit card. I would order shave cream and a cartridge razor.

Duncan stood and undid his buckle. He asked, Is there an endgame?

He said, I know how you value patients, how you pride yourself on seeing good in the worst of men. But you look frail. I don't know what I'll tell the guys, but I'm telling you: I'm worried.

Perhaps you've done your bit. Perhaps the year-end is too far off. Come home now.

It was grief, I know, playing on me, but in Duncan's farewell, I heard something of Miriam.

◊ ◊ ◊ ◊ ◊

The sun was setting as Muscle reappeared to fetch me.

A fifteen-minute walk, he said. He had parked an SUV in a turnout of an old logging road just below.

The light would not last. The path had rocks and roots. We should hustle.

Once we reached the SUV, where would we head?

Back, Muscle said. You're set. Náomi has the Great Man's guarantee.

His guarantee.

It may seem that I was repeating what had just been said, in standard therapeutic fashion. I wonder whether I was not also betraying my patient. The repetition implied doubt about the worth of the Great Man's word. The repetition said that the Great Man's therapist saw him as the world did, fundamentally untrustworthy.

Muscle said, He's ready for you to continue your work.

I was not relieved. Bub or the Great Man was threatening Kareena.

The sky took on a reddish tint. The air had turned cold.

Muscle pursued his own train of thought.

You bring calm.

The Great Man has a similar talent. He makes angry people feel justified. The permission he gives, permission to experience rage, reassures his followers.

Náomi does something parallel with desire. She absorbs lust and even cruelty. She does it by seeing entitlement as foolishness, by smiling.

Remarkable. Under one roof, we have three people who offer acceptance for the unacceptable. It's like in a folktale or comic book series, where heroes with defined powers join forces or engage in combat.

It occurred to me that, whatever our talents, we had not done one another much good.

As if reading my mind, Muscle said, Just now, when she gave the go-ahead to bring you in, Náomi said, *La commedia è finita!*

Your imprisonment raised her level of concern. The retreat to the fortress has been bad for the Great Man. Isolation feeds his paranoia. He needs to be back among colleagues and rivals.

Her marriage needs to end.

You need to be home with your patients.

I need to leave this job.

These views are hers?

She hopes that, should the opportunity arise, you will counsel her husband to venture out.

Náomi had read my books. She knew that I do not tell patients that their fears are overblown.

I won't deny that the prospect of leaving had appeal.

I have been trained to resist what appeals to me. I must not let tempting suggestions influence the treatment.

◊ ◊ ◊ ◊ ◊

This morning, I skied off from the main trail. The spur ended at a small frozen pond. A messy beaver dam blocks the outflow on the far side. The trail continues beyond.

I did not chance the ice. I'm not suicidal. Neither am I hoarding the days.

Using my own fear as a metric, I felt as safe as I had in Providence, on my walks. There, my grief protected me. I was a wild-eyed widower. Here, I rely on my growing competence on the snow.

Unless I'm miscalculating risk and courting danger. Guilt distorts judgment.

In the final session with the Great Man, did I do right by my patient?

He remained vulnerable, but the doctor's job, in every specialty, is to get the patient past the current crisis, to delay the inevitable.

And if we are better off without the Great Man? I'm of the old school—quasi-Kantian. I must not sacrifice a patient for the greater good. I was responsible for the Great Man, and now he is—where?

Not in hell. My daytime nightmare notwithstanding, I see no point to eternal torture, no reason that a goodly portion of the cosmos should be devoted to punishment. On the other hand, if souls are weighed in a balance, I can't imagine the Great Man winning a ticket to an all-inclusive resort.

On encountering his dead body, I had feared that he would appear in New England alongside Miriam. I will see what happens when I return to Providence, but I can say that his spirit has not haunted me in Maine.

I do wonder about the corpse. The Great Man built no mausoleum. Perhaps he could not contemplate his death.

I imagine a half-abandoned western cemetery on a wooded mountain near the Behemoth ski resort. Náomi could have had him buried there, in the wilderness. The remaining EverGreats would need to hike to pay their respects.

He would have wanted military honors. He took most pleasure in receiving what he had not earned.

But I was saying, I worry that I failed in my responsibility as a doctor. I have found returning to the desk—the kitchen table—hard.

I have said goodbye to Chet and Ginnie.

Muscle is the safety valve.

In the transfer, he had entrusted Chet with a special thumb drive, for forwarding to Maury. When he inserts it into a port on his computer, it will create a link to a communications site, notifying Muscle. He or a proxy will contact Chet and arrange for my transport.

I will return home, or law enforcement will find me here. Either way, I'll be gone.

Ginnie has graced me with a turban squash with a green and white cap above a mottled orange bottom. Preparing it for the oven is like breaking into the wine cellar for a grand cru.

I miss Ginnie's company. She never stayed long, but her visits reminded me of how people are, kind and resourceful, considerate and complex. Seeing her, I had been better able to forgive myself—until I learned that my presence had roiled her marriage. I'm short on self-forgiveness just now.

AFTER OUR ADIRONDACK HIKE, MUSCLE walked me to the door of my tiny bedroom and advised me to rest up. Shortly after midnight, as if nothing had changed, I was summoned to the Great Man's bedchamber.

I was made to cool my heels in the recliner, which in practice meant that I had to be roused a second time before being ushered in for what would prove to be my final session with the Great Man. It was a rollercoaster.

The Great Man began by giving me his Sydney Greenstreet look, nose lifted, eyelids half-closed, lips pursed. Had I learned my lesson? Popcorn was scattered over the counterpane. From a bedside bowl, he grabbed a handful of fluffy kernels, squeezed them as if to show his strength, and shoved the mashed mass into his mouth. He wiped his greasy chin on the sheets. I was to wait while he chewed.

He was setting a challenge. You must work with me as I am: unpleasant.

He was enacting a metaphor. I was like popcorn. I could be crushed and swallowed or tossed away.

He glared at me.

Did I disturb your sleep? I haven't been sleeping. Why should you be?

Had he imagined that I could help him while I was locked away? I wondered whether he saw the therapy as I did, ongoing and uninterrupted.

He, too, must have been thinking of my absence because he mentioned it immediately.

While you were away, I exercised my powers.

*Away*—as if I had been back in Providence, as he had falsely told Náomi.

I stirred things up, he said.

And then he entered on a strange monologue.

He spoke of upheaval he had caused, or tried to. This past week, he had redeployed troops under his command. The goal seemed to be to comfort former enemies and distress former allies.

He listed instruments of war: missiles, bombers, submarines, and destroyers. He mentioned cyberwarfare. He claimed to have formed battle plans for complex campaigns.

I thought of the Persians and their meager evidence. What was at stake in the monologue went beyond treason to megalomania. The point was to display his powers. He could be arbitrary on a grand scale, an international scale.

He continued on this tack for some minutes. It made no sense to note down the details—to imagine that he was stating matters of fact. He was boasting. He was intent on overwhelming me.

He referenced the plague. Before, he had claimed that his stance—ignoring science and urging others to join him—had saved millions of lives. Now, he embraced the other side of the argument. He referenced the nations that border ours. The Regime had produced double their death rates, almost double. He had sacrificed our countrymen, many hundreds of thousands.

He starved clinics and let hospitals be overwhelmed. His followers shunned health! He was in sync with them and they with him. No health! He destroyed health. People fell ill, and many died, but the survivors adored him!

He entered a trance, hypnotized by his own voice. *Grandiosity* fails to capture the magnitude of his self-praise. It was as if he were the Lord of the Old Testament and I were Job, with ungirt loins, prostrate before him.

*Canst thou lift up thy voice to the clouds, that abundance of waters may cover thee? Canst thou send lightnings, that they may go and say unto thee, Here we are?*

This globe! Who had put a mark on it as he had?

He had let the streams run foul and the sky turn sooty. The sun beat down, fires raged, glaciers melted, winds howled, dams broke, and cities flooded.

He got stuck on *flooded.*

Cities had flooded before. This time, they disappeared. That was all him.

He could leave the land in ruins and remain beloved.

He had made history. He was the end of history.

I recalled my ride to the fortress and my thoughts of Archie, who, after he killed his wife and daughter, could no longer face—could no longer be—himself. I had worried that a man who had *ruined the world* would be in deep denial, unable to acknowledge his own actions. I had thought, As the delusion lessens, self-assessment will turn painful.

I had not reckoned with the Great Man. His denial, if denial it was, took the form of embracing disaster. Catastrophe was cause for pride, provided that the scale was unprecedented.

He had made the ground to tremble and the wind to howl.

*Incalculable* was another word he got stuck on. The scale of the damage he had caused was *incalculable*.

Was I still conducting a therapy?

In the face of this long lyric poem, this extended aria, this roar of thunder, I did have one stray thought. The Great Man had found his own way of telling me that he had no intention of discussing local harm: my time in the oubliette, the threats against Kareena, and whatever had gone on between him and his wife.

Or else he was discussing those very subjects. He was reflecting my own views back to me. You see me as destructive on a vast scale. Why should you be surprised when I injure you?

Or he was defending against a sense of vulnerability. It would emerge in time—or soon—that the Great Man had lost his authority over our troops. They no longer obeyed his orders. He was about to be stripped of power. He was howling in terror.

Or else, nothing had changed except in the therapy. Having banished me, having shown cruelty in action, on my return he had been moved to reveal or amplify this aspect of the self, to see how much unpleasantness I could bear. I declined to be horrified. I remained in a supportive posture. In perverse fashion, my patient was acknowledging his misdeeds and shortcomings. Perhaps we were making rapid progress.

◊ ◊ ◊ ◊ ◊

I have a confession to make, the Great Man said.

I was so struck by the statement, so stunned by the notion that he was preparing me for an admission of fault, that I repeated the key word: confession.

I feel better about you, the Great Man said. Time away was good for you, I see that.

I had been right that my consignment to the oubliette had been part of the therapy. The Great Man had needed to show himself that he could restrain and punish me. His having taken control allowed him to proceed. That, and his having roared in my ear.

I had a brother, the Great Man began. Have I mentioned my brother?

He had not. I knew of the brother only from Náomi, the time she called him Sean. Had the Great Man's brother been the father's favorite? Had he died young of a drug overdose?

*Chip* was my dad's nickname for him. He seemed a chip off the old block.

My dad traveled a lot when I was young. Liked time away from my mother—our nanny was his gal Friday—long story, for another day.

Did I startle at the word *nanny*? Was she an earlier one, before Lotty? Did the father sleep with all the help?

I was astonished altogether. How did we get from rising oceans to a small tale from childhood?

I have a memory, the Great Man continued. Never shared it with anyone.

I must have been five, clever little fellow. My father's been absent for what seems a long time. At home, it's me and my mom and Chip, who would have been nine.

She was not in good control, my mom. She would go out for most of a day, shopping and drinking. Different era. Not unusual to leave a youngster in charge.

Me, Chip, and a yippy little dog—long-haired dachshund bitch—Brownie.

We lived in a suburb—not for long. This day had to do with our leaving.

Chip was a chubby kid, big, twice my size and more. He found it amusing to sit on me and eat greasy food, and wipe his fingers on my face. Or he might sit on me and fart while he read comic books.

*Greasy fingers*, I wrote on my pad. *Farts. Immobilization.* The narrative contained, I thought, a hint of apology, on the lines of *tout comprendre c'est tout pardonner*. I had never heard the Great Man apologize.

One day, I wriggle free. Quickly, I put a leash on Brownie and walk out. In those days, it's nothing to see a five-year-old walking a dog.

On the pad, I wrote, *pl.* Recalling his childhood, the Great Man was sounding uncharacteristically pleasant.

Immediately, his tone shifted—harsher voice, faster pace, as if he regretted having embarked on the story.

My brother rushes after me. He's terrified that my mother will come home and find me gone. Most basic job in babysitting. Keep track of the kid. Chip's failing at it.

My pad says *¿?*. The narrative had shifted from truth to invention.

Chip catches up and grabs the leash. He goes, You're running off? I'll show you to run off!

He leads me down a hill. The street ends at a small park, narrow, grassy, along a dry stream bed. Maybe there's a trickle. At one point, a path crosses a culvert, a big cement pipe that once directed the stream. The pipe has screens on both ends. They're on the order of chicken wire, but with thicker metal, meant to catch trash, maybe, or keep kids out.

On the downstream end, the mesh has been bent outward at the bottom. Small opening, scarcely noticeable. Chip slips a couple of dog treats through the screen, unclips the leash, and watches Brownie slither in after. Chip pushes the mesh back in place and rolls a stone against it to prevent reopening.

He gives me a whack and tells me to keep my mouth shut.

That's about it, the Great Man says, and he rushes the conclusion.

The Mom returned home. The brother said that the dog had run off. The Great Man was silenced with more blows.

The next day, hearing whimpers, a man walking to work saw Brownie and called the dog officer. The mom reclaimed Brownie, but she was never the same. Brownie peed on bedspreads. She snapped at Chip. Shortly, poor Brownie disappeared. Given to an owner without children, the explanation went. In reality, the Great Man said....

He did not complete the thought.

As the telling proceeded, the Great Man's energy flagged. I think he saw that he was painting himself into a corner. The invention made him look bad. A brave boy would have stood up to the brother and saved the dog by revealing her whereabouts.

So difficult! I said, meaning to cover both the failure in storytelling and the events from childhood.

I was with my patient, staying local, with the canst-thou-send-lightnings diatribe fully behind us. And then I thought, No, the Biblical rant, the grand embrace of evil-doing, had been a prelude to this memory of private shame.

I had never seen this parlay before, the confession of killing hundreds of thousands as an attempt to contextualize mistreatment of a pet. Who but the Great Man could create this sequence? It was exciting in a way, so late in life, to encounter a new form of narrative in therapy.

AS THE GREAT MAN TOLD his yarn, I understood that, at an early age, he had harmed the family dog. He had been prepared to say as much, almost ready, and then he veered off.

As the Great Man spoke, I imagined a parallel account.

He had found his way down the hill, coaxed Brownie into a culvert, trapped her there, and made his way home undetected. He was punishing the mother for leaving him at his brother's mercy. The brother would be blamed for the dog's absence, and all the more once a neighbor happened on Brownie and returned her.

Or else, the final story, the one that the Great Man would tell in time and stick with, if we worked together long enough, was worse. Children can do terrible things. I blocked myself from pursuing this line of thought.

Even so, my mind turned to sociopathy. That's where children who mistreat animals often are headed. I dislike the diagnosis—tried to avoid it in my work with a prison population. Once we call patients sociopathic, we are inclined to imagine that they are untreatable. I prefer not to give up on anyone.

Patients who behave like sociopaths sometimes recall having been driven to extremes in childhood. They were pushed hard by a domineering relative and responded by acting in ways that made them experience themselves differently. The affect includes a mix of shame, if they are capable of it, and pride or a sense of freedom. They crossed a line and turned bad.

I found that, for prisoners, recollections of harm to pets are not rare. The revelation may come in stages. The payoff is in the efforts at disclosure. The patient is learning to aim for honesty, to trust the doctor and the process, to come to face himself.

Hearing the censored telling of the Brownie story, I was struck again by how difficult it is to maintain perspective. The image of the abandoned dog unnerved me more than the memories, from news that had filtered through, of thousands of Southerners—and their many pets—recently lost to flooding. The Great Man's indifference to the public good, his strategic use of know-nothing takes on science, his laziness in the face of disaster—surely these grave flaws should disturb me more than talk of a childhood sadistic streak.

It is hard to ignore harm to a trusting dog.

Perhaps my progression, and the Great Man's, would be from the personal to the political and from the long-ago to the present-day. We would begin by tolerating memories of private cruelty. Later, we would confront marital discord and, only then, the unchecked spread of plague, and structural harm, like the death of democracy. Am I displaying my pollyannaish side when I say that in mentioning Brownie, the Great Man had made a little excursion in the direction of self-awareness?

◊ ◊ ◊ ◊ ◊

Pleased with his performance, the Great Man dozed off smiling, only to wake moments later.

Where is it that you work? We'll be heading to your office. I want to lie on that couch.

The miracle, he said—that's what I need.

I said, You've decided to visit Providence.

Doubtless, yesterday, when Náomi was negotiating my amnesty, she had re-familiarized the Great Man with Trude Nilsson's mythmaking—the notion that I worked magic on my home turf.

The décor, he said.

Náomi's word for sure. In her book, Nilsson had waxed ecstatic about the room that Miriam had designed. The hypnotically complex oriental rug, the nostalgia-inducing engravings and woodblock prints, the tranquilizing shade of wall paint, a pewtery gray-green.

Had Náomi made the setting out as a luxury good? The Great Man would have access to the famous consulting room. He had control of the doctor. If the combination worked, perhaps the office contents, like all that chinoiserie, could be shipped to the fortress or wherever the Great Man would settle next.

Náomi will follow, the Great Man said.

Once he had found refreshing sleep on the couch, he would want me to work with him and his consort together as a couple.

His idea was that I would convince her to resume relations.

You've made a good start, he said. Tell me—I know already, but tell me—you had a word with her yesterday.

I considered protesting that I had been locked up but thought better of it. Introducing reality would only cause him to turn on me.

Seeing me hesitate, he shifted gears and reprised his routine from our pre-oubliette session, a lubricious account of what Náomi had provided him that morning.

I wondered whether she had given him some consideration in exchange for my safety. Had she sashayed before him? Let him sniff her flesh up close? I took him for a renifleur. Not rare, by the way, in my practice, for men to take sexual pleasure in smell.

I guessed that what Náomi had offered was only the agreement to join him on the road trip. He had hoped for more, and now was presenting me with his imagining.

I'm heading east anyway, the Great Man said.

A meeting with kleptocrats outside Boston, would be followed by a rally in New Hampshire. He listed goals: tapping the wealthy, energizing the base, inspiring the nation.

I'm a hero back east. Love my toughness, love my standing up for regular people.

*Regular people* was a code that the Great Man used in public. I thought that I understood. I did not inquire. It was not my job to discuss politics.

The arrangements for the rally suggested that the Great Man knew how much he was hated—how much at risk he was when he went out in public. He would be addressing a pop-up crowd. Bub would announce the visit at the last minute through email blasts sent to known supporters.

Were even they reliable? The Great Man's regular people included the deprived, the enraged, the resentful, the heavily armed. In New Hampshire, the lakes were dry or polluted. Just now, as I write, snow may be plentiful, but in recent winters, the mountains had gone bare. Life was hard throughout New England.

The Reaper had suggested New Hampshire. The Reaper was all over the idea.

I heard weakness in the Great Man's voice, weakness and eagerness. He was a child again, the boy out to please a self-absorbed parent. I was his father, sending him down an icy couloir.

I don't say that I understood the plots against him if there were any. I know that I heard false notes when he shared his plans for leaving the lair.

There was a hotel in New Hampshire that Náomi had liked—back in their courtship days. What romance!

Or was that Vermont?

Never mind. Probably shuttered. If only the health departments had followed his plans!

He would ask the Reaper. Buy the hotel. Executive necessity, housing for security guards. Staff the place royally for one suite, one night.

What Náomi had done to him in New Hampshire! The pleasures he had known!

His monologue was full of fantasy about reconciliation.

Hearing the Great Man enthuse over Bub's plans for him, my mind turned to my patient Ahmed. He is suspicious of any deal. His mantra is, *If it's good for them, it's bad for me.*

Ahmed scorns all solicitations, from offers of friendship to coupons from retailers. The only bargains he trusts are ones he proposes, and you wouldn't want to be on the other side of those.

The group can spin out counterexamples. Some marriages are win-win. A man can believe, correctly, that he's fortunate that this woman considered him at all.

Ahmed understands the arguments, but the mantra sums up his attitude. He schooled the group in mistrust. In session, it's a bit of a thing for guys to say, *Sounds like a deal*, to warn a member about an offer that's too good to be true. Often, it's Ahmed they're addressing. As I say, paranoia deserts you when you need it most.

AS THE GREAT MAN TALKED up the trip, I recalled the teachings of a psychoanalyst whom Hans Lutz admired. This colleague made it a point to allow patients to find their own way. But there were exceptions. If a patient seemed intent on self-destruction, if he had talked himself into a choice that would almost certainly cause him great harm, Hans's colleague would cry out, *Merciful God! Let us consider what will follow that!*

Should I have cried out?

Vera/Marya had led me to suspect that Bub had it in for his master.

I doubted that Náomi wished her husband well.

The Great Man's guards included Persians. They were on the lookout for a convenient ending, like a mishap outside the fortress, beyond anyone's control.

From my patients, I understood how hard profits were to come by. The kleptocrats might resent being strong-armed for bribes. They might favor regime change and have the means to make it come about.

And then there were the locals. If New Hampshire was anything like Rhode Island, there would be residents ready to take matters into their own hands.

Other therapists might set these concerns aside, but I had been trained in toggling—in taking outside knowledge into account, some of the time.

I did not cry out in warning. Instead, I listened empathetically, registering my patient's enthusiasm. I picked up countervailing undertones as well, related to self-destructive impulses. I did not point to them.

The Great Man elaborated his fantasy. So much love from Náomi. So much love from the people.

I thought, He knows. He is composing his eulogy.

I wondered whether the earlier performance, with the Biblical rant and the Brownie story, had been an attempt to make himself unlikeable so that I would give my blessing to what amounted to a suicide.

I catechized myself. Unconsciously, was I seeking revenge for the small injury the Great Man had done when he caused me to phone Luiza? Perhaps it was only that I lacked strength of character. I could not bring myself to forgo what I wanted, time back in my office on Prudence Street.

To sit passively, to leave my patient to his own devices.... Let's not pretend. I was no Kantian. This time it was I who chose to do injury to my profession.

I EXPECTED MORE ENTHUSIASM, THE Great Man said. Why aren't you celebrating?

He must have previously hit a bedside button, because Bub appeared, looking the worse for wear.

The bad penny, he said. He wanted me back in the oubliette.

The Great Man enjoyed conflict between subordinates, but he had a wish and was impatient to act on it.

Reaper, he said, on the way to the rally, I am considering an expedition, to—where is it?

Providence, I said. Did that one word implicate me further?

I have business with...Pomerantz...Komaroff—the Wizard here. We will confer in his office. He has promised to bring me sleep.

Bub is not blessed with a poker face. He ran scenarios. When the inner computer finished its calculations, he brightened. The smile was at once malicious and subservient. It said, *Yes, master, willingly master*, but with barely suppressed glee.

I've seen the consulting room, Bub said. It has an aura. A fine and private place.

I believe that I heard him say those words. I did not react. I was a co-conspirator.

The Great Man explained his plan. He would meet with me, first alone and then with Náomi. He'd do fundraising outside Boston, on Route 128, with her on his arm. Important, when you court kleptocrats, to display the quality wife. Then, the grand rally in New Hampshire. Náomi had consented to stand at his side. On the way back, refreshed by the first visit, coffers full, ego boosted, he would return to my office for a second marital session.

*Stealth* was a word the Great Man used. Bub was to keep the private meetings invisible.

And there was this one hotel...romantic.... He had been there before....

I can arrange it, Beelzebub said. A ghost journey—invisible hours—on short order—time for intimacy—my specialty—my privilege.

So as not to appear overeager, Bub lingered at the bedside, reviewing logistics. The Great Man would head to the rear of my office building and arrive early. Time alone in the iconic room might prove helpful. I would follow, walking the final block and arriving at the front door, as if returning to routine practice after a medical absence. Planning for Naomi would be more delicate. Would it be too much to ask her to travel in disguise? She might enjoy playing a trouser role. Women rarely entered the building. We did not want to attract attention.

Exits were a complex matter. And so on.

Was Bub grasping an opportunity? He had planned mischief for New Hampshire, but how perfect for the Great Man to die in a shrink's office! The location would confirm what every objective observer suspected, that the Great Man was a head case. Bub would claim credit for having kept the boss on track, partly on track, during the long reign. The story would be one of progressive mental deterioration, a figurehead propped up by senior staff and finally coming to a sad end.

While Bub feigned loyalty through attention to detail, I was convincing myself that travel might benefit my patient.

In terms of mental structure, he was not different from other criminals I had treated. He had no greater level of paranoia, no greater level of abuse in childhood. He did lie more and insist more on being believed. But finally, he got round to sharing memories that were distorted in ways that I found familiar. There was still hope that I could work with him.

The therapy might be well served by a change in venue. In Providence, I would be far from the oubliette. I would sleep nights. If I was well rested, if I felt safe, my mind would be sharper.

I did have more mojo in that office. I had been prepared to make that argument in the initial interview with B. In my own chair, I would have easier access to memories of parallel cases. That's what experience means, isn't it, the experience we value in our doctors—their recall of how it went for this or that past patient in similar circumstances?

Embracing the fantasy—the magic of the couch—allowed me to ignore my awareness. Yes, in Providence, I might be more alert, but would my patient survive? The Great Man was being played.

Say better: he was allowing himself to be played and had been when he had agreed to the New Hampshire foray.

Bub's voice sharpened. He was discussing dicey details—which houris to send to the hotel, how to suppress information if it leaked out.

No houris! the Great Man said. No need for houris! Honeymoon suite, champagne and caviar, roses in the snow!

Bring me a list of hotels, top hotels, luxe.

He might recognize a name.

The Great Man's voice cut through my trance. You're excused! Don't you know when time's up?

I rose to leave.

Not you, Finkelstein! So quick are we?

A rant ensued. Weren't therapists meant to understand people implicitly? Why could I not grasp the object of a simple command?

He banished Bub. Reaper, that was your exit cue.

Bub did his proud man's version of the bow and scrape. I found myself alone with the Great Man.

He said, You really are bad at what you do.

◊ ◊ ◊ ◊ ◊

By the way, the Great Man said, good news. The rebellion is over. All but over. *Quashed.*

Fantastic word, quashed.

Quashed or squashed.

Was this news from the outer or inner world? Perhaps militias were in retreat. Perhaps a paranoid delusion had lessened. It occurred to me that the therapy might be benefitting my patient, in preliminary fashion.

WMFGG. Have you heard of them? You're a sad, isolated man, Greenberg. White Men for Guns and Greatness. They have quelled the uprising. Quelled it!

I'll be back at the center soon. You'll like it. Not all that different from the fortress. Big barricades. Tanks. Lots of tanks.

You'll feel very safe.

I do. Safe at the center.

Safe and cozy, with the barricades and the armed helicopters and the little low flying things, like a kid's toy.

When you succeed as much as I have, people get jealous. Can't be helped.

Chaim, the Great Man said, you're a wise person. Tell me, how can a man be *perfect and yet not…*?

He sought a word for what he was not.

*Perfect and not…*, I said, repeating the Great Man's words but moving the negation closer to the delusion.

Certain medications that are effective in the long run can be dangerous early on. Suicides spike a week after the first dose. Sometimes, a patient's energy returns before the despair and self-hatred lift.

Is psychotherapy different? Patients may experience new feelings before they develop the capacity to tolerate them. I had invited my patient to finish his partially stated thought. But what was the proper completion?

The Great Man knew that he would never be respected, not by anyone on whom the hypnosis failed to work. He was hated, and with reason. In his own terms, he was the boy who killed Brownie. He was the screw-up his father has seen him to be.

As if hearing that thought, the Great Man returned to diatribe mode. He did not finish his *perfect* sentence. He stimmed on *chaos*.

I use chaos as leverage. I have made chaos normal. Chaos engenders chaos. The chaos I wreak now opens the door to the vast chaos to come. I revel in chaos.

What is life's goal, Einstein? To be the last free man, the freest man, to act outrageously, to claim license.

I incarnate possibility, the Great Man boasted.

He was an existential rebel, standing up to the gods.

He was Krishna, destroyer of worlds.

I thought back to the *perfect and yet not* formulation. Why had I echoed it, reminding my patient, in effect, that he was unloved?

Did I have in mind his coercing me, through threats to my daughter? I hope I'm not vengeful, but I am no saint.

The Great Man raved, he barked. And then he collected himself.

He glared at me.

You're blind, he said. You don't see what's before you: brilliance, drive, accomplishment.

He said, You'll do better in that burg, the one we're heading to.

Was he asking me to dissuade him from his appointment in Samarra? I should have said, *By no means!*

I chose not to stand in his way.

◊ ◊ ◊ ◊ ◊

Dear, dear Henry. How I thank you for entrusting me with your memoir, if I may call it that. Do you prefer *autofiction*? I mean your account of your time with my Krishna.

I appreciate the service that your Maurice rendered by posting fragments. Because they were of the moment, they captured our interest, but how much more like you the complete version is! I am pleased that you are letting me shepherd it along toward publication—the original, I mean, the text that you forwarded to Maury via that darling farmer woman, your Ginnie.

I KNOW HOW YOU HATE for your books to have introductions. I am composing my thoughts in the form of an afterword.

I so wish that you would undertake the writing yourself and complete the story. Since it seems you won't, I have set myself the task. I'm no author. My efforts at self-expression were in theater. I interpreted lines that others wrote. On stage, I was at ease. Writing, I'm at loose ends. How do storytellers know what to put first?

You, sweet Henry, just jump in, nickname at the ready: *The Great Man was found dead....* You want your books to mirror your clinical work. Starting a therapy, you motion the patient into the consulting room. Treatment begins, without instruction. Impressions form in due course.

Perhaps, in that metaphor, I would do well to claim the role of the patient. I imagine you sitting across from me, inviting me to begin as I please.

What pleases me is to face an audience—your readers and, now, mine. I will turn to them—address them as *you*, and call you Henry, although I do hate to avert my gaze. You're my inspiration.

IT OCCURS TO ME THAT I did once fancy myself a writer. In a small theater troupe, I was cast as understudy in the Emily Dickinson one-hander, *The Belle of Amherst.* Midway through rehearsals, I turned into a poet. That was the experience. Fantastic words and images came to me. I noted some lines down.

It's good that I was never called on to take over in performance. Physically, I was wrong—not birdlike and virginal, not likely to have been rejected by boys at seventeen. But I was good at memorizing. The script is long. I served as prompter.

For the duration of the run, I flattered myself that I had a special skill with language. I wonder whether when empathizing with a car salesman Henry imagines that he can close deals and, if so, how long the illusion lasts. My confidence has vanished, and yet I intend to persist at this task. I tell myself that composing an afterword is like acting: I'm out to give new life to someone else's work.

I'LL START THERE—SAYING HOW I came to ask for the privilege of publishing this memoir.

You (beloved reader) will be aware that in the wake of my husband's death, I left for New Zealand at the invitation of Sunny, as I call her—the Prime Minister.

What a good friend Sunny is. I first met her years ago, when she had her country's economic development portfolio and my husband was globetrotting, hawking his businesses. I bonded with her. Like me, she was struggling with a horrific marriage. If you have seen the documentary, *Breaking Through the Clouds*, you know all about Sunny's troubles. Her husband continued to abuse her even as she advanced politically.

Shortly after she divorced, Sunny invited me to join her in New Zealand and take up residence. As my husband consolidated his political power, she became insistent. I must make a public statement by ditching him.

I doubted that my walking out would have an impact. Dozens of officials had deserted the Regime. My husband maligned them. Nothing changed. I would be made out as unstable, the hysterical divorcée. My testimony would be dismissed.

I stayed with my husband and pled with him for scraps of charity for those in need.

There is no charity, Sunny said.

I DID, YES, CALL MY husband the Great Man and, later, Krishna. I had in mind the role in *The Mahabharata*, Krishna, the wise and noble god, my husband's opposite. *You must learn to see with the same eye a mound of earth and a heap of gold....* Fat chance.

In the final months in the fortress, I sensed that my Krishna had become a desperado. That's when I arranged to summon Henry. I was not out to reform Krishna's character altogether.

Unlike Henry, I lacked that level of hope. Krishna needed calming. He needed being brought back on track.

Meanwhile, with Sunny's support, I began forming an escape plan. We both knew that I might not act on it. She was certain that I was shackled by whatever psychic chains bind women to bad men. Perhaps I was. I will tell my story in time. Following Sunny's lead, I may authorize a documentary.

As Henry has reported, I was molested in childhood. In a hard-to-define way, the marriage felt like a continuation.

I can list elements.

The sneering and sarcasm. The incessant sexual pleas. The sadism and deviousness and bullying. The stench—I'll get to the stench in a minute.

The physical unattractiveness did not help. What an ugly man.

Every brutal element was worsened by the sense of endlessness. No way out. To abandon him was to leave the nation and the planet—and democracy, that fragile beauty—at his mercy. I was chained to the devil.

Henry worried that I was being beaten. He was not far off. I did feel battered, but the bruises that Henry mentions were incidental. While complaining about the marriage, my husband made an aggressive arm movement. When I flinched, I slipped. In my effort to regain my balance, I slipped again and banged against a corner of a dresser.

Krishna's arm sweep was meant claim space, to express contempt.

I am trying to be precise in my report. He never struck me.

Did that misadventure nonetheless send Henry to the clink?

When Henry first asked about the bruises, I looked confused because I did not understand how he had seen them. I had meant to keep them covered. I suppose I should say *meant consciously*.

Once I understood the impression Henry had formed, I took advantage. So long as he suspected domestic violence, I had his attention. I moved the information-gathering phase of the therapy along.

That's my confession. Without lying outright, I misled Henry. I fear that the deception was consequential, that it caused him to lose sympathy with his patient.

The small and private injury, the bruise, was so vivid as to make it hard for Henry to ignore the grand injuries, to the country and the planet. I complicated Henry's effort to treat my husband as just another patient, one who had sinned but might yet be redeemed.

In defense, partial defense, of my deception, the bruise marks served as external indicators of my inner state. I am thinking of what Henry wrote about Knausgård, how he justifies the passage where the wife beats a donkey. I left my bruises unexplained in hopes of capturing *an atmosphere of menace in the marriage.*

Look, you all lived under my husband's rule. How did it feel?

Have I strayed off topic? I was saying how Sunny lent encouragement. As soon as she learned of Krishna's death, she sent a note. *Join me.*

I wrote that I was worried for her reputation.

She said that she trusted me implicitly, trusted me to have done right. Even if I'd acted rashly, she'd still rather have me down under, out of the Regime's reach.

In public, she doesn't come off as that type, the loyal gal pal. She is.

Sunny had a government plane waiting for me in Montreal. Glue drove me there direct from the crematorium and accompanied me on the long flight. There was no fuss. We just went.

The notoriety of the legal system back home makes it easy to claim asylum in New Zealand. The Regime is on a list of rogue governments. The presumption is that the judiciary is an arm of a corrupt executive branch. As a matter of law, I can't be extradited from New Zealand, no matter the charge or evidence against me.

If I am granted citizenship, I will be safer yet. Sunny is rushing papers through. By the week's end, I will be a Kiwi.

Public sentiment is on my side. The Great Man is reviled here, as he must be in every island nation. As the oceans rise, the populace is forced inland. Wellington sits on a peninsula. Street by street, the city is moving west, uphill.

How generous Sunny has been. This morning, as I write, I am in an apartment carved out of the upper floors of the stately home that was her residence when she served as a Member of Parliament, before she moved to Premier House. I have distant ocean views.

When Sunny greeted me, I asked whether Henry and others—his family and Muscle—might be invited as well. She checked with aides and gave the go-ahead.

It helped that Henry is well loved here. His blog posts begin with what the Kiwis consider a joyous occasion, the liberation of the planet from a destroyer. Religious congregations prayed for Henry's safety.

I understood the premise, baked into the memoir, that while Henry was hidden away, correspondence with him was impossible. Nonetheless, I sent Maury a message. If ever Henry did make contact, would Maury let him know that he was welcome in Wellington? And please, please, would Maury forward me Henry's memoir entries in their entirety? The blog posts seemed fragmentary.

Parenthetically, I am not the source of the bespattered manila envelope that familiarized Henry with his readers' responses. I'm guessing that they came from Ginnie. That's why sweat moistened her brow. She was concealing her role as the assembler of the online comments. She'd printed them out because she was disturbed by how acquaintances (or neighbors in a hardware store) were receiving the blog posts.

Despite my own frustrations with the posts' incompleteness, I had followed them intently. Before reading the blog, I hadn't known what my husband had told Henry or what Henry made of him.

I had not known how Candide-like Henry was. The least hint of self-awareness on Krishna's part led Henry to imagine that he could treat him, and in a deep sense, total reform. In our conversations, I found Henry considered in his judgments. In the blog, the moment he turns to patient care, he becomes a cockeyed optimist. Perhaps you need to be, in that line of work.

He got me right, mostly. I did flirt with him. It's how I engage men—I see that.

In Wellington, a morning drive-time radio host took to reading Henry's posts aloud, in the local accent. Knowing Henry's voice, I found the alteration funny, no matter how sober the subject matter. Along with my new neighbors, I breakfasted to Henry's words.

I gather that, back home, too, the blog was a phenomenon. How not? It had seemed that my husband would govern forever, and then—whoosh!—everything shifted. Henry's unhurried account of the lead-up to the event must have stood out from the breathless news coverage. It could not have hurt that the testimony was by a psychiatrist. People wondered about my husband's mental state. *If only an expert could offer an opinion!* Henry was that authority. Who would not wish to hear him weigh in?

But Maury's stripped-down offerings were simplistic. In them, the Great Man was a monster, with Henry as his victim. I had read Henry's books. More, I had sat with Henry. I was sure that with my husband and in the writing, Henry had been accepting and non-judgmental.

Strange to say, I found the blog posts too much on point. In his books, Henry meanders. He circles back. He shares daydreams. In the blog, stray thoughts and inconsequential details were lacking.

I didn't doubt that Maury considered the posts to be Henry's act of witness or resistance. Reading, I thought, Henry can do better. I was certain that he *had* done better. His mosaic, his tessera, the real one, remained hidden.

Even in Maury's redacted version, with certain topics I was able to read through the posts to a reality that they were meant simultaneously to conceal and represent. To give a minor example, my husband's digestion was fine. He had an iron stomach.

As everyone knows, he did eat chicken tacos by the bucketful. Giving him another favorite food, like pork rinds or tofu, would be, to borrow a common metaphor, like depicting Napoleon as a six-footer.

But my husband did not fart, not more than the next man. He had off-putting halitosis, and he loved to put his face right up to yours and let you suffer. He showered too little. He loved the smell of his own armpits and sniffed them regularly, even in public. But primarily, my husband's stench was spiritual. Being near him made people gag, and not just me. You felt his moral rot in your core.

While we're discussing imaginative translation, let me make a note about the houris. Henry hadn't needed to work hard to invent them. His account reproduces a rumor that circulated in the villages near the fortress. His visiting patient, Duncan, may have brought Henry the story.

Henry must have considered it a ready-made objective correlative, what he calls *a fit proxy*, for all I had told him about my husband's sexual predilections, shortcomings, and misdeeds, a lifetime of off-putting behavior, starting well before Krishna and I ever met.

Think of the houris as beaten donkeys. I'm guessing that Henry felt barred, professionally, from exposing his patient in precise fashion. Henry's a blancher—he blanched at tales I told him.

*Houri* expresses his horror. As for the real details…if I write my memoir…if I collaborate on a documentary…we'll see.

I heard imaginative translation, too, in the blog posts about Chet and Ginnie. *You won't publish what I'm about to write*—hmm. On the contrary, Maury seemed to give us those sections complete.

For me, the telltale was the conversation about squash vine borers. It's like the period details that playwrights include to lend verisimilitude—the black cake whose ingredients Emily Dickinson catalogs to demonstrate her domestic bent. We're as ignorant about black cake as we are about species of squash, but the recipe sounds true to the time and place.

My guess: a patient of Henry's once groused about pests overrunning his kitchen garden in Barrington, Rhode Island, and explained how he had resorted to growing Asian varietals. Henry, in writer mode, stashed away the details for future use. Coming upon *pepo* and *moschata*, I thought, No snow-covered trails, no fresh venison, no country cottage.

Maury published descriptions of Chet and Ginnie and the cabin because there was no risk that they or the path interrupted by a beaver pond would be found. They did not exist.

Had Henry refused to leave Providence? Maury had defended mobsters who had chosen to disappear in anticipation of subpoenas. Perhaps he asked one for access to the off-the-grid hideaway he had used in his own time of need. Or else Providence has a Chet-and-Ginnie team, Regime opponents who provide safe haven to resisters on the run. So long as Maury could say truthfully that he had no way to contact his client, the sanctuary's whereabouts would not matter.

Had Henry managed to see Nina and Tammy? Difficult, but not inconceivable.

From Henry's books, I know how keen he is to convey feeling states. The release from the fortress was exhilarating. Continued distance from communal life—from his guys—brought a sense of isolation and vulnerability. *Skiing alone* expresses those contrasts.

Once Henry had established the structure, snowscape and bungalow, he used it to contain and reveal his emotional life. In Providence (if that's where he hid), was he concerned about his effect on those who looked after him? Did he come to admire a particular good woman who was frank but unobtrusive? It occurred to me that Henry hit it off with one of his minders, his Ginnie. Did he worry that he was drifting away from his late wife, the sainted if sometimes mendacious Miriam?

Or else Henry did in fact set his laptop on a kitchen table in a snowbound cabin that had sheltered AWOL soldiers. I'm willing to be wrong, willing years from now, when the cottage in Maine has become a tourist attraction, to visit and smile at the bronze plaque affixed to a stone, Henry Farber, Diarist, Wrote Here.

For our purposes, what matters is that I suspected that Henry might not be as hard to reach as the blog suggested.

I contacted Maury. I asked, Don't you worry that Henry will be discovered soon?

Cops and journalists must have been on his trail. I wanted Maury to extract Henry from the hideout and get him to safety here in New Zealand.

I thought I could sell Henry on Wellington. It's like his beloved Providence as it once was, before my husband brought the nation's cities to ruin. The scale is similar. The housing stock too. Neighborhoods of single-family homes abut the business district. Wellington is a seat of government and a university town. It has water views. It's artsy, neighborly, walkable.

From Maury, I received the expected response—no way to reach Henry. But soon after, Maury posted the final blog entry, and Henry reappeared in Providence. Days later, a link to this memoir in its entirety appeared in my inbox. The site had an auto-burn feature. Paragraphs disappeared as I scrolled past them. I stayed up all night poring over the file—the memoir you have just read. In it, I recognized the Henry I know.

I sent Maury an additional request. I wanted to publish the memoir. It was a resource, a document of our time, an intimate and disinterested account of the Great Man and his effect on those close to him in his final days. I mean, as disinterested as you can get. Henry struggled hard to be fair.

If there was censorship back home, I would publish the book in New Zealand. Had Henry written more, or was he about to? He might be busy, submitting to or resisting official interviews and catching up with patients and his family. But the memoir needed a final entry, to wrap things up.

I received an immediate response. Maury asked whether I could arrange a secure setting for an 'encrypted video chat. Morning in Wellington and afternoon in Providence, after Henry's nap, might be best.

Sunny put me in touch with her communications guru. Only a brief slot was available. You can imagine the frenzy in Wellington as Kiwi diplomats worked to make sense of developments in the States. I took what I time could get.

Henry joined from his office, relying on the technical apparatus his patients had provided. The quality of the video was poor. Perhaps encryption slowed the transmission process. Perhaps we were being hacked.

I had been in Henry's consulting room the morning of my husband's death (I will describe that visit presently) so I was familiar with the furnishings. Still, it was remarkable to see Henry in his chair. Give Miriam credit. Even without the iconic couch, the setup draws you in.

Flirting with Henry in the fortress, I had felt us to be contemporaries. I forgive men their age—I had forgiven my late husband his. On video, Henry looked old. Did he have an asymmetry about the lips? Perhaps the right corner of his mouth drooped. Had he suffered a small stroke? Any change was subtle. His speech was clear.

I've missed you, I said. Are you well?

He stared, turtle-eyed.

Seeing Henry look confused or distracted, I remembered his account of his final conversation with his mentor, Hans Lutz. Demented, Hans had still succeeded in getting Henry to think aloud about himself. Henry was having this same effect on me.

So much to tell, I said. I was ready to pour my heart out. But then, he seemed to be aware of the time available, as I suppose therapists are trained to be.

He said, You find my notes incomplete.

They need an ending.

He agreed, but he was done with the blog. Did I know that Meg Galliard had died while he was in hiding?

How sad for you, I said.

She had succumbed to late effects of plague—more of my husband's baneful heritage. Henry had learned of Meg's death when he worked his way through his email, on his return to civilian life. He had missed the funeral. He wanted to complete his final collaboration with Meg, the book on medical error.

Reading his memoir, you may have the impression that Henry uses silence to draw people out. He does pause when he's lost in thought, but mostly, Henry engages actively. It's only that his speech affects you—affects me, anyway—like a classical psychoanalyst's grunts and hmms. The whole time that Henry is talking, he is waiting for something. You find yourself heading in unexpected directions.

So it was in our video chat. I imagined that I was making a simple request, for Henry to finish his memoir or allow me to publish it as it was. Instead, he was waiting for me to realize that I must volunteer.

I will write the ending, I said.

He did not want me to expose myself to harm.

I'll write the ending, I said, if you will let me publish the rest.

I thought that it would ease his mind if there was a deal, if I seemed to be getting something I valued in exchange for my contribution.

When he hesitated, I said what he had hoped to hear. I wanted to add my own tile to the Resistance mosaic. I would place my tiny fragment beside his more substantial one.

SOON, MAURY ENTERED THE FRAME. He looks younger than Henry. All that hair, pulled back in a ponytail! Maury is quick and forceful.

He wanted to fill me in on the murder investigation. A patient of Henry's—anyway, a man, Daniel Saba, who said he was a patient—had confessed to killing my husband. The police had not determined how to proceed. In the meanwhile, Saba's ex-wife, Noelle, had asked Maury to defend him.

Maury had agreed to appear for the early proceedings. If Henry were indicted, Maury might need to pass Saba's representation on to a colleague.

For Saba's defense, Maury wanted a full statement from me in pocket, for use in negotiations with prosecutors. How much I made public, in connection with Henry's memoir, was up to me.

I asked Maury to pitch in with any information that the police had shared about his client, Saba. I wanted to know what the authorities knew so that, where possible, I could respond to their concerns.

Henry must have already told Maury that my testimony was likely to be exculpatory for his client, because Maury agreed immediately. He would send the police dossier and a file of Henry's memoir entries, the complete set, unedited.

Henry reappeared. He was concerned about my participation. He did not want my asylum jeopardized.

I assured him that I would be fine. It was this Daniel Saba we did not want endangered.

Did I mind, then, Henry asked, if he expressed a preference? As much as possible, the memoir should resemble his books, the ones characterized by imaginative translation.

The statement that Maury wanted, the testimony that he hoped to keep under wraps—I might want to prepare that separately. For the book, if I did provide an ending—best, perhaps, to frame it as fictive elaboration, so as to maintain narrative unity. The Great Man should remain unnamed, and so on. As for factual details, I was to take liberties, just as he, Henry, had.

I understood Henry's concern. If I offered conventional testimony, I might find myself in trouble, through perjury or self-incrimination. Best to afford myself leeway.

As Henry went on, I began to believe that he thought me guilty of mariticide. Henry had used fiction to protect patients while still depicting reality as he understood it. He was inviting me to dissemble for a more banal purpose, to avoid the consequences of my actions, as he imagined them.

Alternatively, in autofiction, I could confess in public without swearing to anything. Permission to invent was an invitation to candor.

I heard Henry out. I feel so tied to him. I wanted to flow through the ether and be reassembled in Providence. I wanted to offer comfort and receive it in return.

Instead, the screen flickered. We waved goodbyes. The audio feed continued for a few more minutes. Maury took advantage of the secure hookup to fill me in on his client the confessed killer.

◊ ◊ ◊ ◊ ◊

That poor man who sits in jail! How I feel for him, as I feel for any bystander caught up in in the affairs of my late husband.

In deference to Henry, I have given Maury's client a pseudonym, Daniel Saba. From here on, I will refer to him by his first name. I will alter the details of his circumstances and identity as well—mechanically, I fear, as I cannot claim Henry's hypnogogic inspiration. No matter. Anyone with an internet connection will know whom I mean when I write *Daniel.*

At the time of my video chat from Wellington, the police had pulled Daniel in for questioning and held him on suspicion of attempted murder.

Shortly, news of his apprehension leaked out, and the media began digging into his background. I will be drawing on that reporting, the parts that sound credible, as well as on my chat with Maury and the briefing file that he transmitted. The police provided Maury with phone logs and interview transcripts. He may have sources within the Department as well. It would surprise me if he didn't.

Daniel is innocent. The evidence the police presented to Maury proves nothing. I can make that contribution, providing exculpatory testimony. Regarding my own actions, will I alter a detail or two? Henry was right. I will want leeway.

I FIND HARD IT TO write about a man I have not met. I'd love to give a first-hand impression of Daniel Saba, to say how he strikes a person—how he struck me. Instead, I must begin where Henry does in the memoir, with a photograph.

I've seen the standard one, copied from Daniel's faculty member home page on the Brown University website. Are there others? Perhaps not many. Our Daniel must be camera shy.

The shot we have suggests that he favors the unkempt wild-eyed professor look. The hair is brown, the skin is young, and he's wearing a cardigan instead of a lab coat, but the facial expression, teetering between wonder and alarm, brings to mind the Christopher Lloyd character from Back to the Future.

We like energy and enthusiasm in our teachers, don't we? Based on the image, I see Daniel as at worst erratic or mercurial. I detect no other signs of mental imbalance, but what would be the tell? I have family members who go off the deep end regularly. In my wedding photo, you would be hard pressed to distinguish them.

What should murderers look like? Any image we have comes from news photos of the poor—ill-kempt men, dark-skinned, scowling, scarred, tattooed, often in prison garb. Henry writes of having worked with white-collar killers. He must have his own, different impression. My only experience is with men who kill at a distance and on a massive scale. They were unremarkable altogether, unless you are close enough to smell the rot.

I'm presentable, and I have confessed that I was ready to do my husband in.

And yet, are we capable of believing that pictures tell us nothing? Daniel looks mild. If he proved violent, we would wonder whether he had been driven to act against his nature. Nothing about him appears studied or calculating. When the university asked for a photo, Daniel must have had a teaching assistant grab a snapshot with his phone.

As for the rest of the webpage, the CV testifies to steady employment with substantial production and achievement. Assistant Professor of Literary Arts. Many writers' residencies.

Daniel has three e-novels to his name, a dozen scholarly publications, and a volume of criticism with the enigmatic title *A Walk in the Park*.

The Literary Arts Department faculty page informs students that Daniel is a programmer as much as a wordsmith. He is said to be known for his *obsessive works of fiction in which hot links lead to subtexts with unexpected and revelatory plot shifts*. One blurb proclaims that, like his principal characters, as an author, Saba is a master of deception.

It's not a characterization you would want attached to you during a murder investigation. But if Daniel is, in fact, one of the guys that Henry writes about, I can see how he must have taken pleasure in his patient's ability to repurpose his paranoia.

For now, poor Daniel is in the soup.

Shortly before Henry reappeared in Providence, Daniel's ex-wife—I have called her Noelle—phoned a local hotline with a tip. She was a regular, calling repeatedly with reports of conspiracies against her, so the police were slow to follow up. She caught their attention at last by promising to identify one of Henry's patients.

When a homicide detective visited, Noelle said that she had reason to believe that her former husband, Daniel, was represented in Henry's blog posts. Duncan, the tech wizard, appeared to be a composite, with some traits drawn from Daniel. He was subject to anxiety. He haunted Henry's office, camping out there nights. But Daniel was also Miguel. In depicting Miguel as a hanger-on rather than a group attendee, Henry had, so Noelle believed, engaged in deception. He hoped to draw attention away from his patients and divert suspicion to an imaginary non-patient, never observed on Prudence Street.

Despite the divorce, Daniel had confided in Noelle regularly. Like the fictive Miguel, Daniel had been agitated about Henry's absence and, later, the silence from his electronic devices. Daniel had known or concluded that Henry was treating the Great Man. Daniel had access to weapons. Daniel wished the Great Man harm.

On the basis of the interview with Noelle, the police obtained a search warrant. Since the divorce, Daniel had lived in an apartment near campus. His digital files were impenetrable. He owned a pistol and a concealed carry license, as did may Rhode Islanders, what with the upsurge in urban crime. Nothing in Daniel's rooms appeared incriminating.

But Daniel's DNA, taken from bathroom items, proved to match up with sequences from samples on a syringe found inside a greenish plastic bag in a dumpster on the direct route from Henry's office to the apartment. The syringe contained traces of a tree-nut slurry like one found in the Great Man's nostrils and gullet on the day of death. The tip of the syringe carried remnants of the Great Man's saliva. The plastic bag had Daniel's prints on the outside and, on the inside, the Great Man's hair pomade.

An excess of incriminating objects.

Daniel is a Muslim, a member of the local mosque. He teaches in its religious school.

The Great Man would have had a heyday with those facts.

The coroner had still not ruled on the cause of death for the Great Man, but given his tree nut allergies, a charge of attempted homicide seemed likely.

While Daniel's house was being searched, he was in Mexico City, presenting at a conference on digital fiction. Rather than tip him off while he was abroad, the State Police waited and apprehended him at Green Airport.

When confronted with a photo of the syringe, he responded with annoyance.

I carry a handgun, he said. If I'd found the bastard alive, I'd have shot him.

Daniel shut down and asked for a lawyer. But after a few minutes in custody, Daniel motioned to the corrections officers. He said that he wanted to change his story, to confess. The syringe was his. If anaphylactic shock was the cause of death, he was guilty.

Then he clammed up. He was willing to own the crime, but not to provide details.

To their credit, the police recognized the complexity of the situation. Their suspect was an armed, paranoid, divorced, single Muslim male with a grudge against the victim, recent statements (to Noelle) of intent, access to the place of death, and a willingness to cop to a crime. They had his DNA on the bag and syringe. But it was not clear that the Great Man had died of allergic shock or asphyxiation. The confession was skimpy, and it came from a man who, for all anyone knew, might be hearing voices that commanded him to seek punishment.

Thoughtful as they were, the local police could not hold out against pressure from the public. Why had they made no progress on this death, the most important ever likely to occur in their jurisdiction? Any day now, Daniel might be charged with murder.

The press went to work, interviewing Daniel's students and colleagues, combing through his writings, besieging Noelle. Meanwhile, she had developed compunctions and changed course. She phoned Maury, the well-known criminal defense lawyer. Would he speak to Daniel? Noelle had tried to reach Henry as well. Could he get Maury on board?

I can guess at Henry's reaction. Returning from hiding, he will have expected to be named as the prime suspect in my husband's death. Mercy Goodenow's kindliness notwithstanding, Henry must also have considered this other eventuality, accusations against a patient. How easy, in the post-truth judicial system, to pair murder and mental illness. But Henry may not have anticipated so advanced a legal case, buttressed by physical evidence and a confession.

Henry was convinced, as I am, that Daniel had no hand in the death of the Great Man. And if Henry had doubts?

I can imagine Henry's train of thought. If Daniel did something rash, the responsibility is mine. I disappeared without preparing my guys. I failed to get out ahead of their ailments. Hubris caused me to try to treat paranoid men, and with unproven methods.

Something on those lines. It would destroy Henry to see one of his patients suffer for a crime he had not committed—or one he had—and all because Henry had kept his practice open too long. Henry had experienced imprisonment. It is oppressive, even for a man schooled in equanimity. He could imagine the rest, a show trial and the chair.

He urged Maury to take charge of Daniel's defense. If Henry himself would be deprived of counsel, if conflict-of-interest rules required that Maury choose—let it be Daniel who got the best representation.

I'm guessing at the course of events that led Maury to take on Daniel as a client and then contact me. Maury and Henry believe that my act of witness will serve their campaign to save man who is almost certainly innocent and who in any case deserved more in the way of protection than Henry had managed to provide.

◊ ◊ ◊ ◊ ◊

Here, then, is my testimony. I will start with the moment when Muscle let me know that he had located Henry and sprung him from the oubliette. Normally, I avoided the room that Henry calls the boudoir, but that day, I joined my husband there and negotiated.

I asked that Henry remain unharmed, Henry and those he loved. I was not up to date on the threats to Henry's daughter-in-law, but I knew my Krishna.

My husband's initial demand was for me to appear at the Massachusetts fundraiser and New Hampshire rally, but soon he began to focus on Henry and his possible uses. We would work with him to restart the marriage. Why not in Providence, I said, since we were headed east?

As yet, I had no plan. I wanted to get Henry home—to put him out of harm's way and put my husband in it.

Throughout the marriage, I had been strategic in a general sense. I was like an intuitive player of a complex game like chess or go. Some arrays of pieces looked favorable. I tried to create set-ups where good things might happen.

Krishna latched on to the idea of a romantic weekend. In Henry's presence, we would hash out our differences—that is, Krishna would bombard me with complaints. The evening would be like a second honeymoon. I would parade before him, and on and on.

I gave grudging consent. Let Krishna think that he had bullied me into acquiescence.

Outside the fortress, perhaps Bub would take matters in hand, Bub or a wily kleptocrat. In New Hampshire, security guards would turn on the Great Man, or the crowd would, or someone in it, a lone gunman. I had every intention of making the rally's location known—leaking the details early. The Great Man was widely hated.

How he imagined that he could appear in public was beyond me. Did he still believe that he was adored? Was he content to die? When you have ruined the country and the planet, what more is there? The Great Man was not made for efforts that require patience, application, or persistence. He had come to the end of the road.

An intermediate understanding is possible. My husband wanted to relive his glory days. He would bask the adulation of admirers, however few. He yearned to roam the land, thump lecterns, and deliver rambling speeches full of self-praise. If in the process, he exposed himself to the wrath of detractors, so be it. He would die a free man.

I preferred not to take action myself, but I think I understood already that if none of the likely assassins did the job, I would need to shoulder the burden. I was resolved that my husband would not make it back to the fortress or, worse, our capital. But then, who knows finally if she has the courage to act?

If I made a move, it would be after the rally, when we were far from Henry. I did not want him implicated. I had not chosen a method. I would improvise. I hoped to be clever. I had no desire to wear the noose.

I wish I could say that it's ironic that a plan designed to shield Henry from suspicion should end by further entangling him, but I would be shading the truth. It had occurred to me that my husband might die in the iconic office. I could see Bub making that move.

For a second time, or perhaps the nth, I had proved willing to complicate Henry's life.

I made a pledge to myself: if I got Henry into trouble, I would get him out.

I justified my resolution in this and other ways. There was no ending the Great Man's rule without drawing innocents into the vortex.

KRISHNA ELABORATED PLANS. HE WOULD arrive at the famous office alone and see whether he drifted off. Henry would join soon after. If my husband was not yet asleep, together they would try to reenact the Trude Nilsson scenario, with Krishna on the couch, responding to Henry's mojo. I would arrive later, to meet a husband who was rested and vigorous.

He wanted reassurance, and he wanted justice. I had done him wrong.

I'll let it all out, he said. Your besotted lover boy will see you for what you are.

I did not protest. We were in the final days or hours.

Bub handled logistics. He had confiscated Henry's office keys. Bub would supply Muscle and Glue with duplicates. In the name of secrecy, Vera—Henry's Marya—would chauffeur Bub and the Great Man.

Bub was like a stage play director, sequencing entrances, blocking scenes. Vera would stand guard at the building's rear. Bub would walk the Great Man up the back stairs and then come around to stand guard at the front door, intercepting any patients hoping to enter.

Muscle would bring Henry and relieve Bub of guard duty. Glue and I would follow. Bub would return later to fetch the Great Man to attend the fundraiser and rally.

Off we all went to Prudence Street, Providence.

The Great Man left the fortress in the wee hours, headed for the legendary couch.

Henry set out next. He would practice his craft and be rewarded with family time.

I was meant to be the last to leave and the last to arrive.

Did I have a sense that together we had devised a loose variant of a locked-room murder mystery? The endlessly unlocked room. Three times of entry. Three sets of keys. Motive aplenty.

On the night before the fateful trip, I did not sleep. Instead, I had Glue fetch me early, as soon as my husband was out the door. My thought was to surprise him at the Prudence Street office. I had nothing specific in mind. I only knew that it was a mistake to let Bub or my husband control a schedule. I would appear before he had his mind arranged. Perhaps I would get my two cents in.

If he was not long for this world, did it matter whether he caught up on sleep?

I had dressed in disguise, not as a man but as a frump, with a mousy wig, dowdy sweatsuit, running shoes, and cut-rate sunglasses. I had packed dress-up clothes for the fund-raiser and rally and entrusted Bub with the suitcases. For the couple consultation, I thought a silk caftan dress—what Henry calls a muumuu—might be easy to slip into. I set one, along with a pair of heels, into a carry-on bag. I would bring it to the back room of Henry's office and change there.

On the drive in, I reviewed my thoughts about the back-up plan, uxoricide. What weapon would I use?

A line from Hamlet came to me: *Thoughts black, hands apt, drugs fit, and time agreeing*. In the play within a play, the murderer says it, as he prepares to pour deadly poison into the king's ear.

If my husband survived the rally, he would demand that I join him in his hotel bedroom. I wanted to avert that horror. I had no fit drug, but I had had a good notion where I might find one. Before leaving the fortress, I had lifted a ten-pack of syringes from the fortress dispensary.

With Glue at the wheel, I searched for stores that would be open before sunrise. On the pretext of needing a headache remedy, I asked Glue to make a detour. We stopped at a mini-mall with a twenty-four-hour pharmacy that emphasized health food and supplements.

Glue stationed herself just inside the glass door, minding me from a slight distance.

It had been years since I had shopped in person. I had not anticipated the half-empty shelves. Krishna loved tariffs the way some people love crosswords. He was always at play with them. And then came hyperinflation and the weak dollar. There were no imported goods, and I had not realized how shoddy domestic ones had become. Evidently, graphic design was an expense that manufacturers skipped.

I grabbed a plastic basket from the stack and checked out the headache section, in case Glue was following my progress. I picked up a box of Aleve equivalent, not yet a year past its expiration date. From the natural toothpaste aisle, I grabbed a mouthwash cup. Under a *Peanut allergy?* banner, I found what I had come for, containers of almond and cashew butters.

After paying for them, I asked for the rest room. With warm water as a softener, I made a nut-butter slurry in the cup and drew the mixture into syringes. I nestled them back in the open cardboard box, grabbed a fresh liner bag from the restroom waste basket, wrapped the box in the liner, and dropped it into my handbag. I washed the jars—the outsides—as well as I could. As I left the pharmacy, I deposited them in the trashcan of the adjacent pet store.

I trusted Glue but not so much that I would let her see how far I was willing to go. Glue's professional responsibilities included protecting the Great Man. I did not want to put her in an uncomfortable position.

Note to any officials wondering how much fiction I have inserted into this testimony: check the strip malls near Gloversville, New York. How many pair a pharmacy with a pet store? I had a scarf over the wig, and I wore dark glasses, but that will be me on the video, if a surveillance camera was working. The digital files should help get Daniel Saba off the hook.

Krishna's tree nut allergy reactions were dramatic. Once, he bit into a chicken taco that, unbeknownst to him, had been dressed with an almond mole. His face erupted with hives. By the time the ambulance got him to the ER, his skin had gone from blue to purple to blue again. Another five seconds, the doc said, and we'd have been phoning the morgue. For a week, the skin on Krishna's back and belly had the texture of an orange peel.

The fortress was nut-free. The dogs at the gate included two trained to sniff out tree nuts.

You may wonder how it felt to be traveling with an instrument of death in my lap. I felt discouraged. I felt resigned.

I spent years play-acting, first on stage and then in the marriage and the public performances it entailed. No part I have attempted was as burdensome as the one I was assuming, potential murderer. The Great Man made each of us worse than we otherwise would have been, made us too timid or too angry, too obedient or too corrupt.

I did anticipate relief—at being rid of the sense of complicity that I felt constantly for not having killed him so far.

I worried that I would enjoy seeing him writhe.

I have never played *Murder in the Cathedral*—as written, all the roles are for men—but I know that line, the one that says that the greatest treason is to do the right deed for the wrong reason. I wanted a purity of purpose. I wanted to kill my husband because he had destroyed so much and would destroy more.

I did not have purity of purpose.

I asked Glue to pull over. I thought that I might need to vomit. She asked whether we should visit another pharmacy. Did I have what I needed?

I did.

Here's an odd confession: trying to settle my stomach, I thought about Hitler.

Henry writes of Hitler's youth. If he'd gained admission to the art academy, so much suffering would have been averted.

What of his adult life? The plot to blow up Hitler in his plane, in 1943—don't we wish it had succeeded? How do we judge officers who failed to join the subsequent plot, a year later? Shame must attach to them—and all the more, perhaps, if they held back on moral grounds.

I have not read Kant, but based on Henry's account, I want to say there can be no Kantians in the foxholes—nor in the military headquarters.

Killing Hitler—what could justify holding off?

Henry has considered the argument that, in a democracy, political assassination muffles the voice of the people. But Hitler was elected. When democracy goes off the rails, may no one hit the reset button? How far does this *anti-democratic* argument extend?

As I say, not intervening had caused me to feel complicit.

In the car, behind Glue, I thought of Hitler in the *Führerbunker*, seeking safety from the turmoil he had called forth.

Tell me that there is no parallel.

I comforted myself with thoughts of Hitler, and still my stomach churned.

Like staying married to my husband, killing him was a sickening duty. I did not know whether I would be able to trade one for the other.

About my indecision, will I be believed?

What villainy do we not ascribe to women? Earth mothers, ice queens, cheerleaders, and weather gals will do you in. We mistrust the female sex.

I would get a chance to confront the Great Man in Providence before deciding finally whether to finish him off in Lexington, Manchester, or Nashua.

I could get lucky. I very well might. Someone would beat me to it.

◊ ◊ ◊ ◊ ◊

I had Glue avoid Prudence Street. Bub was scheduled to be at the front door. I did not want him to spot the SUV and intercept me or warn my husband.

I took the office keys. Glue waited in the car. She would approach the building only much later, at our appointed time, the third slot.

I entered by the alley and toted my carry bag up the rear stairs. No Vera/Marya. Evidently, mine were not the only plans that had changed.

As quietly as I could, I opened and relatched the rear upstairs door. Hearing no snores, I guessed that my husband was resting, waiting for sleep to come.

Henry's back room was tidy. His guys must have tended to the dusting. I slipped off the travel outfit. I pulled on the caftan and shoes. I freshened my makeup.

Only then did I notice my suitcase, the one with the clothes for the afternoon fundraiser. Bub had been by.

Still no snores.

I opened the door to the office.

The room does have the feel of a New York City apartment. High ceilings with crown moldings, built-in bookcases, chair rails, Persian rugs. Intense quiet, with only a hint of early morning city sounds from without. I could see how patients might nod off.

Approaching the couch from behind, I could partly make out my husband's form, the general sprawl, the leg extending beyond the roll arm.

He had been granted his wish, I thought, deep sleep.

I tiptoed round and saw the strange angle of the head and the slackness of the whole.

Dead—dead and thanks be.

If I had a fear, it was that he might move, might waken, might prove to be alive after all.

I sat in what I took to be Henry's chair, the one facing the couch. As he has written, other than by placement and extra wear, it is indistinguishable from the chairs for patients.

The Great Man did not stir.

He had a heart condition. His stamina was not what it had been. Climbing stairs winded him. He had clogged vessels everywhere, in the heart and in the brain.

I assumed that he had died peacefully. He lay down for a nap. His heart skipped a beat or did whatever else hearts do when they fail.

Did it occur to me that Bub might be responsible? Not immediately. The scene was so calm.

For an instant—that long only—I wanted for my husband to have died of natural causes.

Was Miriam's design casting its spell on me? I felt contemplative.

However convenient, the ending was wrong. The Great Man should have died a violent death and perhaps a public one. Certainly, he should have suffered.

Perhaps he had, when the heart seized up.

I stared at the corpse. In death, my late husband looked like a man whose neck had been wrung. He looked like a man who had fallen from a height.

Those fates should have been his.

I thought of the misery he had caused. I felt ashamed that I had not killed him myself. I should have done it then, and then, and then, days and months and years before. Last chance. I could do it now, symbolically.

Standing to the side, so as not to be seen from the street, I pulled back the front window curtain. The angle was uncertain, but it appeared that Bub was not at his post. Plans must have changed. He and Vera had left early. I was alone, although perhaps not for long.

I reached into my handbag and removed the syringes.

His mouth was wide open. Without disturbing the corpse, I stuck a syringe far back and emptied the contents. Then another and another and another. I took care to plug up the nostrils as well.

What was my intent? To dam up his air passages, so that if he came to, he could not breathe? To put those violent allergies into play?

I wanted to guarantee finality, yes, but finality had arrived before I ever did.

My acts were gestures of solidarity. I intended to ally myself with the event. To *like* it. To *heart* it. To subscribe to it. To signal approval.

I acted out of weakness. I acted from regret. I felt powerless. I had failed.

It seemed wrong that the Great Man should have fallen without my having given the shove.

I am finding memoir difficult. I have omitted dimensions of my response.

I felt blessed. I wanted to connect myself to the goodness of the day.

Did it occur to me that I was taking death by natural causes and turning it into murder—potentially, if the coroner focused on my contribution?

Here, I'm with Maury. It was always going to be murder.

A craftsman's mark. That's what I added, even if I was signing some else's work.

Perhaps better: I was annotating it or adding red-pencil exclamation marks in the margin, like an appreciative reader.

A clever coroner would know as much. Are coroners clever? Or is that only on TV?

When I pressed the plunger, no rash appeared. The face did not turn florid. No blood moved to circulate whatever there is in nuts that my husband's immune system could not stand. The nut slurry did not kill him. It was an artistic flourish.

I should have run off, but I was disinclined. I wanted to absorb what I was experiencing. I had long looked forward to this moment.

What is one meant to feel in the face of death? Henry uses the word *wrenching*. Should I have been wrenched? I felt relief and a livelier emotion, call it joy. So much joy!

Climate disaster, financial depression, recurrent pandemic, continual threats of civil strife—none of those burdens had eased, and yet how clear the sky seemed, how bright the day!

I thought of the operetta, *The Merry Widow*. Why *merry*? Does the widow's coming into a fortune explain and excuse her happiness? Is what I gained, liberation, a lesser inheritance?

I know that there's no escaping that other widow trope, however poorly it applies. *Black widow* is a slur on women, isn't it? Our desirability makes men helpless—and then we do them in, poor dears. I mean, when we're not whipping donkeys.

I am not voracious, quite the opposite. Rarely hungry. Certainly not hungry for prey. Bemused. That's how I would describe myself.

If I felt pangs of sadness, they were for Henry. He would arrive to discover that he had lost a patient. The goal, getting my husband to know himself, would remain forever beyond reach. Likewise, for the answers to any questions Henry had about diagnosis or motivation.

Then again, Henry continues conversations with patients in their absence. In every book, he says that he does. He might make progress through daydreaming—conjuring—if he was willing to spend more time with the Great Man.

I was thinking not. My husband's nature was no mystery. He was greedy and egotistical. Henry's photo tells the whole story: a smug slob.

Krishna was a familiar type, *great* only because he rose far.

Did I just mention Napoleon? I am recalling the time I played Natasha in a stage version of *War and Peace*. The director read the cast passages from the novel.

Tolstoy denies Napoleon's genius. When war sweeps through Europe, when all forces push toward destruction, through chance, one man will kill and destroy the most, and he will be celebrated.

Say (Tolstoy asks us to imagine) that, in a flock of sheep, a farmer separates out a ram, puts it in a special pen, and fattens it for slaughter. Seeing the ram get extra feed, the sheep will think him a genius, a superior individual, based on his qualities. The sheep lack the proper framework for analysis, the human, or roast mutton, framework.

Just so, Russians think Napoleon a genius because they ignore the causes of events. The conflict engulfing Europe would emerge under any leaders, and one side would happen to prevail. If there is a lucky congruence, if Napoleon has traits that allow him to succeed in the historical moment—someone always will.

Do I buy Tolstoy's analysis? Not on the upside. We were blessed to have inspired leaders at critical moments: the Civil War, the Great Depression, the Second World War. To repurpose a line of poetry: *It could have been otherwise.*

But regarding destructiveness, Tolstoy is plausible. There is a generous supply of bad and violent men. In the right conditions, one will come out on top.

Randomness! If little Krishna had possessed natural balance, if he had impressed daddy on the slopes, the Great Man would, just maybe, have been less of a dick. If he had been less of a dick, he would not have convinced my mother to sacrifice me. I would not have married him. He would not have risen to ruin the country.

Some other dick would have filled those niches.

Don't we need to be Tolstoyan to that extent? To know ourselves that well? We should acknowledge our proclivity for government by dicks.

There is no end to sociopaths. Like viruses, they are with us always.

My husband's father was a sociopath. From the little I know, his father may have been as well. In another time and place, Krishna would have been like them, cheating his business partners and amusing vulnerable women before making their lives a misery.

The culture was ready to be dominated by a man with his mix of braggadocio, bullheadedness, celebrity, cruelty, prejudice, know-nothingness, and, yes, narcissism and sociopathy and paranoia. My husband glommed on to a ready host, to our society with all its flaws and weaknesses, and the glomming made him great.

Success amplified his baleful personality traits and locked them into place.

My thoughts turned to the willing victims.

My mother knew what she was doing.

I knew what I was doing.

The nation knew.

We handed power over to a grifter.

Analyze us.

Suddenly, I was downcast. Not because my husband was dead. I was downcast because I had married him. I was downcast because I had rarely managed to stay his hand. If he had died of natural causes, in my life I had achieved nothing at all.

Yes, at the end, when Krishna seemed inclined to put himself in harm's way, I had encouraged him to do just that. My contribution seems minor. If Bub killed him here, he would have killed him elsewhere.

I did hope that I had done something useful with the syringes. As between the two arrangements, Krishna dead of obscure causes and Krishna dead with the nut slurry on board, the second struck me as more promising. If Bub had used a subtle poison, if he had wanted a verdict of death by sudden cardiac arrest, I had cast doubt on that resolution. Once murder was in play, Bub would be the last known person to have seen the Great Man alive. I did not want events to go just as Bub had planned. Whatever plot Bub had devised, I had thrown a spanner in the works.

If someone else was the murderer, some modest, invisible hero, and I contaminated the crime scene and muddied the waters—isn't that muddying a close cousin to clarifying? The nut butter shields our benefactor, and it speaks to what the nation dreamt of, foul play.

I had come upon what I took to be a *tableau vivant* in which the only actor happened to be dead. I had made a subtle adjustment in the staging.

I wondered whether my husband's body had been laid out just so, to tell a story. Not to undercut our respect for Henry's vision as a photographer, but the theatrical sprawl that exposes my husband's aspects, commanding and slovenly and, finally, ridiculous, may have been staged—by a murderer or by whoever came upon the body first.

It's true that the consulting room's décor is conducive to daydreaming or free association—whatever it is that Henry deals in. Seated in his chair, staring at my husband's corpse, I picked up echoes of the famous painting of Jean-Paul Marat. Marat advocated for the poor in the wake of the French Revolution, and for his sins, he has just been assassinated. He lies his medicinal bath, the slim body slackened, the head canted at a fearsome angle, the right arm hanging limply over the tub's edge. The 1960s play *Marat/Sade* culminates with a replication on stage of that image.

I did not think, not seriously, that that whoever adjusted the position of Krishna's corpse had that precedent in mind although with Bub and his pretensions to culture, anything is possible. Perhaps some other noble death was being parodied. What a pantaloon our great man was! For me, that's a feature of Henry's photo, an implicit contrast with conventional representations of heroism.

I once played Charlotte Corday, the young woman who murdered Marat. I inhabited that role too. I felt capable of anything. In real life, when called upon, I turned out to lack every one of Corday's virtues, decisiveness and courage and conviction. A complicated variant of *first time tragedy, second time farce*. On stage, I lifted a kitchen knife high and thrust it into a visionary's chest. In life, I squirted nut butter up a dead clown's nose.

In the process, I endangered Daniel. I can't say that I didn't anticipate fallout. To guard against unintended consequences, I decided to bring the emptied syringes with me. I swept them into my purse—all but one. One must have rolled away.

If some innocent was later set up to take the fall, I would produce the exculpatory evidence. Even then, before Sunny wrote, I expected to head for New Zealand. Once I was free of the Regime, my testimony would be hard to suppress.

In his blogs, Henry tries to convey the duration of his thought processes—how long it took, at the bedside, to run through a train of observations that fills paragraphs on the page. My calculations took no time at all.

I injected the nut slurry, corralled the syringes, sat down, enjoyed the moment, and began weeping. A chapter in my life was closed. It had consumed my youth and the prime of my life. Despite my best efforts, I found myself complicit in the crime of the century—not the murder, but the Great Man's rule.

I wept, and because I was weeping, I switched chairs. I was another of Henry's patients, in need of solace.

◊ ◊ ◊ ◊ ◊

To Daniel Saba: my apologies. Your arrest is the unintended consequence of my folly. In my notarized statement, I have given Maury enough to go on. A quick visit with the DA should secure your release. I am holding the physical evidence in reserve.

If the judicial system works, you will be free—free to return to the famous office with Henry and the guys. If the system is balky, perhaps this afterword will mobilize public opinion on your behalf.

◊ ◊ ◊ ◊ ◊

The sound of a door closing downstairs roused me. Henry was arriving.

I stood to greet him.

Henry entered the consulting room from the waiting room. When he saw me, he startled. He beamed. He hesitated.

He'd caught sight of the corpse, with the cruelly twisted neck and lolling tongue.

I'm sure that, in medical school and internship, Henry had seen his share of dead bodies and newly widowed wives. His instinct was to console. How was I faring? How could he help?

But Henry was not the only new arrival.

Leave, Muscle said.

I began to explain myself—the basics. I had come upon the corpse. No one knew of my change in schedule.

Muscle nodded. I should go now. Was Glue nearby?

I repeated, He was dead when I got here.

Muscle shooed me.

He and I had been close. Even so, about the events in the office—I'm not sure that Muscle believed me. He seems not to be considering Sunny's offer of refuge in New Zealand.

In response to Muscle's urgings, I slapped on the wig and glasses and took the rest of what I'd come with. The suitcase Bub had brought stayed behind. I left by the back stairs and let Glue spot me.

HENRY'S MEMOIR BEGINS *IN MEDIAS res*, between his recruitment to the fortress and his supposed exile in Maine. Facing the Great Man's corpse, Henry collapses into his chair. He finds himself overwhelmed and wonders why.

The starting point allows for omission. We hear nothing of Henry's entry into the consulting room. We hear nothing of me.

Does Henry consider me a quasi-patient? Enough so, it seems, that he was willing to take this extraordinary step, concealment, to avoid exposing me to harm. Enough not that, with a real patient at risk, Henry is inviting me to confess.

I'm recalling the passage in which Henry writes of his returning to the milk box to retrieve a thumb drive. He worries that, through incompleteness, he has betrayed his readers' trust. Omissions can constitute bad faith. When he wrote those lines, I'm sure that he was worrying also about this large breach, his failure to mention my presence in his office. How that deception must have pained him!

Describing the distribution of the iconic photo, he writes of the need to reach Glue, *hidden in the welter*. I don't doubt that Muscle sent her the photo, but as soon as I got back in the car, on the main point, Glue was in the loop.

Driving to Bristol, when Muscle spoke of the Hiroshima bombing and the three sets of crew members who knew that history had swerved—did he then refer to me, or to Bub and Vera?

The goal of autofiction is honesty. Hiding me, Henry failed that standard. Arguing in his favor, I would say that Henry announces up front that to shield patients—and certain non-patients—he alters facts. He tells readers that he has been acting on his late wife's advice, to take liberties. He is not Kantian in this sense: he would lie to protect Miriam, or me.

Henry did not want to stir up speculation about my guilt. His mentioning my presence would only send readers down a false path. He believed what I said: I had not committed murder. Or he partly believed. Perhaps, as he continued to write, his doubt increased.

REPORTING ABOUT THE DAY OF Krishna's death, the media makes my journey appear seamless. The plan had been for me to meet my husband in Providence and proceed together to the fundraiser. When the police got through to Glue, they told her that Krishna had died and that the corpse was being removed for forensic investigation. We determined that I would do best to turn back and head to the capital, to help plan the funeral.

Making that choice, did I appear cool? A more caring wife might have ignored instructions and hastened to her late husband's side.

So much the better. I am known as an ice queen, as self-absorbed, in my way, as Krishna. I followed protocol and arranged a dignified memorial.

I dressed in a suit that mimicked the famous one, worn by that other widow, sixty years prior. A waist-length jacket with tasseled buttons. A pillbox hat with veil.

I have a looser, broader figure. I intended homage, not parody, but the line separating them is thin.

Or I intended both. Again, tragedy replayed as farce.

That widow personified grace. As for me, *Who does she think she is?*

How beloved the young leader was! How gentlemanly he appeared. By inviting a comparison—that is, a contrast—I cemented my husband's legacy: slob, shyster, oppressor, buffoon.

Why presume that I am unaware of the impression I make? I am a stage actor.

For the length of the grand avenue, I walked behind the casket and braved jeers and brickbats. Mostly, the mood was celebratory. I marched in subdued mock mourning amidst a carnival of boisterous mock mourning. Transgender widows—the grand street was lined with them. Who knew there were so many drag queens? Ladies, you did me to a T.

I had arranged the procession. I had said, Let the people march.

Yes, Ms. Curry from Dubuque, there were unicycles and jugglers and men in high hats and ringmasters' uniforms, all asparkle, to signal the contrary of grief.

I was tempted to join them.

The performers seemed spontaneous. They had been beaten down, perhaps, by disease, poverty, and terror. They reveled in release from oppression.

My heart was with those who spoofed the ceremony. Before security guards pulled her away, a petite woman managed to approach me and dance a manic jig. She had large hoop earrings and a bluebird tattoo near her left collarbone.

If you read these words, sprightly dervish, know that you expressed what was in me.

My performance had its sincere aspect. It is time for a return to ritual. To the observing the form of respect for the dead, whatever their sins. To adult behavior in the public sphere.

That calm walk was another demanding part. I doubt that I could have pulled it off if I hadn't got my licks in earlier. Desecrating the corpse gave me equanimity and, so, allowed me to help—to try to help—to guide the nation back toward its ideals.

A futile effort? My craft is built on them. Actors roll the stone up the hill and are joyful doing it. Doesn't that image express one view of freedom, freedom in the face of the arbitrary? Don't undersell futility.

The two performances compose a single piece of art. I squirt nut butter down a dead man's gullet. In his funeral procession, I maintain decorum.

I LOVE HENRY'S NOTION THAT I would bury my husband in an inconvenient rural spot, to get his followers out hiking.

As everyone knows, I had Krishna cremated and took possession of the ashes. To honor his wishes, I said. To hold him close. Who can contradict the grieving widow?

There were murmurs. What if new forensic techniques were developed? What if the samples preserved by the medical examiner were insufficient? I had made further investigation difficult. EverGreats had been deprived of a shrine.

My husband had wanted, I said, to be the air we breathe.

That much is true.

For the rest, he had resisted discussing plans for a burial.

I have no intention, he said, of giving you something to look forward to.

He did not know how to think about a world without him in it.

I should confess, I do not have the ashes.

I tossed them in a body of water, a lake or stream, on our way north. A lake or stream or mudpuddle or rest stop toilet. If there is a locus for Great-worship, it will not be one I have created.

I announced a private memorial service, close friends and family only, and suggested that I had sent out invitations. There was no service. He had no friends.

I HAVE MENTIONED BUB'S ABSENCE. His story is that the Great Man dismissed him as soon as they arrived at the doctor's office. The doctor and his guard would be along soon. Meanwhile,

Krishna wanted the full therapeutic experience—time alone on the couch and, later, psychotherapy, without minders at the ready. Afterwards, on the trip north, his wife's guard would provide security.

Vera drove Bub straight to New Hampshire to supervise preparations for the planned rally. They learned of the Great Man's death when the public did.

As for what really happened, perhaps Bub deserted his post taking Vera with him. She was tasked with his safety. She was afraid of crossing him, knowing that he might come into power.

Sources tell me that Bub stopped in Lexington, to meet secretly with the kleptocrats, to discuss contingencies.

Bub has gone underground, and Vera with him. He knows he has no public support. Doubtless, he's negotiating in secret, lining up power brokers.

The next regime will determine whether Bub and Vera testify under oath. Bub hopes to be leading that government.

MY HUSBAND NEVER FELT SAFE. That part of Bub's account is implausible—unless Henry's office had that salutary and finally deadly effect, interrupting Krishna's paranoia. As Henry says, it deserts you at the worst moment.

MEANWHILE, POOR DANIEL SABA WAS heading for trouble.

You who follow the news will have a fair sense of the sequence. Let me reconstruct it, but this time with the certainty that Daniel is innocent.

On the fateful morning, he walks to his office at the university. He grades digital literary projects and then crosses the campus green and enters the classroom, to teach. Imagine his surprise when his pocket monitor picks up a signal from one of Henry's devices. Daniel checks his screen and finds that the good doctor is back in the office on Prudence Street.

We know what happened. To photograph the body, Henry had activated the trusty e-tablet.

Daniel's literary arts session has moved from lecture to practicum. The kids are working on short shorts about dating: a conversation in a dive bar that leads, through clickable hot links, to revelations about the participants' impulses and second thoughts.

It takes time for Daniel to extricate himself from the lesson. He tracks down his teaching assistant, puts her in charge, and dashes off. Since his car is parked at his home, Daniel walks to 190 Prudence. By the time he arrives, Henry is gone.

When Daniel checks the office, he sees the body. He knows that Henry just left. The signal from the tablet, now switched off, suggests as much.

Thinking to protect his beloved therapist, Daniel scours the room for incriminating evidence. He spots and retrieves the syringe that got away from me.

Does Daniel find it hard to believe that Henry has committed murder? Admiring the doc as he does, Daniel may well think that Henry has risen to the occasion. Certainly, the weapon is low-tech.

Daniel entertains a strange notion. What if, appearances notwithstanding, the Great Man is not dead?

Daniel's wife, Noelle, emerged from the divorce with rights to the couple's dog, Nelly, a scruffy-looking border terrier. The pet custody proceedings were acrimonious—that word seems to attach to divorce, doesn't it?—but since Noelle travels often, she has had to extend an olive branch. When she is out of town, might Daniel fill in with Nelly? Because he sometimes walks the dog, Daniel carries compostable grocery produce bags in the pockets of all his pants.

In case his doctor has botched the job, Daniel decides to slip a bag over the Great Man's head. Cinching the open end below his victim's chin, Daniel looks for signs of breathing and sees none. He feels relief—pleasure in certainty.

Or else the gesture is symbolic. Daniel knows a corpse when he sees one. He positions the bag to know what it would have felt like to do the deed.

Like me, Daniel is mesmerized by the scene. What a dream, to have his hands around the tyrant's neck. To think that the oppressor is truly gone!

Immediately, anxiety returns. Daniel removes off the bag, drops the syringe into it, and stuffs both into a coat pocket.

As Daniel heads home, his dread worsens. What if the police are on his trail? Daniel feels *paranoid*. That self-awareness is an indicator of how successful the group therapy has been. When catastrophic thoughts intrude, Daniel is able to label them. Paranoia never succumbs completely. Daniel tries reviewing the assurances that the guys offer when panic sets in. It's no use. He hears cars approaching, and footsteps too.

Daniel catches sight of a dumpster. Turning impulsive, he tosses in the bag with the syringe.

He returns home, washes up, and waits for the hammer to fall. When it does not, he sets off on his trip to Mexico.

On being arrested, Daniel's first thought is to brazen things out. But is there hope for him? If he is going down, he might at least save Henry. Daniel reverses course, confesses, and turns mum—as he must, since he has no knowledge about how the Great Man died. Daniel's life has been difficult, and now it will be redeemed. He can perform a noble act. He will protect his doctor.

It makes no sense that Daniel committed murder. He had no notion that the Great Man would be in town. En route from the college to Prudence Street, how would Daniel have gotten hold of syringes and nut butter? Where are the other syringes or, if there are none, the jars of spreads—enough syringes or supplies to deliver the amount of gunk in the gullet?

Is allergy or asphyxiation even the cause of death?

Nothing except the bogus confession connects Daniel to a murder. To prosecute or, worse, convict him would be an injustice against a man who is both impaired and radically altruistic—doing good at enormous cost to himself.

Krishna and Daniel stand, do they not, as exemplars of the range of paranoia? My husband was narcissistic and uncaring. In contrast, Daniel pairs paranoia with selflessness and loving devotion. Daniel is Sydney Carton welcoming execution so that another can go free. That sacrifice is the negation of the Great Man, of his corrupt values. To reboot, the country could do worse than to honor Daniel.

If Daniel is not the murderer, then who? Not Henry. He arrived after me, and the Great Man was dead before I entered the office. Not me either. If the tree nuts had killed Krishna, if he had suffered an allergic crisis, wouldn't the famous photo show mottled blue skin? Bub? He has alibis. Boston kleptocrats? They had all arrived at the meeting site early, to be vetted by security.

Did the Great Man die from natural causes? Which?

We have the makings of a murder mystery or would, in different times.

Murder mysteries are built around facts. A murder took place at a certain time and was committed in a certain way—with a blunt object. The force and angle of the blow reflect the perpetrator's strength and height. A statue of a falcon is missing. On the page of a newspaper, a boat's arrival time is circled. A blouse is torn and bloodstained. Facts are clues.

Necessarily, authors delve into personality and motive. They make mysteries fun. But many characters will have distinctive personalities and compelling motives. Until the bloodstain is explained, we will not finally know who acted and why.

The French new novelists highlighted this primacy of fact by subverting it. In their books, chronology slips, so that an event that precedes the killing in one telling follows it in another. The position of an object shifts, or the object disappears entirely. The mystery may be solved, but in a way that does not accord with the clues.

The Great Man performed a similar subversion. Like the Red Queen, who pronounces the verdict before conducting the trial, the Great Man determined who was guilty and then ascribed motives and adduced invented facts. The corrupt judicial system and its appendages followed the Great Man's model. That's why, days on, we have no coroner's report. The doctor must know who is guilty before he can determine a cause of death.

He is a man of Henry's age, I believe, this coroner—a man who wishes, no doubt, that he'd had the good sense to retire. I see him as prudent in nature, formal in speech, and testy in manner. In the past, he was stubborn in the name of science. He could not be swayed, hurried, or cajoled. In this political age, he puts his temperament to different use. He will issue a report when authorities name the murderer. Until then, forensic results will remain pending.

EXPLAINING THE DELAY, THE EXPERT alludes to difficulties familiar to us from the plague years. A lack of reagents. Poor standardization of critical tests. He lies without embarrassment. His performance suits the exigencies of the times.

Imagine a novel in which Hercule Poirot or Miss Marple walks through the boat or train or village, interviewing and overhearing suspects. In the post-fact world, an additional step precedes the awaited dénouement. The brilliant detective asks the boss—the captain, the conductor, the capo, the local oligarch—whom to pin the crime on. A clever narrative is then crafted to suit the required result.

I'm thinking first of Bub. By the old style of mystery, he would be eliminated because he was elsewhere when the crime, if there was one, occurred.

By Bub's account, he last saw the Great Man at the waiting room door. The Great Man dismissed him. Soon, Bub received an upbeat text from the Great Man. *The room is magical!*

Bub has submitted the correspondence files for forensic analysis. The time and location stamps will confirm his account. Bub was well into Massachusetts when the Great Man died.

Time and place. How quaint. The old authors had characters use Dictaphone tapes to create false evidence concerning their whereabouts. Today, IP addresses and origination stamps can be monkeyed with.

The Great Man's cell phone is missing. Apparently, the only certain way to know where a text was sent from is to check the phone. The happy missive—*magical!*—may be as fictional as the recent vote counts.

We haven't forgotten the Persians, have we? They wanted the Great Man dead for patriotic reasons.

In one mystery outcome, Vera does the deed. She has access to a subtle poison, or she uses a plastic bag, in the fashion that Daniel later happened to duplicate. The Great Man had forced her to do evil. This last cruel act will close out the set.

Vera knew that Bub would create an alibi for her, to avoid suspicion himself and to prevent exposure of his treasonous acts. Certainly, the Persians have the technical capacity to craft fake texts.

If Bub succeeds my husband, his flimsy evidence will become ironclad. He and Vera will be off the hook. Bub will be free to name a murderer.

Daniel is a convenient choice. He put a bag over the Great Man's head. Manipulation of fact is scarcely needed. Asphyxiation becomes the cause of death. Daniel incarnates the Other.

Better yet might be a cabal of Henry's patients—the group members as conspirators. The implication might be that the Great Man was like them, that he was the sort of person Henry took on as a patient. Bub tried hard to right the ship of state, but a maniac was at the helm.

Bub may prefer to name Henry, an East Coast liberal, a man of the mind, a Jew who harbors Muslims.

Or Bub might want to deify the Great Man. He was a visionary, gaslighted by an undermining wife. That snake Naomi—herself disturbed and erratic—urged this most stable of leaders to see a shrink. Not content with making the Great Man doubt himself, she did him in. No wonder she fled justice!

There is always the passing stranger. An aggrieved citizen spots the Great Man, slips into the building, and finds the intended victim unguarded and asleep. Regime change arises from glitches in a lone wolf's brain. Perhaps the assassin can be assassinated before trial, as happened once before, the crazed offing the crazed.

And if Bub loses out to his rivals? His airtight alibi will be found to be full of holes. The medical examiner will serve the new masters. The cause of death will be poisoning, with a high-tech chemical obtained from rogue military allies. Or asphyxiation, after all—I'm thinking a crushed windpipe. The skin will show bruises shaped and spaced like Bub's fingertips. The time of death will be early, in advance of my arrival and well before transmission of the fake e-missive presented in Bub's defense.

Personally, privately, I find a guilty verdict for Bub appealing. The ancillary evidence points to him. Muscle wondered, How did the media know to start telling truths? Large-scale plotting had preceded my husband's death.

And if Bub is not guilty, still, given the harm he has done others, he cannot be wronged. How delicious to see him tagged with the death, even, or perhaps especially, through a miscarriage of justice.

But wait. Does that resolution serve the country? If the death resulted from murderous political infighting, we would become a nation where that sort of event occurs. The precedent would be set for attempts at political advancement through assassination, something we have never seen before.

And if the country gets back on its feet—why should Bub, that unspeakable man, get the glory?

We're left with death by natural causes. That verdict would mesh well with the ME's preliminary report, full of words like cardiopulmonary. What if the final version is the same—arrhythmia? Will we feel cheated? How can a man die of natural causes when so many would have been content to pull the trigger? It will make no sense. Raise your hand if you would not have done the deed. Motive was universal.

If a truth-and-reconciliation government emerges, a result much to be desired, a determination of death by old age will help move us all ahead. We can nod our heads. Of late, he seemed not to be getting enough oxygen to the brain.

In this narrative, all the actors will have been well meaning in different ways. Bub was out to end the internal exile, to bring the country's leader back to the normal seat of power. Henry worked to give the Great Man ease and, perhaps, a speck of rationality. I was open to reviving the marriage. The kleptocrats want only to tend to charitable foundations. Daniel becomes a small-city everyman, a teacher and a writer, spun about by forces larger than himself, as we all have been for what feels like ages.

You may protest that facts are facts. Someone did or did not cause the cardiopulmonary event. I say: that objection is not of our time. There is no evidence, no motive, and no psychology separate from political necessity.

It occurs to me that there is another reason that the murder mystery is dead. We have been burned by nostalgia.

In World War II, murder mysteries were all the rage. They reminded citizens of what they were fighting to defend, a nation exemplified by its rural villages, full of wise widows, kindly widowers, quirky shopkeepers, plodding constables, observant gardeners, wry farmhands, gossipy housemaids, loyal secretaries, fussy clergymen, and the occasional fresh-faced, plucky young couple.

In contrast, sentiment for a simpler world has been our undoing. Supporters were attracted to the Great Man's evocation of a noble past, whiter and more manageable. What an expensive buy-in! Deaths in every locale.

For the last, unsolved death, the one a crime writer would have us puzzle over, must we name the perpetrator?

By modeling hatred, wasn't the Great Man responsible all the way down the line? For those whom the Great Man never fooled, there will only ever be one culprit. On every front, Krishna was the killer. Henry's Mimi speaks for us all: Krishna ran a thanatocracy. We could do worse than to call his death self-inflicted.

On my list of suspects, only Henry's name fails to appear. His tessera depicts a doctor's attempt to maintain a professional demeanor with an unpalatable patient. It was hard not to want to kill my Krishna, and Henry worries that he did not fully master the impulse. He knew that psychotherapy, in the early going, can perturb patients. Perhaps self-awareness—the least hint of it—had made my husband despairing and impulsive. And then: if Henry contributed to his patient's demise, it was through passivity, through not blocking him from embracing his fate.

But finally, I would frame Henry's guilt differently. To remain attentive, well-meaning, empathetic, and self-critical in the face of provocation was to reject what Krishna stood for, contempt, division, egocentricity, and the rest. There was a Marxist contradiction or dialectic—the seeds of its own destruction—in Henry's therapeutic stance. To care for the Great Man was to contend against him.

◊ ◊ ◊ ◊ ◊

I have mentioned my unease in approaching this afterword: how to begin? I should have anticipated a more perplexing problem, the ending.

Am I there? My husband set the stage for violence, almost everyone wanted him gone, and we are best off without a clear resolution. Finis. Curtain.

The other sort of conclusion strikes me as socially corrosive: the naming of a culprit, Bub or Daniel, that will leave us forever in doubt, inciting further divisions and recriminations.

DEAR HENRY, THIS WORK WOULD be easier if you were here with me.

I imagine you walking Providence's streets, from Benevolent to Prudence, kicking at pebbles like a boy, talking to yourself and daydreaming. At Nina's insistence, you have given up your practice, although only in a manner of speaking: you no longer call yourself your patients' doctor.

When you reach the office, the guys are there, in session. You sit with them as one among equals.

You refuse payment. Nonetheless, the guys pitch in to a fund for your benefit, run by Arthur.

You have kept your doctor's license for one reason, to maintain privilege, to keep the right to stay silent if questioned.

I wonder about the décor. When we spoke by video, the famous couch was absent. You had given permission for the forensic lab to ship it directly to the Smithsonian. Do you have a replacement?

Allow me to fashion one: decades back, when your Miriam put the finishing touches on the office, her brother, Aaron, visited. He was so taken with the furniture that he asked Miriam to order identical pieces for a den in his pied à terre in Boston. On his death, the copies went into storage. Aaron's daughter, your niece, retrieved the duplicate couch and had it shipped to you so that, missing prints aside, the room looks as it always did.

When you leave it, you revisit old haunts. At Zervas Place, Addie switches out your order.

You commune with your wife. You scroll through case notes in hopes that the peculiar abbreviations will spark memories. You write about error. You roll out an old bike and accompany Tammy, whatever her age, on the rail trail.

You remain a suspect in the death of the Great Man. You want that sword hanging over you, just as I want it hanging over me.

Can we explain that preference to others? Krishna victimized so many that we who survive him would think less of ourselves if we lost our vulnerability.

While I am addressing you, let me turn to what is unfinished between us. You depict me, that morning in the rundown park, as ready to parade before you. I may or may not have been, even I don't know for certain, but let me speak to the impulse. It was not sexual only. I understand you to need a woman, and not just in memory. You need the sight and the touch of flesh. You need to be tied to the world in that way.

Would you do me a favor, in your future writing, and devote some chapters to sexual abuse in childhood? I fear that mine left me numb. I know that it appears otherwise. I am seen as outward-facing and energetic—focused on my sexuality. Perhaps it's only that I search for sensation. Or that precisely because I have lost desire, I do not differentiate well among partners. I will accept an old man as readily as a young one, a villain as well as a saint.

I mention my numbness because it seemed to diminish in your presence. It was your calm, I think, and your permissiveness. As much as any man, you left me to my own devices, and I came to realize that I have them, along with wishes and plans and the rest. In that sense, too, you are responsible for my husband's death. Around you, I finally chose to act, to send him out among his countrymen, where he was bound to be done in.

Regarding a woman's touch: is the wish yours, or only mine for you? In Providence, there must be divorcées and widows aplenty. Or spinsters. I suppose that the word comes to me because I just wrote about classic murder mysteries and their busy villages.

I want for one of those women, an old friend of yours or a longtime admirer, local, in Providence, when she reads this memoir or before—right now—to approach you and seduce you and berate and belittle you and let you feel newly at home.

Or should I be thinking of Ginnie? She resembles your Miriam in her love of autofiction and her curatorial eye—for vegetables, more than mid-century lithographs. She's not a mafia wife, I hope? It would be late in life for you to manage that complication. Is Ginnie ready to leave her husband, whatever his calling? You depict her as diffident but dignified, with plenty of backbone. You like a woman who calls you on your missteps. Ginnie's suited to you, don't you think?

Ginnie or the longtime admirer will say, You make too much of age. You're a walker. You're a writer. You still have *mens sano* with, mostly, *corpore sana*.

She will say, Now that they've read your blog, prospective patients are lining up at your office door. They are, as you yourself say, duly informed. Your age is no secret, or your tendency to nod off in session.

She will say, I love Nina, but she is not always right.

Conduct interviews. Open a second group. Resume the mantle of doctor. Do what you love.

Didn't your Mimi predict that the community would supply you a second wife?

To my reading, your memoir, the tessera, is romance, romance and elegy: grief in the age of the Great Man. For you, his death is the end of a journey that starts and ends at home. By interrupting your routine, he made you round out your understanding of your marriage. You've seen the good and the bad. You've had a final ecstatic encounter.

Do shrinks still speak of closure? I doubt that you ever did. Whether or not: time to move on, my love.

What if—here is my fantasy—the country returns to normal governance, the kind that does not intrude daily? Leaders who pretend to modesty, who style themselves public servants. A functioning economy, with low and tolerable levels of graft and corruption. Imperfect laws, imperfectly enforced. An underfunded health care system run by experts with good intentions. Unconscious racism, called out as it surfaces. Half a chance for the poor and needy. High aspirations. Compromise.

If we get that society, you need to live in it, to do your work in it. I want your blog-memoir, when we publish it, to have the proper form. Shouldn't the book end with a wedding?

I HOPE THAT IT WILL—BUT only if democracy returns. If the Regime clings to power, or if its fate hangs in the balance, as writers we will need to retain our focus on the death of the Great Man and the circumstance that flows from it. I doubt that the authorities will crack the case—not in the old-fashioned sense, where clues and testimony click into place in believable fashion.

In time, political necessity may supply a murderer—or here, in these notes, you and I will get there first. We will control the narrative.

Henry, help me to craft an ending.

YOU ARE HELPING ME. YOU conjure your Miriam and, following the example, I conjure you.

The encounter is unlike our prior ones. There is no tension to it, no sexual energy, no urgency to move events along. Facing me, you are at ease, serene and—why do I search for this word?—tolerant. You treat me like a patient. You wait me out.

You seem to suspect me. I worry that you do. In kindly fashion, of course. If I killed my husband, you would not judge me.

I might judge you for having the thought, Henry. Have you fallen for the black widow trope? Men have trouble ignoring it, and you are a man. I fear, Henry, that even for you, my face and figure are my fate.

You are not entirely wrong about my character. I have confessed as much. If it's a matter of psychology, then yes, not just on stage, but also in the world, I have the make-up of a murderous wife—that potential, anyway.

To be fair to you: patients first. You must save Daniel. What if the limited confession I sent Maury is not enough, the admission that I came upon my late husband's body and stuffed nut butters down the gullet?

Am I paranoid? I mean, about the significance of your passivity?

In *Must We Be as We Are?*, you call *The Scarlet Letter* an American gospel. It conveys our values or a value of American psychotherapy, moral autonomy. One cannot confess for another. Hester Prynne must not reveal Arthur Dimmesdale's sin. The physician, Roger Chillingsworth, is wrong to coerce Dimmesdale. He needs to decide for himself, own up or no.

In your ease, your serenity, you seem to be asking me to dig deeper. Am a wrong to sense a hint of prejudgment—a leaning?

Henry, I fear that you expect further confession.

Or do I mistake you? What you want—what you wait for—is more ambiguous.

I CAN SEE WHY YOU like writing as a form of contemplation. Composing this afterword has had a healthy—salubrious—effect on me.

I find myself thinking about your Daniel Saba, how generous he was and is.

Daniel's confession—his selflessness—obliterates the Regime.

I want to be Daniel, minus the paranoia.

I HAVE COME TO REALIZE how jealous I would be if Bub got credit for setting the country and the world aright. To go down in history as having killed the Great Man!

I can testify to the accuracy of Henry's depiction of Bub's character. Power—domination—turns him on. How he loves to grind people under his heel! Bub's ambition is to succeed to the dictatorship and turn arbitrocracy into frank tyranny. If he killed my husband, it was not for the glory.

But what if Bub fails? If he is convicted of murder and is jailed or escapes abroad...? The glory would be there.

WRITING HAS MADE ME WANT to tell another story. I am inching toward it.

HENRY, LET'S RETURN TO THE morning of my husband's death and consider a different entry into the office on Prudence Street.

I have headed east early. On arrival, I notice that Vera is absent.

Curious, Glue says.

We walk through the alley and get a view of the front porch. No Bub.

Chauffeuring Bub and Krishna, Vera drove a yet grander Escalade. Where is it parked?

I know my husband. He has dismissed his entourage.

He will nap. He will waken to hopes of a couple session that suits his taste. He will lodge complaints against me. I will see the error of my ways. Chastened, I will accompany him to the fundraiser and rally. On the drive, in the back seat of our makeshift transport, Muscle's Malibu, Krishna will paw at me.

Who knows what all he is imagining?

I know. I feel queasy.

It's good that I am ahead of schedule. I will surprise him. We will have it out, wife and husband. I will ask him to step down from office, to end the Regime and leave, and in a way that gives democracy a chance. He must open the door to restoration.

We will discuss the aftermath. I have in mind a truth and reconciliation process. He will confess his crimes, perversion of justice, corruption of the electoral process, graft, and, yes, treason.

He colluded with other—foreign—autocrats. I have no doubt.

Few have the chance to alter their place in history, and for the better. Having shown us our vulnerabilities, having humbled us, now he will remind us of our old ideals, the ones that we were too ready to betray.

As a first step, the Great Man will sacrifice Bub. He is easily exposed. What does Bub have on my husband? Only the truth, and we will move toward acknowledging the truth.

I ask Glue to stand by the rear door. If something is amiss, I will cry out.

I enter the back room, wash up, and change. I look fine. I am confident.

I see my husband splayed on the sofa. He snarls, even in his sleep.

I whisper the code word that gives Glue the all-clear. She can monitor the building from a distance.

Imagination is one thing. Seeing Krishna in person is another.

From him, there can be no truth. With him, there can be no reconciliation.

I mean with the nation, but with me as well. I cannot sit beside him on that couch.

The moral stench has accompanied him to this tidy suite. I want to be free of the nausea.

I want to fulfill my ethical obligation and help my husband to fulfill his. While he lives, there will be no freedom and no justice.

The Great Man snarls and gasps, and his breathing stops.

If only the pause would continue!

I can make it happen.

Krishna will not back off. He will not recast his role in history.

His motto is not *Excelsior!* It is *Entropy!*

I have enabled him. It is incumbent on me to stop him.

Give Bub credit. He knew that if he left a vacuum, a nemesis would fill it. A patient, perhaps, or quasi-patient. Miguel would come upon the Great Man and do the necessary. Poor Miguel. If he is en route, let me spare him. The responsibility is not his.

I tell myself that I would not kill the Great Man for private reasons, to end the marriage or to punish him for threatening my mother. But there is the nausea. For how long can it be borne?

I attempt something like what you, in your account of the oubliette, call self-hypnosis.

Kierkegaard says, Purity of heart is to will one thing. Henry, I want to be like you in that way. To will only healing,

I will kill, if I must, in the interest of all.

Might I trust Bub to do the job later, in New Hampshire? He has not succeeded at much, but he has a fair track record when it comes to disappearances.

Bub was never a match for Krishna. I will shoulder the burden.

I watch for a pause in my husband's breathing. I extract the plastic bag from my purse, roll out the syringes, and set them on the side table where you take notes.

As in a horror film, my husband seems to stir. Is he aware of my presence? But no—the breathing stops again.

I will extend a natural process. I slip the bag over his head. The stench! But I am resolved.

I hold the bag in place. It brings relief from the halitosis. Much of the effect must be psychological. The air is fresher without his polluting it.

My own breath is in play as well. I exhale slowly. I experience immense calm—and love, love for the battered world.

My husband's neck expands and contracts, slightly, rhythmically.

Between my hands, the movements stop.

Somewhere in your books, Henry, you write about the *oceanic feeling*, of being in touch with a reality larger than our petty daily one. My love is oceanic.

I do not yet know about the tiled mosaic of resistance, I lack that metaphor, but I am aware that time with the bag is my small contribution to a project of reclamation. I feel lucky to be able to do my part.

Am I weeping? I'm a weeper. As my husband relaxes into nothingness, tears course down my cheeks.

We think that the dichotomy, good and evil, makes choice simple. But, no—evil complicates the moral universe. To end an ongoing evil, a great evil, may we disobey a categorical imperative? Then it would not be categorical.

Like you—more, like your Mimi—I can't see my way to being a Kantian.

I know only that my husband must not continue to govern.

Like the police, I possess a plastic bag that has traces of the Great Man's mucus. Mine is clean of nut butter, which came later.

FROM HERE, THE STORY IS much the one that I have written already. Having suffocated Krishna, I think, *belt and suspenders*, and reach into my purse for the syringes. When it comes to my husband, there was no such thing as too dead.

The nut butter slurry is my signature, my artist's chop.

I want to complicate the makeup of the murder scene.

I want for there to be more than one answer, more than one agent.

I want viewers to think, It was done and done again. One did it and then, for good measure, another.

HENRY, YOU ARE RIGHT. DIGGING deeper is better. It feels good to re-imagine the drama and put myself at the center.

I trust that you will know to read this scene as fictive imagining.

I trust and do not trust.

I have tried to assume the burden of autofiction, honesty. Certainly, the casting is honest. I can see myself in the part, could act it to a T.

If you print the confession as I've written it, most readers will simply conclude that I'm guilty. But unlike Daniel, I am no Dickens hero, doing a far, far better thing. I don't mind the limelight, I like knowing that I've sold the performance, and, dear Henry, I can assure you that I do not risk the guillotine. New Zealand does not extradite in capital cases. That law will hold up even if the Kiwis reconcile with us and would otherwise be ready to ship me home for trial.

About reconciliation: Wouldn't it imply that we had reestablished the rule of law under an independent judiciary? I long for that result.

You must not imagine that you have pushed me toward self-abnegation. In your work, you hope to create spaces for contemplation. From half a world away, you did that for me. You write often about feeling relief. I do now, at the thought of making amends, partial amends. My intentions were sometimes virtuous and sometimes selfish, but it all comes to the same thing. I enabled a monster.

In the event that I face imprisonment, I trust that you will coach me in self-hypnosis. My trance in the presence of my husband's corpse suggests that I have talents in that direction.

I FIND MYSELF WANTING TO withdraw from the role that I have assumed, final arbiter of this memoir's afterward. Henry, I am putting the book back in your hands. Conclude with this new account, stop with the prior one, write your own, or publish the collection of endings just as I have written them and leave matters unsettled.

If you choose a different final scene, I have this request: please don't let the death be from natural causes. I want human agency. Someone crafted a resolution to our crisis. My husband needs to have been murdered.

Similarly, whatever happened in your office that morning, you, dear Henry, are not responsible. I encouraged my husband to leave the fortress. I was Bub's ally in that effort, even if we did not conspire. If you had dissuaded Krishna, one of us would have coaxed him out with a different temptation.

If you insist that you collaborated with us, I will not rob you of your involvement. You played a role—and good on you!

Together we have discovered a new Thanatos syndrome, the near-universal wish for my husband's death. If a metaphor is permitted: the wish doubled and doubled, sweeping the country like the plague. There is no shame in admitting that finally, despite your earnest efforts and your near-Kantianism, you were not immune.

IN FAVOR OF MY BEING the murderer: I am not of the Resistance and not quite of the Regime either. I am not a Jew or a Muslim or a person of color or a gay man or an immigrant or a sufferer from mental illness. Your kind words about me notwithstanding, I am not an East Coast intellectual.

The death becomes a domestic matter. The possibility of abuse enters the picture. In private, as in public, the Great Man was cruel. He got the end that he deserved.

We worry about truth, you and I, but surely beauty is a value too. There is beauty in a story that meets the moment's needs.

One flaw: the *woman* aspect, our having him killed by an overly emotional creature, a schemer, a bitch, and a witch. I hope, at least, that we can pair the black widow trope with what I call the glory.

WHAT'S BETTER, HENRY, TO ASSIGN me the leading role or leave me in the wings?

*Everyone did it* may be the best ending. Shouldn't we all want to be complicit in an imperfect good deed or a beneficial bad one? The Great Man brought us together in the end. His reign was like one of your therapy sessions. We learned about ourselves, and the lessons were disconcerting.

In our time, many truths are hard.

The Great Man came to rule because we hated the facts of our lives. Desperate for change, we put our fate in the hands of a pathological narcissist. Since I am not a professional, I see no need to hedge and say that I use the term loosely.

We had let our fellows live in poverty and despair. We so disrespected our neighbors as to bring ruination upon ourselves. There is no lack of tough realizations.

My husband flattered himself that with a session or two in your office, he would make me appreciate my good fortune and turn me back from Náomi to Naomi. I had a complementary hope that, in the course of the trip, we would find ourselves rid of him and effect that same metamorphosis: no more tears.

Henry, you know that change is not easy, not in marriages, not in selves—and not, it turns out (no surprise), in nations. I am weighed down by what we have endured and how we have extricated ourselves. I worry that we have failed in that last step, worry that we will discover that we have not escaped.

I am still your Náomi. I still weep.

# ACKNOWLEDGMENTS

Thanks to my early readers: Rachel Schwartz, Goldie Alfasi, Paul Summergrad, and especially my friend and colleague Michael Stein. Each offered insight at a critical juncture.

Thanks also to my literary agents. Andrew Wylie encouraged me to undertake the project and let me know when the typescript was ready to circulate. Andrew Blauner brought the book to publication.

I am grateful to Debra Englander for seeing the book's promise and to Post Hill Press for going against the grain and adopting a novel whose political themes seemed to make other publishers leery.

Writing this book has reminded me of the influence of my psychotherapy instructors. They shaped me as a doctor and a person. So did my patients. How lucky I was to work with them.

# ABOUT THE AUTHOR

**Author photo by Matthew C. Kramer**

Peter D. Kramer is the author of eight books, including *Ordinarily Well*, *Against Depression*, *Should You Leave?*, the novel *Spectacular Happiness*, and the international bestseller *Listening to Prozac*. Dr. Kramer hosted the nationally syndicated public radio program *The Infinite Mind* and has appeared on the major broadcast news and talk shows, including *Today*, *Good Morning America*, *The Oprah Winfrey Show*, *Charlie Rose*, and *Fresh Air*. His essays, op-eds, and book reviews have appeared in the *New York Times*, *Wall Street Journal*, *Washington Post*, and elsewhere. For nearly forty years, Dr. Kramer taught and practiced psychiatry in Providence, Rhode Island. He now writes full time and is Emeritus Professor of Psychiatry and Human Behavior at Brown University.